SHELTER OF THE MOST HIGH

This Large Print Book carries the
Seal of Approval of N.A.V.H.

CITIES OF REFUGE, BOOK 2

SHELTER OF THE MOST HIGH

CONNILYN COSSETTE

THORNDIKE PRESS
A part of Gale, a Cengage Company

Farmington Hills, Mich • San Francisco • New York • Waterville, Maine
Meriden, Conn • Mason, Ohio • Chicago

LIBRARY OF CONGRESS CIP DATA ON FILE.
CATALOGUING IN PUBLICATION FOR THIS BOOK
IS AVAILABLE FROM THE LIBRARY OF CONGRESS

ISBN-13: 978-1-4328-5850-6 (hardcover)

Published in 2018 by arrangement with Bethany House, a division of
Baker Publishing Group

Printed in the United States of America
1 2 3 4 5 6 7 22 21 20 19 18

For my precious chickadee, Corrianna, whose voice lifted up in song to the King of Kings is among the most beautiful sounds in my world.

I am blessed to have a front-row seat to the metamorphosis of my sweet-cheeked little girl into the beautiful, curious, courageous young woman who will someday, all-too-soon, spread her wings and fly!

Then the LORD spoke to Joshua, saying, "Speak to the sons of Israel, saying, 'Designate the cities of refuge, of which I spoke to you through Moses, that the manslayer who kills any person unintentionally, without premeditation, may flee there, and they shall become your refuge from the avenger of blood. He shall flee to one of these cities, and shall stand at the entrance of the gate of the city and state his case in the hearing of the elders of that city; and they shall take him into the city to them and give him a place, so that he may dwell among them. Now if the avenger of blood pursues him, then they shall not deliver the manslayer into his hand, because he struck his neighbor without premeditation and did not hate him beforehand. He shall dwell in that city until he stands before the congregation for judgment, until the death of the one who is

high priest in those days. Then the manslayer shall return to his own city and to
his own house, to the city from which he
fled.' "

Joshua 20:1–6

The Great Sea
Tyre
Mt. Hermon
Laish
Kedesh
ASHER
NAPHTALI
Hagor
EAST MANASSEH
Sea of Kinneret
ZEBULUN
Megiddo
ISSACHAR
Golan
WEST MANASSEH
Dotan
Shechem
Beit She'an
Edrei
Shiloh
Jordan River
Ramoth-Gilead
EPHRAIM
GAD
DAN
Gilgal
BENJAMIN
Jericho
Jerusalem
PHILISTINES
JUDAH

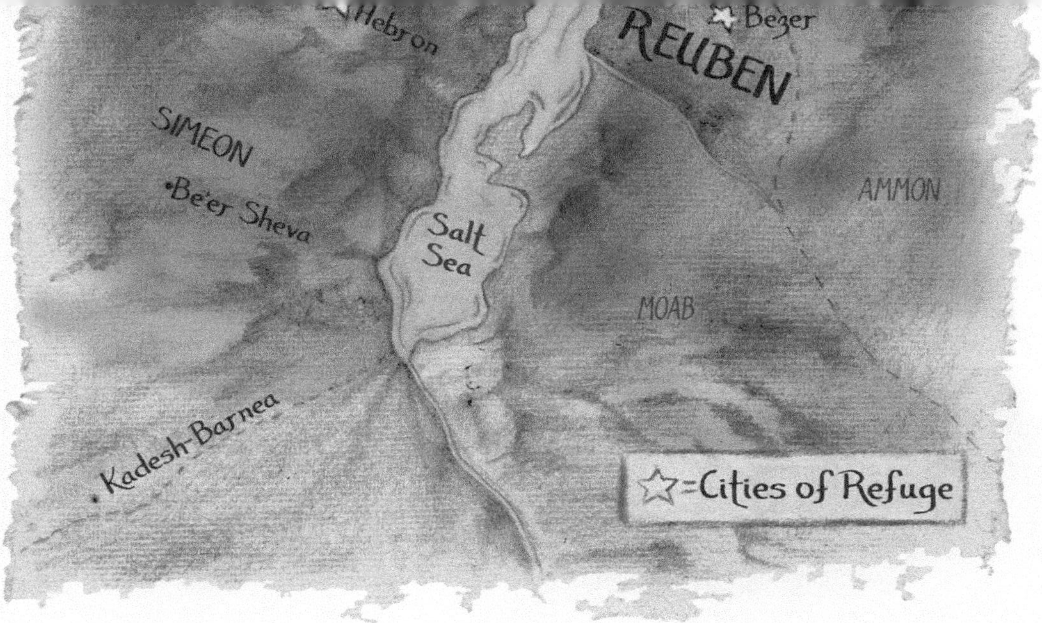
Hebron
Bezer
REUBEN
SIMEON
Be'er Sheva
Salt Sea
AMMON
MOAB
Kadesh-Barnea
☆=Cities of Refuge

Chapter One

Sofea

Island of Sicily
1388 BC

The pulse of the sea pressed me forward, urging my body deeper into its embrace. I obeyed the nudge and kicked my legs, peering through water-rippled light at the hidden world inside this secret cave. Sea grass slithered along my skin, half-heartedly grasping at my ankles. I fluttered my toes as I cut through the water like an arrow flung from a bow, air bubbling from my nose with measure practiced over every one of my sixteen years.

Sensing that I had cleared the entrance, I allowed my body to float upward until my head broke the surface. The voice of the waters amplified and echoed within the surprisingly large enclosed area, a shush of constant sound at once soothing and exhilarating to one born of the sea. I can say I was born of the sea, for it was into this blue expanse I was delivered, with the clouds above to oversee my birth.

Impatient as always, I'd entered the world within minutes of my mother's first surprised cry at the break of her waters. Surrounded by the other women of our village, who'd been enjoying an afternoon of swimming and combing the pebbled beach for telline shells, I'd been received not by the waiting hands of a midwife but the salty embrace of the ocean.

My mother said I had contentedly floated beneath the surface, unaware I'd even emerged from her body until lifted above the waves with a furious cry at the violence of being removed from my liquid world. *"Born of water and sky and with brine for blood,"* she'd said, and truly this secret grotto felt much like a womb to which I'd returned. My prayer to Posedao, the god of the sea, whispered back to me from the cave wall, echoing my gratitude for the discovery of this treasure to which he'd surely led me today.

With a splash and a light gasp my cousin Prezi's head popped above the water, her dark hair swirling around her. "Sofea! Why did you not wait for me? I was not sure how long to stay beneath the surface before coming up."

"And yet, here you are." I offered her a little grin and a teasing splash.

Blowing water from her lips with a noisy rasp, she blinked her eyes to clear the salt water from them and then splashed me back. "No thanks to you."

"I cannot help that I swim faster than you." I swirled around to take in the algae-slick rocks around us, noting again with pleasure the sound of the water lapping against stone as each gentle swell pushed me closer and closer to the back of the cave.

Prezi muttered something that sounded very much like "full of herself," and I ignored it. I *was* faster than she was and able to hold my breath far longer when diving for mussels — one born of the sea had no choice but to be one with it. Prezi was patient with my compulsion to explore every cave along this stretch of the shore, even when I'd insisted on pressing a little farther north than she'd been comfortable with. She'd much rather be lying out on the white-pebbled beach with her toes pointing to the sky, basking in the sun, long dark hair fanned around her. Where my blood was half seawater, hers was half sunshine, and the depth of her golden-brown skin attested

15

to such. Having been born only one cycle of the moon apart, we were as close as sisters. Closer.

"Are you done here yet?" She gathered her dark hair into a twisted tail as she braced against another wave, her lithe form swaying with the insistent force of the water.

"Not quite. I want to see what's below us."

Prezi rolled her eyes. "This cave is no different from the last one, Sofea, nor the one before, nor the one before that. And I am getting hungry."

"Please? Just a bit longer?" I pleaded with matched fingertips pressed beneath my chin. "Perhaps I'll find a magnosa."

Although her brown eyes narrowed, I knew she would capitulate. I'd always been able to sway her to my course, and she loved the delicate flavor of a magnosa. Although finding one of the shy eight-legged creatures among the craggy cave bottom might be a challenge in this dim light. She let out an exaggerated sigh that ricocheted off every slanted surface of the cave, and I seized on her moment of indecision to dive and explore the muted world beneath my feet.

Orange-striped donzelle and sea bream with black spots at the hinge of their tails darted among the anemone fronds swaying in the gentle current. A bright red starfish hugged a coral bed, as if desperate to keep from being washed away with the tide. When my chest burned with the effort of clinging to the last of my breath, I pushed to the surface again.

"Did you find one?" Prezi asked, one hand gripping a nearby outcropping.

"No, I'll go back down." I pointed at the far edge of the cave. "There must be at least one or two in here."

"We need to return to the village. Our mothers will be searching us out."

"They know where we are. We cannot return empty-handed. Give me a few more moments, I'll find something to bring back."

"But the men will be back soon. And we will be needed to help clean and salt the tuna."

Prezi was right. Even on this, the third day of the traditional mattanza hunt, there would be many fish to haul to shore from the boats, to gut and salt, and to lay out on the mats for drying. The men would be exhausted from the effort of herding the multitude of enormous tuna into a series of ever-smaller nets between their longboats and slaughtering the flailing creatures within the bloody corral. We women were needed to help finish the job. And then tonight we would again feast as we praised Posedao for guiding the schools of tuna near our shores, as he had for as many years as our people, the Sicani, had lived on this island.

After telling Prezi to go on and wait for me out in the sunlight, I dove again to search along the western wall of the cave for one of the stalk-eyed lobsters among the pitted rock. Coming up without a prize in my hand, I sipped another mouthful of air before arching my body through the mouth of the cave, knowing Prezi would be annoyed that I'd tarried so long.

Shattered light glittered on the water, blinding me as I blinked my eyes and swiped the salt water from my face. The sun peered with such direct glare that I could not see Prezi within the tiny cove we'd emerged into. I called her name and swam forward. She must have become aggravated with my delay and headed back to the beach. I pushed hard against the persistent tide until I was free of the cove. Then, standing in the waist-high water, I called her name again, lifting my voice to overcome the whoosh of the ocean and the piercing cries of seabirds circling above.

A hand reached to me from a hidden nook between two sea-pitted boulders, and turning, I laughed, "Prezi, you fright—"

18

But it was not my cousin's hand that snagged my elbow and jerked me nearly off my feet, and not her face I stared into as realization slammed into me like an errant wave. Grasping panic snatched the breath from my lungs. An enormously tall man, dressed only in a rough-woven brown kilt, had Prezi smashed into a crevice with his body, an obsidian blade to her throat.

With dark eyes as wide as sand dollars and waist-length wet hair tangled over her face and around her bare torso, my cousin shivered violently.

"Two!" said the man, his unfamiliar accent digging deep into the word. A leering grin split his pitted and scarred face as he took in my naked chest. "As if you girls were just waiting for me here."

"Please . . . please let her go." My strangled plea was nearly swallowed up by the crash of the waves against the rocks around us. I curled my arms around myself, as if they could allay the feel of his eyes on my body. If only I had heeded Prezi's insistence that we not enter this one last cave . . .

He ignored me and gestured with his bristled chin. "Those your tunics on the beach?"

Heart beating so furiously I barely heard his question, I nodded.

"No one else with you?"

"No."

His mud-brown eyes narrowed, and he pushed the point of his knife deeper into Prezi's flesh. "One lie and she dies."

"It is just the two of us. My cousin and me. Please, take me and let her —"

Again he sloughed off my pleading. "You go on ahead, back to the beach, and me and this beauty will follow. Don't bother running, or the fish will feast on her corpse."

Prezi's eyes begged me to comply with the brute's demands, so I turned and made my way through the waves. Digging my nimble toes into the pebbled ground, I fought the surf out of the cove and followed the rocky outcropping all the way back to the beach.

Another man waited on the shore, arms folded over his chest, severity in every line of his sun-browned face. His head was shaved clean, and a white scar slashed through one black brow above the cold gaze he directed at the three of us as we emerged from the water. Thankfully I'd chosen to swim with a linen wrap around my hips, to at least cover the bottom half of my body — as if it mattered when these strangers had already seen the two of us bare-chested, the way we always swam in the ocean. Somehow it had never bothered me until now.

"No others with them, Akato?" asked the man with the scar, his eyes skimming over Prezi and then coming to rest on me before darting away again. Prickles traveled across my skin that had little to do with the breeze off the sea. Something about him seemed vaguely familiar, but my scrambled mind could not fit the pieces together.

"No, they say it's just them." Akato pointed his blade at Prezi's jawline. "Should I just take care of them here, Seno?"

A shiver expanded from the center of my chest. Would they kill us? Or worse?

Seno glanced up at the ridge, toward the direction of our village, a look of contemplation on his face. If I screamed, would someone hear us and come to our rescue? Or would the breeze simply carry my voice out to sea? These men must have come from some rival tribe nearby, for Seno, especially, spoke our dialect with ease.

"No." Seno turned to look straight into my eyes, some strange emotion lurking in the piercing gaze. He lifted a large bag from the ground near his feet and hefted it over his shoulder, the metal items within clanking against one another. "We will take them with us."

Akato stared at the man he obviously held

21

as an authority, disbelief on his face. "But —"

With bridled fury in the look he directed at Akato, Seno took one menacing step forward. "I said, we take them."

"Your decision," Akato said with a shrug, but tension still seemed to vibrate between the two men. He pushed Prezi forward with a jerk. "Put your clothes on, and be quick about it. But if either of you try to run, we will kill the other . . . slowly." The way his eyes flared as he drew out the word assured me he would enjoy such a thing. Although he released my cousin's arm, his knifepoint hovered near her throat. There was nothing to do but comply.

Plucking my sun-bleached white tunic off the ground, I slipped into it as quickly as I could with trembling hands and a wet body, then secured my leather belt around my waist before sliding the necklace I'd recently made back over my head. Holding the purple-and-white mussel shell that hung from its center between my thumb and forefinger, I rubbed at its rippled back while silently begging the gods for deliverance.

Tears streamed down my cousin's beloved face as she fumbled with her own belt. Reassuring her with my eyes, I pressed her fingers away from the snarl her nervous hands had wrought and retied the braided leather rope about her waist.

As soon as I'd finished, Akato snagged Prezi's elbow again. Seno gestured for me to lead the way back up the rocky trail that led to our village. Why would he lead us that way and not to wherever they'd come from? Before we'd even reached the lip of the hill the answer was made clear. It would not have mattered if I had called for help. There was none to be had.

Smoke billowed into the sky as our homes burned and my whole body shook with horror. A ship perched off the coast, patched sails flapping in the ocean wind and men streaming between the shore and their vessel, using our longboats to transport spoils. All the tuna that had been hard-won in the mattanza over the last few days was being ferried away. These men were no rival tribesmen — they were sea marauders, a ship full of thieves and murderers who made their fortune razing villages and plundering the many trade ships that traversed the Great Sea.

Screams sounded from every corner of our village as we approached. Men. Women. Children. I longed to slap my palms to my ears and block out the desperate keening, but Akato ordered me to move forward on the path, toward the devastation.

Bodies lay everywhere. Every one of them someone I knew. Someone I loved.

At the edge of the village, one of my father's six wives lay unmoving with her arms around her three small boys, a trail of blood near her feet. She'd dragged herself through the dirt to pull them into a final embrace while they had breathed their last. Grief seared my throat, a sob building into a scream within my core just as my eyes landed on my mother's sister Jamara and my uncle Riso facedown near the entrance to their caved-in and smoldering hut. Prezi's five older siblings were nowhere to be seen.

Before I could warn my cousin to turn away from the sight of her murdered parents, I vomited on the ground. Prezi folded into a faint against Akato, who grunted as he held her upright and then shook her until she came to.

"Let's go," he snarled at her. "You do that again and it'll be you on the ground with the rest of them." Although she remained standing, her legs wobbled as the man pushed her forward.

The two men guided us down to the shoreline and away from the horror — away from my home.

Although my terror-stricken mind

screamed that I flee somehow, get back to my little round hut, to my mother and brothers and sisters, I could not abandon Prezi. The sounds of agony behind us and the smell of smoke and burning flesh assured me that if they were all not dead already, they would be before I could do anything to help them.

My numb body was incapable of doing anything but walking forward, past the broken bodies along the beach and past the corpses floating in the surf — the men of our village who had rushed to its defense. As the chief and high priest of our village and a powerful man among the other Sicani on the island, my father's head would be a prize for these pirates. But somehow I suspected that his body would not be found among the brave men who'd died on this beach. No, he'd save himself first.

After a brief discussion, in which Akato again questioned Seno's decision to keep us alive, he lumbered off to join the chaos and Seno directed us to a longboat beached nearby. We clambered aboard to sit on the floor among the giant fish carcasses, bundles of flax that the women of our village had spent weeks preparing, and the casks of wine that had been awaiting a celebration that would never happen. My cousin and I tangled our fingers together, gripping each other in icy, trembling desperation — neither of us able to speak as Seno climbed aboard and used an oar to push off the beach.

Matere. My mother, with her sun-kissed hair and warm skin and midnight lullabies, was gone. My two little sisters with their frizzy golden braids and my tiny brown-eyed brothers would never grow to marry or have children of their own someday.

These evil men had stolen everything. Only death and ashes remained.

Hot anger burned in my body as the boat pushed off the beach, each dip of the oars stirring my fury higher and higher as my mind conjured the grisly images. Had they suffered? Or had the brigands had enough mercy to make quick work of slitting their throats?

If I'd listened to Prezi and returned earlier instead of heedlessly frolicking in the waves and satiating my ridiculous curiosity in the underwater grotto, my blood would now mingle with theirs as it sank beneath the skin of the island that was my entire world. I had the overwhelming urge to lunge from the boat and swim back now, to greet death alongside my family.

But for my cousin, I sat still. For my cousin, I kept my eyes trained on the ship looming larger and larger ahead of us as we sliced through the crystal blue water. For my cousin, the only person I had left, I would do anything.

CHAPTER TWO

Prezi and I stood together on the deck of the ship, wet-haired and shivering in the salty breeze. As our captor climbed aboard behind us, still carrying that large sack over his shoulder, another of the men sauntered up, appraising our bedraggled state with an off-balance smile that curdled my stomach. He was quite a bit older than Seno, with a gray-stubbled head and his kilt and bare chest stained with blood. The feral gleam in his eyes made it apparent that he'd reveled in the slaughter. "Well now, what do we have here?"

"Leave them be, Porote." Seno moved to stand in front of us. "They are mine."

Porote's eyes flared as he took in the larger man's defensive stance. "Yours? Aren't we to divide the spoils, Seno?"

Seno took a step forward, the thump of his sandaled foot on the wood planks vibrating beneath my bare toes. "This is *my* ship.

I decide what spoils are divided and what are not." He stood very still, and from the shock on Porote's face I gathered Seno's expression was fierce. "I expect the rest of the crew to be notified of such things as well."

Porote's troubled gaze flicked to me one more time before he shook his head and walked away, seeming just as confused as Akato as to why Seno would go to the trouble of taking captives from a village where everyone else had been slaughtered.

Without an explanation for his strange behavior, Seno ordered us through the hatch in the deck and down the ladder into the hold of the ship. I'd rarely seen such vessels as this one, built for long trade across the sea, with sails that billowed like the ever-changing clouds.

The dark space belowdecks was barely tall enough for Seno to stand upright. He ordered the two of us to sit along the wall behind two large barrels and then wound a length of rope around both our wrists, binding us together.

"Stay put. This may be my ship, but these men have been a long time away from home. And from the pleasure of women." He lifted his brow, the one sliced in two by a thick white scar. "You understand my meaning?"

Molten fear traveled through my extremities.

He took our silence as understanding. "Good. We won't be much longer. My men are nearly finished loading the fish." A sinister smile curled on his lips. "A nice haul this season. My buyer will be pleased."

So it was for the tuna my family had been slaughtered? The fish that our village was so skilled at herding into the mattanza nets must be worth much for Seno to direct his ship here.

"It was one of the things I remembered most about this place, at least until I set foot on the beach. How my father and uncles would prepare those nets for months, and the blood . . . so much blood in the water as they killed the tuna. It used to frighten me as a boy, but I'd been so proud when they finally let me go that I swallowed my disgust at all that gore. . . ." His voice trailed off.

"I don't understand. . . ." I said, stricken by his confusing tale. "How . . . how would you remember our village?"

He stared at me, the light from the hatch highlighting only one half of his face. "You don't know me, do you?"

"How could I — ?"

"I am Seneturo."

With a gasp, Prezi went stiff, and my jaw gaped as Seno lifted his finger and touched the white scar that sliced his eyebrow in half.

I did that.

"I did that," my mouth repeated. "I cut you."

"Yes, you did." A sardonic smile ticked his cheek. "And I thank you for the bit of ferocity it adds to my appearance. Most assume it was some wicked blade that caused the scar and not the sharp edge of a shell during a diving game."

There had been so much blood that day, I'd thought Seneturo might die with the way the wisps of red had curled through the water and how it streamed down over his eyelid. I remembered wondering why he didn't cry out even though the gouge looked so painful.

With profound confusion cluttering my thoughts, I took in the sight of my childhood friend melded with the man who'd just slaughtered our village. His home. My family.

"How can this be?" Prezi trembled as she leaned against me.

Seno lifted his palms and I noticed another thick and ragged scar slashed across his hand. One certainly not made by a little girl roughhousing in the water with her friends. "You were there that day. You saw what they did, how they offered the ten of us boys like sacrifices. Traded like goats by our own people, by *your* father." His lip curled, as if the words tasted of gall.

A chain of memories from eight years ago floated to the surface. A group of young boys being led out of the village. Seneturo, only twelve at the time, his boyish shoulders straight as he was loaded onto a boat similar to this one. The trembling of my mother's hand as she held mine and the fury in her eyes.

"So this is vengeance?" I asked.

"Perhaps." He shrugged one shoulder. "Or perhaps I simply remembered the mattanza and had an eager buyer lined up."

"But why . . . ?"

"Why did I save the two of you?" He looked away, his voice soft. "Your mother."

He paused. "She pleaded with your father not to allow us to be traded to the pirates, even though my own parents said nothing. She was the only one to stand up to him. I will never forget her face as she accused him of cowardice for not fighting back. And knowing him, I am sure she paid the price for her rebellion."

His knowing gaze held mine. He spoke

the truth. I'd not been surprised by the bruises on my mother's face, the cut in her lip, and the way her arm hung limp at her side the morning after Seneturo had been traded away, but now I knew why those wounds had been inflicted. I'd endured my own fair share of bruises at my father's hand and learned from a young age to find escape in the sea whenever he came around.

"When I saw you girls on that beach, just like when we were children . . . I couldn't . . ." His jaw twitched as if he were grinding his teeth. "She and your siblings were dead before I could get to them. I had planned on sparing them, for her sake. But now there is only the two of you."

Prezi wept openly, and an echoing sob shuddered in my chest, demanding to be let free, but I clamped my mouth shut, determined to be strong enough for the both of us.

Seno dropped the bag on the floor, the clatter of metal echoing in the cargo hold. "Your coward of a father was hiding in one of the caves up above the village," he said. "He must have run off as soon as our ship hit the beach. Little did he know that I knew exactly where he kept his stash. I explored every one of those caves as a child and discovered it long ago." He nudged the bag of spoils with his foot, and his dark eyes flared wide with satisfaction as he leaned in close to me. "I paid him back for every moment of degradation I suffered at the hands of the men who bought me that day." His whisper was rough and frightening. "And I took my time until he begged and cried like the dog he was."

Although I was unable to summon any grief for the man I'd called Father, Seno's ruthlessness terrified me, and I blinked against the burn of tears as I considered our utter vulnerability. "What will you do with us?"

"I haven't decided yet." His tone was curt as he stood and brushed a hand over his shaven head. "There's nothing to do now but take you with us."

"You could let us go," I ventured, my plea rushing out. "We'll run and hide, find another village that might take us in."

"No. Akato and Porote have already seen you. I cannot afford to show leniency. One glimpse of my underbelly and the two of them would feed me to the sharks. I won't lose my ship." He stood and walked to the ladder that led to freedom. "For your sakes — for your mother's sake — I wish Akato had never spied your tunics lying on the shore."

CHAPTER THREE

In blackness, Prezi and I clung to each other, mourning together in silence. There was nothing to say as the ship bobbed in the bloodied harbor, no words to soothe the persistent ache as the men above us shouted orders and raised the anchor stones, and nothing that could erase the agony as we sailed away from everything we'd ever known.

At the first port we anchored in the next day, Seno stood guard over us while his men unloaded all the tuna my village had died for. After ensuring that we had food and water, his eyes stayed fixed on his men and his jaw remained set until they clambered up the ladder without so much as glancing our way. Each time rations were divided among the sailors, the process was repeated. Seno's determination to protect us in spite of the way he'd ordered the destruction of our village baffled me.

On the third night of black silence, he descended into the hold alone, accompanied by lewd encouragement from the men above. He returned a threat of violence should any of the lechers attempt to follow him, making me consider just how insufficient the leather hinges on the latch would be, were they determined to disobey Seno's orders.

After retrieving some stale bread, a small jug of watery barley beer, and dried fish for us to eat, he placed an oil lamp on the ground between us and lay on the floor, his hands behind his head, saying nothing. Prezi turned away and pretended to sleep. Although confused by his presence and still terrified of him, I welcomed the silence and instead listened to the now-familiar sounds of wood, water, and metal as the ship cut through the sea.

Without preamble, Seno began to tell the story of his first days at sea. He'd been enslaved on a ship much like this one by ruthless marauders who beat him daily, refused him food often, and took pleasure in pillaging vessels and terrorizing villages all around the Great Sea.

As he grew older, Seno learned the ways of the pirates who'd tortured him as a child, learned to fight and steal and outwit. After a few years, he was allowed to earn his freedom, and because of the lessons he'd learned watching other pirates, he had saved his portion of the spoils instead of whoring and drinking them away.

He'd purchased this ship only a year ago and spent the last few months working to establish his authority over these men, authority I suspected may have been damaged by his actions back at the village when both Akato and Porote had challenged him for saving us.

Our presence gave Seno the opportunity to unload his stories on captive ears. Some of them were fascinating, some horrifying, and some made me desperate for a swim in the sea to wash myself clean of the details. It was evident that nearly a decade of piracy had twisted the innocent boy into someone who barely resembled the Seneturo I had known. He'd survived through any means necessary and seemed to regret none of the lives he'd ended in doing so. I wondered what my own choices might have been if forced into the same situation. Perhaps two days ago my answer would have been different, but now there was nothing I wouldn't do to protect my cousin.

When he finished his tale, Seno sat up and put his elbows on his knees. Picking up the nearly empty beer jug in his hands, he turned his head toward me, a new expression lighting his face. "Do you remember the day you challenged me to drink a mug of seawater?"

Startled by the abrupt question, I nodded, even as the memory caused the corners of my lips to twitch. "You gagged and heaved all over the sand."

"But you would not let me collect the prize until I drank it all."

"Of course not. That would be unfair."

He shook his head. "You always were a bossy one."

As Prezi reminded me frequently.

"You remember what the prize was, don't you? When I finally got that entire mug of awful water down?"

I did, but I would not speak it out loud. *"You have to let me kiss you, Sofi."*

I pressed my lips together and his eyes followed the action. He remembered it too. Even though it was only a quick and awkward brush of childish lips, Seneturo was the only boy outside my family I'd ever allowed to kiss me. I'd told Prezi that night that I would marry him when I was old enough.

We both stayed quiet, lost in our own memory of that day — the day before the pirates came and took Seneturo away.

He glanced at Prezi, as if ensuring that she truly was sleeping instead of pretending this time. "It wasn't only your mother's kindness that saved you the other day." His voice dipped low. "It was that the last innocent moment of my life was there on that beach with you."

"Seneturo is still inside you," I whispered. "It's not too late."

He sat up, cursed, and heaved the clay jar at the hull. It shattered, splattering the remains of the beer down the wall. Prezi startled but did not open her eyes. Shrinking back, I stared at him, my breath coming in short spurts.

He leaned down, his face nearly as close as it had been the day he'd kissed me, his mouth curled into an ugly snarl. He smelled of sea and wind and bitterness. "Heed my words, Sofea. Trust no one. Especially not me."

It had been seven days since Seno had come down into the hold for more than a few moments. Each time he'd barely spoken to us but ensured we had food and water before ascending the ladder. And tonight he had not come at all. For hours we'd listened to the sounds of revel above us: drunken shouting, scuffling, even music from some sort of stringed instrument paired with heavy-footed dancing. Perhaps Seno had overindulged and was sleeping off drink somewhere, having forgotten the tied-up, hungry girls down below. Stomach protesting and eyes weary from peering into blackness, I leaned my head back against the wall and attempted to sleep.

The soft, rhythmic sway of the vessel told me that we were anchored. I longed for the sun, for the sweet caress of the sea on my skin, for the murmur of the waters upon the pebbled shore of my beach, and for my family. The hatch opened and the now-familiar shadow of Seno descended into our prison. My stomach snarled in response.

"Are we in a port?" I asked.

"We're off the coast of Tyre. There's a fire festival tonight, so we are anchored until tomorrow morning."

He knelt down in front of us and placed his oil lamp on the ground. "It's time for you to go." He slipped a knife from his belt and worked at the ropes he'd bound us with.

"Go? But how?"

"You'll have to swim."

"Swim? Why?"

"My men are sleeping off their celebration. It's your only chance to get off the boat."

"I don't understand. I thought you planned to —"

"Plans have changed. Akato and Porote are suspicious. Get up." His gruff tone was laden with the smell of wine.

"Where will we go?"

"That's not my concern."

My mouth gaped at him. "Seneturo —"

He towered over me, speaking as if to a child, the weak light from his oil lamp casting eerie shadows on his face. "My name is Seno."

Prezi pressed closer to my side, her fingers gripping mine, and I had little doubt my expression matched her terrified one.

Seno's lips pressed together in a tight line, and I was not sure if it was regret or anger in their shape. "I will help you get into the water. But this is the last and only thing I can do for you. I *won't* lose my ship." He spun around and climbed out of the hold, assuming we would follow.

"What will we do?" Prezi's voice warbled.

"We swim," I said. "He's giving us a chance. We have to take it."

My legs shook as I walked to the ladder, wobbly from the lack of movement for the last eleven days and thrumming with a

41

mixture of fear and cautious hope. With a deep breath, I climbed up the wooden rungs, wholly unsure what I would see when I emerged on deck. The cool night air hit my face, causing me to drag in a fresh salt-laden mouthful that burned my lungs. *Delicious.*

As my eyes adjusted to the world outside our black prison, a half-moon lit the deck with a subtle glow. Men lay along the edges of the boat, deep into drink-laden slumber. It seemed only Seno was awake to keep watch tonight. Many points of light flickered on the far horizon, evidence of the fire festival taking place in Tyre.

Prezi emerged from the hatch, the miserly moonlight highlighting panic across her features. She immediately searched out my hand, and I squeezed her fingers, hoping to infuse us both with a measure of courage.

Seno nudged me forward, his command barely a whisper. "Go. Now."

Thankful for our bare feet, I held my breath as we carefully navigated around a few men that lay across the deck, their chests rising and falling in steady rhythm.

We reached the low railing that edged the boat, my skin tingling with nervous anticipation at the thought of diving into the black sea. I turned back to whisper thanks to Seno but something grabbed my ankle. Looking down in horror at the last man I'd stepped over, I saw that it was Porote, the grizzled older man who'd questioned Seno when we'd first climbed aboard.

He released my ankle but sprang up and grabbed Prezi's wrist, then pointed a dagger at my throat. "What's going on here?"

Seno came up behind Porote, his expression calculating and his eyes blank. "Looks as though these two are trying to escape."

Everything inside me went still. *"I won't lose my ship,"* he'd said. Seno had turned on us.

I yanked Prezi closer, shuffling until the backs of our knees struck the railing. "Please, just let us go."

Porote sneered. "I don't think we will. Isn't that right, Seno?"

Seno's gaze met mine, and in it was a brief glimpse of the regret I'd wondered whether he was even capable of anymore, along with a hint of the debt he felt he owed my mother. But then the boy who'd kissed me on a beach eight years before shook his head, turning back into the pirate who'd snatched us off that same beach. "No."

"What are you waiting for?" Porote said to Seno, even as his eyes remained locked on me, challenge clear in his tone. "These slaves need to be taught a lesson."

Without a word, Seno unknotted the leather belt that looped twice around his waist. Large metal beads were knotted into the tasseled ends, a tool for a man who ruled his ship with no mercy. With eyes devoid of any feeling, he doubled it in his fist, stepped forward, and raised the whip high.

In one horrifying moment, he brought down the lash, and Prezi spun on me, a mixture of gut-wrenching apology and fierce determination in her expression as she slammed her palms into my chest and knocked me backward over the railing. Heels over head, I crashed into the surface of the sea, my arm stinging every place where those dangerous tassels had met my skin before Prezi took the brunt of the blow.

The shock of cold water hitting my body made me suck in a wet gasp. I twisted until my head was above water, spitting and choking. Prezi still stood by the railing, outlined by moonlight and arms raised to protect herself from the whip Seno brought down on her again and again. My mouth filled with water as I screamed at him to stop, begging him for mercy. Once more he lifted the whip, but instead of lashing her again, his fist slammed into her face. She toppled over the railing, landing in the water with a splash.

I screamed her name, my throat already tender from the salt water, and swam toward the place she'd gone under, my heart pounding. Had Seno killed my cousin? Calling her name again, I flailed around with hands numb from fear and cold. She would not drown. I refused to let her drown. When my fingers connected with floating tendrils of hair I gripped them tightly, yanking her toward me in desperation, regardless of the pain it might inflict.

Ignoring the furious shouts coming from the deck of the ship where it seemed Porote and Seno were now locked in a battle of words and knives, I tugged her close, making sure her head was above the water. "Can you hear me?" I whispered. Although I could not see her in the darkness, she coughed and gasped. I thanked Posedao for not dragging her to the bottom of the sea. I did not wait for Prezi to catch her bearings, could not even wait to see if she was truly alive before I looped my arm around her chest and swam. A loud curse caused me to toss a wide-eyed glance over my shoulder just as Seno's body crumpled over the side of the boat and slipped beneath the black surface, taking his regrets with him into the sea. Porote had won himself a ship.

With no time to waste mourning my child-hood friend, nor the man who'd spared our lives, I used my free arm to pull at the water and kicked with all my might, pushing against the black swells so intent on forcing us back toward the boat, and hoping that Porote counted us as lost or at least not worth the effort of lifting anchor to pursue us.

"Swim," I ordered Prezi, hoping she would hear the command through her half-conscious haze.

Her hand gripped my arm suddenly and she coughed again. "Just let me go. Get yourself to shore."

"Never," I vowed. "We will survive. Both of us."

She did not answer, but she did begin to kick her legs, and soon we were far enough away from the boat that it became only a dark silhouette against the night. Turning my face away from it, I peered in the direction I hoped was the shore and swam, do-ing my best not to guess what sea creatures might be lurking beneath us and how very far away the lights seemed to be.

For what seemed like hours we swam, every so often pausing to float on our backs and rest, and then swam again. We pushed south, away from the torchlights and bon-fires that winked along the coastline, away from the port where Seno's men were headed and where others might spot us.

Just as the sky began to lighten, we were caught in a current that pushed us toward land, moving us with astonishing speed toward the shore. Grateful for the assistance of the gods of the sea, I sent out a prayer of thanks, but just as quickly rescinded it. We were headed directly toward a barrier reef that jutted out of the water. The white crash of waves against the rock and the roar of the sea against the perilous outcropping made my empty stomach churn.

"Swim!" I yelled, pushing Prezi away from me. "Go!" The first touches of dawn on her pale face revealed that her cheek was swollen and purpling. Seno had hit her on the side of her face, as if he'd aimed for her cheekbone instead of dead-on. I wondered if he'd done that on purpose.

With the last bit of our strength, we attempted to cut across the current that dragged us closer and closer to the deadly rocks, but accomplished nothing but fatigue. Our bodies were sucked into a swirl of churning water and we both cried out, grabbing for each other as the sea thwarted us, ripping us apart. I was pushed one way and

Prezi another, and then just before I reached her she was dashed against a large boulder and released a scream that chilled my already frozen blood.

"My leg," she cried.

"Hold on," I said as I gripped her wrist. She grasped the back of my tunic with her fingers, and then with the last of my strength I towed her toward a break in the rocks, hoping the swell of the sea would push us clear before any more damage was done to either of us.

Although continually battered against the sharp rocks, somehow we managed to get around the other side of the treacherous barrier, where the water was much calmer. The sun had nearly risen by the time we dragged ourselves onto the pebbled beach. We lay on the shore, panting.

"Can you walk?" I asked as I examined her leg. There were long scrapes on her shin and her ankle was already swollen. "We need to get out of sight."

"I don't think I can stand."

"You must," I said. "We've gotten this far, we have to keep going."

She sighed, a painful sound that ended on a sob. "There is nowhere to go, Sofi. Nowhere. We have no food, nothing to trade for food, and I may have broken a bone in my leg." She began to cry, her hands on her bruised and swollen face. "I wish they'd killed us back in the village."

Kneeling above her, I yanked her hands away from her face. "No! I won't let you give up," I said, my tone brooking no argument. "Let's get off this beach."

Although her expression remained tortured, she allowed me to prop her up. With a groan of frustration mixed with dogged determination, I yanked her to standing and drew her arm about my shoulders, my stomach wrenching each time she hissed in pain from the welts Seno had inflicted on her back.

With a strength I did not think I even had left in me, I half-dragged, half-carried my cousin across the wide beach and into the trees, where we both collapsed into an area thick with undergrowth and, regardless of the danger that surely surrounded us, passed into beautiful oblivion.

CHAPTER FOUR

Thirst woke me. My mouth felt as though I'd swallowed some of the sand that cradled my bruised and aching body. Prezi was awake too but had not moved from the place where she'd fallen asleep on her side, her face drawn with pain and despair.

I shaded my eyes against the high sun glaring down at us, the narrow-trunked palm trees doing little to block its assault. My skin was tight from the salt water, my hair a knotted mess around my body. Sitting up, I attempted to smooth my salt-encrusted curls but could do nothing more than push the matted tangles behind my shoulder.

"We must find water," I said with a painful croak. I tried to wet my lips, but the skin was cracked and tender and my parched tongue only aggravated the soreness. "Then we can search out food."

Prezi said nothing, her blank eyes taking me in with silent resignation.

"We can't just sit here and die, Prez."

"I can't walk," she said with a voice as flat as her expression. She pointed to her ankle, which had swollen to twice its size, the skin mottled red and purple. "And you certainly cannot carry me. Even if I could move, we have nowhere to go."

I stood, swiping at the gritty sand that clung to my skin and tunic, and looked north, where Seno had pointed out the city of Tyre. I could see nothing but trees and thick underbrush and wondered how far south we'd floated. Behind us was only a long curving beach and the crash of waves on the shore. We were stranded, clueless as to where we were or if there was any help to be had.

Panic began to press upward, but I forced it down, resolving that for as frightened and resigned as Prezi was, I would be equal amounts determined.

"We have no choice but to move. We are too exposed here. We will have to walk into the city. Perhaps we can find someone who will help us there."

"No one will help us, Sofea. We'll be forced to sell ourselves into slavery to survive."

"I won't give up. I'll go look for water and food."

She shrugged a shoulder and dropped her cheek back to the ground, covering her eyes with her arm and lying so still it was as if she were dead already. I headed back toward the beach, taking note of a distinctive mound of rocks near the edge of the tree line so I could find my way back to her.

After scavenging for something edible along the edge of the water for what seemed to be hours, I found nothing more than a few clumps of seaweed. Not willing to leave Prezi for too long, I made my way back along the shore, ignoring the sting of seawater against the abrasions on my toes and calves. Looking west, I shaded my eyes against the bright sun and wondered how far away I was from my island and whether I would ever see its white-pebbled shores or explore its secret grottos again. Stretching toward the horizon, the sea curved away from my vision, as if my home had been completely swallowed up by the ocean, the bodies of my family claimed by its greedy depths.

Kneeling in the surf, I sent a desperate prayer skimming across the water. "What can we do?" I begged. "Prezi will die without help. We have no water, no food. Nothing." Perhaps my cousin was right and we should have died back at the village. Better a swift death by sword than starving or wasting away with no fresh water to quench our thirst. But what could Posedao do? Would Atemito deign to answer? Or what of the Furies that swept like invisible birds through the air to stir the clouds? Was there even a god who could hear me in this faraway land?

My only answer was the constant swish of the lapping waves, the rasp of sand under my knees, and the distant cry of a few gulls searching, like me, for something to sustain them along this rocky, inhospitable seashore.

I breathed in the salt air, inhaling it deep, deep into my lungs as if it could quench my thirst. I grasped the shell necklace that miraculously still hung around my neck, drawing circles with my thumb into its smooth hollow. I had no token of my gods, just this beautiful purple-and-white shell, the only remnant of my home besides Prezi. Then I stood to return to my cousin with only a handful of dried seaweed and not one more answer than I'd carried away with me.

Low voices drifted from the thick stand of trees where I'd left Prezi. Deep masculine voices that spoke words my ears could not decipher. Had Porote and his men found us? Dropping the seaweed behind me, I ducked low and slithered through the trees, careful to step only in the sand and away from any twigs or stones that might betray me. With my breath locked in my chest, I peered around a large white-flowered bush.

My cousin still lay where she had when I walked away, her body curled in upon itself, her face as pale as the sand beneath her, and a large man standing over her with his back toward me. Unmoving, Prezi looked up at the hulking stranger like a hopeless, wounded animal. Clamping my lips to keep myself from crying out, I crouched even lower, keeping myself pressed as far into the sweet-smelling bush as possible.

The prayer I'd tossed out to the gods of the sea and the earth and the air came back to jeer at me. Nothing had heard my supplications but the water and the sky. Prezi and I, the last survivors of our village, would die today.

I would not let my cousin die alone.

I darted from my hiding place, slipped around the giant of a man, and threw myself over Prezi. "Leave her alone!" I shouted at him, and to my surprise the man took two steps backward, his hands aloft, as if he were surrendering to me.

He said a few words, none of which I understood, so I screamed at him again to

54

leave my cousin be.

"Are you all right?" I asked her.

"I woke up and they were here." Although she'd seemed resigned to her fate, her body was shuddering.

"They?" Dread swirled through my bones as I lifted my head to look around. My heart sank like an anchor stone. Six men stood in a loose circle around us now, faces drawn, all heavily armed. I recognized none of them from the ship, and they looked nothing like the bare-chested, tattooed men who'd snatched us from our home. Nonetheless, they were just as dangerous.

Another man stepped forward, his hands upraised, and spoke in that strange language. His words lifted as if he were asking me a question. The sea air drifted through his dark brown hair, making it flop into his eyes. He scratched at his shaved chin as he waited for me to answer. He seemed to be the leader of this group.

"I don't understand you!" I said to him.

He took another step closer to us, and I tightened my grip on Prezi.

"I think they were watching while I was sleeping," she whispered. "I didn't even hear them."

The hulking man spoke to the dark-haired one, gesturing toward Prezi's leg. They both frowned, as if somehow concerned at the largely swollen ankle. As if they cared.

I shook off the notion and yelled again, waving my hands for emphasis. "Leave us alone. I won't let you hurt her."

Again they conversed in that strange tongue, the lilting words grating against my senses as I strained to pick out something, anything I could understand.

The dark-haired man put his hand on the hilt of his sword, drawing it from a leather scabbard. I could almost feel the remainder of my breath seeping from my body.

But instead of slashing at us, the man laid the sword in the sand. Then he gestured to the other men who surrounded us. All of them drew swords or daggers and laid them on the ground, then lifted their palms as if displaying that they had no intention of hurting us.

Confusion rippled through me.

"What is happening?" Prezi whispered as she pushed her body upward to a sitting position. I kept my arm curved around her shoulder, unwilling to allow them to divide us.

"I don't know."

Taking the time to slow down his movements, as if to avoid startling us, the dark-haired man knelt down in front of Prezi. A few threads of silver shimmered at his temples; he looked to be similar in age to my father. But instead of the hard glint I'd seen in Seno's eyes as he drew that whip last night, this man's eyes seemed almost . . . kind.

Baffled, I shrank back, pulling my trembling cousin closer. The dark-haired man gestured toward Prezi's ankle, saying something again in that language that dipped and swelled in ways I'd never heard. I lifted my chin, surveying his companions, but none of them moved, all seeming deferential to this man as their leader. They stood like statues, weapons at their feet, with eyes displaying something akin to sympathy.

The hulking one said something, then slowly approached again, and as he did so, he drew a full goatskin bag from his shoulder and held it out to us. Wary, but desperate for water, I snatched it from his grasp and pressed it into my cousin's hands, insisting she drink first before bringing it to my own lips. The water was lukewarm, as if the giant of a man had been carrying it over his shoulder for hours, but it was wet and soothed my parched throat.

When I finally sated my thirst, I held the bag to my chest, somewhat loath to return it in case he was like Seno, dangling an offer of help and then turning to snatch it from my grip. But the dark-haired man smiled. A wide, warm smile that displayed grooves in his cheeks that made him seem much younger than the silver in his hair would suggest.

The man gestured again toward Prezi's wounded leg, as if asking permission to survey the damage. Although I was terrified of his touching her, I held still as he took my silence for assent and reached out to gently scoop my cousin's foot in his palm.

Slowly he lifted her ankle off the sand, tilting his head to survey the swelling. The big one made a comment and shook his head, and then they seemed to have a conversation about the injury.

The dark-haired man laid Prezi's foot back on the sand, but even though he was gentle, she sucked in a tortured gasp, and I suddenly felt it necessary to beg these men for not only our lives, but also to help my cousin.

"Please," I said. "We have nothing to give you. And I know you don't even understand us, but we have nowhere to go and I can't help her. Please. I'll do anything." The thought struck me hard in the gut — but yes, I would do *anything* if it meant Prezi was safe.

The dark-haired man tilted his chin, assessing me. He pointed toward the north, toward the city that I knew lay somewhere beyond sight, and asked a question. Was he asking if we were from Tyre?

I shook my head and pointed toward the water, waving my hand numerous times to indicate we were from far away, across the sea. His eyes flared wide as he followed my gesture, and I sensed he understood my meaning. He sighed, running a palm down his cheek, his gaze locking with mine. Then he nodded as if he'd made a decision.

After saying a few more indecipherable words to the six men around us, he gestured to the hulking one, who moved forward and then crouched next to Prezi, a question in his eyes as he stretched out his arms.

"I think he wants to carry you," I choked out.

She sucked in a wobbling breath, her trembling even more pronounced. "But where will they take us? Are we to be enslaved?"

"Does it even matter? If we stay here, we will die. Better slavery than the underworld."

Although she protested, I unwrapped myself from her grip and stood, taking a couple of steps back to make it clear I would allow him to help her. Without hesitation, he slipped his enormous hands beneath her broken body and lifted her into his arms. Then he stood, my tall, willowy cousin looking very fragile and terrified in the clutches of someone who looked more like a wild beast than a man. Her bruises, along with the welts Seno's belt had caused, must be aching, but she kept her lips pressed tight against crying out at the pain.

The big man said something to her, a grin forming on his stubbled face, and then let out a quiet but rumbling laugh. Although I flinched, it was a pleasant sound, nothing like the lewd laughter of the men on Seno's ship.

My gaze darted to the dark-haired man, and he gestured for me to walk beside the one holding Prezi. All the men slowly bent to pick up their weapons, lifting them with care and brushing away the sand before placing them back into their belts. Then the six strangers came closer, their circle collapsing around us. Instinctively I moved toward the huge man and Prezi, my heartbeat thundering in my ears.

The dark-haired man said something to me, the sound reminding me of the soothing words my mother had spoken whenever I'd been frightened of an oncoming storm as a small child. Then he began leading the men east, farther into the trees, away from the beach and the waves, away from my sea. With only one last glance toward the waters that glittered brilliant beneath the sun, I followed.

CHAPTER FIVE

EITAN

City of Kedesh
7 Iyar 1388 BC

As I lowered the mold into the trough, the hiss and pop of the clay meeting with the cool water overpowered Nadir's voice for a moment.

". . . No one would ever know, Eitan," he finished as the sizzling dulled to silence. I imagined the way the molten bronze inside the mold would dull as well, from a blooming red-orange to its shrunken, blackened state. I lifted it out of the water with two strong acacia sticks and laid it on the ground next to the trough, giving the metal inside a few more moments to cool thoroughly.

"I'm not going with you," I said as I tossed the smoldering sticks aside and deflected his suggestion by putting him to work. "Pass me that mallet."

Nadir handed me the tool that I used to hammer off the earthen mold, revealing the rough outline of a knife as the pieces crumbled away. I brushed away the dust with a finger, the metal warm in my palm but cool enough to handle. Hard to believe it had been white-hot liquid only a little while ago.

"I told you, I've done it before," said Nadir, lifting soot-blackened palms high. "Look, I am here. Alive."

Nadir had been trying to convince me for days to sneak out of Kedesh and go with him down to the lake just east of the city. I'd brushed off the suggestion time and again without truly explaining my reasons, but it seemed he had little intention of leaving me alone.

"It's dangerous for you to be out there, Nadir. It's well beyond the two-thousand-cubit boundary." Although I knew Nadir missed his days as a fisherman on the Sea of Kinneret, the risks should far outweigh any desire to spend a few hours on the shore of a lake.

He swished a dirty hand at me. "It's been a year," he said. "Medad's family is not hunkered down outside the city walls waiting for retribution. They know what happened was an accident. And they respect the law. What reason would *you* have to worry?"

Nadir was a manslayer. Convicted of the accidental killing of a man from his village during an ill-fated fishing excursion. For months he'd kept to himself, no doubt reliving over and over again the heated argument that ended with his business partner drowned and himself sentenced to life here in Kedesh. It was only recently I'd gotten him to even share that much with me, and he hadn't yet admitted what led to the two men exchanging blows other than to insist he had been trying to defend himself.

"I can't," I said, sidestepping any further questions about my reasons for staying inside the city. "There is too much work to be done. I promised Darek that when he returned from Tyre, I'd have these weapons finished for his men."

I blew the last of the dust from the knife and held it up to the light, turning it back and forth. A good cast. Straight and true, no bits of charcoal caught in the metal. It was possibly one of the best knives I'd cast over the last few months. Since copper ore was scarce and tin only rarely brought in by foreign traders, I usually had to make do with melting down broken weapons or tools that Darek and his men recovered during their travels, and this recast knife was no exception. I could not wait to see how it'd look after I filed away the jagged edges and blemishes, polished it to a shine, and honed it razor-sharp. Although I'd become proficient in carpentry due to the scarcity of metals, smithing was where I found the most satisfaction.

With a low laugh Nadir scrubbed at his head with both hands, dislodging the sprinkling of sawdust that had settled in his brown curls. "Work. Always work. Do you ever relax, my friend?"

I used my shoulder to swipe at the sweat dripping down my cheek. "I'll relax when these knives are finished."

He lifted his brows. "And *then* you'll come fish with me?"

I shrugged, noncommittal, weary of the conversation, and very much wishing I could agree. But I should no more pass that boundary than Nadir. I'd vowed not to do so when I was nine, and I'd honored that promise by rarely even approaching the boundary markers more than a handful of times over the past eleven years. The vow to not leave the city also included a pledge of secrecy about my past, an agreement made for my protection, and even after all these years my mother held me to it. There was no way to explain to Nadir without break-ing my word.

A small voice called out, and I turned my head to better discern the sound with my one good ear. As I suspected, it was Malakhi, my youngest brother, scurrying toward us and the foundry where I'd begun an apprenticeship when I was not too much older than he was now.

"Eitan!" he called out as he approached, stopping on the very edge of the boundary I'd established for his safety. "*Ima* says to come home for the meal." His large gray eyes traveled over the tools laid out on my workbench and the smoldering forge in the center of the open-air foundry.

Although I sometimes allowed him to help with filing or sanding down various tools and objects, Malakhi was well trained to stay away whenever the forge was lit. Yalon, the metalsmith who'd trained me, had given me the same rules when I'd first begun watching him when I was a boy of nine, fascinated by the glowing metal, the rasp of tools across bronze, and the wicked gleam of a polished sword in the sunlight.

I'd never wanted anything more than to work alongside Yalon back then, and it seemed Malakhi might be of the same mind. The thought inspired pride to cinch tight within my chest.

"Tell Ima I'll be on my way shortly," I told Malakhi as I laid the knife on my stone anvil and untied my goat hide armguards. "And let her know Nadir will be joining us."

My brother nodded and sped back the way he'd come. I smiled at the sight of his sling dangling from his belt, flapping behind him like a tail. Since the day I'd fashioned the leather-and-cord weapons for him and our brother Gidal, who was two years older than Malakhi, both boys kept them on their person at all times — just as I did.

"I don't want to intrude —" Nadir prodded a stick inside the mud-brick forge to spread and cool the ashes.

"It's the least I can do to thank you for all the help you've been these last few weeks." Having offered to help work the pot-bellows one day, soon after I'd met him in the marketplace, Nadir had shown up at the foundry nearly every morning for the past two months. With a sturdy frame strengthened by years of heaving fishing nets into boats and a deft hand with a woodcarving knife, he'd become an invaluable partner. Along with manning the bellows, helping me fell trees, and constructing mud-brick forges, Nadir whittled handles for the various tools and weapons I cast. I'd been twice as productive lately, and yet he asked for minimal compensation for all his assistance, claiming he needed something to occupy himself since he no longer had the freedom to spend his days on a fishing boat.

"Besides," I said, "have you forgotten that my mother likes nothing better than feeding people until they can barely move?"

He grinned. The few times he'd accepted invitations to our family inn, my mother had practically stuffed food into his mouth with her own hands, delighted with his large appetite and appreciative murmurs between bites. "I would not want to disappoint your mother."

Chuckling, I tossed the armguards aside, grabbed the unfinished knife up again, and tucked it into my belt. I'd not be foolish enough to leave the weapon here in the foundry. I only made that mistake once, a few weeks ago, and still mourned the disappearance of the knife I'd worked on for days. Even in the City of Refuge, surrounded by Levites, there were those who ignored the Torah's command not to steal.

"However —" I snagged a waterskin from a hook on the wall and tossed it to Nadir — "we'll need to wash before we step foot in that inn, or she will feed neither one of us."

He laughed. "*That* would be a tragedy indeed."

I'd not even opened the door fully when I was accosted by two little girls. Abra and Chana each attached themselves to one of my legs, giggling as they both wrapped all four limbs around my calves and sat atop my feet.

With a grin, I took a few exaggerated steps, which made my sisters giggle all the louder. "I must be more tired than I thought," I groaned. "I can barely move my legs."

My mother stood near the table, wooden spoon in hand and mirth dancing in her silvery eyes as she watched the three of us. After tugging at their long black braids, I tickled the girls, which made them release their hold on my legs. Shrieking with delight, they scuttled off to obey Ima's directive to wash their hands all over again after tussling with me.

I stepped forward and bent down to kiss the cheek of the woman who'd taken me into her heart and home without condition eleven years ago. Even when I'd called her Moriyah instead of *Ima*, I had long considered her my mother. She reached up to pat my bearded jaw, radiating maternal affection.

"I've brought Nadir with me, Ima. The poor man wept with joy when I offered him crumbs from your table," I said with a mocking frown.

She narrowed her eyes and feigned a slap at my shoulder with her spoon. "Ridiculous boy. I should allow *you* only crumbs for such a falsehood." She smiled over at Nadir. "Shalom. I am glad you are with us, you are welcome anytime." She gestured toward the collection of cushions scattered around the large room that served as a gathering place for both family and guests at the inn. "We'll be eating inside today. It looks as though a storm is headed our way."

Nadir dipped his head with a quiet murmur of thanks. Although over the last few weeks I'd managed to drag him out of the shell he'd been hiding in, he seemed much more reserved around others — my mother in particular.

"I am famished, Ima." I bent over one of the large cooking pots she'd placed on the ground at the center of the room, breathing deeply of the spicy scent that emanated from beneath the clay lid. My stomach ached with anticipation. "What have you made?"

Instead of answering, she grabbed both my hands, turning them over to inspect my palms where slight traces of soot still gathered in the deeper creases. "You call *this* clean?" She looked over at Nadir with motherly censure in her expression. "If yours are anywhere close to as filthy as Eitan's, you'd better follow him outside and scrub."

Sheepishly we obeyed. I knew better than to talk back to Moriyah, even though at twenty I towered over her. Nadir and I made use of the small cistern out in the large central courtyard, ensuring that not only were our hands and arms completely free of dirt and charcoal but our faces and beards as well. I even dipped my head beneath the surface, relishing the coolness of the rainwater after hours working the searing-hot forge. The gathering storm clouds above us made it clear that my mother had been wise to refrain from eating in the courtyard today.

Nadir eyed me as I twisted the water out of my elbow-length hair, squeezing as much moisture out of the dark tangles as I could before allowing it to hang loose to dry. "Don't you tire of all that hair?" he asked. "How long will you hold to that vow?"

"I don't know," I said, feigning an indecisive shrug. Although I'd come to regard

Nadir as a friend, I had no desire to reveal my reasons for taking the Nazirite vow. However, his interest stirred memories of the conversation that led to it, the argument that made me realize every hope I'd had was for naught and that my mother's husband saw me as little more than a burden to bear. . . .

Tal and I had talked of little else than being soldiers since the moment we'd become friends, soon after I'd come to live in Kedesh. We'd spent hour after hour slinging rocks from the rooftop of the inn, whacking at each other with sticks for swords, and discussing the day we would join the ranks of the men who defended Israel. So, in our fifteenth year, we gathered our courage and decided to approach Darek one morning, certain that he would be thrilled about our eagerness to place our sandals on the path he'd trod since he himself had come of age.

Darek and Baz, his friend and fellow warrior, were deep in conversation in the shade of the eaves with their backs propped against the stone wall of the inn. As we approached, Darek threw back his head, laughing heartily over something Baz had said. Buoyed by his seemingly light spirits that bright morning, I stepped forward and with sober respect asked for a few moments of his time.

The corner of his mouth twitched, as if my formal request amused him, but he stood and gave me his full attention. I did my best to ignore Baz, whose enormous height always made me feel like a locust before a giant, and stood tall, willing my voice to deepen and my trembling limbs to still as I laid out our desires to volunteer as his and Baz's apprentices, with the goal of someday serving beside the two men we so greatly admired.

All humor washed from Darek's face, and for that matter, Baz's.

"That is not possible," Darek said. "I'm sorry, Eitan."

My knees wavered, but I locked them in place. "Tal and I are able-bodied, and many of the other boys our age are already learning how to fight." I pulled my shoulders back, my chest lifting in what I hoped was a display of rugged resilience. "We take our duty as men of Israel seriously. We will defend our people."

Darek's gaze flitted to Tal beside me, hopefully seeing my own determination mirrored on his face, before resting back on me. "Tal is of the priestly line; he is prohibited from serving in this manner. And you know the reason why you cannot be a solider. You cannot leave this city."

I bristled, six years of restlessness leading

to my sharp retort. "I was not sentenced here. There's no law keeping me here."

"My brother has little respect for the law. You must stay in Kedesh, safe within these walls."

"But the High Priest is old, he could die any day —"

"The High Priest's father, Aharon," he interrupted, his expression stern, "lived to be one hundred and twenty-three years old, and Eleazar has not yet seen his eighth decade."

"But —"

"This is not a point for discussion, Eitan. Your place is here with your mother, where Raviv cannot reach you. A boy who cannot pass outside the two-thousand-cubit boundary around Kedesh is useless to a commander."

I flinched. *Useless.*

His tone softened, and he reached out to put a hand on my shoulder. "You have been a great help to Yalon in the foundry. Smithing is a valuable skill, and he has spoken highly of the aptitude you've shown for both metalworking and carpentry."

A tinge of pride lifted my chin at the praise, but as much as I enjoyed my apprenticeship with Yalon, it was Darek who I revered. And Darek who I longed to emulate. "But I want to be a scout. A warrior, like you and Baz." I attempted to clear the curving plea from my voice and failed. "And if I am with you, nothing will happen."

He shook his head. "I'd be forced to look after you, and I can't afford any distractions. You would only be in the way."

My tenuous hold on self-control wavered, and I jerked my shoulder from beneath his hand. "If you won't train me, then I'll ask Chaim's father. He has told me before that I am as good a shot with a sling as any soldier."

"That is not a possibility. My word on this is final, son."

Fury seared my veins, turning my hero worship of Darek to ash and causing my words to come out in a heated rush. "I am not your son. You are my mother's husband."

Shock passed over his face, along with another expression I could not interpret, before his mouth hardened into a grim line. "Be that as it may, your life is here in Kedesh, at least until your mother is free. This conversation is over."

Within weeks of that argument I'd taken the vow, resolved that until my mother went free from this city, I would hold faithfully to the regulations of a Nazirite, neither cutting my hair nor partaking of any fruit of the vine — a perpetual consecration and a fitting atonement for someone who carried the weight of two deaths on his soul.

I had determined that if I could not train my body to fight the enemies of Israel, at least I could beat it into submission for the sake of Yahweh. Since I was not of priestly lineage like Tal, who was even now in Shiloh learning his role at the Mishkan, the vow had been my only choice. And from that day, the distance between Darek and me had only grown, until all that was left between us was a strained respect bridged only by mutual love for my mother and my skill in creating weapons of war.

The sound of Abra and Chana squealing broke into my thoughts, their small voices pitching high with excitement. The noise must have startled our infant sister, Tirzah, who began crying in earnest. I was grateful for the distraction from more talk of my vow.

"What is *happening* in there?" Nadir asked as he patted his face dry with the neckline of his tunic.

"Those three girls make more noise than an entire flock of geese — and I'm half deaf." I clapped Nadir on the back with a laugh. "Let's go see what has their feathers ruffled now."

As soon as I stepped into the house the reason for my sisters' gleeful shouts was made clear. Darek had returned from his mission to Tyre. He'd been gone for weeks, and we hadn't expected him back until after the new moon. What could have brought him back so early? I'd hoped to finish those last two knives before he and his men returned.

My sisters, along with Gidal and Malakhi, who'd also joined the ruckus, were all talking at once, tossing questions at Darek about his journey, even though he'd barely made it inside the doorway. A brief memory of my own boisterous welcome after one of his missions when I was a child ran through my head.

Back then there'd been nothing better than listening to Darek regale me with tales of his exploits spying among the Canaanites, skirmishing with bandits, and traveling the length and breadth of the Land under the commission of Yehoshua. Now such stories were a thorn beneath my skin instead of the welcome diversion they'd once been for a boy dreaming of a life outside these walls.

Ima waved the children away with her wooden spoon. "Let your father in the door before mauling him to death," she said. Then, ignoring her own directive, she went to him, slid her arms around his waist, and kissed him long enough that I glanced away to playfully roll my eyes at Nadir.

The two of them had never been shy about expressing their affection. Although I usually groaned and teased them about it, it actually filled me with an odd sense of pride — a feeling I'd had since the day Darek asked for *my* blessing to marry Moriyah. Even though the ground between us had always been littered with debris, I'd never doubted his unwavering devotion to my adopted mother.

Without letting go of Ima, Darek craned his head around to call for Baz, who was standing outside the doorway for some reason. "I've brought some extra guests, Moriyah. We found them on the beach near Tyre."

Darek's enormous friend stepped through the doorway, ducking his head to enter and turning sideways to avoid knocking the dark-haired young woman he carried against the doorpost.

"Oh my," said my mother, her hands outstretched to the girl, whose leg was splinted and wrapped with rough bandages that looked to have been cut from some-one's woolen mantle. Scratches and yellow-ing bruises marred every one of her limbs, and a terrible mark slashed violently across her cheekbone. "What happened to her?"

The girl's narrow-set eyes, as dark as her

long, straight hair, timidly took in the scene in the room: the long table laden with food, the children gawking at her, and Nadir and I standing across the room doing the same. Her hand trembled on Baz's shoulder as she shrank back against him.

"We think she was in a shipwreck," said Darek. "Her ankle is so badly damaged she cannot walk. She also seems to have been beaten, so it may have been some sort of slave transport."

"You carried her all the way from Tyre?" my mother asked Baz in astonishment.

He shrugged one of his bear-like shoulders and I noticed that, like Darek, Baz was beginning to wear signs of age around his eyes and in the white patches at his temples. "Wasn't a burden at all. She's fairly tall but there's not much meat on her scrawny bones."

Ima frowned in consternation. "Don't talk about such things in front of her —"

"Not to worry, *ishti*," said Darek. "She doesn't speak our language. Neither of them understand a word we say."

"Neither?" My mother stood on the balls of her feet, craning her neck to peer past Baz and through the doorway. "Oh! Shalom," she said, her voice gentle and inviting as she gestured for someone else to enter.

"We won't hurt you, dear. Come in, it is going to rain any minute."

In response, a roll of thunder sounded in the distance as another young woman stepped over the threshold, immediately going to stand next to Baz, whose enormous height dwarfed her. Golden brown waist-length hair curled gently behind her shoulders, and her sun-darkened skin set off eyes the color of a brilliant cloudless sky. She, too, sported a few bruises and scratches, but it seemed the darker-haired girl had suffered most of the effects of whatever trauma the two had endured.

With their knee-length white tunics stained and tattered and their bare feet encrusted with dirt and muck, the two strangers looked as though they'd been dragged all the way from Tyre. The diminutive young woman placed her hand on the arm of the one Baz still held, a move that spoke of protective reassurance. Then, as if she were staring down the whole of Yehoshua's army, she cast a slow glance around the room, jaw set and body braced for battle, those vivid eyes full of silent warning.

It took everything I had not to let my mouth sag open. Who was this mythical creature Darek had plucked from the sea?

Chapter Six

Rain pattered the roof, and oil lamps pushed back the gloom as our entire family gathered together in the main room to partake of a meal for the first time in months. Binah and Sarai, the two women who worked alongside my mother at the inn, had excused themselves from the room, taking little Tirzah with them.

My mother had taken our unexpected guests into another room to give them privacy to bathe and put on fresh tunics. When she'd returned, she informed us that long welts marked the taller girl's back, as well as the blue-eyed girl's arm, the still-healing injuries lending credence to the idea that they were escaped slaves who'd been whipped. Now the two girls sat huddled together on the floor, sharing one large cushion. The shorter one's gaze did not stop roving around the room, but the other's vacant stare remained latched on her lap, and she did not touch the food my mother set before them.

"They truly don't understand us?" Malakhi said, speaking around the too-large piece of bread he'd shoved into his mouth and earning a stern look from my mother. He wiped a bit of oven-char from his lips with feigned contrition, followed by an endearing grin that never failed to assuage Ima's ire.

"They do not, son. We have been trying for days to communicate, with little success," said Darek. "We do think that the taller one's name is Prezi and the other is Sofea, but we have no idea where they came from or how they ended up on that beach."

"What made you decide to bring them back here?" asked my mother.

"I couldn't leave them there. They were frightened and alone. Sofea made it clear they were not from Tyre, but somewhere across the sea. It seems they have no one. Once they accepted we weren't going to harm them, or perhaps because they had no other choice, they came willingly."

My mother laid her hand atop his, warmth in her expression. "You were right to bring them here, my love." She turned to Sofea and Prezi, who sat pressed together as if joined at the hip. "We are glad you are here," she said. Even if they could not understand her, I hoped that her soothing tones and bright smile might help them be more at ease.

In confusion, the girls looked at each other, and Sofea spoke softly in a language I'd never heard from any of the foreign traders who streamed through Kedesh on a regular basis. I tilted my good ear toward them, wishing I could understand the rolling tones that flowed from Sofea's full lips.

They did not look similar enough to be sisters, although I supposed they could be, but Prezi was tall and willowy, all legs and arms and jutting angles, her hair and eyes much darker. Sofea's head would barely come to my shoulder, but there was nothing fragile about her. Her arms were lean and finely muscled. A leather cord hung around her throat, a purple-and-white shell dangling from its center and shimmering slightly in the lamplight.

"Have you finished those knives, Eitan?" Darek's question dragged my attention away from our guests. He jerked a thumb at his friend, who was busy devouring a third helping of my mother's stew. "Baz here has been harassing me for one for weeks."

"Nearly," I said, again mourning the loss of the stolen knife. "I cast another this afternoon. It'll take at least a few more days to complete. Nadir has been a great help with the forge, and he's a skilled wood-carver."

"All I did was keep the pot-bellows pumping," said Nadir. "You're the one with the metalworking skill."

"I thought you were a fisherman before you came to Kedesh. Did you work in carpentry as well?" asked my mother as she refilled his bowl with thick, fragrant stew.

"No," said Nadir, a shadow passing quickly across his features. "My father was a fisherman, and when he died a little over two years ago, I took over the business he'd built. My partner and I constructed two new boats, which is how I learned to work with wood." He dipped a piece of bread into the stew and took a large bite, as if eager to end the conversation.

To shift attention away from Nadir's obvious discomfort at discussing his life before Kedesh, I asked Darek whether he and his group of spies had encountered any trouble as they scouted on the coast.

"Nothing much to speak of. Yehoshua sent us there because there had been rumors that the king of Tyre was expanding his army, perhaps with the aim of marching this way."

My mother caught her breath. "Oh,

Darek, you don't think they will —"

"No, no. We are quite safe here, *ishti*. We've stationed soldiers in Beit Anat and Merom and up near Laish. The cities of Naftali are safe from incursion for now." I didn't miss how he'd qualified that statement but decided to wait until later to press him for more information. Baz shifted uncomfortably, keeping his gaze away from my mother, but when it snapped to mine I knew there was much more that Darek was not divulging.

"More concerning," he continued, "were signs that the tribe of Asher has been trading with the Canaanites. We even encountered a group of young Hebrews on their way to attend the fire festival in Tyre honoring the goddess Ishat."

"Why would they do such a thing?" My mother's tone was pure horror.

"They told us they didn't see the harm in befriending Canaanites who wanted only to live in peace. With the amount of foreign goods streaming through the port at Tyre, they felt it was best to keep trade flowing with the nations that surround us." Darek pursed his lips and shook his head. "I reminded them that Yehoshua, and Mosheh for that matter, had forbidden such dealings with the enemy, and that mingling with their gods is an affront to Yahweh. But they ignored us and continued on."

"How can they have forgotten so soon?" she said, placing her palm over the scar on her face. "It's been less than twenty years since Jericho."

Baz scowled. "With Yehoshua nearing the end of his life, it will only get worse."

"Our High Commander has a few good years left in him, my friend," said Darek, clapping Baz on the shoulder. "Even at over a hundred years of age, he still insists on sparring with the younger men. His mind is as keen as ever too. The way he's going, he may outlast the mountains." He lifted his cup of wine to drink to Yehoshua's health, and we all mirrored his tribute to the ancient warrior, as well as to Calev, who remained just as faithful and fearsome as when the two had spied out Canaan so long ago.

No one mentioned a salute to the health of Eleazar, the High Priest whose death would mean immediate release for all the manslayers trapped within this city, including my mother.

With her usual skill at deflection, my mother stood to refill everyone's wine cups, passing by mine as usual. The smell of the wine teased my nose, but I took another

86

long, satisfying drink of cool water. After five years without any product of the vine touching my lips, even the unfermented sort, I was rarely tempted. Although everyone else was used to my abstention and therefore ignored it, I caught Sofea's gaze dropping to my cup. When she raised her eyes to mine, a question brewed in them. Perhaps she was as curious about me as I was about her.

With a frown she glanced away, a slight tinge of color on her high cheekbones. I smothered the smile that begged to spring to my lips and hoped it would not be too long before she learned some of our language.

I turned to ask Nadir whether he'd be available to help me at the foundry in the morning and realized that his gaze too had been on the intriguing woman at the other end of the table.

I lifted my brows — a question.

He returned the gesture — a challenge.

I raised my cup again, tipping it toward him with a nod. *Challenge accepted.*

SOFEA

Adjusting my position on the too-soft bed, I slid my arm beneath Prezi's neck and, mindful of her bruises and welts, pulled her closer. Her body was tense, too stiff for sleep. She'd barely spoken since we'd left the beach four days ago. I wished she'd say something — or even just cry. This empty, implacable silence frightened me.

"I truly don't think they mean to hurt us," I whispered into her ear.

She did not respond.

Tomorrow these people would doubtless put us to work, as they seemed to have taken us as slaves, but at least for tonight they'd fed us, clothed us, and provided a bed in the corner of a tiny but private stone-walled room. But how would Prezi fulfill any sort of duties with her useless foot? It may be weeks, or perhaps months, before she'd be able to walk freely again — if at all.

To my astonishment, Darek and his men had not laid one finger on either of us, with the exception of Baz, who'd carried my cousin in his arms for four days and gently tended her wounds, slicing off a section of his own cloak to use for bandages. In fact, they'd gone out of their way to ensure we were warm, sharing their woolen mantles with us at night, and they had fed us and ensured our thirst was sated throughout the journey.

And now they'd brought us to this very large house in a city fortified by the tallest walls I'd ever seen. Built from stone and mud-brick, the dwelling was a two-level structure, nothing like the little round huts my family had lived in. Even now I heard footsteps above us, as if someone were walking on the flat roof. With a home of such large proportions, this family must be exceedingly wealthy and powerful indeed.

Through the high open window, the sounds of the city wafted inside — animals lowing, wagon wheels creaking, laughter, chatter, and a newborn's wail. I wished I could close my eyes and imagine I was back in my own village, but the soothing murmur of the sea was missing, as was the brush of the breeze through the beach grasses and the palms.

This place was nothing like my home.

One of Darek's wives had fussed over us, giving us fresh clothing, aiding us with washing our aching bodies, and exclaiming in her strange language over the lash marks on Prezi's arms and back, along with the vicious black-and-purple swelling of her ankle.

To drown out the foreign sounds and the pulsing, aching loss that seemed to be a permanent layer beneath my skin, I continued whispering into Prezi's ear. "The head wife seemed to be kind. The brand she wears must be the symbols of her gods, wouldn't you think?" The old scar looked to be a crescent moon and a sun-wheel curved around her cheek, one ray slashing across the corner of her eyelid. Imagining the pain of such a branding made me shiver, as did the thought that she, like my mother, must be a priestess of the highest rank. Did these people worship gods like those from my island? Were their rituals and sacrifices similar? Or worse?

Not eager to add to Prezi's distress, I did not voice such disturbing questions and sighed, wishing my cousin would respond. "Those two younger men don't look related to each other, and the shorter one with the thick beard seemed a bit ill at ease. I saw the tall one, with the long hair, speaking with the woman after the meal. He hugged her. Perhaps she is his mother. . . ."

Both of the young men had watched us throughout the meal. The shorter one kept to subtle glances, but the tall one seemed not at all abashed, leveling intense hazel-eyed stares at me between animated conversations with Darek and Baz. I'd never seen such long hair on a man — darkest brown and reaching past the middle of his back. When we'd first entered the house, it had been wet and loose, clinging to his arms and chest in ropey waves, but before we'd sat down to eat, he'd caught it up into a loose twist at the nape of his neck and bound it with a leather tie. None of the other men in this city seemed to wear their hair like his. And why, when everyone else at the table drank the wine the woman offered, would he pointedly drink only water?

Annoyed by my own curiosity and realizing I'd stopped talking to muse about the man, I shifted my whispers to another topic. "Perhaps when your foot is better, we can —"

"Go to sleep, Sofea." Prezi's interruption was terse, raspy from disuse of her voice.

"But we need to decide —"

"There's nothing to decide. We are stuck here. Stop talking."

I blinked into the darkness, swallowing hard against the clench of hurt in my throat. Prezi had never spoken to me like that — ever. But even more than the curt demand, it was the utter bleakness beneath the words that made me sense something was desperately, irreparably broken inside my cousin.

CHAPTER SEVEN

EITAN

"We should call up the men of Asher, Naftali, and any other tribes that care to defend Israel, and push north. Why wait? We should strike first, ask questions later." Baz's low-toned challenge to Darek greeted me as I ascended the staircase toward the rooftop where they'd stolen off to after the meal, taking the rain-slick stone steps two at a time.

"It's not the time, Baz," said Darek. "Yehoshua ordered us to conquer the cities within our own territories, not cast our sights outside our boundaries."

"But if we don't take the fight to them, they'll come here."

"Who is coming?" I said as I strode over the last stair. Standing near the hip-high stone parapet that surrounded the inn's rooftop, the two men snapped their attention to me, expressions wary, as if I'd

92

surprised them. Unlikely, as these two had spent the last eleven years spying for the armies of Israel among the various leftover tribes of Canaan. Darek's men were trained well in the arts of silent observation and stealth. It was likely they'd both known I was approaching before my sandal had landed on the second stair.

"No one," said Darek, waving a dismissive hand. "Baz is exaggerating."

I stared at Darek, my fingers curling into fists at my sides as shadows of our argument five years ago floated to the surface. "I am no longer a child."

Darek raised his brows. "I am well aware, Eitan."

He'd always been too careful around me, keeping the truth of his missions close to his chest, doling out tales to entertain the children but always stopping short of any gruesome specifics. I had been starving for details, as any man of full fighting age would be. I would be satisfied with crumbs no longer.

Therefore, I matched his unyielding expression with one of my own. Not since that day we'd clashed when I was fifteen had I dared to stand so firmly against him. Surprisingly, his stance softened after a few moments. He dropped his head and folded his arms over his chest, as if he was actually considering whether to reveal what he knew. Tentative excitement stoked in my blood. If he was willing to open a window to his secretive world, would he finally yield and invite me inside the circle of his most trusted men?

"All right." He released a long, drawn-out sigh. "I will tell you what we know. But you will keep this to yourself, understand? I have no desire to spark panic among the people unless the threat becomes more dire."

Although victory crackled in my veins, I simply dipped my chin in stoic acknowledgment.

"We are surrounded by enemies, Eitan. To the south, Egypt's vengeance simmers. To the east, Ammon and Moab's long-held jealousies build day upon day. To the north, Aram beyond the Euphrates licks its chops as it waits for Yehoshua to be gathered to our fathers. And among us, the remaining enemy tribes chip away at our foundations. The tribe of Asher has been far too amenable to peace with our enemies; the Benjamites have instituted a tribute from the Canaanites instead of banishing them, and Manasseh has flouted Yehoshua's command and cut a treaty with Megiddo."

"There are also tensions between the

tribes, arguments over boundaries and the like," said Baz. "Simeon is none too pleased with their lot, surrounded as they are by Yehudah's cities and close enough to the strongholds at Gaza and Ashkelon that they are vulnerable to attack by the Philistines."

Darek nodded, his expression dour. "Dan is highly dissatisfied with their portion as well, especially since they've only been able to inhabit one valley due to the strength of Yaffa's army. There's a rumor they plan to send scouts north to search out a new place to pitch their tents."

I stayed quiet, absorbing the flood of information they'd finally entrusted to me. For all these years I'd believed that the victories Israel had claimed, before and after Jericho, were enough. That the sons of Yaakov had their territories well in hand, were enjoying success in driving out the Canaanites, and that with the Ark at our core, our fledgling nation had little need to fear incursion. I may no longer be a child, but I'd certainly been naïve. Protected within the thick walls of Kedesh, I'd been duped into believing that such safety encompassed the borders of Israel as well.

I yearned to use the bronze dagger now tucked into my belt, like the ones I'd crafted for Darek's men, against the enemies of Yahweh. Every bone in my body begged to be used in such a battle.

"Teach me." I slipped the weapon from its leather sheath and held it out to Darek, praying that his arguments from five years ago had withered with time and that I'd proven myself to be useful, worthy of the effort it would take to share his expertise. "Train me to use these weapons I've been creating for the past few years."

Darek accepted the dagger. Then, holding it up in the waning light, he turned it back and forth as if he were examining a rare jewel. It glimmered like a flame as it reflected the sunset. Gripping it by the wooden hilt, he swiped the blade through the air a few times, getting a feel for the balance of the piece. I could tell by the satisfied look on his face that he was impressed. Pride swelled in my chest, threatening to erupt into a shout of triumph as he admired the product of my labor.

After handing the knife to Baz, who also expressed appreciation for my craftsmanship, Darek scratched at his stubbled chin, his beard finally filling in after a few weeks of shaving to approximate the odd fashions of the Canaanites. "I suppose we should," he said, his tone uncertain. "You'll need to defend Kedesh should anything happen. If

Yehoshua dies and the Arameans come south —"

"No." I clenched my fists at my sides, determined to not give in this time. "Not just to defend the city. I want to go with you. I am ready to be on the front lines of this war, to scout with you. To be of service to my people. I am tired of hiding behind my mother's skirt."

"You know that is not an option, Eitan. You must stay in the city."

"I was a child! Who would know — or care — if I left?"

"Raviv lives within an hour's walk —"

"Is he sitting at the gate waiting for me? It's been eleven years, Darek. Eleven years. If you haven't noticed, I don't look the same as I did when I was a boy." I gestured with a sweep from the top of my head to my feet, bringing attention to the fact that I now stood nearly a head taller than Darek himself. "I've endured being trapped in this city since I was nine, and I've kept my mouth shut about why, for Ima's sake. But I can't bear sitting on my hands while you wield the weapons *I make* against our enemies."

"You don't know my brother. It doesn't matter how many years it's been." The line of his mouth hardened. "He will never

97

forget your part in the death of his sons. He will never let it go. You are in mortal danger if you slip one toe over that boundary line, and I have little doubt that he has spies within this very city."

"I can take care of myself," I scoffed. "And if you train me, then all the better. In fact" — I narrowed my gaze on him — "you should have begun five years ago."

Darek grabbed me by the arms, shocking me into stillness with his thunderous expression. "Baz and I will train you to defend Kedesh, but you will *not* leave this city. Moriyah would shatter if you were killed, Eitan. I know you don't consider me your father, but you *will* honor your mother."

Releasing me with a jerk, he strode away and disappeared down the staircase, leaving Baz and me in stunned silence. The last of the sunlight flared over the western hills, and the haze of twilight gathered around us.

Suddenly Baz released a deep-chested laugh and slapped me on the back. "Excellent work, young man."

Annoyed with his joviality after such a heated confrontation, I turned a confused scowl on the man I'd known, and practically worshiped, most of my life. Baz had been a help to my mother during her escape from Shiloh when her life was in peril. Then after his young wife died in childbirth, he'd joined Darek and served alongside him for all these years. Since Darek's own brother had disavowed him and declared a blood feud on his wife and her son, Baz had stepped into Raviv's role, filling the empty space with his enormous personality and unswerving faithfulness.

"I haven't seen Darek that worked up since Moriyah was on trial for murder. When I arrived in Shechem to bring him word that the trial had been delayed, I thought the man might rip my arms off. Not much gets beneath Darek's skin. I've seen him take on one of those vicious giant Anakim alone without so much as a twitch of his little finger." Another story I'd never heard — and wagered that Ima hadn't either. "But he won't tolerate a threat against someone he loves, not for a moment."

"I can handle my mother, Baz. I have no intention of threatening her peace of mind."

"I wasn't talking about Moriyah, boy. I was talking about you."

I had no response to such an idea. Darek had married my mother a few months after we'd been moved from Shiloh to Kedesh, and although wary of him at first, I truly had revered him as a boy. But I'd always known that in his eyes I was Moriyah's son, not his. Not to mention that it was my fault his own flesh and blood had turned on him . . .

Brushing off the reminder, I strode across the rooftop to the city wall where it abutted the inn. Leaning my elbows on the stone, I peered over the rampart into the dusk. Something about the deepening blue of the western horizon reminded me of Sofea and I grasped at the distraction.

"Tell me about those girls you brought here," I said. "The whole story this time."

Baz leaned next to me, his back to the wall and the hazy landscape around Kedesh. "Not sure how much more I can tell you. I found the tall one, Prezi, sleeping beneath a palm tree, curled into the dirt like a sand crab. I didn't mean to frighten her, but her eyes flew open and I thought she'd scream, had myself prepared for some loud squalling. But instead she just looked up at me, all quiet, as if she'd already accepted I was going to hurt her and didn't even care." His brow furrowed. "A strange reaction. But then the little one, Sofea, came tearing out of the bushes, not minding my size a bit as she threw herself between us. She's like a tiny wildcat, that one. Claws out, hissing and flaring her tail." There was subtle admiration in Baz's laugh. "Darek did his best to calm them, and we tried speaking every local dialect we've learned over the past few years, but they were just blank faced, like we were braying donkeys instead of men."

"Why do you think they came so willingly with you?"

He pushed out his lower lip, contemplating. "The only thing I can think is that they just had nowhere else to go and no one left. They didn't try to flee, even though they have had plenty of opportunity over the past few days. Sofea could have run at any time, but she's so protective of Prezi that I doubt she'd leave her for anything."

"I wonder what happened to them," I mused.

Baz shook his head, thick concern on his brow. "I don't know, but I have a feeling it was something awful. The Great Sea is no little puddle and can turn wicked fast." He went quiet, perhaps conjuring the same horrific images I was of the two of them being tossed about by the waves, enduring the splintering of a vessel, and perhaps watching others drown around them.

Baz spoke again, his voice low and hesitant. "From what I've seen of Tyre, the men who command those trading ships are not at all gentle with the maidens, if you catch my meaning."

The thought gutted me. I'd considered the shipwreck, but not whether Sofea and Prezi had been violated. I'd been helpless to protect my own loved ones for far too long, and I had the sudden, overpowering urge to destroy whoever had hurt these women.

"I'm not backing down on the training, Baz."

"I know. I've been telling him this for months." He handed the knife back to me. "It's not that he doesn't have faith in you, Eitan. Hear me in this."

"Then why?"

"This place" — Baz gestured with a wide sweep at the high-walled city around us — "this city has not only been a refuge for you and your mother. It is here that Darek can retreat from the horrors he's endured. The filth that marks the cities of Canaan. The reminders of bloodshed and war. We took a large portion of this land fairly quickly, you remember, and most of us expected that the rest would fall easily into our hands, that the peace and bounty that Avraham was promised would already be achieved. I think perhaps Darek hoped it would be over by now, that you'd be spared the savagery of battle."

I'd only been seven when Yehoshua gathered the Hebrew multitude at Shechem to set up a white memorial stone and renew the covenant between Israel and Yahweh, but I remembered thinking that the fight was over then, that we had conquered the whole land, and our enemies had been vanquished. Had Yehoshua, the mighty man of God I'd considered practically supernatural as a child, failed in his quest? Perhaps he *was* human after all.

"He won't admit it," Baz continued, "but I think Darek looks at Kedesh less like a prison and more like a shelter from the storm, with his family tucked safely inside. It's becoming increasingly clear that idea was only an illusion. Like he said, there are enemies all around us and enemies within. If the tribes continue to mingle with the Canaanites, allowing the creep of idolatry to ensnare us, it will only get worse."

"Then teach me to protect myself, my family, and my people. Eleazar won't live forever."

Baz dipped his chin. "I agree. We start tomorrow."

Chapter Eight

SOFEA

8 Iyar

Prezi refused to get out of bed. I'd done everything to coerce her to rise, but she simply rolled over, blank-eyed face to the wall, mumbling something about no longer wanting to be pushed around by me.

Would our masters be furious we'd slept too long? The sun had already risen, reaching through the high window to paint the opposite wall with morning gold. She may have seemed kind the night before, but the mistress of this grand residence very well might swoop in soon to demand that my cousin begin her service, regardless of her lame leg. I was determined to keep attention off Prezi as long as I could. I would do the work of two for as long as it took for her to heal.

If Prezi lay crosswise on the stone floor of

the room we'd been given, she'd likely be able to touch both walls, but there was a low bed in the corner, a small table that held a pot of water for washing, and a three-legged stool. I'd been so exhausted from the long days of foot travel with Darek's men that last night I'd barely noticed our surroundings, but after standing on the stool to peek through the window, I discovered that our room was situated on the bottom floor of the inn and that our door led out to a large central courtyard.

Ignoring my own bruised ribs and tender feet, I stepped out into the morning. A large number of people I hadn't seen last night were gathered around a long, low cedar table. Seated on pillows and partaking of a meal, they all spoke that strange language and seemed oblivious to my presence in the courtyard.

Darek, Baz, and the two younger men from last night were absent, but I caught sight of the head wife, the one with the brand on her face, standing with her back to me, patting dough between her hands and slapping rounds of it inside the gaping mouth of a towering stone oven. The other two wives were weaving in tandem on a large linen loom beneath a shelter in the corner, shaded by the palm-branch roof and trading quiet laughter as they worked side by side.

At least Darek's women seemed to get along, unlike my father's wives who were near cutthroat in their competition for his attention and the power that came with it. Being the most beautiful of the lot, my mother had never had to fight for his favor, and she'd borne him eight children, five who'd survived past infanthood.

Catching sight of the stone stairway that led to the second level of the building, I marveled at the way these people lived, stacked on top of one another like mud-bricks. Another stairway above led to the rooftop that was surrounded by a stone parapet. Curiosity sparked, and I was suddenly consumed with a desire to climb those stairs to the roof, survey the landscape around this city, and explore this foreign place I'd been taken to.

Although the journey here had been grueling, the towering white-headed mountains I'd seen on the northern horizon fascinated me, as did the sweet, rushing streams we drank from and the thickly forested hills that we'd traveled over to reach this high-walled city. This green and fertile land seemed to go on forever, nothing like the world I'd been born into, which had been surrounded by the sea on every side.

The two little girls who'd stared at Prezi and me as we ate yesterday were playing a game in one corner of the courtyard, something that involved rocks and circles drawn on the ground with charcoal. I had the ridiculous urge to join them, to partake in the innocent activity and their girlish laughter — anything to forget the sound of keening that rose up in my mind every time I thought of my brothers' and sisters' bodies lying exposed beneath the relentless sun, decaying. Swallowing hard against the nausea that surged with the conjured memories, I turned away from the girls. It was time to lock such thoughts away and accept my lot. Nothing could ever bring the dead back to life, nor could innocence be reclaimed. If anything, these last two weeks had taught me such things. Prezi needed me to be a bastion of strength. I would not succumb to pointless mourning, no matter that I had barely slept since we washed ashore, in fear of the horrific images that lay in wait behind my eyelids.

Spying a small pitcher at one end of the table, I strode over and grasped the handle. Some variety of juice sparkled inside the earthen vessel and the sweet, tart smell of the liquid made my mouth water. I began to walk around the table, bending to fill cups as I went, eyes averted from those I was serving. By the fourth cup I'd filled, the chatter around the table began to fizzle, then faded to a halt. The hair on the back of my neck rose as I scrambled to understand what I had done wrong.

A vision of Seno's face as he raised the whip flashed through my mind. Would my back soon carry the same marks as Prezi's? I was nearly grateful at the prospect — she'd taken that beating for me, and although I could never repay her, I would empathize better with her pain if I bore stripes of my own.

Someone put a hand on my arm, and in my shock at being touched I jerked sideways with a cry, dropping the pitcher to the ground. The vessel shattered, spraying dark red juice all over my feet and flooding the gaps between the stones like rivulets of blood. With a gasp, I dropped to my knees to snatch up the shards of the pitcher.

Long fingers reached down to grip my wrists, stopping my frantic efforts to clean up the disaster I'd created. I flinched, pulling away and dropping my chin. Would they punish Prezi too for my mistake?

The hands, which I realized belonged to a woman, again wrapped around my wrists.

She spoke to me in words I could not understand, but the tone of her voice was unmistakably gentle. In shock, I lifted my eyes to meet those of Darek's head wife.

With long black hair that gleamed in the sunlight and eyes the color of rain clouds reflecting on the sea, the woman looked like the Egyptians who had once landed on our shore, eager to trade beads of glass and a blue stone they called lapis. The scar on her cheek looked to be old, faded from time, but the rippled cultic pattern was still a stark contrast to the smooth golden hue of her skin.

She tugged at me, indicating I should stand, and I obeyed, head down again, remembering the way my father had flogged any slave who dared look him in the eye. I would submit, difficult as it was, for Prezi's sake.

The woman removed her hands from my wrists, but then placed a finger beneath my chin to lift my face until my confused gaze locked with hers. She spoke again, a question in her tone. With astounding gentleness, she unrolled my fingers and removed the pieces of pottery I'd been gripping in my palms. She dropped them to the ground, as if she cared nothing for the broken pitcher.

One of the jagged shards had left a small cut on my palm, and she surveyed the damage with furrowed black brows, pulled a small linen towel from her belt, and blotted the blood that had dripped down my wrist before tucking the cloth inside my palm and indicating that I should squeeze my fingers around it until the flow subsided.

She spoke again and then led me to the end of the table, indicating that I should sit down on one of the cushions. Astonished, I obeyed.

Then, to add to my confusion, she began to serve me. After filling a bowl with a thick barley porridge and then a layer of mashed dates, she handed me a wooden spoon and a round of warm, pillowy flatbread. Lifting her gaze, she pointed to the door of the room where Prezi was and asked another incomprehensible question, to which I could only reply with a perplexed shrug.

Offering me an assuring smile that contradicted the wicked scar on her cheek, the woman filled another clay bowl with porridge and headed toward our room. After her strange behavior toward me, the only explanation I could land upon was that she was going to feed my bedridden cousin.

Impossible.

Why would this woman, who was obviously Darek's favored wife and an honored priestess, serve a slave? Bewildered, I kept my eyes on the bowl I'd been given, even as the chatter around the table resumed.

Who *were* these people?

Chapter Nine

EITAN

Whether I would make any progress on this knife today was heavily in doubt. Everything hurt. I scraped the rasping stone over the flat of the blade, from tang to tip, arm muscles screaming with the effort, lower back aching as I bent over the anvil.

I'd labored as the town's only metalsmith over the past two years, after my mentor, Yalon, passed from this life to the next, so my body was in no way soft. But Baz had ushered me out of the gates of Kedesh before the sun rose and forced me to run around the city so many times I'd lost count. He'd thrown off training for torture.

But I would not complain. Even when he'd made me carry a large rock above my head on the last two times around. I was too grateful that he would take the time to teach me what he'd learned while spying among our enemies. It would take much to prove my worth to Darek, but I was determined to work harder than any other trainee until he acquiesced and allowed me to serve alongside his men.

Three more passes with the stone rasp and I was forced to stop. A hiss escaped my lips as I kneaded the back of my arm.

Turning his attention from the mallet handle he was whittling from oak, Nadir looked over his shoulder. "Trouble?"

"Nothing my agonized death at Baz's hand won't accomplish." I switched to massaging the other abused arm.

Nadir laughed, pointing the half-formed wooden handle at me. "You asked for it. Did you not?"

"I did. And I'll ask for it again tomorrow." Ignoring his incredulous stare and my body's protests, I picked up the rasp again and resumed my work. After the loss of that knife a few weeks ago, I had to push through the pain in order to finish the final two before Darek and Baz were sent on another mission for Yehoshua. Hopefully one of their last without me.

Regaining my rhythm with the stone, I worked to remove the burrs left on the edge of the blade from seepage around the mold. Nadir and I slipped into companionable silence as we worked, and my mind began wandering back toward the inn, wondering whether a certain blue-eyed woman was settling into her new home. Lost in thought when someone called out my name from behind, I startled and nearly dropped the knife.

I turned toward the exuberant greeting and unsurprisingly Yoram stood nearby, waving his square palm at me, a brilliant smile on his wide face. "Eitan! Ima say I can watch you!"

Although Yoram was a few years older than me, his mind seemed to be more on the level of eight-year-old Malakhi's. Along with his elongated chin, his overly broad forehead, and the widened stance of his short-statured body, Yoram's speech was affected, as if his tongue was too large for his mouth. But there were few people in Kedesh I liked more.

I returned his smile. "Of course you can, Yoram. In fact, I saved a job for you."

He placed both hands over his mouth, his small brown eyes sparkling with pleasure. He spoke through his fingers. "You did?"

"Indeed." I set aside the knife and gestured for him to enter the foundry. "Nadir has been carving handles for me, but I am counting on you to polish them for me."

A shadow of confusion passed over Nadir's features. "Are you sure that's a good idea?" he murmured.

"Of course!" I clapped a palm down on Yoram's wide shoulder. "This man is the very best finisher I know. When given an assignment, he will not stop until it is completed."

Yoram beamed beneath my praise. It was not idle flattery either. When he'd begun appearing at the foundry a few years ago, I'd given him a nonessential job or two just to appease him, not expecting him to stay focused on the task. But he'd surprised me time and again by applying himself to jobs with relish and following my directions with extraordinary precision. I still didn't quite feel safe letting him near the forge while it was searing hot and, like I'd done with Malakhi, I instituted a boundary line, but on days when Yoram appeared, eager to please, I welcomed his help. It had been a few weeks since he'd come around, having been busy aiding his elderly father and mother, but I always welcomed his animated chatter and persistently joyful nature.

I showed Yoram the knife handles I'd laid out on the workbench for him, reminded him of the best way to oil the wood so it'd stay resistant to water, and left him to his task, completely confident he'd follow my instructions to the last detail.

Although Nadir turned back to his own work, the low hum he released as he did so was tainted by disapproval. However, I believed that once Nadir worked with Yoram a few times, he'd come to see that, in spite of the differences in his appearance, there was innate goodness within his compact body.

Yoram jabbered away as he dipped the linen cloth into the pot of flax oil again and again, describing his wanderings through the marketplace this morning as I'd suffered beneath Baz's training regimen. I chuckled as he described an encounter he'd had with Huleh, the woman who sold eggs at the center of the marketplace. Three of her prized geese had escaped the cage she'd placed atop her stall table, and after attempting to corral the happily liberated birds herself, Huleh had begged Yoram to retrieve them. Around stalls and under tables he chased them, upsetting a few other traders hawking their wares in the market. "I catch every one." Yoram grinned so wide every one of his gapped teeth showed. "Huleh give me six eggs! Ima happy!"

"I'll bet she was," my mother said as she approached the foundry entrance, Sofea trailing in her wake, with a jug in her arms.

"I'd be all too grateful if Eitan brought home eggs from Huleh. That gaggle of hers is famous for laying double yolks. No wonder she was in a state."

Yoram dropped the stained linen cloth he'd been using and ran to embrace my mother. She kissed him on the head as if he were one of her well-loved children. "Don't let me interrupt your work," she said, nudging Yoram back toward his workbench. "I simply heard three rumbling bellies all the way from the inn and was compelled to bring food to head off the threat of an earthquake."

"Thank you, Ima. Baz's idea of training seems to include starvation, as the barley porridge from this morning is only a delicious memory." I wiped my hands on my tunic and she eyed them with a frown. "No soot this time," I said with a grin, but I obeyed her silent command and headed for a pot of fresh water and a clean towel.

Nadir thanked my mother for her generosity and then greeted Sofea. The young woman said nothing, but blue eyes flicked from Nadir to me and back to my mother as she hung back just beyond the shadow of the eaves. A pinch formed between her brows, as if she were desperate to understand but was wary of stepping foot inside, even though the foundry was merely three hip-high stone walls and four oak corner posts to hold the roof aloft.

She turned to cast a slow survey over the bustling marketplace, her long, unfettered curls twisting in the breeze, shimmering in spirals across her face and lips. She smoothed them away and pulled the bulk of her hair to one side, letting the fall of golden brown cascade over her shoulder. My attempt to avoid staring failed miserably.

A few girls had caught my eye over the past couple of years, and lately I'd even considered being more intentional in pursuit of one in particular, but no woman had ever drawn me like this one. Even standing still she seemed to be fluid, and her striking blue eyes, silken sun-bronzed skin, and perfect rose-colored lips combined together to set her apart from any Hebrew woman. But even more than her foreign beauty was the loyalty she'd exhibited that first night, her fierce expression making it clear to all of us that she'd gladly give her life for Prezi. Her eyes roved over the milling crowd in curiosity, as if our mundane marketplace were some strange wonder to behold.

Had she never seen a city like this? Kedesh was small by most measures, but every year more stalls joined the market and more foreign traders were drawn here, where a large portion of the inhabitants were barred from leaving the city and therefore were desperate for news and goods from outside the walls.

My mother gave Nadir, Yoram, and me each a linen-wrapped package from the basket she carried. I sat on a stool in the corner of the foundry and leaned back against the low stone wall before unwrapping the offering — a green apple, a large chunk of crumbly goat cheese, a handful of olives, and oven-warm bread.

My mother then handed each of us a clay cup from her basket and after taking the spouted jug from Sofea, who'd been holding it close to her body as if fearful of dropping it, poured us all a serving of barley beer.

"She thought she was a slave," Ima said as she pressed the stopper back into place and set the pitcher on my workbench.

"Why would she think that?" I glanced at Sofea, who still stood watching the traders hawking their wares and the melee of wagons, animals, and people in the street with open awe. She flinched when two pipers struck up a merry tune nearby and a group of three older children began clapping and singing along.

"Considering Darek found them on that beach half-drowned, then brought them here without the ability to explain what was happening, it must have been a perfectly natural explanation in their minds."

I hummed agreement as I took a drink of the beer, then swiped the back of my hand across my lips and asked my mother in a low tone how she'd figured out Sofea's assumption. It was unsettling to talk about Sofea when she was well within earshot, whether she understood our conversation or not.

My mother seemed to feel the same way. She turned her back, blocking my view of the young woman as she spoke. "When she appeared in the courtyard this morning, she took it upon herself to fill everyone's cups with pomegranate juice."

"She wasn't just being helpful?"

"It wasn't the act of pouring juice that was concerning. She refused to look anyone in the eye, and practically hit the clouds when I touched her arm. Then, when she accidentally dropped the pitcher, she acted as though I would beat her." Tears sparkled in my mother's eyes. "Poor girl. I wish I knew what happened to her. . . . And even worse, Prezi refuses to move from the bed. She only stares at the wall, wouldn't even touch the porridge I brought her. Something truly awful happened to them."

My mother lifted her eyes and was silent for a while, her palm laid over her heart. I held my tongue, familiar with the far-off expression on her face. Then, with certainty in her every word, she said, "Yahweh brought them here, Eitan. He brought them here to heal. To be lifted from the depths."

I did not respond to the declaration. I'd long understood that these confident pronouncements from my mother's lips came from deep within, a reflection of her soul connection to Yahweh. My stomach wrenched as my gaze moved over the shadows beneath Sofea's eyes and the perpetual downturn of her full mouth. She may not be nearly as broken as Prezi, but it was clear that grief clung to her bones. What horrors had this lovely woman endured? And how long would it be before I could coax a smile from those beautiful lips?

Suddenly, her head jerked, gaze pinned on something down the street, her lips parted in surprise or confusion. Then, before any of us could react, she ran, curls floating behind her like a wave.

After a shocked glance at my mother, I bolted out of the foundry and followed as Sofea dodged carts, people, and even a large white dog on her frenzied path through the marketplace. My first thought was that she'd been attempting to flee, yet she was not heading toward the gates, but farther into Kedesh. She moved toward a stall, one that sold dyes and perfumes. A woman stood in front of the table and Sofea approached her, both hands stretched out. I skidded to a halt, overused thigh muscles aching, stunned by Sofea's strange behavior.

The woman's brown eyes were large and round as she faced Sofea. I'd seen this same tradeswoman a few times, both this year and last, at times with an elderly man who I guessed to be her husband, or master. Her bright red hair stood out among the dark-headed people in the market, and her painted lips and clinging dresses did much to entice customers to her stall. Although I did not know her name, I'd heard the dyes she offered were imported from Tyre, the bustling seaport my father had just visited — the city where Sofea had been found.

The two were speaking to each other in another language. Words overlapping, they gestured with their hands. Nearly bursting with curiosity, I stepped closer, moving to where Sofea would see me, but not wanting to intrude on their animated conversation.

After a quick glance toward me, Sofea

spoke to the woman again, her smooth voice stringing a long line of words together, like a necklace of finely polished gemstones. It didn't even matter that I could not understand the words, if only she would continue talking in that lilting tone with those captivating lips.

The tradeswoman turned to me, dipping her head in greeting. "Shalom. I am Kitane. I come from a land far to the north and across the Great Sea. This young woman says I speak a language similar to hers. She heard me chastising my little son." She pointed to a small boy whose big brown eyes peered at us from over the table. "I tend to speak my own tongue when I am angry. Loudly." She waggled her finger at the boy with a wry laugh. "Lozano knows my language well."

"Does this mean . . . ?" I marveled at the coincidence. "Would you translate something to Sofea for me?"

Kitane shrugged. "As long as my husband does not return while you are here and no customers stop by."

A thousand questions vied for supremacy. I was desperate to know everything about Sofea, to discover where she came from, to understand what sort of ordeal had landed her on that beach, to know why her blue eyes held such sorrow, but somehow I came up with only one thing to say.

"Please — tell her she is not our slave."

CHAPTER TEN

SOFEA

Not a slave.

The man whose name I now knew was Eitan had been adamant on that point. His family did not consider Prezi and me slaves, but only guests in their family inn. The relief was overwhelming. My knees trembled as Kitane continued to translate his words to me, telling me that Moriyah, Darek's wife, was his mother and how concerned they all were for Prezi.

No wonder Moriyah had seemed so shocked by the catastrophe with the juice this morning. She'd been trying to help me and I'd acted as though she were no better than Seno or Porote.

Although I did not understand his words, Eitan gestured widely, his voice animated and his smile reassuring. He kept his hazel-eyed gaze on me as he spoke, instead of Kitane, as if he were speaking directly to me.

The intimacy of the gesture provoked an uneasy feeling in my belly, so I took a step backward and again shifted my gaze to Kitane.

"He says that you and Prezi are welcome to stay as long as you like," said the tradeswoman with an inquisitive tilt of her head. "He would like to know where you come from and how you came to be on the beach where Darek found you."

With halting words I explained, leaving out the worst details of my village's bloody demise and filling in only small pieces of Seno's connection to my home and his betrayal on the ship's deck. By the time Kitane finished translating our fight against the sea, Eitan's expression had devolved from intense curiosity into devastation, as if he had somehow watched the horror play out in front of his face.

Moriyah, Nadir, and the other man who'd been at the foundry, the short one with different features, had gathered around Eitan as I spoke. Moriyah's hand was on her son's arm in a gesture of surprise. He placed his own over hers, and the sight of his obvious love for his mother revived that odd twist inside my stomach. I turned my attention back to Kitane, determined to ignore whatever draw this man, this long-haired stranger, had on me.

Moriyah spoke, and Kitane relayed that she had invited the tradeswoman's family to a meal that evening. "They seem most interested in making you feel welcome, Sofea," said Kitane. "I am happy to come tonight, but the caravan that my husband and I are traveling with is leaving in a little over three weeks, directly after the festival."

"What sort of festival?"

"These people are called Hebrews," she said. "They will give thanks to their god, Yahweh, during a harvest festival they call Shavuot."

"Who is this Yahweh?"

She shrugged, dismissive. "They insist he is an all-powerful deity without region or boundary, and that he caused many disasters to fall on their enemies, freeing them from slavery in Egypt nearly sixty years ago."

She patted her neckline. "I have my own goddess, but I keep her amulet well hidden here. They don't tolerate other gods in this place." Her brows lifted with subtle conspiracy. "Imagine, these people worship only *one* god. So very strange. And their laws are just as inexplicable. Overbearing and restrictive."

A shiver built at the base of my spine. "What sacrifices do they offer this god?"

My mind conjured the screams of a young girl as her body was pushed over the tallest cliff to the sea below, a desperate offering by our village after a poor tuna yield and a period of severe drought three years ago.

"I don't know, I've never witnessed this festival. There was another celebration a few weeks ago where lambs were offered and then consumed, but they said uncircumcised foreigners are not allowed to take part."

When I asked what that meant, her explanation inspired equal parts horror and fascination. I screwed up my face in disbelief. "Why would they do such a thing?"

"Your guess is as good as mine. But my husband was not about to have such a thing performed on him!" She cackled. "You should have seen his face! Besides, we are only traveling through, not here to worship their 'One God.'"

Two women walked up to Kitane's stall to peruse her large variety of dyes and perfumes, their appreciative murmurings indicating their interest in the goods. "I must tend my customers," she said with a wide trader's grin toward the new arrivals. "We will speak more this evening."

I nodded my head. "Thank you. I don't know how you came to be here, or how it is that you speak my language when you do not even come from my island," I said. "But I am grateful."

She smiled, showing a wide gap between her front teeth. "Perhaps my goddess brought us together." She brushed her fingertips over the neckline of her tunic.

"Perhaps," I allowed, wondering which goddess she served. Was it Atemito, the goddess my mother venerated? The one worshipped on the sacred hill back on my island? I brushed away the unsettling thought to consider how I would talk Kitane into taking Prezi and me with her when she left. Although this land seemed plentiful and far from stricken by drought, I would not take the chance that they may have brought us here only to sacrifice us to their One God.

The courtyard was full of people speaking a language I could not understand, but through Kitane, I was finally able to communicate. Moriyah sat near us, asking question after question about my homeland, my people, and pressing for more details about how Prezi and I had landed on that beach.

In turn, Moriyah told me about how Darek and his men had been scouting in Tyre that day, how they'd happened to come across us as they were leaving, having been spying during the fire festival in the city. What would have happened to us if they had left the night before? Or taken another route? Perhaps Prezi and I would still be there, our desiccated corpses becoming one with the sand.

My cousin had refused to come into the courtyard this evening, although Eitan had offered to carry her, and still moved from the bed only to relieve herself in a pot. Although she had submitted to my insistence that she wash her body, her lackluster responses and blank stares made my chest ache. It was as if her body was present but her mind far away. It seemed that besides Seno, Posedao had claimed another victim that day, but stolen only the best parts of her. Prezi's laughter, her kind nature, and our sister-deep connection had been devoured by the sea.

"Tell me of your mother and father," Kitane translated as Moriyah looked on. A woman who seemed to be so interested in my homeland surely could have no intention of offering Prezi and me up as sacrifices for their festival. Perhaps my fears were unfounded. My muscles began to relax, and I took another sip of date wine and a few slow breaths before allowing myself to answer.

"My mother was the most beautiful of my father's wives — his favorite," I said. "She was as serene as a placid tide pool most times. She doted on me and my little brothers and sisters. . . ." I cleared my burning throat, pressing hard against those blood-tinged images, pushing them down deep enough that they could not pick away at my determination to be strong for Prezi.

"How many wives did your father have?"

"Six. And four concubines. He was the chief of our village and the high priest of my people."

Moriyah's eyes grew round. "Six?"

"Does Darek have more than just the three of you?" I pointed across the courtyard to the two other women I'd seen working around the inn, one an older woman with black curls threaded with silver and the other a slight young woman with a sharply pointed chin and a perpetually cowed expression in her brown eyes.

"Three of us?" Moriyah's eyes followed my gesture and then she laughed. "Oh! No. Darek is the husband of only one wife, as Yahweh commands. Binah and Sarai are women who have taken refuge in this city, and I employ them to work in this inn."

My mouth gaped. "But this home . . ." My gaze circled the inn around us. "Darek is wealthy. Why would he have only one wife?"

Moriyah laid a warm hand on mine. "You have much to learn of our ways, Sofea. But Darek and I are bound, body and soul, for the entirety of our lives. We are one."

What did that mean? Did Darek control her so fully that she had no will of her own?

"Since your father had so many wives, you must have many siblings. Is Prezi one of your sisters?" she asked through Kitane.

"No, she is my cousin. Our mothers were half sisters."

"What can we do to help her?"

The unexpected response stunned me for a moment. My answer unfurled slowly. "I don't know that anything can be done. She left her soul at the bottom of the sea. Posedao consumed her."

After squeezing my hand in a gesture of reassurance that I immediately slipped away from, Moriyah left to intervene in a squabble between Abra and Malakhi. It seemed as though Malakhi took great pleasure in tormenting his twin sister. Kitane turned away as well, delving into a conversation in Hebrew with an inn guest beside her that I was helpless to understand.

I was grateful for the quiet to consider Moriyah's revelation, and a few things I'd noticed since our arrival now made much more sense. I'd not seen the other two women even approach Darek; they deferred only to Moriyah, fulfilling their duties and keeping mostly to themselves. And this afternoon, after we'd returned from the marketplace, I'd caught a glimpse of Darek and Moriyah talking together on the roof, shoulders pressed together, fingers entwined.

The man who'd saved us on that beach, by all appearances a hardened warrior, seemed utterly devoted to his wife, his eyes following her around the courtyard as she served her family and her guests. As I surreptitiously watched the two, I noticed the interchange of secret smiles — a private language that spoke of deep affection.

Even though my mother was my father's favorite and a priestess in her own right, on nights when my father called for her, many times she returned to our little hut with bruises. The man was brutal in every way, and the chief he'd promised me to in a neighboring village was rumored to be just as ruthless. A shiver formed between my shoulder blades as a traitorous thought began to form in my head. *Seno and his men saved me from that marriage.* And yet my mother, my sisters, my brothers . . . I refused to be grateful for the price that had been paid for such freedom.

Feeling the effects of the two cups of date wine I'd consumed and Moriyah's lovely meal sitting in my belly like a stone, I stood, desperate to move away from the questions and the happy chatter in words I did not understand.

Although tempted to go inside and try once again to rouse Prezi from the sleep that she'd retreated into most of this day, I caught sight of the stone staircase that led up to the rooftop, and felt the compulsion to explore.

The stairs led me to a wide, flat rooftop that overlooked the entire courtyard. I peered over the parapet wall to the gathering below. Animated voices carried upward on the breeze as the children played a game of chase. A few men stood off to the side, deep in conversation, Eitan among them.

After our translated conversation this morning, I'd been even more conscious of his presence. I'd forced myself to refrain from watching him during the meal tonight, but my ears rebelled against the restraint, searching out his voice again and again as he spoke with his young brothers who sat on either side of him at the table, vying for his attention. Now from my perch on the roof, I allowed myself a few moments to appraise his tall form, the dark hair that trailed down the middle of his muscular back, and the easy laughter that flowed from his lips.

As if he could feel the weight of my attention, he lifted his eyes, catching my inquisitive gaze, and the corners of his lips twitched upward. Flustered at being caught watching him, I turned and walked to the edge of the wall. Standing on the balls of my feet, I leaned against the rough stone, peering down to the ground below.

Although I'd never feared diving from cliffs into the sea, something I'd been doing since I was a small girl, somehow the long drop to the rocky ground made my stomach uneasy and I backed away, choosing instead to watch the colors bleed from the sky. After brushing the chill from my bare arms, I wrapped them around myself, wishing it was my mother's embrace curling around me instead.

A male voice came from behind me. I spun, heart pounding, expecting Eitan — but it was his friend Nadir who'd appeared on the rooftop. I retreated a few paces, keeping the staircase in the corner of my vision. Maintaining his distance, the man didn't seem to be aggressive, but neither had Seno. I would not chance being taken unaware again.

In many ways, Nadir was the opposite of Eitan. He stood nearly a head shorter than his friend, and his curly brown hair was cropped short above a very thick beard. Like Eitan, he was handsome, but with a wider, more rugged cut to his face. His skin was a deep bronze and fine lines around his eyes attested to a life squinting against the sun. Something about him reminded me of the men of my village who spent their days battling the sea for a regular yield of fish.

Nadir spoke a few words but then stopped abruptly, no doubt remembering I could not understand. With a pinch between his brows he looked around, as if searching for a way to help me understand. His gaze snagged on my shell necklace.

He pointed at it and asked a question. Then, moving his hands in a motion that mimicked waves, he made a shushing sound. Was he asking about the ocean?

I nodded my head and repeated his motion, to tell him that indeed I had lived near the ocean. I touched the necklace, brushed my fingers over the speckled shell at the center, and said the word for *sea* in my language. Then I repeated the motion for waves.

He smiled and repeated the word, obviously pleased with our little interaction. Then he pointed off to the southeast, made the wave motion again, and pointed again off into the night.

Standing on the balls of my feet, I lifted my body to see that he was gesturing toward a glint of moonlight reflecting on the horizon. It seemed to be a small lake, shining in the light of the nearly full moon. I made the wave motion again to tell him that I saw the lake. He gestured to himself and with one hand made the motion of a fish flitting through the water, and then with his other hand, he scooped up that "fish."

Understanding bloomed immediately. Nadir was indeed a fisherman, just as I'd somehow sensed before. I repeated his moves and gave him the words in my own language. I was strangely satisfied by the connection we'd made in our little game. I leaned back onto the stone ledge and turned my gaze back to the small lake that I could now more clearly see sparkling there like a blue-black jewel under the night. Would it reflect the eyes of uncountable stars like the sea did in the tide pools? How deep was such a body of water — enough to swim in?

I longed for the cool slide of water on my skin, the tang of salt in my nostrils, the pull of the tide luring me out into the sea and calling me to explore its mysteries.

Nadir began to speak quietly, his words foreign but the lull of his deep voice tugging at something inside me. If Nadir was a fisherman, why was he here in this city? Was that lake he'd pointed out the one he fished? He must, for what was a fisherman with no boat, no nets?

Although Nadir had been helping in the foundry this morning when Moriyah dragged me along with her to the market, it was Eitan who seemed to be the metalsmith in this town. I'd caught a glimpse of the weapon he'd been working on and wondered how he'd learned such a skill. For the brief moments I'd watched him converse with his mother, I'd been frustrated by my lack of comprehension and suspicious that they'd been discussing me.

But what did any of that matter? I did not welcome the attention of *either* of these men with their strange language and their strange customs. I could no more trust them than I should have trusted Seno. I needed to look after my cousin, survive these next three weeks until the Hebrews' festival, and somehow convince Kitane to take Prezi and me with her.

Ignoring whatever gibberish Nadir was speaking, I turned away, slipping down the staircase and into the house without once glancing Eitan's way. These Hebrews had nothing to offer me but more grief.

CHAPTER ELEVEN

EITAN

2 Sivan

Tipping my head back, I guzzled the cool water, letting it spill past the corners of my lips and down my bare chest, relishing every drop until the waterskin was dry.

Baz slapped me on the back, leaving a sting where his enormous paw met skin. "Giving up, are you, boy?"

"You wish, old man." I dropped the deflated goatskin bag on the ground. "In fact, I'll wager you that I can make one more loop around the city before the sun finishes cresting those hills."

"Oh?" With a roguish expression he glanced at Darek, who'd come this morning to observe my lessons. "And if you don't?"

"I'll do another two loops with your favorite torture device." I gestured to the rock they'd made me carry my last few times around.

Baz shook his head slowly. "I've something much better in mind."

"Oh? And what would that be?"

He clucked his tongue and pointed to the eastern ridge. "Getting lighter, my friend."

He was right, I had no time to argue. I ran.

Following the trench that encircled the city, one of the defenses built into Kedesh by the Canaanites long before Israel had captured it, I pushed past the burn in my legs and lengthened my stride. These past three weeks I'd challenged my body in ways I'd never thought possible, but Darek and Baz assured me this training was no different from how Yehoshua trained his own men. And I would not complain. In fact, I was determined to run faster and longer than any other soldier. I'd not shame myself in front of Darek. I'd prove that I could hold my own against Raviv and that I would be anything but a distraction among Darek's men.

Passing beneath my mother's window, easy to spot due to the lamp she kept burning there day and night, I wondered whether Sofea had joined her yet to prepare the morning meal as she had since she'd arrived. For the thousandth time, I pondered what exactly had happened on the roof between her and Nadir that night. She'd come floating down the stairs with a blank look on her face and her blue eyes shuttered against whatever storm she was fending off. Nadir said he'd given her ample space and merely talked about nothing of consequence, knowing she couldn't understand a word, and that suddenly she walked away as if he'd somehow offended her.

Much to my chagrin, she hadn't been any more receptive to my offer of friendship than Nadir's. I'd learned a few words in her language from Kitane, but yesterday when I'd approached her with a greeting, instead of giving me the smile I'd been craving since that day in the foundry, she flinched and walked away without so much as a glance over her shoulder.

She knew now that we were not her captors. I'd asked Kitane to make that very clear from the start, but she was still in a strange land with strange people — it may be that only time could assuage her fear of us. But in the meantime I would do what I could to chase the haunted look from those intriguing sapphire eyes.

The air was sweet this morning, cool on my bare skin and full of birdsong as the sun slid higher into the sky, chasing shadows from behind trees and away from the city walls. A large herd of sheep, one of those cared for by the Levites who administrated the city of Kedesh, huddled near the city wall and blocked my path. Frustrated by the obstacles, I jogged through them with gritted teeth, trying not to startle the ewes as I picked my way past, and nodded a greeting to the four shepherds who were driving the herd around the city and toward the olive grove to the north.

Three of the men waved to me, calling out a friendly "shalom," but the other shepherd watched me intently as I passed. He was not yet a man, a boy of perhaps fourteen or fifteen, without much of a beard on his sun-browned face. Something about his perusal unnerved me, and I glanced over my shoulder when I finally made it past the woolen blockade. His gaze was still pinned on me, even as a trio of ewes broke free of the herd to wander off toward the tree line, and I surmised that he was irritated by my intrusion.

The sun had nearly risen past the eastern ridge, and I had no time to contemplate the strange young man or stop to apologize. However, the rough-hewn staff he carried had given me an idea for a way to bridge the gap between Sofea and me. . . .

Rounding the southern curve of the city walls, I picked up my pace near the gates, already opened wide to welcome early-morning travelers and those in need of refuge in Kedesh. Chaim, the commander of the guardsmen and a friend of mine for the past eight years, lifted a palm in greeting as I passed, but determined to win this wager, I lengthened my stride, ignoring both him and the screaming burn in my thighs and shins.

The glare of the sunrise blinded me for a few moments as I searched out the place I'd left Darek and Baz. The big man was hard to miss, and even from twenty paces away I could see the broad smile stretched across his thick-bearded face. Darek was leaning against one of the terebinth trees, arms folded and humor in his own expression.

Baz's grin grew impossibly wider as I skidded to a stop in front of them, heaving as I forced air into my burning chest. After a sly gesture toward the fully risen sun, he clapped his beefy hands together. "This will be entertaining."

A groan slid from my mouth as I bent forward with my palms on my thighs, still gasping for breath. "What are you going to do to me?"

Baz grinned with menacing glee and a conspiratorial wink toward Darek. "Patience has never been among your strengths, my boy. I think it's time we show you how to be still."

SOFEA

"What *is* he doing out there?" Leaning my chin on the sill, I peered through our window into the courtyard to where Eitan had been standing motionless since early this morning. All through the meal, he'd stood at the center of the space, eyes on the far wall, saying nothing, doing nothing — just standing.

Moriyah and the two other women who worked here in the inn simply maneuvered around him, going about their chores without so much as a glance his way — as if it were perfectly normal for a man to stand in a courtyard for hours on end. The only people to pay any attention to him other than Nadir, who'd stopped by for a few moments but left after Eitan refused to respond, were Abra and Chana. The girls held hands and did a little dance around his long legs, singing a chanting song that spun faster and faster until they tripped over their own feet and fell down. Then they stood in front of him for a while, making faces and

145

doing their best to break his composure. From the disappointment in their expressions, he had not been swayed by their silly game.

Before they'd given up, however, Chana had pulled a wide stool over to him and climbed atop it. Then she'd untied his hair from the large knot at the base of his neck. It spilled down his back, a waterfall of deepest brown that rivaled my own in length. The girls had then taken turns standing on the stool, twisting the long strands into a multitude of small braids, tying each with a snip of thread. Eitan had not moved one muscle throughout this treatment, allowing the girls to delight themselves in grooming him. Was this some sort of dare he'd taken on? To stand in the courtyard without moving or speaking?

"Why do you care?" Prezi startled me by responding to my mumbled musings from her seemingly permanent spot on the bed. "I thought you wanted to leave this place."

"I do." I kept my voice measured and my expression flat as I answered. "Simple curiosity."

Her extended silence goaded me to step off the stool I'd been standing on to look out the high window. Crossing the room to collect her used bowl and cup from the little table by the bed, I avoided the suspicious look she turned on me.

"Sofi —"

I spoke over the question I knew she was asking. "I'll be asking Kitane to take us with her when she leaves after the festival."

Although she narrowed her eyes, she let the matter of Eitan drop. "My foot is still not able to carry my weight. How will we go with her?"

I brushed off her concern with a wave of my hand. "I am sure they will let you ride in their wagon. We cannot let this chance to return north pass us by. Kitane can help us find others who speak our language. We cannot stay trapped here with people who can't understand us."

"And if she refuses?"

"She won't." I had full confidence in my powers of persuasion.

Prezi shrugged a shoulder, her expression blank as always. "It matters little to me."

Heart aching from the drastic shift in my cousin's behavior, I stacked the cup inside the empty bowl, grateful that Moriyah had somehow convinced her to finally start eating again. "Will you come to the festival?"

"I can't walk, Sofi."

"You can lean on my shoulder. Please, I don't want to go alone, and Kitane said that the entire city will take part."

"You don't serve these people's god. Why go?"

"I am curious to know what kind of god they worship. Kitane says they only venerate one. It's very strange, but she says —"

"Don't you remember the last time you forced me to go to a ritual with you?" she spat out, a dark shadow passing over her countenance.

I flinched hard as the memory loomed, and as I did so, the wooden cup tipped out of the bowl in my hands and clattered to the stone floor with a hollow sound. I'd been ten when I convinced Prezi to sneak through the night with me, to follow the pounding drums and wailing chants up a high hill near our village. My mother had gone with my father, his other wives, and a large group of revelers to venerate the goddesses of fertility, and I'd always been desperately curious to know what transpired during such rituals. What the two of us had witnessed in the sacred grove so confused and shocked me that I was unable to look my mother, or Prezi, in the eye for many days. The two of us had fled within minutes, and I cursed myself for dragging my cousin into such foolishness for the entire silent trek down the hill and all the way back to our dark village, where we slipped silently under our blankets. We'd not spoken a word about that night since.

My throat burned with bile as I blinked away the disturbing thoughts. "I don't think this festival is the same." I did not add that I was clinging to the hope that the priestess we'd come to live with had no plans to offer us to her One God. Whether she counted us as slaves or not, I spent every moment I was not with Prezi helping with meals or aiding Binah and Sarai as they cleaned the inn, hauled water, and worked the looms, desperate to display our usefulness just in case I was wrong.

"You have no way of knowing that. And like I said, I cannot walk, and I won't be carried about like a child." Her disdainful tone, so opposite of the soft and kind one I was used to, somehow sparked a frisson of anger in me.

"Are you planning to stay in this room for the rest of your life? Will you simply curl up in a ball and wait for death? I lost my family too, you know. Even though I did not see them —" I cut myself off, knowing neither of us needed the reminder of the sight of her parents' bloodied corpses. I saw enough of it whenever I closed my eyes. And from Prezi's moans and the shuddering that shook our bed each night as I lay awake next to her, dreading sleep, the same demons plagued both our dreams.

I softened my tone. "You are all I have left, Prez. I am scared and I am lonely for my friend. My sister."

Her jaw tightened and she glanced away, her dark eyes not revealing anything. "You should have let me drown," she said, so low I barely made out the words.

For the rest of my days I would never forget the sight of my sweet cousin's body jerking in agony as Seno lashed her back for my sake, nor the despairing void that had consumed me when she sank beneath the waves after his fist knocked her unconscious.

"I will never let you drown," I said. "I will always fight for you. To my last breath."

Chapter Twelve

Festival of Shavuot
6 Sivan

Every shred of hope that I'd clung to over the past weeks melted away as soon as I awoke to find Binah at the door with two pure white tunics slung over her shoulder. Deep lines surrounded her pursed mouth as she regarded us from the doorway with mud-brown eyes, her demeanor suggesting she did not relish the task of retrieving us.

After setting a large pot of water on the small table in the corner, along with a towel and a chunk of natron, she scrubbed at her own black curls to indicate that Prezi and I should wash our hair along with our bodies. In silence, she spread the simple white tunics on the bed and swept out of the room, taking the remnants of last night's rare peaceful sleep with her. The sickly sweet smell of flowers wafted from the water pot, a harbinger of the awful truth.

A renewed vision of that girl hurtling toward the rocky seabed, garbed in pure white, locked into place. At my father's insistence, her body had been ritually washed and anointed with fragrant oil before he himself pushed her over the cliff — a fitting offering to the god of the sea, a beautiful maiden dressed for death.

Moriyah had lulled me into complacency, luring me with false interest in my family, false concern for my cousin, and a pretense that we were merely guests in her home instead of oblations for this harvest festival. No matter how hard I'd worked at proving my worth in this household, we would die today for the sake of Hebrew crops in the year to come. A deep throb of pain pulsed in my chest. We'd been betrayed yet again. What could I do? What would I say to Prezi?

Two mornings before, as I'd gone to leave the room, a stick that had been leaning against the wooden door clattered to the ground. After looking back and forth to see whether one of the children had been playing a game with me and seeing no one in the courtyard, I plucked the stick off the ground to examine it, thinking perhaps it was a shepherd's staff someone had misplaced. The long stick was tapered, finely sanded, and fitted with a cross bar at the top that was wrapped in soft wool. When its use was made clear in my mind, I'd laughed aloud. Someone had fashioned a crutch for Prezi, which would allow her the ability to move about without being carried while her mangled foot healed.

It had taken me hours, but I'd finally convinced her to try the apparatus, and by the time she'd become proficient at walking around our small room, the tiniest spark of life had bloomed in her eyes, and gratitude for whoever had made such a thing filled my heart to overflowing. She'd even conceded to my pleas to attend the festival. If only she were not stepping out of her room for the first time in weeks to be destroyed in the name of some foreign deity who called for our blood.

There was nothing I could do to avoid this fate. We were trapped inside a city with high, thick walls and heavily guarded gates. Surrounded by warriors like Darek and Baz. I could only hope that whatever method of death they had planned for us would be swift.

It would profit nothing to frighten my cousin, so instead I measured my breaths as I took my time scrubbing my body, then dressed in the linen tunic and helped Prezi do the same. If only the sweet-smelling water could wash away my terror as well.

A stoic Binah appeared in our room again and, with a brusque jerk of her head, indicated that we should follow her. Each slap of our sandals on the stone floor, each echo of my cousin's wooden crutch clicking through the deeply shadowed and empty inn brought us one step closer to whatever was on the other side of the door. I slipped my hand into Prezi's. If these were our final moments together, I'd let nothing come between us.

To my great astonishment, I realized that *everyone* was wearing white today. From the tiny child perched atop her father's shoulders peering over the bustling crowd to the old shopkeeper leaning on a knotted cane in a doorway, the people of Kedesh were an undulating sea of purest white. Binah kept her pace slow for Prezi's sake, so the flow of bodies moving toward the center of town parted around us. How had I not noticed that she too was clad in a white dress as she led us through the inn?

Many of the people carried baskets of goods — barley, wheat, and various vegetables — and a few of them led goats and lambs on tethers. The children carried long-stemmed wildflowers and fistfuls of barley stalks.

Although seeing everyone dressed in similar garb made me second-guess the assumption I'd made about our role in this festival, the closer we came to the temple at the center of town, the more my knees began to tremble. I gripped my cousin's hand a bit tighter as I wondered how long it would be before they singled us out, dragged us to the altar, and finished whatever Darek had begun by finding us on that beach.

Searching the crowd for the group of people who had become so familiar in these past weeks, I spotted Chana first. Seated high on Eitan's shoulders, the little girl clung to her brother, her palms clamped to his cheeks as if she would tumble backward at any moment. Next to Eitan, Abra bounced on the balls of her feet, again and again, attempting to see over the wall of white-clad bodies. Nadir stood on his other side, watching as I approached. His eyes darted to my cousin, and surprise flitted across his features. Remembering that Nadir had been carving the handle of a knife the day Moriyah and I had gone to the foundry, I wondered if it had been he who had created the crutch for Prezi.

To my shock, Moriyah appeared in front

of us, placing a kiss on Prezi's cheek and then my own. I'd not expected her to be among the celebrants, but nearer the temple where the rituals would be performed. "Shalom," she said, a word I'd come to gather meant she was greeting me. I stiffened, still unsure whether this priestess offered peace or destruction. A wrinkle formed between her black brows, a look of concern that I did not trust, so I shifted my attention to the gathering around me.

Craning my neck, I searched the porch of the small temple but could see no signs of an altar, nor any depictions of the Hebrews' One God. I'd visited the temple on my island twice a year, at each solstice, and remembered well the various carvings set upon pedestals, the gods our people had imported from the ancient homeland we'd come from, as well as those we'd gathered into the fold of worship as we made peace with various tribes and peoples from all around the Great Sea. But here, at the center of Kedesh, there were no carvings, no sacred trees, no smoldering incense burners. What sort of bizarre religion did these people hold to? And now that I considered the lack of gods here, I remembered that I'd not seen any statues or engravings at the inn, nor did the people around us wear any amulets. There were plenty of niches built into the walls, perfect places to set household gods or small home altars, but they sat empty, or were used as shelving for small pots, cups, or other mundane items. Not once had I seen a carving of a deity since I'd entered Kedesh.

They don't tolerate other gods, Kitane had said the day I'd met her, and I wondered if the one she had tied about her neck, hidden beneath her dress, was the only depiction of a deity in this town.

Regardless of the lack of graven images of this unknown god, if this were a festival to celebrate harvest, offerings must be made, and as my mother had told me the day I'd seen that white-clad girl plunge from the cliff and into the waiting arms of Posedao, nothing appeased a god and ensured a plentiful harvest like blood.

A large group of men, clad also in white tunics and white head coverings, stood near the temple, accepting baskets of produce, jars of grains, and jugs of wine and beer. They disappeared time and time again into the temple. Was the statue of their One God located within? This god must be a greedy one indeed for so much food and drink to be laid at his feet. Everyone gathered in this square seemed to have something to give.

Would all of this be burned on an altar inside the temple? It seemed such a waste.

Some of the white-clad priests gathered to the side of the temple porch were making music; the drums, pipes, lyres, and sistra lifted a merry rhythm over the heads of the crowd. A few others began to sing, a multi-layered tune that matched the instruments with perfect precision.

Voices began to rise around us to join in the song that the musicians were leading. Everyone seemed to know the words and the tune, even Chana and Abra, whose eyes shone with pleasure as they followed the melody, lifting their arms and waving the pink and purple blossoms they both clutched in their fists. The music enveloped us, and although I could not understand a word, something about the song gave my heart a buoyant feeling, as if this music were crafted to fill every bit of my body with exaltation.

This worship was nothing like the acts Prezi and I had witnessed on that high hill. In fact, the longer I watched the people around me, their faces reflecting the joyful tones of the song, the more I began to relax. The contrast between this sort of worship and that within the sacred grove on my island was like a night without stars compared to the glory of daybreak. And Moriyah, the woman I'd assumed to be some sort of powerful priestess, was simply part of the joyful crowd, her arms uplifted, eyes closed, and her upturned lips parted in melodic worship of her God.

For the first time since Binah had walked into our room with white tunics that morning, I allowed myself to hope that my assumptions about this festival, and about Moriyah, were wrong.

Then, as I caught sight of Eitan, with Chana still perched on his shoulders, bouncing to the rhythm and singing along with the song as well, the hope blossomed into near conviction. His sister gripped his cheeks harder to keep her balance as laughter seemed to bubble up from her little toes. The morning light on his face made his many freckles more prominent on his sunbronzed skin. As relief began to trickle through my limbs and the joyful song transformed into one that encouraged a group of women to circle into a dance, I gave myself permission to study this intriguing man, if only for a few moments.

He was so tall that Chana jutted high above everyone else's heads, and his dark brown hair was gathered into a haphazard swirl at the back of his head and secured with a leather tie. A large white flower had been tucked into the knot. I guessed Chana had placed it there from the way the blossom drooped by its stem off to one side. I smothered the grin that welled up as he wiggled his shoulders, playfully pretending to unseat her until she released a high-pitched squeal. Something sidestepped inside my chest as I watched the two of them.

My father had never done such things. He'd never embraced me with obvious pleasure the way Darek had his young children the night we'd arrived from Tyre. His kiss had never lingered on my mother's mouth the way Darek's had that night either, the greeting of a man devoted to the one and only wife he'd loathed being parted from. Would Eitan greet his wife that way someday too? As if nothing tasted as sweet as her lips on his? A confusing jolt of longing rushed through my body at the notion.

As if he'd heard my embarrassing thought, Eitan turned toward me, his hazel eyes full of mirth and that ridiculous flower now bobbing at his ear. Caught staring, I went still. His gaze flitted to my cousin next to me, who thankfully was engrossed in watching the celebration, and then dropped to the crutch beneath her arm. When his eyes met mine again, a slow smile stretched across his face, one that made me suspect that I'd attributed the gift to the wrong man.

Did you give her this? I lifted the question into the arch of my brows as I lightly gestured at Prezi's crutch. With a modest twitch of his shoulder, he gave me a nod.

Although he'd been busy training with Baz and Darek most mornings and the rest of his days were spent in the foundry smelting, crafting, honing, and polishing beautiful bronze weapons, somehow Eitan had made time to offer my cousin dignity and freedom by carving the crutch.

"Ah. Handsome, no?" Kitane had found me in the crowd and now stood on my other side, her hand looping through my arm. The tease in her voice made it clear she'd seen the interchange between Eitan and me.

Supremely grateful that no one around us spoke our language, I turned my attention back to the white-capped man near the temple who had begun reading from a scroll with a commanding voice. "I have no cause to notice."

"Telling lies now, are we?" She pinched my arm playfully. "You did notice." She leaned closer, lowering her voice as if it mattered. "And he *noticed* you."

A strange flutter began in my stomach.

Was Eitan aware of me in the way she was insinuating? Was that why he'd made the crutch? To lure me in some way? My lungs constricted. Did he have expectations after having offered such a gift?

Although my fear that Moriyah and her family had tricked us and were planning to offer us as sacrifices had dissipated, and Eitan's kindness seemed genuine, I would not stay around to find out if I was wrong.

I whirled on Kitane, grasping at her sleeve. "Take us with you."

Surprise wrinkled her forehead. "Take you?"

"Yes, now that Prezi has a crutch, she can move. We cannot stay in this city. Take us wherever you are going. Take us to your home, where they speak my language. Please!"

Kitane tilted her head, studying me. "There is no possibility of such a thing, my lovely. We have no room in our little wagon. We travel light and we travel quickly. I'm sorry."

Dread washed down my limbs. "But you must! When you leave, we have no way to talk to these people. We cannot stay here. Please, ask your husband. We will work, we will help you trade, whatever you ask."

She put her hands on my shoulders, a

162

crimp forming between her brows. "No. I cannot. My husband would not even entertain the idea. Besides, I have not even been to my home since I was a little younger than you. My father traded me to my husband for food when my village was starving. The way everyone was wasting away, I doubt if anyone even survived for more than a few weeks after I left with the trading caravan."

"But without you —"

"Listen to me. You have no choice. Learn their language. Make a new life here. These people and their customs may be strange, but there are worse things than living in Kedesh." Her expression darkened. "*Much* worse. I am very fortunate that I am treated as a wife and not a slave."

"Besides" — she smiled again, gesturing with a tip of her head toward Nadir and Eitan — "with those two both pursuing you, it won't be long until one of them comes seeking your hand."

"I don't want that."

She squeezed my arm with a suggestive laugh. "You will. And when you do, language won't matter all that much."

Chapter Thirteen

Eitan

20 Tishri
Four months later

Dirt and sweat stung my eyes, but neither of my hands were free to swipe them away, locked as I was in the violent embrace of a man bent on wrestling me to the ground. The thunder of my pulse and the scream of my muscles blocked out every sound but the rasp of my breath and that of my opponent.

Where had Baz found this man to spar with me? Not quite as tall as me, but wiry, he had a strength that perfectly matched mine. We'd been grappling for what seemed like hours, neither of us giving in to the exhaustion that quivered in our muscles. During the struggle, half of my hair had come loose from the tight knot at my neck. Slick with sweat, it clung to my bare chest and across my face, creeping into my eyes.

Ignoring the irritation, along with the pain where my knuckles had grated over the pebbled ground during the wrestling match, I closed my eyes, focusing on every point of contact between us, holding my breath steady as I waited for the slightest weakness in his stance.

There it is. A shudder in his chest and a minute shift of his leg to gain better footing. I struck, twisting as I grasped his wrist, yanked it hard over my shoulder, and dropped my knee. Off balance, the man wavered, and I used the motion to flip him onto his back and pin him to the ground with a grunt of satisfaction.

After three heavy breaths, the fog of concentration began to lift, and I became aware of cheers around me. What had begun as a small group of soldiers observing our pairing had become a ring three deep of townspeople. It seemed as though half the marketplace had ceased bartering to watch the match.

"Eitan! Eitan!" Malakhi called from the far side of the ring of observers, jumping up and down and shouting my name with glee. His face glowed with the same triumph that sang in my own veins. Gidal was beside him, pride in his dark eyes, although his excitement was less exuberant than Malakhi's, who was announcing to anyone who would listen that the winner was *his* older brother.

Behind the two boys stood Sofea, with her cousin and Binah, all three with market baskets in hand. Just the sight of her knocked the rest of my breath from my already straining lungs. With her golden-brown hair shimmering in the sunlight, her blue eyes were alight with an intriguing mix of humor and interest as her gaze moved down my bare chest and then flicked back up to mine. She had yet to grace me with a full, genuine smile, but it was there, just below the surface, making me desperate to bring it to fruition — and soon.

Four months of waiting for her to learn my language. Four months of watching her skitter away like a mouse whenever I approached her. Four months of growing ever more convinced that there was no one like her and no one else for me. The wait had been interminable, but the way she was looking at me now made the crowd melt away. I moved toward her, drawn by a force that I had no interest in resisting.

The gray shadows beneath her eyes had softened, along with the extreme wariness that had so characterized her first weeks in Kedesh. Thanks to the crutch I'd made for

Prezi, the two women no longer stayed holed up in their room, Prezi joining her cousin in helping around the inn, cooking, cleaning, fetching water from the spring, and running errands in the marketplace. Bit by bit they'd begun to meld with our family, much as Binah and Sarai had done years ago when my mother offered them each refuge.

My siblings adored both women, and Chana especially seemed drawn to Prezi's quiet nature. Abra, on the other hand, was enamored with Sofea, following her everywhere, begging to braid her exotic hair, and taking it upon herself to teach her as many Hebrew words as possible. I'd wondered whether Sofea would tire of the girl after a time, but she endured the endless chatter with no small measure of grace.

And each time she watched over her cousin like a lioness, each hidden smile she shared with my sister, each sweet rise and fall of her stumbling, accented attempts at my language made my appreciation for her deepen even further. I was hungry to know more of her — to delve into the secrets she guarded behind those entrancing blue eyes.

Someone handed me a waterskin and I drank deeply from the spout, still not taking my gaze from Sofea's. And for the first time since she'd stepped her graceful foot across my mother's threshold, she met my stare without flinching, without shying away or passing off her interest in me as fleeting curiosity. I suppressed a victorious grin. My wait was nearly over.

Malakhi spun around. "Did you see?" he asked Sofea. "Did you see how easily Eitan bested that man? There is no one in Kedesh who can pin him," he boasted, his chin lifting higher. "I know it."

"Is that so?" she responded, one brow lifting in challenge as she smirked at me. "Even Baz?" If even that tiny smirk scrambled my insides, what would a full grin from this woman do to me?

"Well, perhaps not Baz," Malakhi conceded. "He's a giant." His gray eyes went round as he considered the veracity of his own claim.

"He is that," she said, her lovely, lilting tone curving in fascinating ways. Although her tongue still stumbled much of the time over our Hebrew words, her understanding of our language had blossomed in past weeks. A pinch formed between her brows as she worked at comprehending the story Malakhi was relating about a skirmish Baz had with some Amorites years ago — a common tale the seasoned warrior liked to tell — and one that Darek insisted was vastly overblown. But even though she most likely understood only a portion of Malakhi's river-fast words, she still looked into his eyes, listening intently and proclaiming astonishment at Baz's impressive exploits.

"But even Baz cannot outshoot my brother," said Malakhi, his small chest puffing out with pride. "There are none of Naftali's soldiers who can wield a sling like Eitan. He can hit a target at fifty paces."

"Can he?" She turned her bright, laughing eyes my way. "I will see this for myself? No?"

I grinned, secure in my skills and plans already forming in my mind. "That can certainly be arranged."

I was distracted for a moment by the sight of that shepherd who'd been watching me as I ran around the walls that morning a few months ago. He stood at the back of the crowd not far from us, his mouth in a deep frown as he met my gaze before he turned abruptly and strode away. A large palm came down on my shoulder, taking my attention from the surly young man.

"I certainly cannot outshoot you," said Nadir. "I have heard much of your skill with a sling. But I find myself unable to refrain from challenging young Malakhi's assertion that none can best you in wrestling."

I laughed, thinking he was jesting. But instead of laughing with me, he narrowed his gaze. "That is, unless you are too weary to fight me?"

Although his challenge sounded nothing but friendly, there was an edge to the remark, as if he might have something to prove. A slight flicker of his attention toward Sofea hinted at his intentions. Nadir had been quiet about his interest in her, and to my knowledge rarely approached her, but perhaps I'd underestimated the nearly forgotten challenge between us the first night Sofea and Prezi came to Kedesh. Before I could second-guess my own motives for doing so, I accepted the match.

"Excellent." Nadir clapped his callused palms together. "In fact, I do believe a wager might be in order."

"A wager?"

"If I win . . ." He scratched at his beard, contemplating. Then he leaned in close. "If I win, you go fishing with me."

I'd pushed aside his invitations to the lake a number of times and had been glad when he stopped asking a couple of months ago, finally accepting my vague refusals as unmovable. If by some chance he did manage to best me, I'd find some better prize to offer and hope he'd not push harder for an explanation about why leaving the city to fish was impossible for me.

"All right. But if I win, you suffer my training regimen. Before dawn. With Baz." I wiggled my brows playfully. "*Then* we will see who is tired. Baz loves nothing better than making me stack rocks or dig holes for no reason at all."

He scowled, knowing how hard my mentor pushed me each day, but he nodded acceptance and then walked to the center of the loose ring formed by the remaining onlookers, all humor wiped away as he faced me. Then, without warning, he charged, plowing into my shoulder with the force of an ox and nearly knocking me off balance. But I held my stance and pushed him back a few steps.

Apparently this was no throwaway match. Nadir meant to collect on his wager — or at the least meant to up his worth in Sofea's eyes.

We circled for a few moments, taking stock of each other, both of us poised to strike. He was built wider than I was, broad-shouldered and muscular from tossing fishing nets and heavy woodwork. But while my physical strength had grown during

171

Baz's training — my body now honed into that of a solider and proficient with a variety of weapons — the most important skill Baz had taught me was patience. I now understood the value of waiting, watching, and weighing out my opponent's greatest weaknesses before striking at the exact right moment.

And I used every bit of that patience now as we grappled back and forth, both of us with heads down, one of my hands hooked around his neck and the other looped beneath his thigh.

"Come now," I forced out after a prolonged struggle during which neither of us gained any ground. My tone was jesting, but I did not allow my hold on him to slip in the slightest. "Let's call this a draw."

"No draw," he grunted, his iron lock on my wrists tightening as he tried to slip my hold. "I won't give in."

In response, I jerked his leg forward and used my body weight to knock him onto his back and claim my victory. He let out a gasp as the breath was jolted from his lungs. The amiable, confident expression that had greeted me a few minutes ago was long gone, replaced by a grim mouth, making me regret having accepted this challenge.

Had this match, or for that matter my

unwavering interest in Sofea, truly damaged the friendship we'd formed?

Standing, I offered him a hand up, but he lay still for a few long moments, his face pinched and jaw set. Perhaps it *was* time to tell Nadir the truth about my past and explain why I never left the boundaries of Kedesh. The only person outside my family I'd confided in before now was Tal, but Nadir had proven trustworthy. I felt certain he would guard my secrets well.

Just as I was about to apologize for that last move that ensured my victory, in case he was actually injured, Nadir released a huff of laughter and grasped my hand to pull himself to his feet.

Relieved, I lifted a note of humor into my voice. "So, you admit defeat, my friend?"

"For the moment," he conceded, his grin wry. "But when I want something, I rarely, if ever, give up." He flashed a meaningful glance over my shoulder to Sofea.

Brushing aside the competitive current still pulsing through my veins — for I had no plans to step aside unless Sofea made it clear that she desired me to — I slung an arm around his neck with a hearty laugh.

"Come now," I said, scrubbing my fingers into his scalp as I would with my own brothers. "Nothing soothes the sting of a thrashing like my mother's food. I have it on good authority that a delicious lentil stew has been simmering over the fire all day. And you'll need all the sustenance you can get before I turn you over to Baz tomorrow."

CHAPTER FOURTEEN

SOFEA

"Zayit," I repeated, flattening the word so my tone would match Eitan's.

"Yes, better," he said, rolling a bright green olive between two long fingers. "Zayit."

"So many words to learn." I sighed, shaking my head in frustration. Although I understood much Hebrew now, my tongue still became entangled with the foreign sounds, and many words were as yet a mystery to me.

"You've come a long way in the past few months, Sofea." He dropped the *zayit* into the half-full basket at his feet with an encouraging smile that warmed my insides. Then, reaching high into the tree, he shook the branch vigorously, unseating more olives from their stems. A waterfall of rose and green tumbled onto the blankets spread below to catch the precious fruit.

All around us the men, women, and children of Kedesh worked together to bring in the harvest, using long sticks to divest the branches of their treasure and cheerful songs to motivate the rhythm of many hands, large and small, at work.

I'd been surprised when Eitan had joined us in the grove today, but thanks to the wager he and Nadir had made yesterday, Eitan was free to help instead of training with Baz this morning, as was his usual routine. Instead, Nadir had been the one to wake before dawn and run loops around the city. I'd even overheard Baz telling a snickering Eitan that he planned to make his friend build a useless wall in the middle of a field and then tear it back down again stone by stone. I'd felt sympathy for Nadir, as he'd been nothing but kind to me and Baz seemed to delight in assigning meaningless but rigorous tasks to his students, but I had little complaint about working alongside the man who'd become the subject of all too many of my unruly thoughts over these past months.

My cousin limped into view nearby, managing an olive basket under one arm and the crutch beneath the other. She flashed me a knowing smile when she caught sight of Eitan, who'd inched ever closer as we harvested the olives and now stood only two paces away.

Although I made an expression that communicated annoyance for her humor at my expense, a swell of affection for my cousin bloomed in my heart. It was almost as if something about Kedesh had done the impossible and slowly but surely raised her from the dead.

Together with Chana, her small but persistent shadow, she headed toward the large press at the center of the grove where our collected baskets of fruit would be smashed beneath an enormous flat stone to produce fragrant, golden olive oil.

Since the day I'd realized Eitan had made the crutch for Prezi, I'd become increasingly drawn to him, and bit by bit my trepidation about his motives had lessened. Normally he kept a comfortable distance from me, our brief interactions always taking place in the presence of his friends or family. But today he'd seemed to be testing my invisible boundaries, staying close by as we harvested, working the same tree, and gradually drawing me into conversation. Enduring my ineptitude with his language with admirable patience, he offered a word whenever I stumbled, only the barest hint of humor in his eyes as he repeated words slow enough for me to emulate and never laughing outright whenever I mangled the pronunciation.

It had become a game of sorts, watching him with his family and straining to overhear his conversations at meals without detection, but all too often our gazes managed to entwine, invariably causing my cheeks to heat as I glanced away. Yet during the times I did manage to observe him without getting caught, I'd discovered Eitan to be intelligent, unshakably loyal, extraordinarily skilled with his hands, and always the first to laugh at the antics of his younger siblings — not to mention I'd memorized his every well-formed feature from afar. Watching him wrestle with Nadir yesterday had been a test in keeping my rebellious eyes from tracing the bare chest that had grown ever wider the longer he trained with Baz. Even the sound of his low voice jumbled my thoughts and heated my blood.

Sometimes, however, I glimpsed an underlying sadness behind his changeable hazel eyes, some inexplicable hurt that called my name and connected with my own grief-laden soul. At times the impulse to comfort him was so strong, I had to turn away before I embarrassed myself by giving in to the desire to go to him, wrap my arms about

178

his waist, and lay my head against his strong shoulder.

A squeal from Abra two rows away broke into my thoughts. "Ima! Malakhi is throwing olives at me!" The accused grinned down at her from his perch among the branches, blatantly unrepentant.

Although I could not hear Moriyah's quiet admonition to her most trying child, Malakhi's mischievous smile faltered, and he called down a reluctant apology. Yet the moment his mother's attention was directed back to her task, two more olives struck the back of his twin sister's head. Accepting that the assault was inevitable, Abra flounced away, but not before sticking her tongue out at the gray-eyed rascal in the tree.

Eitan chuckled. "Now you know why there are more than a few strands of silver in my mother's black hair."

I raised my brows, reaching for another clump of ripe olives. "And none from you?"

The grin he turned on me was nearly as impish as Malakhi's. "Oh, it was I who inspired the first of them to appear."

"As a child you were — ?" Frowning, I fumbled for the correct word. "You not obey rules?"

"Disobedient?"

"Yes. This."

He shrugged, the corners of his lips twitching. "I was . . . active. Never still. Always exploring, taking risks, and acting on impulse — which of course gave her no small amount of angst and frustrated Darek to no end."

"I was same. To explore water was the thing I love most." A sigh escaped as I closed my eyes, grasping at the tendrils of memories that were becoming more and more clouded as days passed. I could barely even remember the smell of the ocean or the sensation of sun-warmed waves caressing my skin.

"You miss the sea," he said, the words low with understanding. "You long for your home, don't you?"

I nodded, his empathetic gaze causing my throat to swell and my eyes to sting. "But my family is gone. All are dead in my village."

He moved a step closer but then stopped, as if compelled to comfort me but worried that I might dash away as I always had before when he approached me. But instead of being a cause for fear now, somehow his nearness smoothed the serrated edges of those blood-tinged memories.

"Last night I have dream," I whispered. "But the words were not Sicani. Only

Hebrew." The vision had been such a strange mixture of my village and Kedesh, the thick walls of the city towering over the beach and our cozy round hut opening into the busy marketplace. But the closer I came to awakening, the murkier the images of my island became, as if my new home had swallowed up the old. The faces of my loved ones were already more mist than memory.

My gaze was drawn to Moriyah as she worked nearby, with little Tirzah strapped to her back and Abra crouched beside her, scooping olives into a basket as she contentedly prattled away at her ima.

"I wake feeling sadness." I laid my hand in the center of my chest, where pain still lingered like a bruise that refused to fade. "Like I lose my mother over again."

Although I did not look back at him, I sensed him moving nearer, silently closing the gap between us until I could feel his warmth at my shoulder. "I am so very sorry about your family, Sofea. I wish I could remake the past for you. Save them. Prevent you from enduring such horrors. But I hope . . . I pray that you will be content here. With my family." His tone dropped to an intimate rumble that scrambled my senses. "And with me."

Had I misunderstood the underlying current beneath his words? Did they offer the promise of something more, or was he simply concerned about whether I'd settled into my new life in Kedesh?

But before I gathered the courage to look up at him and respond to his sweet words of comfort, I saw Moriyah's body suddenly go stiff, the woven basket slipping from her fingers and spraying olives as it landed on its side. Her attention seemed to be locked on something at the far end of the row, near the white stones that marked the boundary line of the city.

Alarmed, I moved toward her, but Eitan was faster, one of his paces matching two of mine. He reached for his mother with long arms, his body shielding her from whatever it was that had made the woman he revered go pale with obvious terror.

"What is it, Ima? What do you see?" he demanded, all his earlier softness pushed aside in favor of commanding vehemence as Moriyah continued to stare through the silver-green lane of trees toward the empty horizon.

Her bleak response, although incomprehensible to me, nevertheless caused a shiver of fear to trail down my back.

"Raviv." She clutched at his tunic, her

knuckles going white as she looked up at her son. "Raviv was there. Watching me."

CHAPTER FIFTEEN

Four large braziers had been set alight in the inn's courtyard, each occupying a corner with flickering firelight to buffer against the chill of the evening.

People were crowded into Moriyah's courtyard tonight to celebrate the olive harvest, with nearly as many gathered on the rooftop. Everyone huddled in groups on the ground: eating, talking, laughing. I hung off to the side and leaned against one of the cedar pillars beneath the shadow of the eaves, knowing that even were I to sit among those gathered here, I would still miss one out of every three words shared between them.

Since Moriyah's strange encounter yesterday, after which Eitan insisted on rushing all of us back to the inn and then promptly disappeared for the rest of the day, I could not push away the unease that followed me home from the olive grove.

When I asked Moriyah about who the man was, the only thing she would tell me was that he was someone who held a grudge against their family. But from the way she and Eitan had reacted to the mysterious stranger, and the way she hedged when I pressed for more information, I was convinced there was something sinister to the story — something that these people did not want me to know.

Therefore, although the persistent nightmares I'd endured during the first months in Kedesh had faded with time, this morning I'd awoken shaking, my pillow wet with tears, and in the clutches of dread that refused to retreat, even with the sun.

I'd considered bringing up the unsettling incident with Prezi but was loath to upset her. After the festival of Shavuot, she'd begun emerging from her self-made prison regularly, but it had taken weeks for her to begin smiling again and for the light to come back into her dark brown eyes. I could not chance undoing the miracle of my cousin returning from the dead.

She had found her place next to Moriyah at the table tonight, a spot she'd come to occupy on a regular basis these past months. Oddly enough, the more agile Prezi became with the help of the crutch Eitan had made, the more she latched on to his mother. Now every morning she woke with the sun, eager to help prepare the daily bread, and content to hobble around after Moriyah, serving guests.

She'd even befriended Yoram, the little man who shadowed Eitan much of the time, her endless patience with his mangled speech and constant questions earning his adoration. When he wasn't at the foundry watching Eitan, he was usually following her around chattering half-intelligible stories that even Prezi, who was more proficient in Hebrew than I was, could not possibly understand fully.

Something about Yoram reminded me of a baby Prezi's mother had given birth to last year — same wide forehead, tiny eyes, and jutting tongue. Within a few months my father determined the child an abomination and ordered it to be left on the rocks. I shivered off the memory of Jamara's blank, red-rimmed eyes as that baby was taken from her hands on the beach and the way she folded into the sand like a tent without poles. It had done no good to cry for such a thing. As chief priest of our people, my father's rule was bestowed by the gods. His word was law.

A low, all-too-familiar voice spoke behind

me, the sound curling around me like the embrace of a sun-warmed tidal pool. "Your cousin seems to have taken to my mother."

"She is kind to Prezi," I said, not turning around and hoping Eitan would not detect the underlying envy in my words. My cousin had been spending so much time with Moriyah over the last couple of days, preparing for this feast, that she and I had barely spoken more than a few words before crawling into bed each night.

"My mother's wings are wide. She does not turn anyone away from their shelter. Much like Yahweh."

To shift away from talk of his invisible god, I decided to press for answers about the man in the olive grove. I turned to face Eitan but regretted it immediately. He was entirely too close, his long body leaning against my pillar, and I was forced to look up to meet his gaze. "Who is this Raviv?"

He watched me for a few silent moments, his hazel eyes reflecting the light from the brazier nearby and traveling over my face at excruciating length. Schooling my features to minimize the reaction his nearness caused, I lifted my brows. A demand that he answer my question.

His lips dipped into a tense frown. "Darek's brother."

"Your uncle? Why be afraid of him?"

The frown tightened even more. "Darek is not my father."

I had noticed that Eitan's rangy build was very different from Darek's and that his lighter skin and eye color set him apart from Moriyah's Egyptian looks. I'd also noticed the respectful but unmistakable distance between the two men.

"Moriyah took me as her son eleven years ago and married Darek a few months later. My parents died of a fever when I was five years old. I lived with an uncle, a half-brother of my mother's, until I was nine." A twitch at the corner of his tightly clenched mouth told me that such an arrangement was anything but pleasant.

My hand went to my chest again, that familiar knot of pain surging to life. This must be why I'd felt such inexplicable kinship with Eitan from the beginning. He too had lost his family.

"I am sorry." My compassion came out on a whisper, and I longed for more Hebrew words to offer, words that might soothe a small measure of the hurt in him, just as he had done for me in the olive grove.

"I wish I could remember them better," he said, a pinch forming between his brows. "Their faces have all but disappeared from my memory. But I do remember my mother singing me to sleep, running her fingers through my hair. . . ." He gazed into the distance over my shoulder, likely caught up in a haze of memories that I understood all too well. I still remembered my own mother's face, but her voice, her smell, the sensation of her touch were gone, and without a doubt her image would soon follow.

When he spoke again, his voice was deeper, more tender. "Although I wish you had not endured the loss of your own family, I am glad that Darek brought you to Kedesh. I am glad you are here, Sofea."

His accent curved around my name, lending it fresh beauty and a sense of intimacy that I knew I should not desire. But even so, I nearly asked him to say it again so I could watch his lips form the word. As if he'd deciphered my renegade thoughts, he lifted his hand to capture a ringlet of my hair between his fingers and repeated my name. Softer. Slower.

All of me went still. Because we stood in the shadows with my back toward the gathering, no one would have seen the subtle move, but surely my echoing heartbeats were drowning out the conversations taking place all around the courtyard.

Caught between the instinct to pull away

from the moment and the overwhelming urge to lean into him, I simply stared back at him, paralyzed. For months I'd been drawn to him, since Shavuot at least, or perhaps even since the day I'd watched him let his sisters play with his hair. Humor tugged at my mouth as I thought of his dogged determination to ignore their antics and keep his eyes trained on the far wall of the courtyard.

With a playful scowl, he lowered his chin. "What is that look for?"

"Why did you stand so still in the courtyard that day?"

His laugh was not much more than a whisper, but it reverberated inside my bones.

"I lost a wager," he said, twirling his finger into my ringlet in a way that somehow seemed both absentminded *and* quite intentional. "So Baz decided to teach me a lesson about being still."

"And this is problem for you? Being still?"

"Perhaps." He smirked, and then his voice lowered. "But I've been practicing patience for a long while now."

"Oh? You wait for what thing?"

He leaned forward, forcing me to tilt my head farther back to look up at him. "This. For you to be able to speak my language.

So I could say the things I want to say."

"What things you want to say, Eitan?"

He hummed, low and deep. "I love the way you say that, with that little loop on the end of my name."

With my own thoughts from before mirrored so clearly, I nearly forgot what I'd asked him, but then I repeated my question. "What things you need say?"

"Everything." Did I imagine the quaver in his voice?

What *was* this? Why did this man draw me in like the relentless pull of the tides? I'd vowed from the beginning that I wanted nothing of Eitan's interest, but at this moment I wanted nothing more than to live at the center of it. Although my instincts still screamed danger, I no longer cared. So I allowed a smile to curve on my mouth and held his gaze for one breath. Three breaths. Five long, beautiful breaths.

With another resonant hum that bordered on a groan, he let his hazel eyes dip to my mouth. "I've been waiting so long for that smile to turn my way."

A shofar sounded from the direction of the city gates, barging into the moment and making me acutely aware that Eitan and I had not been alone in this courtyard, burrowed together in the shadows. I turned my head to search out the meaning of the ram's call and my gaze collided with Nadir's. He stood next to the flickering brazier, a cup in his hand, his eyes on us.

Guilt assailed me. I'd been aware of Nadir's interest in me for a long while now, and he'd been nothing but kind since that first interaction months ago on the roof. But whatever had been simmering between Eitan and me had boiled over tonight. And from the pained look he was now giving us, Nadir knew it too. Feeling helpless, I lifted a palm in greeting, wishing I could wipe the hurt from his face.

With a wince, he brought the cup to his lips and tilted his head back, draining the contents. Then he turned and walked out of the courtyard. I looked up at Eitan, wondering if he'd seen Nadir's reaction, but his eyes were instead on Darek and Baz near the center of the gathering. The men stood with bearded chins tilted to the side, as if working to discern the pattern of shofar blasts, which were even now being repeated.

Eitan said nothing as he slipped around me, out of the shadows, and toward them. After conferring together briefly, the three men followed in Nadir's footsteps and left the courtyard, leaving the large gathering of guests to stand around, speaking in low, confused tones. Some wore expressions of shock, and others seemed wholly disinterested in whatever situation was happening at the gates.

I made my way to Prezi's side and asked if she knew what was happening. "Someone is at the gates," she said. "Asking for refuge."

Was Kedesh under the threat of attack? Was this why Eitan had been training so hard over the last months?

After a few tense minutes, Darek appeared again and pulled Moriyah aside, their expressions troubled as he conferred with her for a moment before linking his hand in hers to lead her out of the courtyard. Surely Darek would not drag his wife into danger. My fear that an enemy was outside the gates ebbed away, replaced by building curiosity. Heeding its call, I took a step to follow.

Guessing my intentions, Prezi gripped my wrist with a warning to stay put, but I twisted away with a little shrug and a grin, knowing she could not keep up with me on her lame leg, then sped out of the courtyard, through the large main room, and into the night-shrouded street.

The inn was not far from the city gates, a location that provided weary travelers with a comfortable place to sleep. Passing through the wide-open inner gates, I noticed that the enormous outer gates had been closed and locked, leaving the receiving area safeguarded from whomever was on the other side of those thick cedar barriers.

A large group of people were gathered near the gatehouse, a jumble of agitated conversations lending an air of upheaval to the crowd. Catching sight of Moriyah, I made my way to her side, fully expecting to be warned away but determined to understand what was happening.

However, instead of sending me back to the inn, Eitan's mother looped her hand through my arm and gently turned me away. But not before I caught sight of the body of a man lying on the ground nearby, a dagger protruding from his chest. Eitan stared at me from the other side of the crowd with concern plain on his face.

"He was a manslayer," Moriyah said, her lips close enough to my ear that I could hear through the chaos surrounding us. "He was attempting to take refuge here in Kedesh. The son of the dead man caught up to him outside the boundary line and attacked. The manslayer was carried the rest of the way by his brothers, but he did not survive."

"A killer?"

"It was an accident, Sofea. The man shot an arrow in pursuit of a deer and it hit a fellow hunter. There was no malice intended."

"No matter." I shrugged. "Killers deserve to die." The swift judgments my father instituted for such things were always meted out by his own hand, and every time he insisted that the entire village, children included, stand witness to the slaughter.

"Our law differentiates between intended murder and manslaughter. Someone who kills by accident is allowed to run to one of six cities of refuge and take shelter from kinsmen who seek their blood. A fair trial must be held by a council of elders."

My face twisted into confusion. "One who kills you let live?"

"Yes, the manslayer will live out his life in the refuge city, unless the High Priest of Israel dies first."

Profoundly perplexed by such strange ideas, I gestured to the body, my clumsy words tumbling out in a rush. "You say he come here for refuge. Why not those 'six cities'?"

Moriyah shifted to look me in the face, her black brows drawn together. "Sofea, I'm so sorry that we have not explained this to you before now. I know your father —"

She stopped, as if reframing her words before she continued. "Prezi wanted you to feel safe and see that you could trust us before we revealed the truth. Kedesh *is* one of the cities of refuge. Many of the people who live in this town are here because they caused the death of another person."

A ringing began in my ears as I surveyed the crowd around me. My eyes flicked from one man to the other, wondering who among them was guilty of such a thing. There was no way to know. No way to determine who among them had snuffed out the life of another.

Prezi knew all this and did not tell me? Why would she keep me ignorant of the true nature of this city we'd been brought to?

Moriyah's voice was soothing as she stroked my arm from shoulder to wrist. "I know it may seem frightening, but those who have taken refuge here will not hurt you."

"But they are killers!" My voice pitched high, and the eyes of everyone, Eitan included, landed on me, causing my skin to prickle.

"No one will lay a hand on you or Prezi. You have my word," she said.

"How can you say such things? A killer does not change." Seno's final moments of brutality toward my innocent cousin had proven this quite clearly.

"Because, my dear girl," Moriyah said, her expression weighted with a mixture of compassion and regret, "I was the *first* to take refuge in this city."

CHAPTER SIXTEEN

23 Tishri
I stand on the highest cliff above my village,
eyes trained on the azure horizon, breathing
deep of the sea air. I inhale the familiar tang
all the way to my bare toes.
  Home.
  Home.
Home, *sing the gulls as they loop through*
the sky. The sun lazily trails its fingers through
the water, leaving a glittering path to the edge
of the world.
  Home.
  Home.
Home, *sings my heart as the wind whips*
my curls into the sky, across my face. I brush
back the tendrils, tugging the stragglers from
my lips with a laugh, but the wind refuses to
relinquish them, yanking them around my
neck. A smooth laugh wafts from behind me.
My fingers wrench at the rope of hair that
begins to pull tighter and tighter with every

moment. Toes gripping into the pebbled ground, I look down at my tunic. White. Pure white.

Spinning, I register my father's satisfied smirk before his hands lift to my shoulders. What better offering than blood? *asks his sea-blue eyes before he pushes me backward, and I fly, fly, fly to shatter against the granite-hard surface of the sea.*

The salty darkness envelops my broken body, the sky and the seabed trading places again and again. A wicked undertow drags me sideways, slams me against a boulder, my head cracking against its invisible weight. My father's voice slips through the silent, suffocating, churning blackness — "Take her, Posedao, she's worth nothing to me."

With a gasp I sat up, hands at my throat, kicking at the wool blanket that had tangled around my body during the night. Hazy dawn filtered into the room through the wooden shutters as I pulled in breath after shuddering breath.

Jostled by my violent awakening, Prezi sat up as well, her brown eyes wide, a hand splayed against her chest. "What is wrong?"

I shook my head as the last wave of terror rolled through me. "We have to leave this place. We have to go."

"Why would we leave?"

"You know why." A cold knot of betrayal tightened in my gut. I spoke the words through clenched teeth. "You *knew* these people were murderers and you said nothing."

I'd not even spoken to her after what Moriyah had revealed last night. Horrified and furious, I'd walked from the gates, head swimming, and went straight to bed, feigning sleep when she finally came in.

"No." Scooting closer to me on the bed, she wrapped one slender arm around my shoulders. "No, they are not."

I jerked away from her tender touch. "Yes, they are! Moriyah admitted that *she* killed someone! And that man last night was slaughtered within only a short distance of this city. We are not safe here."

She sighed, folding her arms. "Did you ask her about what happened back then?"

"What is there to know? She took someone's life. And she said many of the people who live in this town have done the same. We are surrounded by killers. Surrounded!"

Prezi released a low breath and leaned back against the wall. "I knew you would react this way, considering who your father was, and after what we witnessed back in the village." She paused, her eyelids fluttering as if she were blinking away the horror.

"This is why I asked them not to tell you before now."

Hurt and confusion tangled with my sharp response. "How did you find out?"

"If one is quiet, one tends to overhear certain things. And after working with Binah and Sarai, who tend to gossip much" — a little smirk passed over her lips — "I put together the pieces of the mystery a couple of months ago."

The knot tightened in my throat, cutting my words to a strangled whisper. "Months? You've hidden this from me for months?"

"You need to hear it all, Sofi, so you understand."

I shook my head, which was still filled with those nightmare images of my father pushing me off the cliff. "No. A killer is a killer."

"Even when the death was an accident?"

"The gods demand blood, Prezi, you know this. Justice is a life for a life."

"True. But the Hebrews' God is different from the gods of our island, cousin. Let me tell you Moriyah's story." She reached out, gingerly placing a hand on my cheek. "Please?"

"It will not change my opinion. We must go. We are not safe here."

Instead of arguing with me, she scooted down, laying her head on the pillow and patting mine in silent invitation.

Huffing a sigh, I lay back down and she pulled the blanket over the two of us, tucking it under my chin to fend off the morning chill that had begun to lengthen its stay more each day for the past two weeks.

Forcing myself to settle, I breathed the gamy wool and watched the reflection of the dawn rise against the back wall of the tiny room as Prezi told me Moriyah's story: The tale of a girl, marred in a wicked city that fell beneath the mighty power of the Hebrew god. Of a young woman, pressed to the outskirts of society, shunned and mocked for the blasphemy foisted upon her. Of a betrothal, unwanted but accepted by the maiden to please a father. Of a deadly flower unknowingly placed in a stew. Of two boys whose last moments were full of agony, the manslayer forced to flee for her life, and the grieving father who vowed to spill her blood.

"This city was her shelter, Sofea. Just as it has been for us."

I lay quiet for a few moments, absorbing the story, realigning what I now knew of Moriyah with the jagged path that chased her to Kedesh. "So the boys' lives are worth nothing, then? Justice means nothing to these people?"

"Of course it does. Life demands life. Blood calls out for blood. Moriyah explained that a murderer, one who knowingly and willfully steals life, does indeed forfeit his own. And this city, while a refuge, is also a prison. Moriyah will not leave Kedesh until she dies. Or until the High Priest dies and everyone goes free."

"*All* the killers in this city will go free?"

"They will be allowed to return to their lives, their debt satisfied."

"Why would the High Priest have to die? Shouldn't a manslayer simply go without punishment, then, if they are to be released someday anyhow?"

She shrugged. "If there were no consequences for even accidental killing, perhaps others would be reckless, heedless of others' lives. Yahweh seems to be inordinately concerned with the preservation of life. You've no doubt noticed as much as I that these people do not offer human life at the altar. It is only animal blood and drink offerings that are spilled in worship of the One God."

"This makes no sense. My father —"

Her face twisted as if bitterness had welled in her mouth. "Your father was an evil man. If anyone deserved to die, it was him."

I jerked back a handspan, as much from

the force of her words as from the venom that coated them. "My father was the high priest, given that divine right by the gods. It is blasphemy to say such things!" Even as the protest passed my lips I knew it was a lie. My own dreams illuminated the truth.

Prezi was silent, her mouth pressed into a tight line, but her chest heaved, as if each breath through her nose was an effort. She closed her eyes. "You were there, Sofea. You dragged me to the top of the hill that night, so curious to know what was happening beneath the sacred trees. How can you defend any of that?"

Chills razored up and down my limbs. "That was an ancient ritual to Atemito —"

"It was an evil ritual, Sofea. You felt it deep inside you, just as I did. It's why we've never spoken of it until now. And after living in Kedesh and seeing the way these people live, I cannot help but see it even more clearly."

I had no argument. I *had* felt the weight, the darkness of what we'd witnessed in the core of my being, as if some divine edict against such things had been scrawled on my heart.

"Your father made his own law, Sofi. There was no justice in it. You know this just as well as I do. He took *whatever* he wanted and *whomever* he wanted, equating himself with the gods and justifying himself by their unholy deeds. In our village, maidens were tossed off cliffs to Posedao and babies left to suffer on the rocks." Her voice wavered and she stopped, tears at the corners of her eyes. "Here, women are valued. Daughters cherished. Babies like my little brother, like Yoram, allowed to live and grow. Even the life of a manslayer is considered worth saving. Do you really think Moriyah should be slaughtered for the mistake she made without even a splinter of malice in her heart?"

I'd never heard Prezi speak so many words at one time. The passion in her voice stripped away any response I might have made. How had my unassuming cousin, who'd always followed my lead without question, found her voice?

She brushed her hand across my forehead and down my cheek. "I know this is a shock to you. You've been settling into life here, just as I have, which is why I did not tell you all I'd gleaned about this place right away. After all that happened, with your father, with Seno and our village . . . I begged Moriyah not to reveal it until I felt you were ready for the truth.

"These are good people, Sofi, and I feel

safer with them than I ever did on our island where your father took lives as he pleased," she said. "How can we possibly turn our backs on a family that has done nothing but welcome and protect us?"

Mind spinning with all she'd laid before me, I turned my eyes back up to the ceiling and she did the same.

Twining her fingers into my own beneath the blanket, she whispered, "Given the choice between the gods our people venerated on that hill and the God who offers shelter for even the most undeserving, I know who I choose."

CHAPTER SEVENTEEN

EITAN

Working together, Nadir and I lifted the hip-high jug of first-press olive oil and moved it to the back wall of the dais. The raised platform that formerly displayed an enormous statue of Ba'al now held fifteen jugs of only the purest of oil, given to the Levites as their holy portion from all the villages that surrounded Kedesh. Since the elderly farmer who was hauling the jugs had his wagon break down near the city gate, Baz had volunteered me to transport the goods — entirely on foot. Thankfully, Nadir had offered to help.

Once a Canaanite temple, this building had been ritually cleansed, its blasphemous idols stripped and destroyed. No longer a house of repugnant worship, this building now served as a storehouse for the Levites who administrated this town.

I sat down on the edge of the dais, needing a break from trekking back and forth through town carrying jugs of oil and brined olives, and used the neck of my tunic to wipe the sweat from my face and beard.

"Quite a commotion last night," said Nadir as he slumped to the floor next to me and leaned his back against the knee-high stone platform. "Were you there when they brought the body in?"

"I was. In fact, he did not die until after he'd been brought through the gates." I winced at the memory of the manslayer, blood dripping from the dagger lodged in his torso, as his two panic-stricken brothers carried him to his last moments of life. If only Sofea had not witnessed the aftermath of the altercation. I'd seen her for a moment during the ruckus, pale-faced as my mother had explained the realities of Kedesh to her, but my desperate need to speak to her, comfort her, had been thwarted by her flight back to the sanctuary of her room.

Nadir cut into my thoughts. "Was the Blood Avenger found?"

"He was. Darek and Baz tracked him north, near Laish. There were witnesses who confirmed it to be a hunting accident. The manslayer simply did not make it to the boundary line in time before the *go'el ha-*

adam exerted his legal rights to redemption."

We both went quiet. Nadir was undoubtedly considering his own experience with the boundary line that encircled our city in two thousand cubits of safety. From the few things he'd told me about his manslaughter conviction, it seemed Nadir had been escorted to Kedesh without incident. Nothing like the harried flight Moriyah and Darek had been forced to take here eleven years ago. Because of me.

A rush of unseasonably warm air breezed in through the tall open doors, making the stuffy chamber more like my mother's bread oven than a storehouse. I lifted my thick, sweat-laden braid, entertaining the thought of cutting it, of ending my vow, for the hundredth time since I'd begun training with Baz. But I would hold to the promise I'd made to Yahweh; in fact, I welcomed the discomfort. The weight of the hair on my head was nothing compared to the burden of Zeev and Yared's deaths on my soul, nor the pain I'd inflicted on Darek's family.

"How much more can fit in here?" said Nadir. He swiped a palm across his forehead as he surveyed the tall chamber that had once echoed with the chants of worshipers and other unholy things too disturbing to be imagined. Now jars of grain, barley, and dried foodstuffs lined the walls, stacked high on shelving that I, as a boy of nine, had a small part in crafting during the first year I lived in Kedesh.

"There are two more years until the sabbath year. We've filled the underground storage rooms already with the more perishable items, but there is plenty of space."

I remembered the miraculous abundance of the sixth year in the last *shmitah* cycle well. Trees had bowed beneath the weight of enormous fruits, crops saw neither pestilence nor destructive storms to limit their yield, and herds seemed to multiply overnight. Being only two years old when we crossed the Jordan, I did not remember the taste of the manna in the wilderness, but I would never forget the way these chambers overflowed with provisions for Yahweh's people.

On the seventh year of the cycle, the Land would lie fallow. No planting, no pruning, no harvest. But Kedesh would be well stocked, ensuring that not only would the Levites and their families be well provided for, those imprisoned here would not go hungry either.

"There are two more jugs of oil by the gates," I said, rolling my shoulders back.

"Then we can get to work on the farmer's broken axle."

With a nod, Nadir followed me out into the sunshine, and I blinked against the brilliant blue morning. A flock of geese honked their way over our heads, their formation like an arrowhead pointing toward the lake nearby. Thankfully, after losing our wager the other day, Nadir had said no more to me about fishing; and from his willingness to help today, it seemed as though my victory had not severed our friendship either.

Skirting the busy marketplace in favor of the maze of alleyways between homes, we headed toward the center of town. My hope that this last trip would be swift and relatively painless was dashed when two soldiers turned a corner, blocking our way.

I groaned internally as I recognized one of them. Meshek. A bully of a boy who'd grown into a beast of a man, one who'd taken inordinate pleasure in mocking me in particular. The harassment I had endured as a child had ended only when Meshek came of military age three years ago and left Kedesh to join a regiment of soldiers stationed at Merom as a precaution against incursion from Tyre.

Although the son of a manslayer himself, as soon as Meshek had learned that my mother had been convicted of the accidental killing of two young boys, he'd found no lack of opportunities to mock her and the Canaanite brand on her face, labeling her an Egyptian-bred temple whore.

As a boy ruled for the most part by a quick temper, I'd rarely been able to control the flashes of anger his cutting words instigated. Of course, once Meshek discovered my malformed ear and lack of hearing on my right side, his abrasive remarks shifted from my mother to me.

The older boy had found great entertainment in sneaking up on me and whispering foul words into my deaf ear while his friends laughed. And I, being self-conscious of not only my weakness but also the way people stared at my deformity, usually went hot with rage and swung my fists without considering the cost.

"Ah well, if it isn't the deaf boy," Meshek said, his well-trained stride shifting into a swagger as he approached me.

Determining not to succumb to provocation, I ignored him, stepped to the side, and pressed my back to the wall, giving him and his companion enough room to pass in the narrow space. Although unaware of my history with the solider, Nadir followed my lead.

With a guffaw, Meshek disregarded the handspan of height I'd gained on him since he'd left and crowded me with his bulk. "Aren't you old enough for military service now? Why are you still here?"

"I don't see how that is any concern of yours," I replied, muscles tight and jaw iron-set.

With his head cocked to the side, he appraised me, a razor-edge glint of humor in his eyes. "What sort of coward hides behind walls while others go fight his battles?"

He reached out and grabbed the thick braid that trailed over my shoulder. My muscles coiled, ready to spring, but I held my ground. With a provocative gleam in his eye, he let the plait slide through his grimy fingers. "How appropriate. I'll bet it's lovely unbound."

Still unmoving, except for a surreptitious curl of my fingers into fists, I stared at him, refusing to be goaded by his blatant questioning of my manhood. "Move on, Meshek," I said. "I have no desire to quarrel with you."

His laughter reeked of derision. "Just as I thought. A coward." He leaned closer, his oily words dipping low. "Or perhaps that temple-whore of a mother still has you tucked behind her skirt."

My restraint snapped. Vibrating with fury, I swept my arm out and hooked Meshek by the neck, driving his head into the wall behind me. His bronze helmet clanked against the stone with a satisfying thud and slipped down over his eyes. As he recovered, blinking and adjusting the helmet back into position, I stretched to my full height, silently thanking Baz for the months of speed- and strength-building exercises that had honed my body.

With a growling curse, he lunged. His heft barreled into me at full speed, nearly knocking the wind from my chest and slamming my elbow into the opposite wall. But I spun before he could pin me and swept his feet out from under him, dropping him face down into the hard-packed earth, his helmet spinning across the dirt.

I followed him down, one knee in the center of his back and the other pinning his arm to the ground. Both of my hands were around his throat from behind. Digging my knee into his spine, I squeezed his throat, satisfied when I felt him gasp for breath. Leaning forward, I rasped in his ear, "Never again will a word about my mother pass your lips."

Undeterred by the hold I maintained on him, he spat out, "She's no more your mother than you are a *man.*"

Molten fury flooded my body. The twins' deaths may not have been premeditated, but Meshek's may be another story entirely. What kind of sound would a man make as his tongue was separated from his depraved mouth?

From the corner of my eye, I noticed that Nadir had slipped his dagger free and was holding the other soldier at bay, a man whose wide eyes and lanky frame declared him to be early in his training. I felt confident Nadir would hold him off while I entertained my murderous thoughts.

"Let him go, Eitan" came a command from my left flank. Without releasing Meshek, I flicked a glance over my shoulder at Chaim, another of my childhood acquaintances. Although he maintained detached calm on his face, his brown eyes danced with humor.

"You sure you don't want to get in a swing?" I asked through gritted teeth, menace still swirling in my blood as I dug my fingers into points on my former tormentor's neck that would keep him from squirming. "This worm pounded on you a time or two as well, I recall."

Chaim's stance widened, his expression controlled as he crossed his arms over his chest in a falsely casual pose. "That he did, but now I outrank him. When I tell him to polish my weapons, he does just that." His tone remained even, but a smirk twitched at his lips. Although Chaim had been older than me, he'd always stood up to Meshek whenever he'd caught the tyrant picking on Tal and me.

Meshek struggled against my hold, but I leaned harder into his back. "Now that, I'd love to see."

"I'm sure you would," said Chaim, nodding his head to me with a subtle command. "Let the worm go."

After a few more stubborn moments, I capitulated, and Meshek drew in a loud breath at the release, spitting foul curses at me.

Chaim leveled a scowl at Meshek. "I'll deal with you later," he said, and then dismissed the two men with a tilt of his chin.

To my surprise, Meshek stalked away, his wide-eyed young companion following close at his heels. Again I offered a silent word of thanks that Darek and Baz had pushed me so hard. I'd barely had to exert myself while besting the man who'd left me with more bloody lips and bruises than I could count when we were children.

"Seems to me you might want to step up

the training with your men, Chaim."

He chuckled. "I heard Baz was working you over these past months. I guess the rumors were true."

I ignored the compliment, grinding my teeth. *If only I could put that training to good use.* "Are you stationed here now?"

"We are. At least through the cold months. You still making the best weapons north of Shechem?"

"I do what I can."

"Don't give another thought to Meshek," Chaim said. "I know if you were free to leave here, you'd be the first into battle."

He *knew*? Shock arched my brows.

He answered my silent question in a low tone. "Darek filled me in last year, when you came of military age and I requested that you train with my company."

Frustration and hot embarrassment swelled in my throat. Who else had Darek told about my past? He and my mother had been so adamant that I keep the information secret for the past eleven years. Had it become town gossip without my hearing of it?

Chaim must have seen the confusion on my face. He lifted his palms in a gesture of surrender. "He told me in confidence, and I swear to you I have not told a soul."

I'd nearly forgotten Nadir was still beside me, but now I could practically feel his intense scrutiny on my face. I refused to look his way. We'd become friends since he'd joined me at the foundry, but other than to confide in Tal, to whom I'd sworn a blood oath of brotherhood as a boy, I'd never let the truth pass my lips.

"I appreciate that," I said to Chaim and offered a stiff nod of gratitude before turning to continue on with a silent Nadir in my wake.

"Eitan," Chaim called out, halting my escape after only two paces. "I meant what I said. Your metalwork is extraordinary. I've heard your name mentioned more than once in Merom as a master bronzesmith. And if . . . if circumstances change, I would be honored to have you among my men."

I nodded a silent farewell and walked away, regret and powerlessness twisting into an impossible knot that made my chest burn. Nothing about my circumstances was simple, and if Darek continued to keep me penned up in this city, neither would they change anytime soon.

CHAPTER EIGHTEEN

"I can practically hear the questions knocking against your teeth."

I placed the last jug of olive oil on the shelf. Nadir had not said a thing as we'd collected the last of the farmer's goods and promised the old man we would return to repair his broken axle. Nor did he mention what Chaim had revealed as we walked back through the city with our burdens, but I did not doubt that he'd been silently mulling the mystery.

"Far be it from me to prod." He lifted his palms. "Your past is your own concern."

I slid a covert glance around the dim room and then to the miserly window slits on the far wall, ensuring no one would overhear my confession. "What do you know of my mother's presence in Kedesh?"

His eyelids flickered twice before he spoke. "Only that she accidentally poisoned two boys."

"Yes, they were the twin sons of Raviv, Darek's brother."

His brows lifted in surprise.

"Raviv vowed at the trial that he would find a way to destroy my mother, but he also vowed to end my life as well."

"Why?"

"Because I was part of that tragedy. Although I was not convicted of manslaughter like my mother was, being only a child and ignorant of the lethality of even a tiny amount of oleander, I too was sent here for protection from Raviv."

"And that is why you never leave the city?" His tone was mild, and I appreciated that he was minimizing his shock over my hidden past.

"It is. I vowed to never pass the boundary, even if legally I have every right to do so."

"And why is this a secret?"

"My mother and Darek did not want the taint of such a thing to affect my childhood. I suffered enough scorn for my deformed ear from boys like Meshek. They did not want to scrawl the label of *manslayer* on my forehead as well."

"But you are no longer a child, and now there are plenty of others in this town whose misdeeds are common knowledge. Why bother concealing your part in the deaths anymore?"

"To honor my mother, who has asked me many times to leave the past in its place. But the incident today is just one more reminder that my hands have been bound by those secrets. I am more than ready to fight for my people."

A spark of excitement lit in Nadir's eyes, and I knew he felt a kinship with my constraints. "Then you will leave Kedesh? Join the army?"

"I am hoping that I have proven my commitment to Darek, as well as my ability to protect myself from Raviv, and that the next time he leaves on a mission into enemy territory, he will allow me to go."

"So you will claim your freedom to go wherever you desire?" Nadir grinned. "You'll go fish with me at the lake?"

Annoyed that he would bring up fishing — again — I brushed off the jest. "If he lets me go, I will repay him by continuing to honor my mother's wishes. When I am not actively on a mission with Darek, I will remain in Kedesh."

Frustration flashed in Nadir's expression. "That is not true freedom."

I don't deserve true freedom. "Perhaps, but it is the compromise I am willing to endure for my mother's sake."

He shook his head, eyes fixed on the ground. "I would do anything for my freedom," he said, contemplation in his low tone. "Anything. If only that ancient priest would die so I could go home to my village."

It struck me suddenly that my lot was far better than Nadir's. Yes, I was stuck in Kedesh, but I had my family with me. Nadir had not only lost his freedom and his livelihood, but his family as well. My annoyance over his dogged persistence about fishing faded to nothing. The chance to reclaim even a shadow of what he'd lost by visiting that small lake must be a constant temptation.

"Let's return to the farmer and work on that axle," I said, moving toward the entrance of the storehouse. We both had need of distraction. Hopefully the crumbs of my story had been enough to satiate his interest in my past. I had no desire to dig any further into the wound today.

Wordlessly, Nadir walked beside me as we left the building, both of us blinking in the sunlight after the dimness of the storage chamber. To avoid the chance of any further contact with Meshek, we made our way through the market instead of returning the way we came.

Surreptitiously I kept my eyes roving over the teeming crowd, hoping to catch a glimpse of Sofea, who frequented the market at this time of day. She was always the first to volunteer to fetch articles or food-stuffs for my mother, but I suspected her forays into the maze of stalls and wagons had less to do with duty and more to do with her innate curiosity.

More than once I'd seen her visiting with foreign tradesmen, her lips full of questions about the places they'd been and the wonders they'd seen on their journeys. The longer she lived in Kedesh, the more she'd let down her guard, gradually revealing all the vibrance and inquisitiveness of her natural personality. I smothered a smile as I remembered the feel of her silken curl around my finger and the intoxication of speaking with her in the shadows last night. My step quickened as I planned the fastest way to fix the farmer's wagon. I needed to get back to the inn and see how she fared today.

My mother said Sofea had been shocked over the true nature of our city, but she felt confident Prezi could make her understand. I'd respected Prezi's request that we not tell Sofea about the manslayers in this city, especially after she'd told me about the evil man Sofea had called *Father*, but I was relieved that I could finally speak freely with her about such things. It was time she knew the whole of it. It was time to lay everything, including my heart, before her.

"Does Sofea know?" Nadir asked, as if privy to my thoughts. I'd seen him watching us last night and truly hoped that what he'd witnessed would not hinder our friendship.

"Not yet. After the disturbance last night she discovered what Kedesh is and why my mother is here. I plan on telling my own part in it today." Making a swift decision to forewarn him of my plans, I stopped and turned to meet his gaze. "Along with asking to go on the next mission, I will be requesting that Darek arrange a betrothal."

Nadir folded his arms and settled back on his heels, head down for a few quiet moments before he spoke. "Sofea reminds me very much of a girl I knew back in my village. Her name was Liora. Smart. Beautiful. A thirst for life."

Yes, Sofea was all those things, and so much more. The way she'd looked at me last night as I'd slipped my finger into her ringlet like a lovesick fool, as if she welcomed the pull between us, had solidified my decision to make her my wife — and soon.

Nadir continued, his chin lifting as he met my gaze. "And just as I'd once hoped that Liora would be mine, I hoped for Sofea as well."

My empty stomach churned. Had I lost my friend by declaring my intentions?

"But I could never do that to her," he continued.

"Do what?"

He gestured around us, sweeping his hand toward the city walls that encircled us. "You've seen how curious she is about this land. How desirous she is to explore and learn and see new things. And you also know how desperately she misses the sea. What do I have to offer her, other than a life locked away in this prison?"

Stunned, I scrabbled around in my head for a response — a rebuttal. Even if Darek allowed me to travel with his men, my life was centered here with my family until the High Priest of Israel died and set my mother free. *What do I have to offer her but the same*?

He waved a dismissive hand. "Ignore me. I'm sure you've already considered such things. Besides, I saw you two last night. It's obvious she's made her choice." He clapped a hand on my shoulder with a wry smile. "I won't begrudge your happiness, my friend."

Equal parts relief and confusion pooled in my gut as we turned the corner near the inn. Nadir didn't seem to be angry about my pursuit of Sofea, but he was wrong if he thought I'd fully considered all the ramifications. She had come to settle into life here so well over the past few months — learning our language, working alongside the other women, even indulging Abra's tendency to follow her like a chick all over town — I'd taken for granted that adapting to this city meant wanting to stay here permanently.

Before I could untangle my tongue or my thoughts, a familiar figure caught my eye. The young shepherd whom I'd seen glaring at me as I ran around the walls and during the wrestling match was leaning in the shade of the palm that stood a few paces away from the main entrance to our inn. Although his pose appeared relaxed, the way he was craning his neck made it seem as though he might be peering through our half-open doorway.

Noticing my attention had been diverted, Nadir turned to follow the direction of my gaze. "Someone you know?"

As if the shepherd suddenly felt the weight of our scrutiny, he looked back over his shoulder, eyes flaring wide. He pushed off the tree trunk and headed for the city gates. The first time his reaction to me had been strange, the second time an odd co-incidence, but this time suspicion roared to life.

The young man strode away without a look behind him. His clothes were tattered and his feet bare, his thin shoulders just beginning to widen into manhood. There was little to set him apart from any other shepherd tending the abundant flocks of goats and sheep owned by the Levites, aside from his seemingly keen interest in me.

"No," I bit out, torn whether to pursue him or check the inn first. "Have you seen him before?"

Nadir scratched at his beard. "Can't say that I have. Looks like one of the herdsmen. Odd for him to be in the city this time of day without stock."

"I saw him outside the city a few months ago, watching me as I trained. And then again the day you and I wrestled —" My explanation skidded to a halt as I remembered Darek's words from months before. *I have little doubt that Raviv has spies within this very city.*

"I need to go," I said, my feet already moving toward my mother. "Can you find someone else to help the farmer with his wagon?"

After a swift, curious look divided between me, the partially open door to the inn, and the shepherd who was quickly melting into the swirling crowd near the gates, Nadir waved a dismissive hand at me as he began to move toward the broken wagon. "I'll see to it. Go. Make sure Moriyah is safe."

Ensuring the door was latched tight behind me, I headed through the shuttered main room and out into the bright courtyard. Cool relief trickled into my limbs as I saw my mother at her usual place in front of her stone oven, unharmed. On the heels of relief, however, was jagged alarm. Even after seeing the man who'd vowed to slay her in the olive grove that day, she seemed all too complacent over the threat he posed. At the very least, the door to the inn should not be an open invitation to spies — or worse. How could I ensure that my mother would re-member how vulnerable she truly was, even within the stone walls of Kedesh?

A scheme formed in my mind as she stood with her hands on her hips, a flat spatula gripped in one fist, staring into the coals as if she were chastising the bread for cooking too slowly. Lost in thought, she did not notice as I made my way toward her.

Binah and Sarai spotted me and looked up from where they sat cross-legged in the shade of the roof overhang, chopping vegetables. But when I placed a finger in front of my lips, they grinned, well-acquainted with my antics, and said nothing as they shook their heads and continued their work.

Rolling my feet to keep my steps silent, I came up behind my mother and threw my arms around her from behind, gripping her against my chest as she flailed, arms trapped by the unexpected embrace. I squeezed a bit tighter, ensuring she would not have the luxury of knowing who her attacker was. To my satisfaction, she bucked against me, fighting with surprising strength and insisting she be set free.

With a low laugh, I obeyed.

She spun on me, silver eyes on fire, and smacked my shoulder hard with her spatula. "Eitan! What are you doing?" Anticipating the second slap of her weapon, I dodged to the side and lifted my palms in surrender.

"You nearly made my heart stop beating!" With a glare, she moved to retrieve the flatbread loaves that had curled away from the sides of the oven before they burned on the coals.

"My apologies for startling you." I glanced

back toward the door, wondering how long that shepherd had been standing there with his eyes on my mother's inn. "But you must be more aware of your surroundings. Even here."

"What do you mean?" She must have sensed the gravity in my statement. Her anger seemed to dissolve as she brushed soot from the brown-dappled rounds and placed them into a linen-lined basket. The steamy smell of the fresh bread made my neglected stomach grumble loudly, so she handed me a piece.

Impatient, I tore it in two and shoved one half into my mouth as if I were Malakhi, nearly moaning as its salty warmth delighted my senses. No one made bread like my ima. Reluctantly swallowing, I continued. "Have you seen a man hanging around the inn? A young shepherd, dark hair and eyes?"

She looked up at me over her shoulder. "Not that I know of, but there are so many people streaming in and out of Kedesh these days."

I pursed my lips, glancing back to ensure Binah and Sarai were out of earshot. "I have. I noticed him watching me twice before, and just now I caught him peering through the front door, which had been left open."

"The girls went next door a while ago to play with Surit's children. They must not have latched it." Concern pinched her black brows into a tight line as she set the bread basket on the table. "A guest, perhaps?"

I shook my head. "He sped off the moment he saw me. I have a feeling Raviv may have sent him."

Her hand flew to her chest as she caught her breath. "Have you told Darek and Baz?"

"Not yet. But I will. We must be more diligent, Ima. I should have taken Darek's warning about Raviv's tenacity more seriously." I braced my hands on my hips, unease settling into my bones. "I will do whatever is necessary to protect you."

"Of course you will." She slid her arms around my waist and hugged me tightly. I noticed that her head now fit underneath my chin, smiling as I remembered it being the other way around not so long ago. Moriyah had been a light in my dark world as a boy, and it made me ill to think that Raviv might have sent someone to watch her — or worse, to hurt her.

She looked up at me. "But you must remember, Eitan, it is Yahweh who creates life and Yahweh who maintains it. Your efforts, and Darek's, can only go so far to preserve me from harm. I trust the God who rescued our people from Egypt, the God who brought us through the sea, and the God who shook Jericho to its foundations to protect me."

I admired her unswerving faith. I'd hoped that by consecrating myself body and soul as a Nazirite Yahweh might be pleased, but somehow shame continued to gnaw at me, along with the memory of two boys vomiting blood and bile and poison into the dirt.

She loosened her hold but kept her arms looped around my waist. "Have you spoken with Sofea about marriage yet?"

Startled by the question, I simply stared at her. I'd not revealed my intentions toward Sofea to my mother, but I should have known she'd guessed my thoughts. Not much escaped her notice.

"Eitan, you are anything but subtle." She breathed a laugh. "You've been panting after that girl since she walked in our door."

Heat rushed up my neck. To cover the evidence of my embarrassment, I hooked my hand around my nape. "I have tried to be patient."

She patted my chest knowingly. "I know you have. You've done well to not pursue her until now. Healing does not happen overnight." She glanced up and tilted her head toward the stairway to the roof. "Now that she knows about Kedesh and about me, she has some decisions to make. Prezi said she's recovered a bit from the shock, but she's been up there all morning by herself. Perhaps you should join her, offer to answer any questions she might have?" She leaned in, sniffed, and made a sour face. "*After* you've washed."

"Do you think she will . . ." I cleared my throat. "Accept me?"

"I think she still has some healing to do, son. And she has much to learn of Yahweh. But you?" Her smile was pure mischief. "I have little doubt that she is well on her way to accepting you."

With a grin, I gave her a peck on the cheek and spun away, heading toward my chamber, a pot of water for washing, and my clean tunic. Anxiety, elation, trepidation, and desire stewed in the pit of my stomach. Today I would make my intentions known to Sofea, hoping that when I finally poured out the contents of my past she would not turn away the heart of a killer.

CHAPTER NINETEEN

SOFEA

I felt his presence long before he came to my side but continued watching a swirling black flock of birds dance across the sky in awe-inspiring formations over the valley. The living cloud moved like a wave in the air, rolling up and down, swooping high, stretching wide, before curling in on itself and rearranging into a new pattern, an ever-flowing tide of tiny winged creatures chasing with the wind.

"What are these?" I asked, offering him an invitation to approach. How long had he been standing here on the rooftop, watching me? Although the thought should make me cringe, should make me flee, in truth I'd wondered what had taken him so long to come.

"Starlings." The low answer directly behind me made the blood thrum in my ears. He was almost as close as he'd been last night, but this time there were no shadows to hide the flush of my cheeks.

"Where do they come from?"

"I don't know. But I remember . . ." He cocked his head and peered into the sky, as if searching his memory. "I remember my mother telling me about starlings — how they would swirl in the sky like ink on water, when our people still wandered the wilderness far to the south of here." He paused, gazing in that direction with a faraway look in his eyes. "Perhaps they are on their way now to those deserts to wait out the colder weather."

"Moriyah told you this?"

"No." He turned with a sad smile. "It is one of the few memories I have left of the woman who gave birth to me. Her name was Abra."

"Like your sister?"

"Moriyah and Darek allowed me to name my sister when she and Malakhi were born. I didn't have anything left of my mother, other than those few cloudy memories, so I gave her name to Abra. To honor her life and keep a small part of her with me."

We went silent, listening to the song of the flock as they continued their enthralling dance in the sky until without warning the birds sped away as a unit, heading toward the southern horizon.

"Sofea." He cleared his throat. "I know that you are aware now of where you live. Of what Kedesh is and why my mother is here."

I nodded but kept my lips sealed. I'd spent hours here on the roof digesting all that Moriyah and Prezi had told me. Although still more than unsettled with the idea that I lived in a prison, I was forced to acknowledge that I felt safer in this city, surrounded by killers, than I ever had with my own father.

Prezi was right. He'd been nothing but a murderer. It was common knowledge that to stand against him meant death, and I'd seen more than one man gutted for doing so — it was a miracle that my mother had survived standing up for Seno's life that day. The longer I'd stayed up here, the higher the rot of his deeds piled in my mind. And knowing how I'd excused those actions all my life, attributing them to his divine right as the chief and high priest, how could I possibly condemn someone like Moriyah? Although I was still annoyed at my cousin for hiding the truth from me for so long, my initial overheated reaction had tempered into mild acceptance.

"There is more you need to know," he

said. Something about the way he spoke the words made my insides swirl like that cloud of starlings. "About me. About how I came to be Moriyah's son. About why I live in Kedesh."

He breathed out a long sigh, the sound of a man releasing the knot on a long-held secret. "As you know, my parents died when I was five. The only relative willing to take me on was my mother's half-brother. He was quite a bit older than her, and there were eight years between me and the youngest of his six sons." He stopped. Winced before continuing. "Although he took me into his home, I was treated more like a dog than a child. I lived on whatever was left after the family had eaten. I inherited tunics that had been used by each of the sons, worn until near unraveling. My uncle didn't hit me — in fact, at times I'd probably have preferred that he did — he just didn't care. And his wife was too harried by the enormous task of raising six unruly sons to concern herself with one small orphan. I imagine they didn't even expect me to live long, since my father and mother had been swept away so easily by illness."

I was speechless. I could not imagine this tall, vibrant man being so wholly ignored by his relatives. Everything about Eitan demanded attention. His long, slender body honed by grueling work and training. His animated laugh and the way humor danced in his hazel eyes as he interacted with his loved ones and covertly watched me during mealtimes. The high, masculine cut of his cheekbones. The thick outline of his black eyelashes. His deeply freckled skin. Even the long dark hair that hung down, damp and wavy, about his strong shoulders. No matter that I'd fought it since that first night, I'd always been aware of him, ever attuned to his presence in any room. Nothing about Eitan should ever be ignored.

"But strangely enough, it was their neglect, their disregard for my health and well-being that ended up being my salvation." He turned around and leaned against the stone wall, half facing me. "I spent those years wandering all over Shiloh, looking for food. Entertaining myself. Exploring the hills and climbing trees."

"You have no children to play with?"

He shrugged a shoulder. "A few, but many of them shunned me because of my ear."

I furrowed my brow, confused by his statement. "Ear?"

"Have you not noticed that I only hear on my left side?"

I shook my head, surprised that I had

missed such a thing since I spent too much time studying him whenever he was not looking.

He shifted around and lifted the dark curtain of his hair away from his right ear. The outer ear was misshapen, completely curled in on itself and without an opening to let in sound. No wonder he kept his hair tied very low on his neck; its thickness hid the deformity well. Remembering some of the unkind children in my own village, I imagined Eitan had been taunted for such an obvious difference in his appearance.

"You not hear with it?"

Dropping his hair, he turned his left side to me with confusion on his brow.

"This is difficult? Hearing me?"

"I was born this way, so I've learned to adapt. My left ear picks up sound very well, as if making up for the loss. And I watch lips." As if to prove his point, his gaze dropped to my mouth, making me acutely conscious of the attention.

He seemed to be waiting for me to speak, his eyes targeting my lips like an arrow from a bow. I held still, refusing to so much as breathe until he finally glanced up with a confident little smirk. *He knows the effect he has on me.*

Slouching back against the wall, with his

good ear toward me, he continued his story. "It was on one of those lonely, friendless days that Moriyah's father, Ishai, found me with my mouth stuffed full of his grapes. I'd snuck into his vineyard a few times before, always keeping out of sight of the watch-tower guard, but this time Ishai caught me. Instead of running me off, like most vintners would do to a thief, he put me to work scar-ing off the birds from his crops. Sometimes he even let me stomp the grapes at harvest. Of course you can imagine that I was overjoyed to be paid in food from Moriyah's kitchen."

I returned his mischievous smile. "*No one* goes hungry at her table."

"This is true, and I adored her for it. There was nothing I wouldn't do for her." His brow furrowed. "There were people in Shiloh who treated her poorly for the brand on her face, so I took it on myself to be her defender." A boy who endured such tor-ment for his ear would undoubtedly be highly protective of someone he so admired.

He dropped his chin, looking at the plas-tered roof under his feet. "It is for that very reason that I killed those boys."

Blood rushed in my ears, and I blinked at him in confusion.

"It was me. *I* was the one who plucked

240

the oleander that day, not understanding its true nature. I noticed that Moriyah had accidentally sliced the deadly stems along with her herbs while distracted by Raviv's malicious sons. I placed the poison into the stew when she told me to stir the herbs into the pot. Although I thought it would only make the boys get sick and stop taunting her, I still wanted to see them suffer. Wanted to see them vomit and writhe after the awful things they said to her."

Although I should have been horrified by the admission, as much as I had been when Moriyah told me the truth of this place last night, instead empathy for Eitan welled in my chest, along with a feeling of acute frustration. He did not understand my heart language, and my Hebrew words were so inadequate. What could I say to this man who clearly was still suffering from a grievous mistake he'd made as a child? He'd comforted me in the olive grove, and I desperately wished I could respond in kind.

"For her part in the deaths, Moriyah was sentenced to live in Kedesh, and it was then that she adopted me as her child. She is as much my mother as the woman who gave birth to me, yet I am the reason she cannot go past that boundary line without being hunted." Choking on the last words, he whispered something under his breath and then threaded his fingers behind his neck and bowed at the waist, as if standing were painful.

Helplessly I watched as Eitan slid down the wall, the weight of such admissions dragging him to the ground. Feeling the pull to do something — anything — to lessen his pain, I folded my legs and settled beside him, offering the only gifts I had: patience and silence. Another small flock of birds passed overhead, long-legged white egrets on their way to Nadir's sparkling lake nearby.

"I stayed," he continued, his tone dark and tortured as he kept his head down, his hair hiding whatever bleak expression was surely on his face. "My mother does not know this, but I did not run off after poisoning that stew. I hid around the corner of the house, not trusting that even with sick bellies those boys wouldn't keep calling her names. I watched Zeev and Yared eat that stew, rejoiced when they demanded another bowl from her, and then when one of them began to vomit and moan I felt victory in my blood. I felt like a warrior."

I could practically see him, all legs and spindly arms folded into the shadows like a tattered little spirit of the night, watching the effects of his ill-fated actions.

"Then one of them began to cough up blood. He cried out that he couldn't see, and the other one was affected in the same way soon after their father arrived. I watched as Raviv held one dying son on his lap while the other collapsed, blind, bloody, and convulsing next to him in the firelight."

I could not move, my body had gone as rigid as that little boy in the dark must have as the horror of that night unfolded in front of him.

"It wasn't until both boys were dead, until Raviv began bellowing for Moriyah's blood, that I ran. I ran until my feet were shredded from the rocks, until I was completely surrounded by darkness and could not see a hand in front of my face. I don't even remember curling up in the dirt at the foot of a fig tree or waking the next morning. It was three days before my howling belly forced me to slink back to my uncle's house." He shook his head with a humorless laugh but didn't look up. "They didn't even notice I'd been gone."

In my desperation to soothe him, I placed my hand on his knee, a paltry attempt at comfort offered without much forethought. My heart thudded in my chest as I realized that I was touching him without invitation.

But just as I reconsidered and began to remove my hand, he caught it in his callused one, grasping it tightly. Then his other palm curved around it as well, and he threaded his fingers through mine, braiding our hands together securely. The grip he maintained on my hand reminded me of the way Prezi had clung to me in the sea to keep her head from slipping underwater as her body was thrashed against the rocks. Eitan held on to me as if I alone were keeping him from drowning. And I welcomed it.

CHAPTER TWENTY

When Eitan finally raised his head, we stared at each other, a clash of hazel and blue that caused the air between us to thicken. I'd been working so hard to keep my distance these past few months, pretending that each crossed glance, each brush of fingers at meals, each secret smile hadn't been dragging me farther from shore, closer to this moment. But the pull was undeniable. Eitan was an undertow that I was no longer strong enough to resist. One I no longer *wanted* to resist.

"Do you want to leave?" he asked, his grip on my hand relaxing.

My eyelids fluttered in confusion. "Why for?"

"You aren't afraid?" His expression was agony and his words a plea.

I breathed a sigh, trying to align my thoughts with Hebrew words. "When Darek bring us here, I thought you mean to kill us. And then I think that festival, Shavuot, maybe you want us for a sacrifice. . . ." I dropped my eyes. "Like on my island."

He lifted my chin with a gentle finger, his eyes wide with horrified understanding. "Our God is not the same, Sofea."

"I learned this, but I could not understand your words."

"What changed your mind?"

"The crutch you make for Prezi." I dipped my chin and placed a palm to my heart. "And I thank you." Remembering what else had shifted my perceptions during that festival, I smothered a smile.

"What is it?"

"Also the —" I gestured with my fingers, struggling for the word. "In your hair?"

"Ah, the flower? You liked that, did you?"

I spoke through my fingers to stifle a giggle. "Oh yes. Very beautiful."

He tilted his chin back and laughed, the rich sound echoing off the stone around us and traveling all the way through me. The place where we were seated was hidden from view and, even with the noise of the bustling market nearby, somehow felt very much like our own private world. Like one of the secret sea caves on my island.

"Will you tell me . . ." I bit my lip, hoping he would not be offended. "About your hair?" The locks in question were still damp, the dark waves cascading over his shoulder to tickle the skin on my arm.

"You want to know why my hair is so long?"

I nodded.

"I am a *nazir,*" he stated. I repeated the word, and after he'd patiently corrected my pronunciation, then praised my victory after a second attempt, he continued. "I took a vow when I was fifteen, consecrating myself to Yahweh. In doing so, I abstain from cutting my hair, from eating or drinking any fruit of the vine, and from touching any human corpse, even family members."

"For the rest of your life?"

"Perhaps." His face darkened a bit. "Or until I am able to make the proper sacrifices at the Mishkan to complete the vow."

"For what purpose did you choose this?"

"It's a long story and goes back to when I was nine, when we first moved to Kedesh."

I settled back against the stone wall, indicating my wish for him to tell the tale.

He sighed, leaning his head back and looking up into the bright sky, as if he could see his past written on the clouds. "The only people here were a few Levite families and a regiment of soldiers. So my mother allowed me to wander freely, to explore as the men worked to rebuild the city. It was near paradise for a young boy, a mostly deserted city to ramble around in all day."

"Why did they need to rebuild? Was Kedesh attacked?"

"I forget that you are still learning about our history," he said. "This city was built by one of the Canaanite tribes and was taken by our armies shortly after a decisive battle at Hazor, just to the south of us. Thankfully, this city was left standing for the most part, but there was much work to be done to prepare it for . . . its purpose."

I winced at the veiled reference. *A refuge for killers.*

"I'd made friends with Tal, the grandson of the priest who presided over Kedesh, and we spent many hours shooting rocks off the parapets, searching for trinkets in the empty houses and buildings, pretending that it was the two of us who had driven the enemy away."

I could almost see the two in my mind, scrambling about barefoot, stick swords in hand, searching every dusty corner for treasure. It reminded me of the way I'd dragged Prezi along on my adventures: collecting pretty shells, catching minnows in the tide pools, poking around in every cave and cove I could find.

I tilted my head, confused by the direction of his story. "But what of your hair?"

He squeezed my hand playfully. "I'm getting to that." The false exasperation in his voice and the teasing grin he sent me reminded me so much of his easy, light-hearted manner with his sisters, the very thing that had warmed me to him in the first place. Eitan was so very opposite of any man I'd ever known.

Suddenly, like a sun-warmed wave breaking against a beach, knowledge crashed over me — I wanted that heart-stopping smile directed my way every single day for the rest of my life. Feeling the shift in my core, I allowed the delicious sensation to wash over me, swallow me whole.

With a rush of audacity that I'd not felt since being torn from my island, I let my thumb brush slowly over his and lifted my brows in a taunting gesture. "Well . . . go on, then." Then, just to make sure my message was clearly received, I reached over with my free hand and slipped one finger into a wavy strand of his hair, soft and cool from the washing.

Just as he had done, I twirled that piece around my finger once, not taking my eyes from his. Another loop. He leaned closer, submitting to the gentle tug.

"Finish the story," I whispered. The next two loops brought us face-to-face.

"What story?" The breathy reply paired with the sweetness of honey across my lips and the smell of cedar and hyssop from his damp hair. His warm palm cupped my face, his thumb grazing my cheekbone as he waited, a question in the pause.

My answer was the last twist of my finger that drew his lips to mine. His kiss was gentle, the brush of a feather against my mouth that I felt all the way to the tips of my fingers — and nothing like the bumbling press of lips between two children on a beach long ago.

Eitan exhaled my name, and any restraint I'd had floated away with the sound. I slid my arms around his neck and pulled him to me, forgetting everything but his lips and his scent and the softness of his beard against my skin. I pressed closer, delighting in the feel of his arm snaking around my waist, capturing me against his body. Suddenly, he broke the kiss with a quick intake of breath, and I swayed forward, not ready to relinquish the moment.

"Sofea," he said, gently using the palm on my cheek to put a bit more distance between his mouth and my greedy lips. His lashes fluttered closed, the sweep of them dark against his freckled cheeks, and he waited one breath. Two. Three. Then his eyes opened, the tangle of blue and brown and green brilliant with excitement and reflecting the wide smile curving across his face.

Feeling my cheeks blaze as I realized how I'd thrown myself at him, I inched away, settling back on the ground. "I'm sorry."

"I'm not," he said with a slow shake of his head, his chest rising and falling in quick rhythm. "Not at all. I've waited for that for months. I am simply working very hard to draw on every drop of training Baz drilled into my head."

"What does your training have to do with this?" I gestured between the two of us.

"Because you are all too tempting . . ." He leaned forward, slowly sliding his fingers down the side of my neck, causing me to shiver. ". . . And as Baz reminds me frequently, patience has never been my strength." He came closer to brush a slow, warm kiss across my lips.

"Ah yes, I remember. Baz teach you to be still in the courtyard."

"That he did."

The laughter in his eyes caused an admission to spill out. "Prezi tease me that I stand on a stool, watching."

His brow lifted, smugness in the upturn

of his mouth. "Oh?"

Glaring, I poked his chest. "I only watch your sisters play with your hair."

He made an amused noise in his throat. "Jealous of them, were you?"

My face went hot. He'd hit all too close to the truth. Even now I'd do anything to push my hands back into his hair and let the long smooth waves slide through my fingers. To distract both of us, I huffed out, "What of the story?"

His grin was pure satisfaction. "Where was I?"

"Your friend."

"Ah yes. Along with exploring every building in the city, Tal and I also shadowed the men as they worked. We helped with repairs to the walls and building, farming, shepherding, carpentry, whatever chore they would allow us to do." He gestured toward the parapet opposite us. "Tal and I gathered many of those rocks you see embedded into that patch of the wall."

The pride was evident in his voice. Even as a child he'd taken part in rebuilding this city; he was as much a part of it as those stones. Remembering what he'd told me about his lonely life in Shiloh, I said, "Tal is a good friend. Yes?"

"The best. No brother could be closer."

The words were undergirded with hints of a bond that I sensed was as strong as that between Prezi and I. "He lives in Shiloh for now. He was born of the priestly line of Aharon, the first High Priest of our nation, so he is in training until he comes of age at twenty-five, when he will serve at the Mishkan. When we came to Kedesh, his grandfather, Dov, was the priest in charge of this city, as Tal's father, Amitai, is now. Directing rebuilding efforts, along with administrating a Levitical refuge city, as well as tending to the physical, judicial, and spiritual concerns of the people is no small task. But no matter how busy he was, Dov always took time to fill our eager ears with stories of our ancestors and the wisdom of his long years."

He stopped to look into my eyes. "I would very much like to introduce you to Dov. He saved my mother's life and also gave her this inn."

Although his description of the man was laced with warmth, I had little interest in meeting any sort of priest. I had plenty of experience with a man who wielded such unfettered power.

"It was Dov who told me of the *nazir* vow. He explained that a man or woman could choose to bind themselves to Yahweh in this special way, even if that person was not of the priestly line. When I was fifteen, I decided that I would submit myself to that vow." A shadow passed across his features, a hardening of the lines around his mouth. "And I will not end it until my mother goes free."

Shifting so that I faced him, I lifted his hand from where it lay fisted on his thigh. At my touch, he relaxed, and I slid my fingers between his. This hand created deadly weapons from fire and wood and stone and yet had caressed my face earlier with the tenderness afforded a delicately formed piece of glass. Again I wished for a better command of Hebrew words, ones that might smooth the fractures inside him that I now understood ran just as deeply as my own. Instead, I lifted that strong, beautiful hand and pressed the back of it against my lips. Once for a lonely child with a malformed ear. Once for a boy who'd not understood the consequences of a few leaves in some stew. And once for the man who'd carried the weight of his mother's imprisonment for too long.

The gesture seemed to lighten his mood. "Enough of such heavy talk," he said, bending to brush another sweet kiss on my lips, mischief once again creeping into his expression as his eyes crinkled at the corners. "I have an idea."

Chapter Twenty-One

Eitan

Drawing on the pulse of exhilaration and relief coursing through my limbs, I bounded to my feet and stepped a few paces away. I'd expected Sofea to flee from this rooftop the moment I'd confessed my part in Zeev and Yared's deaths, especially after I'd seen her reaction last night at the gates. Instead, she'd comforted me, soothed the furious grief that consumed me as I relived that horrific night in the shadows, and then, when I was still reeling from the release of baring my soul to her, she'd kissed me. If I lifted from this roof to take wing with the next flock of starlings that happened by, I would not be surprised in the least.

She'd kissed me! And now she was looking up at me expectantly, her blue eyes bright as she waited for me to explain my sudden burst of energy. After dumping all my ugly truths on her, I was desperate to steer us away from the dark reaches of my past and show her a glimpse of who we could be, together.

With a grin, I untucked my sling from my belt, its usual location since those days Tal and I had spent hours and hours hurling stones from this very roof. Holding the braided cords high, I unfurled the weapon. "Do you still want to see me shoot?"

She nodded her head, the amused purse of her lips highlighting a dimple in each of her cheeks that I very much wanted to press my mouth against — and planned to, soon. I could still taste her sweetness and needed a distraction from the memory of her fervent response.

I gestured for her to stand back farther and she complied, her eyes luminous with that avid curiosity I'd come to delight in. Since I always kept a stone loaded in the leather pouch, it took only a flick of my wrist to bring it into motion. Having spotted a cracked pot on the lip of the parapet earlier, one that held a handful of desiccated flowers that must have been gathered by my sisters weeks ago, I made it my target.

The sling whirred like a hummingbird in flight as I circled it through the air to my right and then to my left, propelling the leather and rope in a smooth, practiced track through the air. Loop. Loop. Release. Even though I put little strength into the throw, the stone slammed into the broken pot with such force that it flew off the low wall, spraying shards high into the air.

Her gasp of surprise had me spinning around to catch the expression of wonderment on her face, a look that gave me no little amount of satisfaction.

For all the weapons Baz had taught me to wield over the past few months, the one I'd latched onto as a boy was still the one I was most competent with. And Baz assured me that being left-handed gave me a distinct advantage. Shamelessly, I reveled in the opportunity to impress this woman whose every glance made my heart scamper around in my chest like an untethered pup.

"Would you like to learn?" I asked.

"Me?" She lifted a hand to block the glare of the sun.

Striding back to her, I grinned and dangled the leather pouch in front of her. Her blue eyes watched it swing back and forth for a moment before she reached out to yank it from my grasp.

With a laugh I headed toward a small pile of stones in the corner that my brothers had undoubtedly gathered to fling from the walls themselves. I selected a few small, smooth ones that would be suitable for practice, then walked back to where she stood with her back to me, elbows on the wall, gazing to the east.

"Nadir say there is a lake there." She pointed over the now-harvested orchards and olive groves that painted the valley with vibrant shades of orange, red, green, and yellow, to a sliver of water glimmering beneath the sunlight.

"There is. In fact, the land Darek recently inherited from his father lies adjacent to the water. The valley is very fertile: olive groves, green pastureland, and cedar and oak blanket the hills. My mother said the soil there is rich, and the area is plentiful with streams."

Sofea shifted to look at me, blinking in confusion. "You never go yourself?"

I shifted my gaze to the stones in my palm, rolled them back and forth. "Since moving to this city with Moriyah, I have not been past the boundary line." That two-thousand-cubit radius, marked with large, light-colored rocks, had been my universe since I was nine.

Back when we'd arrived, the boundary hadn't even been delineated. Moriyah had been forced to make it all the way to the gates in order to outrun Raviv, but the Levites were meticulous about maintaining it now, ensuring that the roads leading to this city of refuge were always clear and marked with signs engraved into boulders and trees to make a manslayer's flight to Kedesh as quick and easy as possible. Now that all six cities of refuge were occupied with Levites, an accused killer would have less than a day's journey to safety anywhere within the territory of Israel. Nothing like the perilous flight my mother and Darek had undertaken over a week's time, with Raviv in dogged pursuit.

Sofea seemed to be processing this new information, and I wondered if she'd press for more to satiate her fathomless curiosity, but instead she rotated and gestured toward the north and the three white peaks that lorded over the northern horizon. "What is this mountain called?"

"That is Har Hermon. The Canaanites who populated this area before we came believed that their gods lived up there."

"Where does your God live?"

"Yahweh is the Most High God, Sofea, the Creator of every living thing and the earth upon which we stand. There is no mountain that can contain him. No nation that can stand against his power. No sea that does not obey his command."

Eyes wide at my declaration, her mouth twitched, as if more questions had bubbled to her lips. My mother was right that she had much to learn of our God. But then with a teasing smile she spun the sling in a lopsided circle in the air between us. "I thought you teach me shooting."

"That I will," I said, offering her one of the stones I'd selected. After showing her how to place the stone within the cradle of leather, resting in the small hole at the center, I demonstrated the best way to loop the sling back and forth a few times without releasing the cord that would send the projectile toward its target.

With a small wrinkle between her brows, she attempted to swing the cords the way I'd done. The pouch lobbed through the air haphazardly, the stone dislodging and clattering to the ground. I reached out to take the sling back and show her again, but she shook her head and snatched up the stone. "I try again."

Amused by her determination and enjoying the opportunity to observe her at my leisure, I leaned back against the wall, placing my elbows on the ledge. She attempted the sling a second time, her face a mask of concentration. Her soft curls floated free on the breeze. I was grateful that she rarely tied her hair back. The few times she'd hidden her locks beneath a headscarf while working out in the courtyard or in the gardens outside the city walls with my mother, I'd felt as though a cloud had moved over the sun.

"Our armies are well known for our companies of slingers," I said. "The Canaanites came to fear the speed and precision of projectiles that can hit charioteers at a run and even pierce armor. Most of us begin learning as soon as we can walk. It came in handy when I was chasing birds from the vineyards as a boy, although I usually found a large leafy branch to be most effective."

After a few more tries, Sofea's confidence in her swing strengthened, and she insisted that she was ready to shoot. I moved to stand directly behind her and placed my arms beneath hers. She startled, whirling around to peer up at me, lips parted in surprise. "What are you doing?"

"Teaching you the timing of the throw." Emboldened by the fact that she'd not pulled away from my touch, I shifted closer, her nearness sending heat to the soles of my feet. She blinked up at me with those enormous pools of blue. I wanted to dive into them and never surface again, but I willed innocence into my expression. "I cannot simply tell you. I have to show you."

With one last suspicious glance, she turned around, swept the bulk of her glorious hair over one shoulder, and submitted to my loose embrace. The feel of her slender body in my arms and the smell of her skin was intoxicating, but valiantly clinging to Baz's admonishments that a solider must be in command of himself at all times, I held her hands between mine, swung the sling around twice, and then demonstrated the correct moment to release one of the cords and let the missile fly.

Without enough speed to propel the stone, it dropped lazily to the ground three paces away, but she still cheered, exclaiming loudly in her own language, her joy at such a small victory flowing into my own blood. In that moment my determination to speak to Darek about arranging a betrothal immediately upon his return became etched in stone. From the way Sofea had responded to me earlier, I had little doubt that she was of the same mind, and I was desperate to secure the promise of her hand.

She twisted her neck around to look up at me but did not pull away. "You need to teach the sling in this way?"

"Perhaps not." I shrugged, my hands drifting to her waist, my voice dropping. "But I felt this was a much preferable training technique." I bent forward, letting my mouth graze the curve of her ear. "Don't you agree?"

"Sofi?" Prezi's voice floated from the staircase behind us, and I slid away from Sofea just as her cousin came into view, followed by Abra and Chana. Standing two steps down, Prezi looked back and forth between us, no doubt sensing the moment she'd interrupted still hanging in the air.

"Moriyah has need of us," Prezi said, sending me a glance that somehow communicated equal parts suspicion, protectiveness, and amusement at finding Sofea here with me.

Surprised by the acceptance I sensed in her demeanor, I squelched a smile. "Of course. We can continue our lessons another day."

My sisters slipped past Prezi on the stairs, and after spying the sling in my hand, begged for their own lesson. They clung to my legs, pleading with such big-eyed fervor that I could do nothing but acquiesce. The sound of their cheering conjured a vision of a future daughter of my own — one with golden brown hair and bottomless blue eyes — wrapping me around her tiny finger. "All right," I told them. "A few tosses. But then

I need to get to the foundry. I have a project that needs finishing." One that would find its way to its new owner this very night.

Following Prezi, Sofea peered back over her shoulder before she disappeared from sight, a regretful smile on her lips. She wasn't any more anxious to leave this rooftop than I was to see her go. The wait for Darek to return so I could place the two most important requests of my life before him would seem an eternity.

CHAPTER TWENTY-TWO

SOFEA

Prezi and I approached the spring outside Kedesh where a crowd of women waited to collect fresh water in preparation for Shabbat. Other than brushing aside my concerns about whether she'd be able to carry a full skin-bag while hobbling back into the city on her crutch, she had not said much since she'd found me on the rooftop with Eitan, but her mischievous expression made it clear that she had much to say.

Grateful for the privacy our shared language offered as we awaited our own turn at the spring, I turned to face my cousin, gripping my empty water jar close to my body. "I know you are practically boiling over with questions."

"Perhaps now is not the time." Her eyes flitted to the women around us who were watching our conversation, undoubtedly wondering what the two foreign girls were babbling about.

"They can't understand us, Prez." I fluttered a hand. "Say what you need to say."

Her brown eyes danced in amusement. "You were with *Eitan.*"

I grinned. "I was."

"And he had his hands on your waist!" Her tone squeaked upward.

"You saw that?"

"I stood on the stairs for a few moments, too stunned to speak." Her admission was paired with a little shake of her head. "What were you doing?"

Diving into the deep. I could still feel the way his strong arms had surrounded me . . . his breath on my cheek . . . his lips at my ear . . . I restrained a shiver but fixed an innocent smile on my lips. "He was teaching me how to use a sling."

Her arched brows displayed obvious disbelief. "You are fully aware I won't accept that paltry explanation," she said, folding her arms. "The sun, moon, and stars are sparkling in those big blue eyes. Tell me."

I explained to Prezi about Eitan's childhood, his ear, and then the vow he'd made not to cut his hair until Moriyah was free, but I kept his part in the boys' death, and the heavy grief he carried, to myself. The way he'd clung to me as if he were reliving that night all over again had convinced me that no matter how much I trusted Prezi, it was not my story to tell.

"He is very devoted to his God," she said.

"It seems so." The passion with which he'd spoken of Yahweh as the Most High God had caused an unsettling lift within my spirit. For all the talk of the gods back in our village, I'd never heard anyone, let alone my father the high priest, speak of a god or goddess who claimed power over every living thing and every part of creation. As if he were not only the most powerful of all the gods, but the *only* one worthy of worship.

As if she'd heard my internal musings, Prezi said, "This God the Hebrews revere is very different from our gods, Sofi. Moriyah has explained much to me while we work around the inn."

A twinge of jealousy tugged at me. Prezi had become as much Moriyah's shadow over the past few months as Abra was to me. She rose before dawn each day to help prepare bread with her and seemed content to spend many hours in the courtyard weaving with Binah and Sarai while I entertained the children, helped clean rooms for the guests, and ventured into the market to purchase goods for the inn for Moriyah, who'd discovered I had a knack for bartering. Every day I did so, I looked for Kitane and her little boy, wondering when they would return to Kedesh. Remembering the last of my words to her, one final plea that she and her husband take us away from this city, I realized that she'd been right to insist we stay.

Although the ache for my island had not disappeared, it had waned significantly over the past months. Eitan's family had absorbed us into their life with such ease — feeding us, clothing us, affording us time to heal and rest after our arrival, inviting us into their celebrations, and never once had they demanded anything. Our participation in the household had come on gradually, a result of our gratitude for their kindnesses and a natural enfolding of us into their daily rhythms. I could not explain it, but somehow Kedesh had become a place of refuge. A shelter from the storm that had swept Prezi and me from our home and across the sea.

"Has he asked you to marry him?" Prezi's quiet question blared into my thoughts.

I choked on my reply. "No."

"Does he intend to?"

The remembrance of our kiss tingled on my lips and heat flashed into my cheeks.

She peered at me, amused and expectant.

"I think he might." I bit my lip and lowered my voice, even though no one around us could decipher my words. "He certainly kissed me like he did."

A hand flew to her mouth. "He kissed you?"

I glanced down at my hands gripping the jug — at the finger that had drawn him in, loop by loop. "Actually, I'm fairly certain I was the one who initiated the kiss."

Pink painted her cheeks as she giggled. "Somehow that does not come as any surprise to me, cousin. I've seen the way your eyes follow Eitan everywhere, and you are always the first to volunteer to deliver food and drink to the men at the foundry." She pinched my arm gently. "Subtlety has never been among your strengths. Your heart is all over your face."

A trio of chattering women moved away from the edge of the spring, giving us enough room to finally approach the bank. After dipping my hand in for a quick drink of the sparkling clear water, I crouched to tilt my jug beneath the surface, watching it burble to the rim, and then traded Prezi for her empty skin-bag.

"Do you understand what marriage to Eitan would mean?" Prezi asked. "Moriyah has explained many of their laws to me. Among them is that Hebrews may only marry those of their own kind, or those who choose to embrace worship of Yahweh alone and bind themselves in covenant with his people. Are you prepared for that?"

I tied off the waterskin and then helped her sling it across her back before hefting my own pot of water to my hip. "Posedao nearly stole you from me. And the gods that my parents worshipped on that high hill . . ." I swallowed the burn in my throat. "I want nothing of them. I don't know this Yahweh, but if he commands the sea like Eitan says he does, then perhaps he is more like Posedao than I'd guessed. But if I can have Eitan . . ." I placed my fingers on the lips his had so recently touched. "Then perhaps I don't need a god. There is no such thing as a god who cares about me, but Eitan does. I can see it in his eyes."

Prezi remained quiet beside me as we made our way back through the city gates with our burdens. As she'd insisted earlier, she'd become so deft with her crutch that I barely had to slow my pace. Although I knew our discussion about Eitan was far from over, her way was to turn a thing over and over before speaking her mind, so I allowed her time to contemplate as we made our way toward the inn

The city was readying for Shabbat, the market stalls closing down early, women scurrying home with baskets on head and goods in hand. Pack animals were already penned in courtyards, having been relieved of their burdens and untethered from wagons in preparation for their own seventh-day rest. Over the past months I'd become accustomed to the Hebrews' peculiar weekly tradition, enjoying the peace that settled over Kedesh from sunset to sunset.

Just as we reached the door to the inn, Prezi stopped and turned to me, her mulling apparently at an end. "Eitan cares for you, Sofea. It is evident to anyone within twenty paces of you both. But I think that Yahweh cares for you as well."

I wrinkled my brow at the strange declaration. "Why would you think that?"

"You are here, are you not? Out of all the people slaughtered in our village, the two of us were spared. Then, against every odd, we survived the sea, were found on a remote beach in a foreign land by Darek and his men, and brought to this place — a city designated as a place of refuge. And now, instead of living beneath the tyranny of your father and his gods, we enjoy weekly sabbath rest among the people who have sheltered us, clothed us, and shown us love in spite of our heritage. It's almost as if Yahweh plucked us out of the sea himself and carried us to this place."

The prayer I'd sent skimming across the restless ocean came to mind. Had the Hebrews' One God been the one to hear my plea that day?

Prezi turned to me, her expression solemn. "I was dead on that beach, Sofea. After seeing what Seno and his men did to my family . . ." Her words shuddered to a stop. "I was so angry at you for not just letting me drown. And when I went to sleep in the sand, I hoped that my eyes would never open again. But somehow, through these people — through their God, through their beautiful ways — I came to life again. In truth, I feel like I was never truly alive before now."

Perhaps Yahweh had saved us from drowning that day, but I knew that if it was true, it was for Prezi's sake he'd done so, not for mine. But regardless of the reasons or the means by which we had come here, I was grateful and more than willing to submit to the laws of these people, enjoy their sabbath days, and participate in their festivals as long as I could have Eitan.

CHAPTER TWENTY-THREE

An old man moved to stand at the center of the gathering next to the fire, all eyes focused on him. Braziers flickered in the corners of the space and along with the fire pit cast wavering shadows on the faces of many people scattered in groups on the ground.

I'd been told that this would be a night of stories, a time to bathe in the histories of these people and their ancestors. I'd experienced many of these gatherings in the past few months, although I did not remember this man being the storyteller. However, in the past I'd not understood enough of the language or hadn't bothered to pay much attention, too lost in my own thoughts of fear, or survival, or too distracted by Eitan's handsome face and searching glances from across the courtyard. But after Prezi's admonition that marriage to Eitan would include covenant with his people, and what she'd told me of the shift in her own heart, my curiosity was piqued like never before.

Hushed and expectant, we waited for the man to speak.

"This land is not where our origins lie," he said, the authority in his voice echoing off the stone walls of the courtyard. "Our father, Avram, was not born here. Instead he sprang from Ur, a city far from here." He gestured to the east. "From earliest childhood, he was steeped in the worship of Inanna, of Enki, and Utu, the gods of Sumer, the gods his own father, Terah, fashioned from wood and stone."

The old man's silvery beard caught the firelight, giving him an otherworldly glow as his hands gesticulated his words. Next to me on the ground, Prezi leaned forward, lips slightly parted as if thirsty for more of the story.

"But Avram had heard the whispers about Elohim," the man said. "He remembered the day he'd met Shem, the ancient son of Noach, as a small boy. Although nearly five hundred years old, Shem still lived, and none of the memories of the Great Deluge had withered from his mind. On a night very much like this one, Avram listened to Shem describe how his family alone boarded a mighty ark, withstood the never-ending rains, and listened to the sounds of the condemned as they beat on the walls of the boat as it lifted and then were swallowed by waves that covered the whole face of the earth."

Although a few details of the story were lost to me, something seemed familiar about it, as if there were echoes of the tale in the stories the Sicani had passed down from generation to generation. A devastating flood. A large boat full of animals. Few survivors. Perhaps our histories were not so different from that of the Hebrews. I found myself mimicking Prezi's posture, elbows on my knees and my focus narrowing on the elder's face. His eyes skimmed the crowd, his mouth turned upward as he continued.

"The stories of the Flood clung to Avram, and as he grew he found himself hungering for more knowledge of Elohim, of the One God who'd saved Noach's family from destruction, and wondering how it was that within the lifetime of Shem, man had already turned to gods of their own creation instead of the One who created man — the God whose immense holiness would slay any who looked upon his face and whose enormity and perfection cannot, and should not, be depicted by any human hand."

Images of the gods were as familiar to me as my own reflection in the tide pools. Posedao, Atemito, and all the other gods and goddesses were depicted in amulets, idols, and carvings. Each of our huts had contained an altar with various household gods to ward off evil spirits and provide protection for those within. If such images were not allowed here among the Hebrews, how did they ensure Yahweh would protect them? My mind was a clutter of confusion, and I had the urge to spring up and approach the old man to demand answers for the myriad questions his words provoked.

"Then," he said, "came the day when Elohim spoke to Avram. Telling him to take himself away from his father's tents and follow where he led."

The elder described a journey from the land of Ur here to Canaan, and even how the path had taken a sad detour in Egypt where Avram had made the mistake of calling his wife his sister. He told of the promise Elohim made to Avram, that this land would one day be inherited by his descendants, but that those of his flesh and bone would be held captive in a foreign land before finally being led out of slavery. He told of how his name was changed to Avraham, the father of many nations — a promise to a man without a son.

"And I was there," said the storyteller, "when that prophecy was fulfilled. Although I was only two years old at the time and have only cloudy flashes of memory of that night, my small feet trod the dry seabed after Yahweh congealed the powerful depths into walls as we escaped the wrath of the Pharaoh. I was there when the great Cloud hovered over us, a fiery shelter of protection to guide us to safety, the first steps on a journey that would take us here, to this land, to this city of refuge and hope. And although the Cloud is no longer visible over us, the Eternal One still watches, still protects, still holds fast to his promises to Avraham. We reside, now and forever, in the shelter of the Most High."

As the ring of his declaration faded, I discovered I'd been holding my breath, and my chest shuddered at the release. The crowd around me was silent, as if they too had been lost in the story.

The elder smiled in a grandfatherly gesture that matched the warmth of his eyes as he looked over the people gathered to hear him speak. He lifted his hands and spread his fingers wide. For the first time, I noticed that his palms were scarred, the evidence of long-ago burns.

"And now, people of Israel, sons and daughters of Avraham by birth and by covenant . . ." His tone become richer, more weighty, moving into the proximity of worship. "May Adonai bless you and keep you. May Adonai make his face to shine upon you and be gracious unto you. May Adonai lift his countenance upon you and grant you shalom."

With the blessing complete, the spell of the story was broken and conversations began all around me. Children popped up, free now to expend shackled energies and stoppered laughter. Prezi leaned into me, her eyes bright, her tone reverent. "Do you see what I mean, Sofi? The way they speak of Yahweh . . . I've never heard anything so beautiful."

Before I could answer her or press for answers to some of the questions the story had raised in my mind, Eitan appeared in front of us. Startled, I looked up at him, my neck craning back to take in his height.

"May I speak to you, Sofea?" Although he smiled, his eyes were tight and one fist was clenched. His thumb tapped a quick, nervous beat against the side of his leg.

Nodding, I stood, telling Prezi I'd return soon. Her mischievous grin and slight wink offered encouragement to whatever was happening between Eitan and me, giving me courage. I followed him through the crowd and under the shadow of the eaves, near the same column where we'd spoken before, when he'd made his interest in me clear.

Moving behind that very column, he leaned his back against the wood, a sigh escaping his lips. "I am sorry to drag you away from your cousin, but this is the most privacy I can have with you," he said, and then a smile curved his lips upward. "At least for now." His gaze deepened, flooding with meaning that made warmth spread throughout my body. His eyes were on my mouth as he spoke again, a rasp in his voice. "And in truth, it is for the best that there are fifty people behind me right now, or I'd pick up right where I left off during our sling lesson."

Silenced by the insinuation, I stared at him, unsure what to do with my hands, or my face, or the legs that were suddenly trembling so much I could barely stand. Everything about Eitan called to me — from his enveloping gaze, to the strength of his well-honed body, to the way he'd poured out his heart to me.

"I want to marry you, Sofea," he said, never taking his eyes from my face. "When

Darek returns, I plan to ask him to arrange a betrothal between us."

My jaw gaped as I searched his face for signs of teasing. Just a few hours ago, Prezi had asked whether I would consider binding myself in covenant to Eitan, and thereby his God. My quick answer, that I'd do so if I could have him, seemed flippant in light of the story the old man had told tonight.

A flash of uncertainty moved across his features. "Have I shocked you?"

I dropped my eyes, dragging in a wobbly breath. "Yes."

He slumped against the wood, defeat in the drop of his shoulders. "I should have waited. Given you more time." His fingers moved to his ear, hidden beneath the dark sweep of his hair where it was pulled into a low braid. He tugged at the misshapen earlobe, a rare self-conscious move I'd noticed before today but had not understood until he'd revealed the deformity to me.

Tangled up in equal parts affection and hurt for him, I placed my hand on his forearm and tugged it away from his ear. "You shock me, Eitan, but still, I am glad." I slid my fingers down his arm and wove them into his.

His breath released. He closed his eyes

and gripped my hand as if savoring even the slightest contact between us. He muttered something that sounded very much like a prayer of thanksgiving to his God. Then he opened his eyes, his brows coming together. "Are you certain? Do you understand that as my wife you will be expected to follow our Torah and put aside worship of any foreign gods?"

Somehow between Prezi's revelations and the blessing spoken over us this night, my decision had been made. I still did not fully understand this God of his, but from everything I'd seen, Yahweh was nothing like the capricious and grasping gods of my island. I wanted the protection the old man had spoken of — to hide beneath the shelter he described. And I wanted nothing more than to be Eitan's wife. "Yes, I understand this. My gods are no more important to me. But . . ." I glanced away, gnawing at my lip.

He drew me closer. "What is it?"

"I have nothing to give," I said. When my father offered me to the chief of the neighboring village, a wide array of commodities had been exchanged; the dowry of the high priest's daughter was precious indeed. Now, even the clothes on my back had been gifted by Moriyah.

"The only thing I want is you, Sofea.

Always." His tone was full of sincerity, the words nesting in the deepest part of me. He reached for my hand, lifted it, and placed something in the center of my palm. A delicate copper ring, fashioned with large swirls and small swirls, like waves crashing on the seashore.

"Eitan," I breathed, lifting the ring to study it closer in the firelight. "So beautiful. You make this?"

"I know you miss the sea," he said. "And since living here with me in Kedesh means you will not see it again, I hoped it might remind you. Comfort you."

Teary-eyed, I slid the ring onto my first finger, the copper still retaining the warmth from his palm, and admired the sight of the gift he'd made with his own hands, for me.

"And who, may I ask, is this young woman?"

I turned toward the voice that had broken into our quiet moment, unsure why it seemed so familiar. The old man who'd told the stories tonight stood within a couple of paces of us, a large grin on his face and mirth in his eyes.

"Dov!" Eitan said, a wide smile in his voice, and I recognized the name as belonging to the grandfather of Eitan's childhood friend Tal. Another realization slammed into me in the next moment — the storyteller was not simply an elder, but a priest. I took a step backward.

Unaware of the hitch in my breath, the man came closer and embraced Eitan, then reached up to squeeze his shoulder. "How good it is to see you, my boy."

"Are you well?" Eitan asked. "I have not seen you for weeks."

"I am. I've been in Shiloh," Dov said. "My mother passed from this world into the *olam ha'ba.* We all gathered in celebration of her life there, where'd she'd lived with my brother Avi's family."

Eitan frowned. "I am sorry to hear that. I only met her one time, when I was a young boy, but she seemed very kind."

"There was no one like my ima," said Dov, turning to me as he explained. "She was a midwife. Her hands guided thousands of babies into this world. She was the very embodiment of wisdom, gentleness, and faithfulness to Yahweh." The adoration in his voice was evident, and I had the irrational thought that I very much wished I could have known his mother too.

He tilted his head toward me with a grin. "Are you planning to introduce me to your friend?"

Eitan smiled down at me, a gaze that

spoke a thousand words. "This is Sofea."

"Ah yes. I've heard of you. One of the girls brought here from Tyre, correct?" Dov reached a hand toward me, as if he'd meant to place it on my shoulder as he'd done to Eitan. Instinctively, I took another step backward, the image of my father's sneer somehow bright in my mind.

A frown tugged at Dov's mouth. "I mean no harm, my dear. Forgive me." His words were gentle, reassuring, and nothing like the censure that I expected from such a powerful man. He turned back to Eitan, whose brow was wrinkled with concern for me. "Come, my Rachel will be anxious to see you and give you news of Tal."

Although my instinct was to slip away and find Prezi among the crowd, I followed Eitan and the priest to the opposite end of the courtyard. I had no desire to speak with a priest or his wife, but I had even less desire to leave Eitan's side. My thumb traced the line of the ring on my finger back and forth, the feel of the warm metal against my skin comforting as I was introduced to not only Dov's wife but also his son Amitai and his wife, along with their youngest daughter, Rivkah, who seemed to be about the same age as Gidal. The girl fixed a curious but wary amber-eyed stare on me as I sat down.

Dov and Eitan chatted amiably about Tal, Dov's pride in his grandson's priestly training evident in every word. I wondered what sort of training would possibly take five years to complete. My father had done nothing more than conduct bloody sacrifices, execute unfair judgments, lead disgusting rituals, and collect and discard women. Surely little training would be needed for such activities as these.

"A good boy, our Tal." Rachel's hand went to her chest, as if to cover some pain there. "If only Nurit had lived . . ." Her voice trailed off, and Dov reached over to squeeze her hand, his gaze reassuring and full of such tenderness that my own heart fluttered in response. "Give it time, my love," he said. "Any woman our grandson chooses to marry will be blessed indeed."

Rachel patted her husband's bearded cheek with a watery smile. "That she will. And knowing Tal, he will choose a woman whose kindness will only be matched by her depth of love for Yahweh."

Eitan leaned closer to whisper in my ear as the conversation moved on to the upcoming birth in the family. "Tal's betrothed died last year, only a month before the wedding." His fingers grazed over mine. "I hope one day you will meet him. He is as much my brother as Gidal and Malakhi."

The longer I listened to the priest talking with his family, laughing, jesting affectionately, the more my muscles relaxed. The comparison between this grandfatherly man — who plainly adored his only wife and spoke of each of his children and grandchildren with pride — and my depraved father was stark. There was no calculation in his relaxed manner, no caustic disdain on the edges of his words, no hint of lust in his kind gaze. And the stories that he'd told had steered my imagination in directions I'd never considered before.

Nothing I'd learned of these Hebrews had been what I'd expected, from the way they'd invited us into their lives, to the purity of their worship, to the priests who valued life instead of seeking to destroy it. Embracing worship of Yahweh had certainly brought Prezi back to life. Perhaps binding myself to him through a marriage covenant with Eitan would surpass my expectations as well.

Tracing the curves of the copper ring on my finger once more, I smiled to myself, letting the rest of my fears drift away as hope began to burrow into my bones. The island was my past. Eitan, and Israel, were my future.

CHAPTER TWENTY-FOUR

EITAN

27 Tishri

I leaned against the doorway to the small chamber Darek shared with my mother, watching as he pressed a few days' worth of dried meat and flatbread into the pack on the bed. "You just returned," I said. "Where are you off to so early?"

He'd come into the city after dark, so I'd been shocked when my mother told me he was leaving again this morning, especially since another storm seemed to be gathering. But I was determined to speak to him about the shepherd I'd seen watching the inn, as well as my betrothal to Sofea, before he left.

"Heading back north," he said, his attention not wavering from his task. He added two knives, one of which I'd made, which caused a surge of pride to ripple through me. "A group of Amorites raided some farms near Laish. We need to find out if they are planning another incursion." He reached over to pick up a sword I hadn't seen among the linens on the bed. He held it out to me, his expression dour.

I accepted the weapon, the blade glimmering in the early morning light from the window. "What's this?"

"A Hittite-crafted iron sword."

I raised a brow, testing the heft of it in my hand, examining the smooth lines and polished metal. "I've heard of such things but have never seen one."

"One of the Amorites who attacked north of Laish had this on him." He skimmed a finger over the flat of the blade. "These iron swords shatter bronze ones as if they were glass. Until now, the Hittites have mostly kept these sorts of weapons to themselves, so we were very surprised to find it in Amorite hands. I knew if anyone could figure out how the Hittites made this, it'd be you."

It was clear that this sword was not cast in a mold but wrought with tools and strengthened by hammering. I'd cast iron on a few occasions before but the products we'd managed to mold were nowhere near strong enough to be used for weaponry, especially with the amount of tin we'd had to add to the mix to bring the melting point low enough. Yalon and I had never been able to stoke the furnace hot enough to create such an extraordinary sword.

Encouraged by Darek's confidence in my skills, my mind began to whirl with possibilities. Perhaps a different metal than tin could be introduced to lower the melting point of the ore? Copper perhaps . . .

The reminder of the ring I'd made for Sofea brought back into focus the reason for my presence here, and I lowered the sword to my side. I pictured Sofea's expectant smile from the other night, along with her blue eyes and irresistible silken curls, the image solidifying my determination. "Before you go, I have a request."

"Oh?"

"I want to marry Sofea. I know that it's not conventional, since she is not a Hebrew, and because of the way she came to Kedesh, and of course her parents are dead —" Annoyed with my fumbling words and the infuriatingly stoic look on his face, I stopped.

His expression remained impassive, but he sat on the edge of the bed, arms folded. "Is she of the same mind?"

"She is and has assured me that she is

willing to take part in the Covenant as well."

His brows lifted. "And everything it entails?"

"Yes."

He lifted his eyes to the window, considering. "Since she is not a Canaanite, nor an enemy of our people, I doubt the elders would insist on head shaving, or the like."

I hadn't even considered the possibility, and I was gutted by the thought of her golden-brown curls beneath a razor. I was grateful that Darek did not think she'd be forced to submit to such a thing, but some part of me wondered whether she *would* be willing to do such a thing, for me.

"And does she know . . ." He frowned. "About your past? About why you are in Kedesh?"

"She does."

He was silent for a while, his gaze still latched on the window. Then he gave a slight nod that made my blood sing with anticipation. "Moriyah already informed me of the attachment between the two of you, although it's nothing anyone with eyes would miss." He sent me a knowing glance.

"Since the moment I met her on that beach, she has exhibited admirable strength and loyalty. She is a good match for you," he said. "She's been through so much, but there's no one I trust more to protect and cherish her." The sincerity in his eyes made my own burn with unexpected emotion. "So, if she agrees to the match and understands the consequences, I will arrange a formal betrothal when I return."

He stood with a groan to tie his dagger sheath onto his belt, and as he did so I noticed that gray had begun threading into the dark hair at his temples. Darek had spent the last eleven years leading an elite group of men whose mission had been to spy on the enemy through whatever means necessary. He'd learned every Canaanite dialect and was an expert at sliding into foreign mannerisms — a talent he swore he'd learned from my mother. He'd spent more time traveling between tribal territories than living here in Kedesh with his family. The awareness that all of it was wearing him down suddenly struck me. Would he ever have the chance to simply enjoy rest in this land he fought so hard for?

"How long will you be gone this time?"

He did not look up at me as he finished tying the flap on his pack closed. "I don't know. I'll determine that when I get back up there."

Something about the carefully selected words snagged my suspicion. "Why did you return last night, then, if you were only heading back that way today?"

"I came to retrieve a few more men and to send a message to Yehoshua through the Levites."

My eyes narrowed. I was right. He was holding back information from me — again. "Who is going with you?"

"The fifty men under Meshek's command, and Baz went to Merom to petition for another two hundred."

I flinched, indignation surging high. "Meshek is in *command* now?"

"Not my decision, I assure you." His mouth pursed as if the idea were as bitter to him as it was to me. "If his uncle was not the commander over Naftali's forces, it would never have happened."

My longtime feud with Meshek notwithstanding, two hundred and fifty men being called to Laish was no small thing. "This is more than a few Amorites testing our borders, isn't it?"

His sigh was laden with defeat. "We lost sixty men."

"Sixty?" I pushed off the doorway to step closer. "You said the remaining Amorites went running off north like a pack of whipped dogs after the battle at Hazor. What's changed since then?"

He scrubbed a hand over his beard. "The kingdom of Aram-Naharim, to the northeast of us, has grown stronger, for one thing. Their new king is known for his ruthlessness. He slaughtered his six brothers and their entire families in order to ascend to the throne, then hung every one of their headless bodies from the walls of his palace — from infants to concubines."

The gruesome image turned my stomach.

"He is also very shrewd," he said. "My men and I traveled with a group of traders a couple of months ago all the way into Damascus. Rumor says he is using the Amorites as an advance force, stirring up their latent anger against us for his purposes and promising the return of the territories they feel they have the right to. As you can see, he's arming them with the finest weapons and providing them with supplies so as not to put his own army in harm's way, for now. He's using them to test us, prodding to see where we are weakest."

"Does this mean war?"

His mouth pinched. "I hope not. We are not ready to face a force like that, especially if the Hittites are involved. I'd hoped that the victories we enjoyed since Jericho would discourage such ideas. But this king is young and seems not to know, or care, what

Yahweh did to Jericho, or to Egypt, for that matter."

"Surely the tribes will come together and push them back. Yehoshua assured us that Yahweh will hold to his promises. We cannot be uprooted from this Land."

"It is not Yahweh who has violated the covenant. There have been a rash of intermarriages between Hebrew leaders and Canaanite women — ones not built upon *torah* but on peace treaties with enemy cities within our territories."

Mosheh and Yehoshua had warned that such unions would destroy us from the inside, drag us into idolatry. Was such a thing happening already, within twenty years of our entrance into the Land of Promise?

"This Land is being divided by compromise," Darek said, answering my unspoken thought. "And I fear that if this continues, the protection Yahweh promised will be withheld and the surrounding nations will take full advantage." He picked up his pack and slung it over his shoulder. "If we don't push back now, make it clear that we are united beneath Yahweh's banner, war will be inevitable."

The implications of his statement were grave. Laish was only a few hours' walk from Kedesh. Nearly everyone I loved lived within these walls. Sofea. My mother. My siblings. How could I call myself a man — a husband — if I waited until the fight was at the gates? Determination settled into my bones, grounding me as never before, and I gripped the hilt of the sword tight in my fist. "I'm going with you."

"No, you are not."

I stretched to full height. "I am ready. Baz said I'm as capable as any soldier trained to defend Israel." I lifted my chin, confident in his assessment of my proficiency, especially with a sling. "If not more so."

"I am aware of that. But your place is here."

"My place is with the army defending my people."

"Your skills are needed in this city."

"There are plenty of soldiers to protect Kedesh."

"I'm speaking of your metalsmithing skills. You want to be a part of protecting Israel, I understand that. But this —" He pointed to the iron sword. "This is how you will serve your people. Israel needs the ability to make weapons like this — now."

"I said I would try, and I will, after the Amorites are pushed back north." Unbidden, Meshak's jest poured out of my own mouth. "What sort of coward hides behind walls while others go fight his battles?" *And how can I even stand before Sofea with any sort of dignity if I do?*

"You have no choice! You cannot leave this city."

I scoffed. "I am not afraid to leave."

"You were sent here by Eleazer for your safety."

"I am not a child anymore."

"I did not say you were, but regardless, you will not go past that boundary line."

I stepped closer to him, body rigid and my words sliding into a snarl. "I am going, Darek. My decision is made."

"The decision was made when you were nine." His voice sharpened. "The moment you dropped that oleander into the stew that killed my nephews."

The accusation slammed into my chest, expelling my breath in a surprised huff. Just as quickly, anger and shame melded together in my blood before flaring white-hot. "I. Was. A. Child."

He flinched, and his expression dropped, remorse bleeding into his tone as he lifted his hands. "I know that. That's not what I meant —"

I clenched my fists tight. "I was not

sentenced here like Ima. I don't *have* to stay."

"It doesn't matter. If you step over that line, Raviv will kill you."

"I'm not afraid of Raviv, I am well prepared —"

Conviction hardened the planes of his face. "There is nothing more to discuss here. I've told you before that my brother will not give up until you are dead, and frankly I don't think Eleazar's death will change anything. You must live here for your lifetime."

"I won't cower —"

"No." He threw a palm in the air. "You must stop fighting against the protection you are afforded in this city and accept that this is your permanent home. And furthermore, you need to make it very clear to Sofea that marriage to you means it would be hers as well."

My mouth gaped as his argument knocked me back a step.

"Besides," he continued, "I need to deal with the problem at hand, not worry about whether my brother is trailing us looking for an opportunity to take revenge or whether you will make some impulsive move that will jeopardize my men." He moved past me to the door. "Moriyah told me about the shepherd you saw watching the inn. She said you've seen him before, watching you?"

Too furious to speak, I nodded.

"I knew Raviv had spies in this city. Moriyah is to go nowhere without you until I return. Your place is here, protecting your mother and figuring out how to replicate that sword."

"Nadir can keep watch over Ima." The next words ripped from my mouth in a blaze of fury. "I will go where I please. You are not my father."

He stood in the doorway, his back to me, one white-knuckled hand gripping the doorpost. "I understand that." His voice sounded even more weary than it had before. "But I will not chance your safety, nor the safety of the woman I love more than my own life. I will *not* discuss this with you any further, and Chaim will have orders not to let you past the gates until we return."

My voice rose to a shout, my tenuous hold on fury shattering. "You would imprison me even more than I already am?"

His answer came out flat and cold. "If that's what it takes — then yes."

He walked away, leaving me glaring at the empty doorway, chest heaving, outrage and pain leaking out of me like a frayed wineskin. *The decision was made when you were nine . . . when you dropped that oleander into the stew that killed my nephews. . . .*

Although both he and my mother had assured me back then that Darek held no grudge against me for my impetuous actions that day, it was plain that it had been a lie. A lie I'd suspected from the beginning, which was why I'd kept my distance from him over the years. What use was there in accepting his blatantly false attempts to win me over in those early days of his and Moriyah's marriage? He loved my mother, of that I had no doubt, and for her sake he'd accepted my presence in her life, but anything else was pretense. No man could possibly want a son who'd killed his own flesh and blood. I knew, whether Darek admitted it or not, that he blamed me. For Zeev and Yared, and for his wife being imprisoned in Kedesh.

Nadir was right. I had nothing to offer Sofea. Although my father was born of the tribe of Naftali like Darek, my parents had died before being allocated any land. I had no inheritance to pass on to our children other than a soot-stained foundry and the forever sullied name of a killer.

With all the wild beauty and bold curiosity that I loved about her, how could I trap

Sofea into a marriage that was nothing more than a prison sentence? I'd been selfish in claiming her without more carefully considering the consequences — another impulsive move like the one that had defined my life since I was nine.

With an anguished bellow, I heaved the magnificent sword at the back wall. The flat of the blade hit the stone with a mighty clang before it shuddered off, spun, and clattered to the ground with a pathetic thud.

My entire body trembled as I sank to my knees and dropped my head into my hands.

CHAPTER TWENTY-FIVE

SOFEA

The door rattled on its hinges as a gust of wind swept through the crack above the threshold with a sharp howl. The violence of the windstorm that had been pummeling Kedesh for the past hour reminded me very much of the storms we'd endured on my island, huddled in our round huts, shivering under blankets and calling out to the gods to preserve us from their fury.

Instead of cowering in fear, burning incense, or laying offerings before household altars, Moriyah had organized a morning of walnut shelling to fill the time and keep our hands and minds busy. The cooperative hum of women's and children's voices swirled around the room, rising above the angry wail of the winds and the clatter and bang of debris outside. Every so often someone would lift their voice in song, but even the beautiful lilting melodies did little to soothe my nerves.

My uncoordinated attempts at shelling nuts were interspersed with anxious glances toward the door. Eitan had left the inn before I'd awakened this morning, and I was desperate to hear whether he'd spoken to Darek yet. While I was confident of Eitan's affection for me, I was a foreigner here, an outsider with nothing to offer Darek's family. My worth to my own father had been only equal to the tribal alliance my marriage would have provided.

Determined to distract myself from the flock of questions and worries swooping around and around in my head, I brought a stone down on the walnut in front of me with a bang. It split perfectly this time, the two sides shuddering as they landed on the table. I tapped the halves on the wood until the nutmeats separated from their casing, then set them in the basket between Prezi and me with a flourish.

Prezi laughed at my triumphant grin. "One done . . ." She swept her hand over the long table upon which were set baskets and baskets of unshelled walnuts. "One thousand to go."

I made a face at her and picked up another nut, her sweet laughter doing more than anything to soothe my anxiety over Eitan's continued absence. As I eyed the large amount of cast-off shells already on the table in front of her, a sudden flash of competitiveness prodded me to not only match her rhythm but overtake it. Her knowing grin goaded me even further. I had no intention of losing this game.

The changes in my cousin over the past months never ceased to astound me. The broken, bleeding, dead-hearted woman who had landed on the shore of Tyre had been replaced with one whose smile radiated joy. She dived into each new task at the inn with relish, and instead of shrinking back when new guests arrived at the doors, she welcomed them with food and drink and gentle questions about their travels. It was as if coming into Israel had recreated my cousin into a completely new woman.

I watched her from the corner of my eye as she chatted with Binah, who I recently learned was also a convicted manslayer, and marveled that the changes inside of Prezi had even transformed her face. Beauty shone there that never had before.

Gone was the timidity and reticence that had lived on her mouth, even when we were children, and the light in her dark brown eyes was a distinct contradiction to the underlying hollowness that had reigned there for as long as I'd known her. We'd always been close, from the time we could walk, but in the past few years she'd begun to curl inside herself, becoming even more withdrawn. I cursed myself now for being so absorbed in my own concerns and too busy pressing her to tag along on my adventures in and around the sea to even ask why.

Never again would I take advantage of her kindness, of the sacrifice she'd made for me under Seno's whip. My heart swelled with love for my cousin, and not for the first time I hoped that she would find a husband to cherish her, protect her, and make her feel as desired as Eitan did me.

Rachel, Dov's wife, had joined us today, as had her son's wife and the girl named Rivkah whom I'd met the other day. Having shelled no more than ten nuts over the past hour, Rivkah bounced up, declaring she was tired of the work, and went to search out Gidal and Malakhi. Banned from the room earlier by Moriyah after they'd knocked over a pot of beer, the two boys had removed themselves to the hallway to play with a basket of discarded walnut shells.

A short time later, Rivkah came streaking back into the room, voice pitched high with complaints that Malakhi had invented a game of seeing how many broken shells the boys could lodge in her long black hair.

Moriyah left the room to deal with her wayward sons, returning with a contrite Gidal, who delivered a sincere apology, and a not-so-contrite Malakhi, who mumbled the words but smirked at Rivkah as soon as his mother turned her back. The girl stuck out her tongue at him and whirled away with a huff, making a great show of ignoring the boy who seemed intent on provoking her. I smiled to myself as I slammed the stone down on another walnut. Something told me that Rivkah's parents would have their hands full with that young woman in years to come.

The door behind us swung open and a powerful blast of wind accompanied Eitan and Nadir across the threshold. The sight of Eitan made everyone else in the room disappear for me. Much of his long hair had come loose from the tie at his neck and now hung around his face in a disheveled tangle. It was all I could do to stay seated on the ground and not go to him, eager to pick up where the wind left off and run my fingers through its dark length. As if drawn by the same powerful force of nature that drew my attention to him whenever he was within sight, his hazel eyes sought out mine across the room.

Interrupting the silent connection between us, Moriyah sprang up from her seat at the table and strode over to Eitan. "Where have you been?" The slight censure in her tone suggested that she'd been concerned for her son's safety out in the storm, even though she'd seemed perfectly calm as she entertained the large group of women gathered in her home.

"We went to secure the foundry before the storm hit, but as we were returning we came across a neighbor whose animals had broken out of their pen. Nadir and I have been chasing five goats and three donkeys all over town."

This information elicited some laughter from the ladies around the table and excited chatter and questions from the children.

"How is the foundry?" asked Moriyah, already pouring two cups of barley beer for the men as they dipped their hands in a washing pot in the corner.

"The roof has some damage already." Eitan accepted the cup from his mother with a nod before guzzling the contents and releasing a satisfied sigh. "If this storm doesn't calm soon, Nadir and I may end up having to replace the entire thing."

Another brutal rush of wind slammed against the shuttered windows, followed by a clap of thunder that startled all of us. Tirzah began to cry, so Moriyah strode over to lift the infant from the blanket she'd been playing on, then paced the length of the room, shushing her and cooing words of calm into her tiny daughter's ear. As I watched them, a flutter of something new came to life in me — a desire to cradle Eitan's child within my body.

Since they too were now stuck inside with the rest of us while the storm howled outside, Moriyah asked Eitan and Nadir to put their muscles to good use by bringing in the smaller of the stone mills from the courtyard to crush the leftover walnut shells, which would be used to polish the metal in the foundry, for dyes, and in a variety of other ways around the inn. Moriyah was an expert at making sure nothing, even the shell of a nut, was wasted.

My gaze traveled over the women and girls gathered around this table: Moriyah, Abra, Chana, Binah, Sarai, even sulking Rivkah and her mother and grandmother. I'd been brought to this city against my will, grieving and alone except for Prezi, but somehow over the past months I'd begun to think of these people as friends, and this inn as my home.

If Darek agreed to a marriage between Eitan and me, I would be considered a permanent member of this household. I would be a wife, a sister, a daughter, and someday, a mother. I would be part of a family once again.

Overflowing with hope that today Eitan would announce our betrothal, I smiled to myself, grabbed another handful of nuts to shell, and wondered whether Prezi was right about Yahweh after all.

The storm pounded its fists against the doors and shutters for another two hours, and by the time it quieted its demands we'd nearly finished the walnuts. Baskets of empty shells sat on the floor near Eitan and Nadir, who'd barely taken a break as they crushed the pieces into sand.

Moriyah opened the front door to the inn, frowning in dismay. "It seems to finally be over. The palm tree out front is destroyed, and there is quite a bit of debris in the street. Eitan, you'd best check on the foundry."

Both men stood, but Eitan leaned close to Nadir, speaking so low I heard nothing more than the silken rumble of his voice. With a frown, Nadir glanced at Moriyah, then nodded and sat back down to his task at the stone mill. The odd exchange left me with a feeling of unease.

After Eitan left, the children filtered out of the room, anxious to stretch their legs in the courtyard. Even Rivkah sauntered off to join them, ending her self-imposed isolation.

"If there is this much damage to the few trees within the walls, I can only imagine what the orchards and groves around the city might have sustained," said Moriyah. "Perhaps we should collect firewood."

"Prezi and I will go," I said, anxious to stretch my own legs.

"That would be wonderful. There ought to be plenty of small limbs all over the ground, and we'd best bring in as much as we can before it rains. Nadir, would you mind going with them?"

Seeming uncomfortable, Nadir cleared his throat. "Eitan said I should stay here, make sure you are safe." His expression, and the pointed look he gave Moriyah, was full of meaning I could not grasp.

She waved him off. "I am fine, Nadir. I'll not be leaving the inn today. I have too much work to do inside. I'm sure the courtyard is a mess, but we could really use that wood. Please, take the girls. I'll be safe, I assure you."

Giving in to her argument, Nadir waited

as we collected large woven baskets to carry the tree limbs, then followed us out into the street. Although the wind had toppled market stalls, shredded linen awnings, and ripped shutters from windows, the damage seemed to be limited. And there had been little rain, so the streets were not even wet.

We'd only just turned the corner when Eitan's voice called out to us. I spun, barely restraining my impulse to run to him, slide my arms around his narrow waist, and lay my head against his chest. I hoped that Darek would agree to a short betrothal, for nothing would be more wonderful than having the freedom to greet Eitan so, anytime I chose.

"Where are you going?" he said to Nadir, his brow furrowing. "I asked you to stay with my mother."

"She insisted she wouldn't leave the inn and asked that we retrieve some of the downed tree limbs," said Nadir. "I couldn't let Prezi and Sofea go out there on their own."

Eitan grimaced, his gaze flitting between the three of us and then back toward the inn. Unease shifted inside me. Something had upset him. His mother? Or was it the damage to the foundry? Between the long hair that he'd still not bothered to tame, the streak of soot across his cheekbone, and the bleak look in his eyes, he barely resembled the man who'd kissed me on a rooftop and laughed with abandon as I attempted to shoot his sling.

A sudden feeling of desperation made me step toward him. "Come with us."

His gaze clashed with mine, and if I hadn't been carrying a large basket, I might have fallen to my knees at the impact. This was more than storm destruction. His expression was tortured.

"Please." Dazed by grim premonition, my plea came out as a strangled whisper.

His eyes slipped closed for a brief moment, his lips pressed so tightly they went white, but then he looked over my shoulder to Nadir and Prezi. "I need to speak to Sofea. We will catch up with you at the gates."

Although both of them offered me concerned looks, they walked on. I kept my eyes locked on them until they disappeared into the crowd, desperate to hear what Eitan had to say but at the same time dreading it.

Darek and Moriyah most likely desired Eitan to marry another Hebrew girl, one steeped in the ways of their people. Not the daughter of a heathen priest who reveled in the shedding of blood and debasing rituals.

I was the child of a murderer, a monster, and the taint of it would never wash away.

My lungs began to burn, as if I were trapped deep beneath the surface of the sea. The beautiful waves of copper that Eitan had fashioned into a ring were cold against my skin, a final mocking by Posedao, who'd stolen so much from me already. Had I lost Eitan now as well?

Gathering my courage, I turned to him. "Darek wants you to marry a Hebrew, yes?"

"What?" He shifted his stance, his attention briefly drawn to an ox-drawn cart full of tree limbs passing by. "Oh. No, he agreed to arrange the betrothal when he returns."

"He did?" My knees wavered as relief poured into me, and I placed the empty basket on the ground, needing to steady myself. I'd worried for nothing. "How long will he be gone?"

Eitan took a deep breath. A muscle ticked in his jaw, as if he were grinding his teeth together. "It may be a few weeks. There is a threat building on the northern border of the territory. He came here only to call up more men."

"Is danger coming?"

"For now, no. Although that could change," he said, then told me of the king of Aram-Naharim and the Hittite weapons that had been found among the Amorites.

"Can you make such thing as this iron sword?"

"Possibly. I am considering whether layers of charcoal might help raise the heat in the furnace more. But at the moment I only have a small amount of iron ore to experiment with. And the roof ripped off the foundry, so I'll have to repair that before I make any more attempts."

I placed my hand on his arm, sliding it down to squeeze his wrist in a gesture of comfort. "Darek choose the best man to make such thing. I know this."

He made a noise of dismissal in the back of his throat, his expression so pained that I longed to smooth the worries from his brow. But since we were standing in the street, the crowd parting around us as if we were two boulders in a stream, I stepped back and picked up my basket. "We should not keep Prezi and Nadir waiting."

We walked on, silence keeping pace between us. If Darek had conceded to the betrothal, why was Eitan so troubled? For as long as I'd known him, his emotions seemed so close to the surface. Even when I hadn't spoken his language, I'd nearly always known his thoughts by the way he'd looked at me. Whether it was concern, or curiosity, or longing in his eyes, I'd never had to guess. But today everything was shuttered as tightly as the inn had been during the storm. Perhaps once we were outside the city and able to speak more freely, he might be more forthcoming about whatever was on his mind.

We passed through the inner gates of the city, and I waved to Prezi and Nadir, who stood waiting for us near the gatehouse. Although still unsettled by Eitan's strange mood, I could not wait to tell my cousin the news of our betrothal.

Just as I moved to wend my way through the crowd, Eitan caught my arm. "I can't go with you."

"What do you mean?"

"I cannot leave the city." He pointed toward the group of guards who controlled the flow of visitors and traders through the tall outer gates, which stood wide open at this time of day. "Darek has given them orders not to let me pass."

The acid in his tone confused me. Although I'd always sensed an underlying tension between the two men, I had little doubt that Eitan greatly admired Moriyah's husband. And from the pride I'd seen on Darek's face when he looked upon the man his wife had taken as a son, I was convinced he loved him nearly as much as she did.

"Why would he do this?" I asked.

"I told him I planned to go north with him, to help defend our people against the Amorites."

"But you cannot pass the boundary, no?"

Anger flared on his face. "Only because he does not trust me to protect myself. I was not convicted of anything by the council. Since I was a child, Moriyah shouldered the full burden of blame. Legally, I can go anywhere I please. And it is time for me to fight. To stand for Israel. But now . . ." He jabbed a finger toward the guards, whose wary eyes were latched on him. "Now he's made me even more of a prisoner than before."

"But you —"

He cut me off. "I should not have asked you to marry me, Sofea. Like usual, I made an impulsive decision and I was wrong."

My jaw gaped. "What are you saying?"

"I have wasted months training with Baz, hoping that Darek would change his mind. Hoping that he would see that I am more than capable of joining him. But the only thing I am good for is making weapons to be handed off to the men who have the freedom to fight for Israel, to fight for the ones they love. What kind of husband can't even protect his own family? Marriage to me means you would be trapped in this city like me, Sofea, possibly for the rest of your life. What kind of life would we have? What kind of life would our children have, growing up in a prison?"

"We would have life together," I said, my vision watery. "This is enough for me."

His expression softened. His eyes traveled over my face, as if he were memorizing every feature, lingering on my hair, my cheeks, my lips. I stepped toward him, not caring who was watching us as I lifted my hand to touch his face.

Before my palm could connect with his bearded cheek, he took a step backward, his eyes going hard. "It is not enough for me."

The words lashed harder than the metal tip of Seno's whip against my skin, leaving lacerations that went infinitely deeper.

Eitan turned away, his height making him visible above the crowd as he passed back through the inner gates. Swallowing the violent sob that had been building in my throat, I watched as the man I loved turned the corner and disappeared from view, leaving me with nothing more than an empty basket and broken promises.

CHAPTER TWENTY-SIX

Prezi planted herself in front of me. "Sofea. What is wrong? You have not said a word since we left the city."

I ignored the determined set of her chin and bent to pick up another limb, adding it to the basket that was already half full of wind-torn olive branches. "I am fine."

"You are not," she said. "What did Eitan say to you?"

The sun shimmered through the clouds, blinding me as I looked into the sky. A flock of gray cranes winged overhead, and I watched them disappear over the eastern horizon. Prezi waited for me to respond, unyielding.

"He does not want to marry me," I finally said.

"That is not true. I've seen the way that man looks at you. There's nothing he wants more."

"You'll have to convince him of that, then.

Although Darek gave his blessing for a betrothal, Eitan made it very clear that he's changed his mind." I told her more of our conversation, straining to keep my voice even as I laid out the way he'd destroyed everything with six words.

Dropping her basket, Prezi wrapped her long arms around me. She smelled of rosemary, yeasty bread, and olive oil — the smell of the sea having long washed away from her hair, and along with it, the remnants of our home.

How had our roles shifted so completely? Back among the Sicani, I had been the strong one, the older cousin who chose the games, directed the excursions, and pushed her to dive deeper and swim farther out into the sea. Now it was Prezi's arms holding me together.

"At least this time you weren't in the way of my misplaced trust," I said, my voice trembling. "These wounds are all mine."

"He's not Seno," she said. "Something deeper is going on here. Something we don't understand. I'll talk with him when we return."

I shook my head against her shoulder. "He made everything quite clear."

Nadir approached the two of us, his arms full of tree limbs as big around as my leg and concern on his face. "Anything I can do to help?"

"No." I extricated myself from Prezi's embrace and bent to pick up a few more small branches, determined to not allow Eitan's rejection to wound me any more than it already had. We were very near the area where Moriyah had seen Raviv, the white boundary rock visible through the green underbrush. I frowned as Prezi explained that Eitan and I had a falling-out and about how Darek had forbidden him to pass through the gates.

Nadir said nothing, but I could feel his gaze on me as I lifted my hand to shield my eyes, tilting my head back to watch yet another flock of cranes drift overhead. As their honking calls trailed off, I sighed. "I wonder where these birds fly to. . . ."

Nadir looked over his shoulder at the place where the magnificent animals had vanished from sight. "I know where they are going." He turned to me, a spark of something lighting his expression with anticipation. "Do you remember the lake I showed you from the rooftop?"

I nodded. I'd never forget the day we'd connected, even without language, over our shared love of the water.

"Each year thousands of birds congregate

there on their way south. The entire valley is full of them at this time of year."

"Is this so?" I exclaimed, grateful for the distraction from Eitan's rejection.

"It is."

"You have seen this?"

Nadir smiled broadly. "I have. I've been down to the lake many times. It's at the center of one of the most fertile valleys I've ever seen. The water is so clear all I had to do was walk out a few paces with a small net and wait for the fish to come to me."

Prezi frowned. "I thought you could not pass the boundary."

He shrugged a shoulder. "True. But unlike Moriyah, or Eitan for that matter, there is no one who has vowed to kill me if I do so. Medad's family knows that my part in their son's death was purely accidental. They testified on my behalf. There is no danger for me in leaving Kedesh. I stay here only at the behest of the elder council."

His description of the water in the valley had conjured a deep longing for the caress of the sea on my skin, the pleasant drag of its salty fingers through the length of my hair, the taste of the ocean on my lips.

Seeing the yearning on my face, he grinned. "You want to go, don't you?"

I sighed, nodding. This day, more than any

other, I longed to float on my back with my ears beneath the surface and watch the clouds in blessed watery silence. He looked back toward the city. In the distance, a group of men were carefully shoveling dirt atop a densely packed pile of burning tree limbs. The mound would smolder for days, producing charcoal for the people of Kedesh.

"Let's go," Nadir said. "No one is watching."

"No!" said Prezi. "This is not safe."

"It is less than an hour's walk. We'll be back well before the sun goes down."

My heart picked up its pace. *Could* we do such a thing?

"I am armed," said Nadir, with a gesture to the sword hanging from his belt. "I will protect you. I have been down to that valley many times and have rarely ever crossed anyone's path. I know the way to go where we won't be seen."

"We cannot." Prezi's expression was a flood of worries, an echo of all the times I'd urged her to enter an unknown cave or cajoled her into flinging herself off a low cliff into the sea after I'd already dived in.

"Please, cousin?" I pleaded with my palms pressed together, just as I'd done when we were children. "I am not ready to return to the city or . . ." I lowered my voice and allowed a bit of my devastation to surface. "To see Eitan just yet."

Her brow furrowed as she considered my argument and then lifted her eyes to Nadir. "We will be back before sunset?"

A jolt of excitement made me drop the broken limbs in my hands, and I hugged her, thanking her for understanding. Although she returned my embrace, her smile was tight and she glanced back toward the city a few times as we hid the wood baskets behind a large olive tree and moved toward the boundary line.

"There's nothing to fear," Nadir said, his own eyes flitting back toward the walls to ensure we were not spotted as we made our escape. "Although this lake is nowhere near as large and beautiful as the one I used to live next to, the short walk is worth it, I assure you."

As soon as we passed by the large limestone marker, I felt my muscles begin to uncoil. I slipped my hand into Prezi's, giving it a little squeeze of gratitude. Eitan had pushed me away and smashed my hopes for the future, but at least today the water would welcome me with open arms.

As soon as we crossed over the ridge into

the valley, I sighted the lake Nadir had pointed out from the rooftop of the inn. The glittering water called to me, whispering words of home, of the warm sea and blue tides, of brine and white-pebbled shores.

I gripped Prezi's hand tightly, my steps quickening without forethought, and then with an apologetic grin I slowed, realizing that I was practically dragging my lame cousin along in my wake.

Nadir had not exaggerated the myriad flocks of birds that gathered in the wide basin. Enormous gray and white cranes milled about the valley floor, various groups rising and falling like white-capped waves as they vied for position within the multitude. Their graceful necks and long-stretched legs lent them a regal appearance as they strutted about, searching out treasure among the long grasses at the edge of the lake.

Overhead, swooping birds of all varieties filled the sky with song, welcoming us into the valley with great cheer. I had the foolish thought that Eitan should see this place, that he would delight in exploring here with me. A very foolish thought indeed, for even if he had not set me aside, he still could never leave Kedesh. Yet even so, the idea of building a life and a family with Eitan had been so satisfying that I would have gladly vowed to never step foot over the line for the rest of my days.

When my toes finally met the shore, all my hopeful expectations dissipated. The water was frigid, the bank slick with reddish mud and clogged with marsh grasses. Although the valley and the lake were exceedingly beautiful, lorded over by a majestic snow-capped mountain range, nothing about this place echoed my island, my home. And the promise of a new home with Eitan had now been washed away. My thumb worried the ridges of my shell necklace, as if the familiar movement could smooth away my heartache.

Seeing the disillusionment on my face, Prezi slipped an arm around my shoulders. "I miss the island too, Sofi," she said, her soothing tone causing cracks to splinter the tight hold I had on my emotions.

I had not cried on the beach the day our village was razed, nor as we'd lain helpless and hopeless on the sand. I'd been determined to stay strong for Prezi's sake, to keep a rein on the grief that only overflowed when I was in the throes of a nightmare. But now hot tears spilled over.

"Without Eitan, what is there to look forward to in this land?" I said, my throat seared with anguish. "All that is left is the pain of losing my family. Of losing everything."

My cousin pulled me tight against her side, her hand brushing down my curls over and over as I wept, as I finally grieved the loss of my family, my home, and now my love.

She waited, not speaking until my sobs stilled and I was empty of tears.

"For weeks after we washed ashore I felt the same way," she said. "All I could remember was the blood, my mother and father's bodies splayed on the sand, the smell . . ." She stopped, swallowing hard before continuing. "At times I feel guilty that I am glad that we survived when no one else did." She turned to face me, her expression grave as she brushed a gentle palm over my cheek to wipe away the remnants of my sorrow. "But if I had to choose living in eternal ignorance with my family over knowing the truth all over again, I would still choose Yahweh. No matter what happens, I will always be grateful that he called us away from our island."

We stood silently in the placid water for a long time, until my toes went numb and the sun began to arc toward the western ridge. A whisper of embarrassment curled through me as I suddenly remembered that Nadir had been waiting nearby all this time as I poured out my despair over the man I'd chosen over him.

"We should return to the city before the sun goes down," I said, wiping away the salty trails from my cheeks. Although I dreaded facing Eitan after the things he'd said, it was time to cinch together my courage and go back to the inn.

We turned, searching out Nadir, whom I'd last seen leaning against a terebinth as Prezi and I had gone to dip our sandals in the icy water. I shadowed my eyes against the flare of the setting sun, peering toward the tree where we'd left him.

He was there, but he was not alone.

Five men now stood beneath the shade of the tree. At first I thought perhaps Nadir had been accosted, but then he laughed, his demeanor relaxed as he gestured for the two of us to join them.

One of the strangers, a tall man with close-cropped dark hair and a tightly trimmed beard, turned to meet my curious gaze as Prezi and I cautiously approached. Something about him was familiar, the set of his shoulders perhaps, or his coloring, but his piercing black eyes and the slight frown on his mouth were anything but friendly. I slipped my hand into Prezi's, feeling a distinct urge to run but knowing her leg would not allow it.

"Who is this?" I asked Nadir, attempting to conceal my apprehension. Had he not said no one would see us here?

"There's nothing to fear, Sofea." His tone was reassuring but somehow did little to comfort me.

"We should return," I said, trying to make my voice sound unaffected. "The sun is to set."

The tall stranger surveyed me, head to foot. "So this is she?" he asked Nadir, as if I had not spoken. A pulse of dread cascaded down my back, and Prezi's grip on my hand became a vise.

"It is." Nadir's mouth quirked into the shadow of a satisfied smile. Then he gave me a small shrug, a feeble apology as he delivered a devastating betrayal. "Eitan will come for her, without a doubt."

Fool that I was, I'd walked directly into a trap set for Eitan by none other than Darek's brother Raviv, and taken my cousin with me. Within moments, we were surrounded by his men and herded toward a small group of homes and black tents on the edge of the valley. There was no point in fighting our capture; Prezi was lame and I would not leave her.

Skirting the dwellings by a wide margin, we were led through the deepening shadows to a half-constructed house at the foot of a sloping apple orchard. Raviv's men bound us, hand and foot, and left us with nothing more than a threadbare woolen blanket and the darkening sky above to cover us.

Prezi and I huddled close together on the dirt floor as Raviv ordered two of his men to stay by the door and another to keep watch, ensuring that any hope of escape, or rescue, was fully squelched. All of it was startlingly similar to being locked in the hull of Seno's ship. Except this time, instead of weeping or shrinking in on herself, Prezi merely leaned her head on mine and offered confident reassurance.

"Someone will come, Sofi," she whispered, with echoes of Moriyah in her serene tone. "Yahweh has his eye on us, even now. If we —"

Two voices on the other side of the stone wall halted whatever she'd been about to say.

"It was fortunate that Sofea and Eitan had a spat this afternoon," said Nadir. "It provided me with the perfect opportunity to lead them out to the lake. I knew someone would sight us and send you word."

"How do you know Eitan will come if they were arguing?" asked Raviv.

"He's been lusting after her for months. And now he's determined to marry her. I know him well enough to be sure that he'll find a way out of those gates to chase her down, no matter what your brother says. And fortunately Darek and his men have gone north, so they will not be an issue."

"I guess this is the next best thing, since you failed at luring him out alone."

Nadir's tone sharpened. "I did my best. I told you it would take time to gain his trust. I've been slaving away in that foundry for over half a year in order to do just that."

The truth sickened me. He'd initiated friendship with Eitan *solely* for the purpose of betraying him, even before we'd come to Kedesh. My fingernails dug into my palms as I considered all the times Moriyah had invited him into her home, the meals she'd offered him, and how often I'd seen him laughing or jesting with Eitan. Every moment of it had been false. A ruse to ingratiate himself with the family he'd been planning to betray.

"And what of you?" asked Raviv.

"I intend to be free, just as I told you the day we met by chance at the lake," said

Nadir. "I will take back what was stolen from me — by whatever means necessary. I will return within eight days to collect the reward you promised so I can rebuild my life, far from here."

Their voices faded into the night, leaving behind only the rustle of the night breeze through the leaves, the murmuring of our guards, and the hushed echo of birdcalls from across the water far behind us.

Twisting around, I took in the height of the wall at our backs, searching for climbing niches in the stone, wondering if I might be able to at least reach the leafy branch that hung over the top. But no matter how hard I struggled against the papyrus ropes that bound my hands and feet, I only succeeded in creating abrasions on my wrists. And even if I did get free, there was no possible way Prezi could scale a wall and outrun the guards. And I did not even want to consider what these men might do to her if I left her alone.

"There is nothing we can do," said Prezi, scooting her body down to lay beside me. "Instead of fretting, let's try to get some sleep. Perhaps the morning won't look so grim."

Although tempted to argue, I followed her lead and curled up beside her beneath the blanket. And then, as if we were in our cozy bed back at the inn, she began to sing a Sicani lullaby, low and sweet, and followed that with a few she'd learned in Hebrew until I drifted into a surprisingly peaceful sleep.

Just after dawn, Nadir entered our roofless prison, looking well-rested and smug, followed by Raviv. Dazed from being jolted awake and sore from sleeping on the ground, I fumbled to sit up without the use of my hands.

"Get up," said Nadir, coming forward with a knife in his hand. Shocked, I gasped and jerked backward, but he only laughed and sliced the papyrus ropes from around my ankles. "You, my sweet Sofi, are coming with me."

"No!" I scrabbled against the ground with my heels, pressing myself against the wall. "I will not leave Prezi!"

He grabbed me by the arm and hauled me to my feet. "You will do as I say or she will die."

Terror swept over me. How could I have ever trusted this man?

"I have a task for you," he said, his smile chilling. "Nothing too difficult, I assure you."

Raviv stepped forward. "No, she's the one

Eitan wants. Take the other."

"She is lame. There is no way she can make the journey. Besides, all you need is one of them to draw him here. If he doesn't arrive by nightfall, send someone into the city tomorrow to spread the rumor that the girls were spotted heading toward the valley. He'll come."

Realizing that Nadir meant to separate me from my cousin, possibly for good, I bucked violently against his grip. "I won't leave her. Let go!"

He wrenched my arm behind my back and leaned close, his words dropping into hushed malice. "You will do as I say, or I will slit her throat. And if I don't return within eight days, if you thwart my plans in any way, Raviv will make sure she is never found."

I searched his face for any hint of pretense, or any trace of the man I'd thought was a friend, but instead I saw only my trembling reflection in the eyes of a stranger.

CHAPTER TWENTY-SEVEN

EITAN

28 Tishri

I trusted Nadir to protect Sofea and Prezi, but where could they possibly have gone? Banned from leaving the confines of Kedesh to go out and look for the three of them, I'd spent a sleepless night on the rooftop last night, peering into the dark tree line, watching for any movement among the shadows.

I cursed myself for spending the entire day working out my frustrations on the foundry roof after the storm. Perhaps if I'd returned sooner I would have discovered they were missing and had time to search for them before the sun went down.

And yet the truth hit me between the eyes — it wouldn't have made a difference. Chaim still wouldn't have let me pass through the gates, since his duty to Darek far outweighed any concern for Sofea. At least he'd had enough respect for our child-hood acquaintance to take a couple of men with torches and search the area.

Darek had done this. If I'd not been forced to stay in the city when they went out to gather firewood, I would be with her now. I'd know for certain she was safe. The horrific words I'd tossed at her came back to me for the hundredth time. *It is not enough for me.* Of course she was enough! What had I done by spewing my frustrations all over Sofea? She had not hesitated when I'd told her our days would be lived out here in Kedesh, only reassured me that a life with me was all she wanted. I'd thrown her affection for me back in her face.

Entering the courtyard, I found my mother in her usual place, kneeling on the ground near her oven, kneading out her worries in the dough trough. Her eyes were closed and her lips moved silently as she pressed her knuckles into the pillow of barley bread over and over. The sight gave me a small measure of hope — if Yahweh would heed anyone's prayers, it would be my mother's.

Her eyelids fluttered open as I approached, concern twisting her face. "Anything?"

I shook my head. "I checked with the Levite family Nadir has been lodging with, but they have not seen him since yesterday morning." His room had been empty — save for one bed, a woolen mantle, and a few scattered belongings. I'd actually been surprised that his chamber was so barren, as if he were only a visitor passing through, not a man condemned to life here.

"I have to do something," I said. "I just can't stand around while she's . . . while the three of them are out there." I flung a hand toward the impenetrable city wall.

"We don't know they are in danger, son. They could very well be just down the street. Remember that time you and Tal were accidentally locked in the storage room beneath the old Canaanite temple over-night? We had to practically turn the city over before we found you."

I also remembered the pitch-blackness that surrounded us there and the fear of two young boys, neither of whom would admit to the other how terrified they really were as they waited to be rescued. I dug my fingers into my hair with a groan. "You don't understand. I said something terrible to her before she walked out of those gates. I hurt her. I turned my back —" I choked on the words, my throat surging with fire. "And if something happens to her, I'd never forgive myself if those were the last words . . ." I could not finish the thought and slumped down onto a stool nearby, my head in my hands.

"Perhaps then, if her heart is tender, she and Prezi have gone somewhere to let the sting pass, and Nadir is watching over them." My mother slipped her arms around my shoulders, speaking into my good ear. "We must trust Yahweh, my son. The God who made Sofea sees her."

"I *have* to find her, Ima."

She brushed my hair back from my face like she used to do when I was a boy. "I know, Eitan." Her smile was sad, resigned, as she kissed my forehead. "And I understand. But let's give them a bit more time before you make any hasty decisions."

Unable to sit still any longer, I told her I needed to go speak to Chaim at the gatehouse to see if he'd discovered any trace of them this morning, and if not, I would knock on every door in Kedesh until I found her.

Two half-full baskets of tree limbs had been found tucked behind one of the larger olive trees by the men Chaim had sent out into the surrounding area. With a grimace of apology, he said the baskets looked to have

337

been deliberately hidden, and that nothing suggested that Nadir and the girls had been taken by force. He'd already called off the search since they could have gone in any direction and there was no trail to follow. I left the gatehouse, chest aching as Chaim's words sank into my bones. *"I'm sorry, Eitan. It looks as though she ran away."*

Sofea must have convinced Nadir to help her flee the city after I'd wounded her so deeply. No matter how well Prezi had settled into Kedesh, she would never leave her cousin's side. Since he'd undoubtedly protect them both with his life, Nadir must have taken them somewhere they would be fed and cared for. Somewhere that would be a place of comfort to the woman I'd tossed aside like the fool I was. The only answer that made sense was that they'd gone to his family home on the shore of Kinneret.

The water Sofea missed so much would certainly be a solace after I'd heedlessly pushed her away after my argument with Darek. From what Nadir had told me, his village was less than a day's walk from here — but it might as well have been ten thousand miles, as I could not put a foot past the gates.

Had I lost her for good?

Perhaps it was for the best. Hadn't I known all along that being trapped here with me was not the best thing for her? Now she'd be free to go where she wanted, to explore the lakeshore, to seek out a new life without walls. A life without me.

Either I was wrong and the three of them would come back by nightfall so I could beg Sofea's forgiveness, or Nadir would return to confirm my assumption and put my fears to rest. With nothing else to do, I headed back to the foundry to throw myself into work and pray.

Although dusk had fallen, a few people still ambled through the streets, going to visit friends for the evening meal or carrying out chores that required attention. A few called out a greeting, but I ignored them as my sleep-deprived body moved toward the inn of its own volition. Sarai had come by the foundry earlier to deliver the news that still no word had been heard from the girls or Nadir, and that my family had taken up my cause and knocked on every door in the city but no one else had seen them either. Bereft of hope, I wanted nothing more than to go home, lock myself in my bedchamber, and sink into oblivion.

With my path lit by the flicker of oil lamps

perched in open windows to greet the twilight, I passed the city gates where I'd trampled all over Sofea's trust and stomped on her heart yesterday. I'd likely never come this way again without remembering those sharp-edged words flying out of my mouth or seeing her blue eyes glossing over after the words had hit their target.

Just as I turned the corner toward the inn, a familiar figure darted from the shadows, heading in the opposite direction.

The young shepherd.

I hadn't seen him since that day near the palm tree at the inn, and when I'd searched for him among the Levite shepherds, they'd told me only that he was from up north near Laish. He'd arrived alone and begged for work in order to fill his empty stomach, but he had disappeared after that day I'd seen him watching my mother.

My pulse kicked up as I changed course to follow him, lagging behind about ten paces so he would not notice me. If I could not find Sofea, at least I could confront Raviv's spy and ensure that my mother was protected.

To my surprise, the shepherd stopped just past Dov and Rachel's home and wedged himself into the gap between two homes, his attention turned back toward the open doorway where Binah stood in the spill of lamplight talking to someone, perhaps delivering a message to the head priest of the city. My mother and the woman she'd employed for the past few years looked nothing alike, so there would be no reason for the young man to mistake one for the other. So what reason would he have to follow Binah? Perplexed, I tucked myself into the shadows as well to watch and wait. Only curiosity and Baz's training kept me from rushing toward the young man and demanding that he reveal his connection to Raviv.

After a short conversation, Binah turned away from the threshold as the door closed, her face troubled. She stepped back into the street, the silver in her dark curls glinting in the waning moonlight as she began walking back toward the inn. Before I had a chance to take a step toward her or call out her name, the shepherd lunged from his hiding place behind her, his hand outstretched. Although caught off-guard by the sudden move, instinct took over, and I barreled toward him. He called out something unintelligible, and Binah spun around, hands lifted to fend off the attack and a scream bursting from her lips. With a bellow of fury, I angled my shoulder to plow into the shepherd, but not before he brought down the dagger he'd been holding and buried it in Binah's chest.

The three of us went down, a tangle of bodies and shouts and blood. The shepherd elbowed me in the mouth and slithered away, but I caught him by the tunic and swung him around. He threw a miscalculated punch, making it clear that he was nowhere near as well trained as I was. Catching his wrist in my right hand, I twisted it, dislodging the dagger before smashing my left fist into his jaw. Although he was a head shorter than I was and hadn't yet filled out into a manly build, somehow he held firm. He struggled against my hold on his tunic, cursing Binah, and then kicked me in the knee, which nearly knocked me down. I grunted at the impact, but fury ripped through me, and this time when I swung my fist upward, all the pent-up anger at Raviv — along with my despair over Sofea — hit the shepherd directly beneath the chin. His neck jerked sideways, his eyes rolling back into his head before he slumped to the ground, unconscious.

Someone grabbed me from behind, pinning my arms behind my back with a loud command that made it evident a guard had me in his grip. I did not fight against it, knowing the scene was chaotic and the perpetrator unclear. I dragged in a deep breath, straining to slow the heaving of my chest and the rush of my pulse in my ears. My knee throbbed and one elbow stung, both skinned and bleeding from skidding across the cobblestones. Three more guards gathered around us, ordering curious onlookers to go back inside their homes.

With the air of authority befitting the head priest's wife, Rachel pushed past them, her face pale as she took in Binah's bleeding body. "Help her," I managed to say between labored breaths. "He struck her in the chest with that dagger."

Kneeling in the street, Rachel pressed her hands against the wound, issuing a command for one of the gawking neighbors to fetch the healer who lived two doors down. When the guard released me, I realized that it was Chaim who'd had me constrained.

"That shepherd needs to be tied up before he comes to his senses," I said. "He meant to kill her." Considering the pool of blood shining on the cobblestones, I wondered if he might well have accomplished his goal. But if Raviv had sent him, why would he attack Binah instead of my mother? None of this made any sense.

"We'll take him to a holding cell." Chaim gestured toward my lip, which seemed to be split and swollen. "You'd best take care of that. And get some sleep, there's nothing more to be done tonight. We'll sort this out in the morning."

My body sore and weariness filling the places where anger had reigned during the altercation, I headed toward the inn to ensure that my mother was safe. She would be beside herself when she discovered what had happened to Binah, whom she'd taken into her home and under her wing nearly eight years ago. She'd undoubtedly insist on rushing to Dov's home and aiding the healers in whatever way she could. No matter how exhausted and heartsick I was, the oblivion I craved would likely elude me this night as well.

CHAPTER TWENTY-EIGHT

29 Tishri

I drew in deep breaths of cool predawn air, hoping to infuse my body with vigor as I approached the gatehouse. I'd gotten a few hours of sleep at Dov and Rachel's home while my mother tended to Binah, but woke before the sun, plagued by questions about the young shepherd and desperate to know exactly what had happened with Sofea. I prayed that Nadir would return today and ease my mind. If he'd taken her to his village like I guessed, at least I would know she was safe — even if I'd never see her again.

Shaking away the howling despair the thought provoked, I knocked on the door and Chaim appeared, his expression grim but looking not at all surprised to see me before sunrise.

"Is he awake?" I asked.

Chaim glanced over his shoulder. "Just

coming around. So far he refuses to say anything."

"Binah is alive, but barely." My voice came out rough. My mother was still at her side, her lips moving in constant prayer for the woman who'd become part of our family. "Let me talk to him."

He stepped forward and closed the door behind himself. "I'm not sure that is a good idea, Eitan. I wasn't sure he *would* wake up after that hit you delivered."

"That shepherd boy has been spying on my family, Chaim. He may be involved with Raviv. If Binah dies and he is hauled off to a trial, I won't get the answers I need."

Chaim lifted his palms in concession. "All right. After everything Darek and Baz have taught you, you may be able to get more out of him than us anyhow."

We entered the small room, which served as both sleeping quarters for the guards and as weapons storage. Dwarfed between the two guards who held his arms, the shepherd looked even younger now than I'd assumed. His jaw and right eye were grotesquely swollen from our fight, but I had no sympathy for anyone who would attack a defenseless woman in the street.

Chaim stood in front of him, arms folded across his chest. "What's your name?"

Although a shadow of something like fear flickered through the boy's eyes, he kept his mouth firmly closed.

"Why did you attack that woman?"

Still nothing.

Chaim attempted a few more questions that resulted in only blank stares from the boy. He turned to me with a shrug and a gesture that it was my turn to try. Although it seemed unlikely I would succeed, I took his place in front of the defiant shepherd.

Up close I could see that whiskers were only just beginning to sprout on his face. He could not have been more than fourteen. He'd fought me off fairly well for being so young.

Drawing on that stillness that Baz had pounded into my head, I fastened my gaze on the boy with as much precision as I used when lining up a shot with my sling. Keeping the image of Binah's bloodied body in my mind, I poured fury into my expression and waited. Silent.

For a few moments he stared back, his mouth like stone and hands balled into bloody-knuckled fists. But when I refused to so much as move or blink as I regarded him, his eyes fluttered away. I let my shot fly.

"What sort of coward attacks an innocent

woman in the dark?"

"She's no innocent." A sneer formed on his lips. "She's a killer."

Although surprised by the accusation, I kept my expression carefully blank and waited. Unmoved. Unflinching.

He spat out an ugly word. "I've only delivered justice where it was lacking."

Although it was common knowledge that Binah had taken refuge in Kedesh all those years ago, I knew little of her past. I had no doubt my mother knew the circumstances, since she'd gained Binah's trust and loyalty within the first few months of her arrival. But she was insistent that none of the convicted manslayers in this city be defined by their horrific mistakes and guarded those details zealously, much as she had done for me.

"You could not have been more than five or six when she came to this city. What could you know of the incident?"

"She murdered my mother. Threw her into the fire and watched her burn." He swallowed hard, his lips trembling slightly.

Unbidden, the awful night of Zeev and Yared's deaths surged into my mind . . . the scrape of the mud-brick on my cheek as I hid in the shadows . . . the horrific retching by the boys . . . the keening of their distraught father. I knew *exactly* why this boy had come to Kedesh. Empathy pooled in my gut. "You saw it happen, didn't you?"

All the fight went out of him, and his head dropped forward. "I didn't know her name. Didn't remember her face. Took me months to figure out who and where she was."

That day by the palm tree he hadn't been watching me or my mother. He'd been watching for Binah, waiting for his chance to catch her alone.

"You understand what will happen if she dies?" I asked. "Your life will be forfeit."

He lifted his chin, his brown eyes piercing. "I watched my ima burn. She was with child at the time, so my father grieved himself into the grave within months. She stole my *entire* family." His face hardened back into the resolve from before. "If I die, then so be it."

The complete indifference to his own fate shocked me. How had he survived since that day? I wondered whether he too had been forced to live with a family that cared nothing for him. Slept on the cold floor. Devoured tossed scraps like an animal. Was that what had turned a child into an unrepentant murderer? Was this who *I* would have been without Moriyah?

As if he somehow sensed I was on the

verge of breaking apart, Chaim interrupted. "This was found in the street last night. Where did you get this weapon?" The dagger he held in his outstretched hand was bronze with distinctive scrollwork in the black walnut handle. My stomach tumbled over. A weapon I had made with my own hands was now encrusted with Binah's blood.

The shepherd glanced away. "Someone gave it to me."

"Don't lie to us. You stole that from my workbench," I said.

"I'm no thief," he snapped. "A man found me outside the city and gave it to me."

"Raviv?"

He shrugged. "I don't know his name."

I moved forward, two handspans from his swollen face, my voice like granite. "How long have you been spying for him? Did he send you to kill my mother too?"

The boy's face screwed into a mask of belligerence. "I came here only to right a wrong. I don't know anything about your mother."

"I saw you spying on my family."

"Only enough to find that woman."

Confusion swirled in my head. "That dagger was stolen from my workshop months ago, just after the Feast of First Fruits. You had to have taken it."

"I *said* I did not take it." His defensiveness was laughable in light of the act he'd committed last night, and yet the expression on his face communicated nothing but sincerity.

"This man you claim gave you the weapon — what did he say to you?"

"I woke up with that dagger at my throat one morning. He must've followed me to the place I've been sleeping in the apple orchard. He threatened to kill me if I didn't tell him why I was in Kedesh, so I did. He told me I was justified and then gave me the knife."

Of course Raviv would encourage such a thing. He was undoubtedly dreaming of the day he could do the same thing to my mother. And me. But if he hadn't directed this boy to kill my mother . . . was someone *else* in this city charged with the task? Someone had to have stolen that knife from my workbench. My blood stilled.

"What else did this man say? Did he mention the name *Moriyah*? Is someone else coming after my mother?"

His belligerence flared again. "I told you, he didn't talk about anyone else."

I had to get back to Dov's home, make sure my mother was safe. I turned to go, but the shepherd boy spoke again. "If he wanted to kill your mother, he had plenty of opportunity on his own. He wouldn't need me."

I spun around. "What do you mean?"

"The man who gave me the knife. He was with you when you saw me outside the inn." He gave an indifferent shrug. "Looked to me like you were friends."

My thoughts careened back to the moment I'd seen the boy leaning against the palm tree. My bones turned to water. The only person with me that day was the same man who now held Sofea and Prezi's lives in his hands.

I crept through the room I shared with my brothers, trying not to wake the slumbering boys. Once my eyes were adjusted to the dim light in the chamber, I retrieved my sword from the hiding place between my bed and the wall. The fact that Nadir had carved the handle on this very weapon was not lost on me. Betrayal coated my tongue with bile. If he had hurt Sofea, I would bury this blade in his belly —

"What's wrong?" asked Gidal, interrupting my bloodthirsty thought. Sitting up on the bed he shared with Malakhi, he was sleepy-eyed, night-tousled hair poking out in every direction. "Did you find Prezi and Sofea?"

"Not yet," I whispered, my voice raspy from the fury that had been my constant companion since I'd lurched out of the gatehouse like a madman. "Go back to sleep."

I yanked my woolen mantle from a hook in the wall, then rolled and pressed it into a leather satchel. The air was growing cooler by the day and I'd have need of the mantle's warmth at night. I had no time to say goodbye to my mother. But I'd heard the stories of the ways both Darek and Moriyah had placed their lives on the line for each other during the treacherous journey to Kedesh and knew she would understand my drive to save the woman I loved — she'd intimated as much yesterday.

"Where are you going?" Gidal's voice strengthened, all slumber pushed aside in favor of keen curiosity.

Although I considered deflecting the question, Gidal's gaze was unwavering, full of concern, and surprisingly sharp-eyed for a ten-year-old boy. For as wild and impetuous as Malakhi was, Gidal was his opposite. Steady, quiet, and reserved.

"Nadir is a traitor," I said, the truth solidifying as I spoke the word. A man whom I'd trusted with my most guarded secret had betrayed me, betrayed everyone in this town. "He took Sofea and Prezi. Fled south with them."

Malakhi too had awoken and gasped at my revelation. After glancing at the sword now at my belt, he threw off the blanket, crawled over Gidal's body, and rushed toward me with terror on his face. "He won't hurt them, will he?"

Placing my hands on his small shoulders, I looked down at my youngest brother and into the light gray eyes he'd inherited from our mother. I pressed aside the small twinge of jealousy that niggled at me when I considered my younger brothers following in Darek's footsteps someday. For unlike me, there would be nothing to stop them.

"No, Nadir is not an honest man, but I don't think he will hurt them." Although the reminder of Binah's assault last night did little to back up my words, and my mind skittered through other crippling fears I'd been straining to tamp down. Even as he lied about accepting my marriage to Sofea, Nadir had not hidden his desire for her. A man who had no respect for the life of one woman might well have little respect for the virtue of another. . . . A deep throb of rage began to pulse behind my temples. I slung the satchel over my shoulder and turned toward the door. "I have to go."

"How? Didn't Abba make it so you can't leave?" said Gidal as he slid in front of the doorway and blocked my exit. "The guards won't let you pass." Always astute and watchful, the boy must have overheard a conversation about Darek's edict.

"I'll find a way."

"I know!" said Malakhi, also pushing his little body in front of me. "You can climb out a window like Ima helped the spies do in Jericho! We will help!"

In spite of my urgent drive to leave and make Nadir pay for whatever he'd done to the woman I loved, I laughed at his suggestion and scrubbed his wild hair. "I'm not sure the two of you would be able to bear my weight if we attempted such a thing."

He frowned, his eyes filling with tears as he looked up at me. "But I want to help find Sofea and Prezi too. Can I come?"

"If I could take you with me, I would. But I need you both here to protect Ima and to be a help to her until I return." I divided a stern glare between the two of them. "Can I trust you both to do your duty?"

They nodded their heads, and their solemn expressions gave me confidence that they viewed that obligation as sacred. Although we were not related by blood, the bond I had with these two boys went soul deep. I grabbed them both by the back of the neck and yanked them toward me, gripping them in a tight hug. "Good," I said, an idea suddenly coming to me. "For now though, I could use some help getting past the guards. . . ."

As I had anticipated, Chaim stopped me at the gates, determination etched in his heavy jaw as he placed a palm against my chest, his posture befitting his status as captain of the guard. "I can't let you go, Eitan. I have orders."

My voice whipped out with venom. "He has Sofea, Chaim."

His hand dropped to his side, understanding on his brow. "I know. I gathered by your reaction that it was Nadir the boy was speaking of. But that doesn't mean he would hurt her."

"He not only encouraged the shepherd to kill Binah, he gave him *my* dagger to do it with. Sofea is not safe with him."

He stared at me, scratching at his thick beard uncomfortably, and I knew he was weighing our years of friendship against his duty to Darek. "I'm not asking permission. I *am* going. If you don't let me walk out that gate, I'll find another way. You know this."

Indecision flitted across his face and a low warning growl came from his throat. "This is a bad idea, Eitan."

A surge of victory welled up. "Just make sure my mother is guarded well until Darek returns. If Raviv has someone else in the city, she must be protected."

"I already sent two of my best men to Dov and Rachel's home."

"Thank you." I clamped down on his shoulder to communicate my gratitude. "Now, let me go."

"I can't just let y—"

I glared and cut him off. "Darek only wants to keep me from following him to Laish, and I have no intention of going there."

"He wants to protect you —"

I threw up a palm, again silencing his argument. "What matters to Darek is my mother. And she knows, just as well as you do, that I have to do this."

He studied my face for another agonizing moment, his lips pressed tightly together, then poked me in the chest, his tone lighter. "All right, but if Darek hangs me from the walls, it's your fault."

I smiled briefly, knowing Darek would do

nothing of the sort. "The Sea of Kinneret is only a day's walk. Most likely I'll be back before he even knows I am gone."

His brow furrowed. "What will you do with Nadir when you find him?"

I'd been weighing out all the implications of this revelation. If Nadir had betrayed me by encouraging Binah's murder, what else had he lied about? Since the words had left the shepherd's mouth, I'd been scouring back through every conversation I'd had with him, digging for inconsistencies. I could not fathom how the reserved, unassuming man with whom I'd worked side by side and shared laughs and jokes could have stolen my dagger and put it into the hands of a young killer. Had he hoped that *I* would be implicated in Binah's death?

The night Sofea had walked through the door to the inn, we'd playfully lifted our cups to the challenge of capturing her attention. But he'd never planned to fight fair in the first place. What sort of man would be so callous as to encourage murder in pursuit of a woman? I pinned a hard gaze on Chaim. "All I know is that I'm not coming back without her."

A sudden commotion rose behind me, and Chaim lifted his eyes over my shoulder. My brothers had taken advantage of the time

358

I'd been arguing with him and managed to spook two horses and three donkeys by pelting them with rocks from atop the ramparts. One of the horses reared and a wagon tipped over, spilling wares all over the ground.

With a sly glance toward me as he recognized Gidal and Malakhi, Chaim began shouting, "You boys! Stop!" before stepping to the side to chastise the two culprits. It was the perfect distraction to keep the eyes of the rest of the guards off me as I slipped away, and the perfect story for Chaim to feed Darek when he returned. After two long strides that took me out of the gates, I broke into a run that took me down the road and all the way to the edge of the city's territory.

I glanced back over my shoulder and took a last look at the walls of Kedesh, hoping my mother would forgive me for ignoring the edict she'd given me eleven years ago. Then I stepped over the invisible line that kept me protected from the man who'd vowed to spill my lifeblood when I was nine.

CHAPTER TWENTY-NINE

Since I'd last seen this lake eleven years ago during our journey to Kedesh after the trial, a number of the abandoned Canaanite fishing villages had been resurrected by Hebrews. I'd passed through four so far today, stopping in each of them to ask whether a fisherman named Nadir had ever lived there. Although the villagers were welcoming, a few of them offering hospitality in the form of a meal, no one seemed familiar with anyone of his description.

As I neared the next village on the western shore, my body was nearly as exhausted as my soul. I stopped to rest on a large boulder at the water's edge. After putting my pack on the ground, untying my scabbard from my belt, and removing my sandals, I placed my feet in the cool water.

Children's laughter hooked my attention. Four little girls were wading in the water down shore and splashing one another, while a few men and women worked on the beach nearby, preparing fish to dry on racks in the sun. Seemingly immune to the chill of the water this late in the year, the tallest girl plunged under the surface, her bare toes pointed toward the sky briefly before she disappeared. After a few moments she popped up again, her black hair plastered to her head and a grin visible even from this far away. The innocent girl looked to be about the same age I was when I'd destroyed everything by putting a deadly flower into a stew. Defeated by my futile search, I dropped my head to my hands, pleading with Yahweh to guide me and to spare Sofea and Prezi.

A terrible thought struck me. Considering all the lies Nadir had told me over the past months, what if he'd also lied about where his home was located? Had I been searching on the wrong shore? Sick to my stomach, I lurched to my feet, determined to head north and make it to at least a couple of the villages on the opposite side of the lake before the sun set.

Just as I bent to pick up my pack, one of the girls I'd been watching earlier cried out, jerking my attention back to the shoreline. She pointed to a place on the water where a few expanding circles marred the surface, calling out for help. There were only three little girls standing knee-deep in the water. The fourth, the black-haired one, had disappeared.

With a pounding heart, I plowed into the lake, ignoring the sharp stones beneath my bare soles. I had little experience with swimming, but I could not let the girl drown. I pushed through the water, keeping my eyes locked on the place where I'd seen those ripples emanate. One of my feet slipped out from beneath me and I nearly went under myself, but I caught my footing once again and circled my cupped palms in an attempt to propel myself forward.

Stretching out my arms, I swished my hands back and forth through the chin-deep water, begging Yahweh to help me locate the girl. I took a few more labored steps forward, my confidence wavering when the bottom dropped off abruptly and I lost my footing, but when I kicked my feet to find my bearings, my toes met with something soft and yielding. I gasped, then coughed and spit as water entered my mouth.

Ignoring the blare of warning that I might be drowning myself along with her, I plunged under the surface, forced my eyes open, and reached for the murky form at the bottom. My fingers met with a tunic, and I yanked upward, rejoicing when I felt the tangle of long hair wrap around my forearms.

Breaking the surface, I pulled the girl with me as I blinked away the flood over my eyes, then kicked until my feet met the bottom of the lake. Just as I whirled around, I was met by two men, their hands already reaching out for the girl. They pulled her limp form from my arms and plowed back toward the shore.

By the time I made it to the beach, breathless and spent, the men had the girl on her side and one of them was pounding between her shoulder blades. Her lips were tinged blue, but suddenly a great gush of water spewed from her mouth and she coughed. Relief and exhaustion brought me to my knees on the rocky ground as a swarm of villagers gathered around, blocking my view of the girl.

A silver-haired woman pushed through the crowd and threw a brown wool blanket around my shoulders. My entire body melted into the comfort.

"Thank you!" said the woman as she planted a vigorous kiss on my cheek. "You saved my niece! My sister is furious with her recklessness. She's been told before not to venture out so far, but we cannot thank you enough for coming to her rescue. Yahweh must have guided you here today for this very purpose."

Once my sandals and belongings had been located, I was ushered by the woman and her husband into the enclosed side yard of a small home and ordered to sit next to a cook-fire until my shivers subsided. Once I'd warmed enough to feel my fingers and toes, I asked my hosts about Nadir, again giving my description of the traitorous fisherman.

"Oh certainly! We know Nadir," said the woman, who'd earlier introduced herself as Ahuva. "He grew up in this village. His mother and I were good friends until she died in childbirth when Nadir was about fourteen years old. Poor soul." She frowned. "His father died only a few years later."

I let the blanket slide from my shoulders, the chill of the lake forgotten. "Have you seen him? I've been trying to find him for the past two days."

Ahuva and her husband looked at each other, frowning, and then the woman turned a compassionate smile on me. "No, my dear. Don't you know that Nadir was convicted of accidentally killing his friend Medad? He's been living up in Kedesh for nearly a year now."

"Yes, but he left there two days ago and is traveling with two young women. You've not seen him here in the village?"

"No. No one has seen Nadir since the day he was escorted away after the trial. One of his cousins took over his fishing vessels. What a sad day that was." She shook her head. "Such a shame that a lifelong friendship ended with such tragedy." With a large wooden spoon she ladled spiced lentils into a bowl and handed it to me. "If Nadir hadn't struck Medad when they argued, the young man would never have gotten tangled in the nets and drowned."

"I thought Medad was the one who attacked, and Nadir was forced to defend himself."

The couple glanced at each other in confusion. "No, the witnesses on the shore testified that it was Nadir who swung first. Of course, since Medad went over the opposite side of the boat, no one was able to see what happened next, but by all accounts Nadir dove in and tried to save his friend."

The story Nadir had given me was certainly similar, but the inconsistency did not sit well with me, especially now that I knew Nadir was a traitor who had encouraged the murder of Binah. A chill that had nothing to do with my plunge in the lake traveled through me.

I handed back the full bowl of potage and lurched to my feet. "Thank you for the food, but I really must go. Are you certain no one has seen Nadir in the last couple of days?"

"This is a small village, son," said Ahuva's husband. "If anyone had seen him, it would be common knowledge by now. Why don't you sit back down, eat your meal, and tell us what this is about."

"I thank you, but I must be on my way." I slung my bag over my shoulder and tied my scabbard back on my sodden leather belt, sifting through my head for ideas of where to look next and coming up with nothing more than desperate prayers for a miracle.

Ahuva retrieved two small fish from a drying rack nearby, insisting that I put them in my satchel to sustain me on my journey. "Perhaps —" she began, and then waved a palm, her expression dismissive. "No, there would be no reason . . ."

"What is it?" I asked, desperate for anything that might direct me toward Sofea.

"I just wondered . . ." She bit her lip, looking as though she felt foolish speaking the words aloud. "If Nadir left Kedesh, perhaps Liora might have heard something."

Liora. I remembered Nadir saying that name the day we'd moved those jugs of olive oil into the storage house. He'd told me Sofea reminded him of a woman named Liora.

"Who is she? Does she live nearby?"

"Why yes, she lives with her mother and father. She is Medad's widow. In fact, the three of them, Liora, Medad, and Nadir, were inseparable during childhood. We all thought perhaps Nadir would marry Liora when they were young, since he seemed so smitten with her. But Medad's father arranged the union shortly after Nadir's father died, so he missed his chance."

Just as I had asked Sofea to marry me before Nadir could stake his claim on her.

"Please," I said, "take me to Liora."

Nadir had once compared Sofea to Liora, but besides the fact that they were both women he'd wanted, there was no similarity at all between them. Liora's hair was darker and without curl, but her beauty seemed limited to lush curves and full lips. She had none of the sparkling vibrance that emanated from Sofea's blue eyes.

Instead of exuding strength and boldness, she practically faded into the background, eyes downcast and shoulders hunched as I asked my questions about Nadir. Her father insisted they had seen nothing of the man since the day he'd been taken to the city of refuge.

"If only Medad had a brother," said Liora's father, thick regret in his tone. "Then my daughter would have been protected by the law and given in marriage to the brother next in line. But since he had only sisters when he died, she returned to our home instead." He reached over to pat his daughter's hand with affection. "But I have found another man willing to marry her. She will be cared for and finally have the chance to bear a child, to live the life she was meant to have."

Disheartened by the lack of any new information and sickened by my suspicions, I offered quick congratulations for the upcoming marriage, thanked them, and took my leave. Although within a few steps of their home, I stopped, at a loss as to where to go from here and gutted by the implications. The sun was already going down. Would I be forced to return to Kedesh without ever knowing what happened to Sofea and Prezi?

Someone placed a hand on my arm. I jerked back, startled by the contact, my hand going to the sword on my side. Liora stood next to me, her expression meek, her eyes darting back toward her home, as if she feared someone might see her. "He was here," she said. "I saw him."

I sucked in a sharp breath. "Nadir?"

She nodded. "He left a signal for me. One that we'd used as children when the three of us wanted the others to meet. Only Nadir and Medad would have known our secret place, so I knew it was him."

"Weren't you afraid to meet him?"

"No. Nadir would never hurt me. He . . ." She cleared her throat and looked around again. "He loved me."

As I suspected. "And Nadir was jealous of your marriage to Medad."

"He was. But my father and Medad's father are cousins, so he refused to even consider Nadir as a choice of husband. I was shocked to see him yesterday. I thought it would be years and years before he would be released."

"What did he say to you? Was he alone?"

"Yes, but he was in a hurry to meet back up with his traveling companion. He said he was going to Shiloh, and when he returned he would be a free man."

A memory floated to the surface. *I would do anything for my freedom — anything. . . . If only that ancient priest would die so I could go home to my village.*

"Did he say anything else? Did he speak

of two young women traveling with him?"

"No. Only that he would never again let anything stand in the way of marrying me. Even some old priest." Liora rubbed her palms together and then scrubbed her fingers up and down the knuckles of one hand, a pained look on her delicate features. She seemed far too anxious for a woman anticipating the return of a man she loved.

"Liora, do you want Nadir to return?"

"I —" She stopped and swallowed hard. "We were all such good friends as children. We did everything together. Medad was a good man — bold, full of laughter." Her eyes teared. "And Nadir was so quiet and solemn that they were a good balance to each other. But there were times when Nadir could be . . . intense, even a bit possessive. He watched me, all the time. Twice I saw him outside my window late at night. It was unnerving. One day he came to me, insisting that he loved me and that when he was old enough to take over his father's fishing vessel we would marry."

She scrubbed her fingers back across her knuckles, and I realized that they were red and swollen from the rough treatment. She'd been repeating that nervous action for some time now, and I suspected it had begun when Nadir had returned to this village.

"When I admitted that it was Medad I preferred," she continued, "he turned cold. Refused to speak to me or even look my way for weeks. And then only a month after Nadir's father died, my father negotiated a betrothal. When Nadir discovered the match, he threatened to kill Medad."

"He did?"

She nodded. "Of course, neither of us took the threat seriously at the time. They'd been the best of friends since they were small boys, and I was sure that time would heal the friendship. And it did seem that way for a while. They continued working together on his father's fishing boat until the . . . accident that took my husband from me."

"But you don't think it was an accident, do you?"

She bit her lip, her voice dipping low. "I can do nothing to prove what happened that day. I was not on shore when it happened, and no witnesses opposed his story. It seemed to be a fight that spun out of control and ended with Medad becoming entangled in the nets beneath the boat and drowning." She took a shuddering breath. "But after the trial, Nadir was allowed to collect a few belongings, say his good-byes to friends and family. When he embraced me, he whispered in my ear that he would find a way to return, and that when he did, nothing and no one would ever keep us apart again." Her eyes filled with tears. "So you see, I am not afraid that Nadir would ever hurt me. It seems that even now he is still fixated on me. But" — her voice warbled — "I do believe that he murdered my husband."

Her accusation solidified the idea that had been forming in my mind since the moment she mentioned Shiloh. Nadir had told me once that when he wanted something he rarely, if ever, gave up. He'd already murdered his friend over a woman and encouraged the death of another. Was he planning an attempt on the life of Eleazar, the High Priest, the only man standing between him and freedom? If so, why would he drag two innocent women into the plot?

CHAPTER THIRTY

1 Cheshvan

When I left Shiloh eleven years ago, much of the valley floor had been covered by Hebrew tents. Now the once-dilapidated walls of the former Canaanite city stood strong and fortified, and many new homes encircled the fortress. Flourishing orchards, olive groves, and vineyards clung to the surrounding hills, testifying that Shiloh had dug its roots deep into the fertile soil. It was from this place that the twelve tribes had spread like thousands of streams branching from a mighty river, with the Mishkan, the heart of Israel, at its headwaters.

On its own rock-hewn bluff to the west of the city sat the Tent of Meeting itself, white courtyard walls billowing in the afternoon breeze and the smoke of sacrifice meandering into the sky. Somehow it seemed smaller, not quite the impenetrable fortress it had appeared to me as a boy, although an aura of mystery still surrounded the black-topped structure that had been designed by Yahweh himself.

At the far end of the complex was the beginnings of a stone wall under construction, which I guessed would someday wrap around the entirety of the Mishkan, evidence that Shiloh was to be the permanent spiritual center of Israel, never again to be moved from place to place upon the leading of the fiery Cloud that had guided us to this Land.

Incense floated on the wind, tempting me to breathe deeply of the smell that resurrected a thousand childhood memories, but I had no time to entertain such thoughts. I had to find Nadir. Now.

Without waiting for the wagon to stop, I hopped off the back of the bed and called out quick thanks to the farmers who'd offered me a ride this morning. From instinct my eyes searched out the winding path up to the vineyard where I'd filled my lonely boyhood days chasing birds and digging my toes into the rich soil, and where I had first met Moriyah.

Batting away the impulse to head toward the little mud-brick home among the vines and poplars to speak with her father, Ishai, I tightened the knot that secured my scabbard, ensured that my sling was still tucked into my belt, then pulled my woolen mantle over my head before merging into the crowd of people flowing through the city gates. None of their chatter hinted at shock or grief, so I was confident that, at least for the moment, Eleazar was still alive. But Nadir would have arrived at least an entire day ahead of me, so I had no time to lose. I lengthened my stride and pressed through the crowd without apology.

Today was Rosh Chodesh — the monthly celebration that heralded the first sliver of new moon in the night sky. Although the streets were not nearly as packed as they would be during Pesach, Shavuot, or Yom Kippur, when every man was commanded to gather at the Mishkan, the city was still brimming with visitors.

My eyes roamed over every face, searching for Nadir among the throng glutting the streets. I paused at the center of the chaotic marketplace, sickness rolling in my stomach as I turned in a slow circle and considered the impossibility of spotting one particular man among the hundreds of dark-haired, full-bearded men in this city today. Especially one who was determined to blend into the crowd.

Surmising that the easiest way for Nadir

to make contact with Eleazar would be for him to dress as one of the Levites, I narrowed my search to the sons of Levi, who stood out like white sheep among the varicolored herd. As I followed the flow of the men who served as priests and assisted in the Mishkan, I discovered that they were moving toward the large common area at the center of the city.

A few long tables had been assembled in the gathering place, and many women buzzed around the space preparing for this evening's feast. Each new moon, the Levites would gather here to partake of their allotted portion of the sacrifices. A perfect opportunity for an assassin to gain access to the High Priest of Israel.

Overwhelmed by the number of white-clad men milling around the city, I gripped the hilt of my sword, weighing whether I should rush forward to warn someone or continue my frantic search. However, if by chance someone recognized me as a resident of Kedesh, I'd be detained and questioned. Sofea and Prezi's breaths might very well be numbered alongside Eleazar's, so I could not bow to irrational impulses or they all might pay the price.

Remembering Baz's instructions, I paused in the shade of one of the newly constructed buildings near the center of town and willed myself into watchful stillness. Focusing on my own heartbeat instead of the cacophony of voices around me, I carefully measured each breath until my galloping pulse slowed.

I pulled my mantle a bit farther down over my continuously roving eyes and feigned a casual pose, even though every muscle in my body was prepared to spring into action at the first sight of my enemy. I had little doubt I could overpower him, but if I did not see him in time, all my training would amount to nothing. I considered slipping my sling from my belt, but flinging a stone into a crowd, no matter how certain I was of my aim, would be reckless.

Without warning, an arm slipped around my neck from behind, yanking me into a fierce choke hold that cut off my breath as a low voice growled in my ear. "Did you really think you could sneak into the city and not be recognized . . . Eitan?"

Cursing myself for leaving any gap between my body and the building behind me, I bucked hard against my captor and slammed him backward into the wall. With a gasp, the man released me, and I spun with a growl, pinning him against the brick with my forearm. Through my furious haze I registered only white Levitical garments and a familiar full-bearded face. However, it was not Nadir's throat I'd locked in a crushing hold, but that of Tal, my oldest friend.

Jerking back in shock, I released him. Eyes wide, he curled forward a bit, rubbing at his neck and coughing out a surprised laugh. "Some reunion, my brother. Remind me never to sneak up on you again!"

Mouth agape, I reached out to grip his shoulder, too shocked to answer. I'd not seen Tal since he'd moved to Shiloh last year, and during my frantic journey southward had not even considered that I might run across him here.

A playful grin spread across his face. "Did you finally convince Darek to let you out of your cage?"

Still attempting to force my frenetic thoughts into some semblance of order, I shook my head. "No. . . . No. I'm looking for —" Reminded of my purpose, I broke off and spun back around. Had I missed Nadir in my distraction?

Tal moved to my side, all delight at my appearance wiped away by concern. "What is wrong?"

Scanning the crowd again, which was becoming more difficult now that the sunlight was waning, I heaved a frustrated groan through my teeth. "I am looking for someone."

"Who?"

"Nadir, a prisoner from Kedesh, is here to kill the High Priest. I have to stop him and have no time to explain."

"Tell me how to help," he said without a whisper of doubt in his voice. I chanced only a brief glance at the man I'd been friends with for more than half my life, confident that he would not question my judgment in the slightest.

"Go tell Eleazar that there is a man here tonight who is planning to assassinate him. There's a possibility he is dressed as a Levite."

"All right." Tal took a step forward. "I'll be right back."

I snagged his sleeve and yanked him to a stop. "Wait. No one can suspect that anything is amiss. If Nadir guesses he's been spotted, he'll run off."

"But we need to move Eleazar to safety."

"You can't do that. Nadir has the woman I plan to marry, and he has killed before. I don't know what he plans to do with her or where he has hidden her away. . . ." My stomach wrenched painfully. "You must convince the priests to keep this quiet, for her sake. Just tell them to be watchful and stay close to Eleazar."

With a solemn nod, he disappeared into the crowd and gratitude flooded me for the answer to a prayer I'd not even known to ask. Although still desperate to find Nadir and Sofea, I breathed a bit easier knowing the priests would be alerted to the danger.

Although his death would free my mother, and although he was far advanced in years, Eleazar had been extraordinarily compassionate after I'd admitted to killing Zeev and Yared during my mother's trial. It pierced me through to think of Nadir stealing even one of the man's God-ordained breaths.

A large group of women passed in front of me. Carrying trays of fruit, breadbaskets balanced on heads, or pitchers of wine on their hips, they chattered and laughed as they headed toward the gathering place. Impatient for them to move along, I stood on the balls of my feet until they passed, trying to keep the milling Levites in sight, looking for Nadir's familiar build and carriage among the white-clad men.

Settling back into position, closer to the building this time, I breathed out a prayer that my eyes would be guided to the one person among this throng who would dare to murder the divinely appointed High Priest of Israel.

CHAPTER THIRTY-ONE

SOFEA

Attempting to draw on my heritage as the daughter of a merciless killer, I dragged in a shuddering breath, separated myself from the group of serving girls I'd been walking with, and, with my eyes still downcast, headed for the table of the High Priest. Each wobbly-kneed step that took me closer to my final destination was like plowing through the driving surf at high tide.

Nadir had forced me to stand in front of the enormous tent the Hebrews called the Mishkan during the animal sacrifices this morning, waiting for the High Priest to exit the beautifully woven purple, blue, and red gates so I would be able to recognize him later. I saw him now, silver-bearded and formidable, about twenty paces away, seated at the center of the head table. Power seemed to radiate from his countenance. Apprehension curled around my stomach and twisted hard, making nausea burn at the base of my throat, but my decision had already been made. I would not sentence my cousin to death.

For Prezi.

I swallowed hard and pushed forward. On either side of the priest stood two armed men dressed in white, their eyes roving over the throng of Levites crowded into the gathering area, searching for signs of obvious threat. For his part, the elderly priest seemed relaxed, conversing with another man who sat beside him, unaware that the serving girl who now approached him with a pitcher of wine carried the instrument of his death.

For Prezi.

I did not maintain any hope that I would survive this night, whether I succeeded in this mission or not. The only time I remembered a man in my village daring to threaten my father's life, in hopes of possessing his power and wealth, he'd been gutted in full view of the tribe, a warning to anyone else with such foolish aspirations. His blood-curdling screams still tainted my night-mares. I only hoped the Hebrews would have enough mercy not to torture me before they slaughtered me. Restraining a shudder, I blinked away the images, along with the sting of hot tears.

For Prezi.

Ten cumbersome paces lay between the head table and me, and although I fought hard against the impulse, my eyes were again drawn to the man I'd been ordered to kill. His lips were curled in a smile as he listened intently to the man next to him, his silver beard catching the flicker of firelight, and I was immediately reminded of Dov, the priest who'd told us the stories of the Hebrews' ancestors. I remembered his rich voice as he spun his tales near the fire, his hearty laughter as he joked with Eitan, the way he'd lovingly brushed his scarred palm over his wife's cheek, and the sight of his smallest granddaughter perched on his lap, tugging at his beard.

My heart thundered painfully, and my hands and feet went numb. The price of Prezi's freedom was the death of someone's husband, someone's father, someone's grandfather. And after meeting Dov, I could no longer equate all the priests of Israel to men like my father, who ruled the Sicani according to their whims and those of the bloodthirsty gods they claimed to speak for.

In that moment, I remembered Prezi's last words to me, along with the expression of inexplicable peace on her face as Nadir dragged me out of that roofless house in the valley. *"Have faith, Sofi. Yahweh brought us here for a purpose. He will provide a way."*

Truth collided with my soul.

I was not my father.

I could not kill a man who served the God who brought my cousin back to life. I could only pray that somehow he would save her again.

Even as my resolve snapped into place, I took my last step, closing the gap between the priest's table and me. The two armed men standing behind him ignored me, not seeing a servant girl, nor the wine in my hands, as any sort of threat.

With my heart scrambling up my throat and feeble prayers to a God I did not worship unfurling in my mind, I leaned forward to fill the priest's empty cup, knowing that from somewhere close by, Nadir's eyes were on me. However, as I did so, my hands trembled so violently that the spout of the wine jug caught on the lip of the cup and knocked it over. Poisoned wine splashed onto the table, spreading over the white linen tablecloth like blood.

My clumsiness alerted the High Priest to my presence. He turned from his conversation to pick up the clay drinking vessel. I braced for the impact of his targeted attention, the lash of reprimand over my blunder, and an icy stare like the one my father wielded. Instead, warm brown eyes lifted to meet mine. I was stunned to see evidence of kindness within their depths and many lines from their corners that attested to a lifetime of easy laughter.

"Ah," he said. "I wondered when my cup would be filled again." He gestured over his shoulder toward the men standing behind him. "I do believe my guards here are scaring the other serving girls away."

"Don't drink this wine." The words spilled from my mouth in a whispered torrent. "It is poisoned." The warmth drained from his eyes, leaving behind shock and bewilderment.

Desperate for a moment to make him understand, I feigned an attempt at sopping up the spilled wine with the long saffron-colored headscarf Nadir had purchased to hide my distinctive hair. "Please," I begged without looking up at him. "I had to do this, or my cousin will be killed. The man is watching me now."

Silence reigned for the length of ten violent heartbeats, each one stretched to a lifetime.

"Pour the wine," he said, causing my astonished gaze to meet his again. "Half a cup is plenty." A contrived smile was on his lips as his fingers hovered over the rim of the vessel.

My eyelids fluttered and my breath shuddered in my chest. Holding the jug with both hands this time to control my shaking, I obeyed.

"Thank you," he said, tipping the lethal cup to me as if in true gratitude.

Aghast, I watched him lift the cup and tilt his head back as if savoring a long draft of wine. Then with a loud, artificial sigh of satisfaction, he wiped his mouth with one knuckle, brushing away any trace of poison that may be on his lips.

"I'll wait a while to feign my death," he said with a wry grin. "But I would suggest you do not go far. You and I have much to discuss, young woman." These last words, although softly spoken, made it clear that regardless of the kind eyes that had first greeted me before he knew my treachery, the full weight of his power as the High Priest of Israel would be unleashed upon me tonight.

With a palm on my chest, I nodded my head, ceding to his authority, and backed away as he twisted around to rejoin the ongoing conversation with the oblivious men seated to his left, as if completely unaffected by our quiet, yet monumental, inter-action.

My limbs vibrated with bone-deep exhaustion as I walked away. Once I was outside the glow of firelight and the press of bodies, I found a space between two buildings and slipped into the cove of shadows. Realizing that I still carried the tainted wine, I tipped the remainder onto the ground beside me, ignoring the splash of it on my bare toes, and then with my back against the nearest wall, I slid down into the dirt, let my head drop to my knees, and sobbed. Yahweh may have saved the High Priest of Israel from death tonight, but I had little hope that I would see the morning.

CHAPTER THIRTY-TWO

EITAN

The flood of Levites moving toward the gathering began to slow as the sun slipped behind the western hills. Frustration mounted as I warred with myself over whether to abandon my post and go search among the milling revelers, or stay where I was in case Nadir had yet to walk by.

A sudden commotion at the center of town snagged my attention, but I was far enough away that I could only hear a few men shouting. My heart dropped into the pit of my stomach. Was I too late? Had Nadir already completed his heinous mission? And if Eleazar was dead, what did that mean for Sofea?

Despondent over the priest who'd been so kind to me when I was a child, I stood paralyzed and helpless, watching a few of the white-clad men begin running toward the upheaval.

Yet one seemed to be going against the tide, his head down and his wide shoulders jostling his tribesmen as he made his way toward the gates. Twilight muted his features, but there could be only one reason that a Levite would be heading out of Shiloh instead of farther in during an assassination attempt. It was Nadir. I was certain of it.

Securing my mantle over my head, I followed, determined not to let the traitor from my sight until he led me to Sofea. Only then would I ensure that he was held accountable for *both* his crimes.

He strolled out of Shiloh, the guards not even turning their heads to watch the killer in Levite garb pass through the gates. Thankfully, the ruckus over Eleazar had not yet reached their attention, or the enormous wooden gates would have been shut against my exit as well.

Blocked by a group of last-minute stragglers heading toward the festival, I kept my gaze locked on my quarry, attempting to keep calm as I waited for the chattering revelers to pass through the gates so I could break free of the crowd and give chase.

Within fifteen paces, Nadir's leisurely pace had quickened to a trot, and by the time I was free of the gates he was well on his way down the narrow road and all too quickly getting away.

With only the count of three breaths to make a decision, I slid my loaded sling from my belt and swung, confident that my guess about his identity was correct and that my aim was true.

Without waiting to see whether my target had faltered, I swiped a larger rock from the side of the road and then broke into a run while reloading and slinging it toward the purpled blur of his white garment against the dusk. This time I heard Nadir cry out when my shot hit, and even in the dim light I saw him stumble to the ground.

Just as he lurched to his feet I was on him, my full weight slamming into the man I'd revealed my most guarded secret to only a little over a week ago. We fell to the ground, grappling. With the amount of fury racing through my blood, I easily bested him, one knee pinning his elbow down and the other on his heaving chest.

He gasped for breath, attempting to push me off. "It's done, Eitan. There's nothing you can do now."

My stomach cinched tight, and I slammed his shoulder against the ground. "Where's Sofea?" He did not answer, so I slid my dagger from my belt and pressed it to the place where Baz had shown me that a man's pulse throbbed in his neck.

"I'll send you back to Liora in pieces." I pressed the tip of my knife deeper, feeling immense satisfaction at his hiss of pain. "Where is she?"

"There's nothing to be done for her. The priest is dead. Sofea made sure of that." The victorious grin that spread across his lips was a thing of pure evil. My pulse shuddered to a stop, and my vision tunneled for one long horrific moment. *Sofea* had killed the High Priest?

"WHAT. DID. YOU. DO?" My words came out in a roar as I twisted the point of my knife into his skin, perversely delighted to see blood well beneath the blade and barely restraining the temptation to drive it home.

Nadir paled a bit at the unbridled fury in my expression. "If you don't let me go, Raviv will kill Prezi too."

The revelation struck hard, making me almost bleary-eyed with confusion.

"Raviv? How did you . . . ?"

He scoffed. "You thought you guarded your little secret so well, didn't you? I knew before I ever offered to help you in the foundry, fool."

Not only was Nadir a liar and a murderer, he had been colluding with the man who'd vowed to hunt my mother and me down, all while enjoying her hospitality and working beside me every day for months. Just as the threads of their warped conspiracy began to untangle in my mind, two of the guards from the gate yanked me off Nadir, snarling at me to drop my weapon.

"He was involved in the death of Eleazar!" I yelled as the guards twisted my arms behind my back and Nadir scrambled to his feet. "Don't let him run!"

Thankfully, another swarm of armed men encircled us, preventing his escape. Three torches burned among them, affording enough light for me to see Nadir lift a hand to his temple, wincing from pain. A large welt had appeared where my stone had struck him down, and blood trickled down his neck. A twisted sense of pride made my lips curl upward as I glared at the coward until he looked away.

"Why would a Levite want to kill Eleazar?" asked one of the guards.

"He's not a Levite. He's a manslayer from Kedesh."

"So are you!" Nadir spat out. "A killer of two little boys."

I struggled against the guards, eager to add another victim to my account, but then I heard a familiar voice above the rush of blood in my ears.

"Take them into custody," said Tal, his expression grim, the flash of concern in his eyes barely discernible as he looked me over. "The High Priest wants to speak to both of them."

Shock slackened my jaw, and I ceased my endeavor to break free of my captors. "He is alive?"

"Indeed." Tal's voice remained unaffected, as if we'd not spent our boyhood spitting over the walls of Kedesh together, whacking at each other with wooden swords, and sneaking sweet treats from my mother's kitchen.

Nearly weak with relief at the news that Eleazar lived, I silently cheered Tal's caution. It would not do to explain our friendship to the men who surrounded us now. He may have been shy and softhearted growing up, but no one's wits were sharper. I trusted him implicitly.

Chancing a glance at my friend as the guards bound my hands together and divested me of my weapons, I lifted a brow. Conversation flowed wordlessly between us, a practice born of eleven years of blood-oath brotherhood. *Is she safe?*

His lips pursed and his chin dipped ever so slightly. *She is.*

I suppressed a relieved moan by clamping my teeth together, lifted up silent thanks to Yahweh, and allowed the guards to march me back into Shiloh.

CHAPTER THIRTY-THREE

SOFEA

Escorted between two stern-faced guards who'd found me crouched in the alley, I'd been ushered to a two-level dwelling on the far side of Shiloh. Although I expected the High Priest's residence to be a raucous display of wealth, the large home was sparingly outfitted and very much brought to mind the warmth and welcome of Moriyah's inn.

I was led into a large chamber where Eleazar sat at a small table scattered with papyrus documents and numerous potsherds with writing scrawled across their smooth surfaces.

The guards vacated the room as soon as Eleazar acknowledged my appearance with a casual flick of his fingers, so I was left alone with the man I'd very nearly killed tonight, only the scratch of his quill across papyrus filling the silence. He took his time writing the missive, dipping the feather into the inkpot time and time again, not once glancing at me.

Once he'd finished the message he was composing, he rolled it, put a small bit of wet clay onto the edge, and pressed his signet ring against the lump, a seal to confirm his identity on whatever important document he'd just written.

He strode across the room and handed the missive to someone standing just outside the doorway. "As soon as my seal has hardened," he said, "take this to Yehoshua."

Would the high commander of Israel's armies be the one to slay me now? Or did Eleazar, like my father, take pleasure in carrying out his own judgments? The hair on my arms and neck rose as the idea took root.

The High Priest turned to stare at me, his arms folded across his body. He'd not changed his clothing since the incident, and a dark red stain trailed from his waist down to the hem of his white tunic, the remnants of the spill my trembling hands had caused.

The silence stretched so long that my knees began quivering again, just as they'd done on my walk to his table, and my fingers found their way to the shell necklace at my throat. I rubbed my thumb over the time-worn edges again and again, willing my pulse to slow.

"So you came here today to kill me, did you?" He peered at me, his fingers running over the length of his silvery beard.

Eyes downcast, I nodded, my mouth too dry to speak.

"But you changed your mind?"

I offered another vague nod.

"Explain." The firm demand provoked a shiver to slide down the center of my back. I'd come into Shiloh today with the express purpose of poisoning him. My father would have had no leniency for even the thought of such a thing, so I expected none now.

"Please," I said as I sank to my knees in front of the elderly man, my head down and tears spilling over. "I have no choice. They kill her if I do not do this awful thing — she is all I have." My tongue stumbled over the hasty explanation, clumsy words tumbling over themselves in a mad dash of panic. "I deserve no mercy. . . . I have no sacrifice except my blood. But please . . . ask Yahweh for to protect Prezi, her life is more important than me."

A large palm curved beneath my chin and I squeezed my eyes shut, anticipating the pressure of his hand squeezing like a vise and the haughty sneer of a man whose eclipsing power far overshadowed anything my father could have even imagined. But instead of crushing my jaw in an iron grip, Eleazar gently lifted my face, waiting until my eyes fluttered open in surprise.

The High Priest did not look down on me with disdain. He did not chide me for my foolishness or my ignorance. Instead, he looked me straight in the eye.

There was no contempt in his countenance. None of the arrogant mockery that characterized nearly every interaction I'd ever had with my father. There was only a deep compassion in his warm brown gaze, so full of unexpected tenderness that my chest ached.

"What makes you think your life is worth so little?" he said, his voice soothing, as if he were speaking to a child. "The Almighty Creator spoke your being into existence. How could you be anything less than precious?"

Dumbfounded by the question and his benevolent tone, I could only stare at him in wonder.

"From the accent in your speech, I assume that you hail from a foreign land."

"Across the sea. Men destroy our village."

"Ah," he said. "Then you are a bit like Avraham, the father of our nation. Do you know of him?"

I nodded, remembering the firelit evening when Dov spoke of the way Elohim had whispered to Avraham, how he called him out of a distant land and out of the worship of gods so similar to my own.

"Although you did not hear the Voice like he did — and I suspect your journey here was not easy — I believe Yahweh has called you here for some purpose. I do not know what that purpose might be. Perhaps it was only to save my life today, perhaps some effect of this night will be echoed in generations to come. We may never know. But I have no doubt that his eye was upon you, even in that foreign land across the sea. He calls you by name, even if you have not yet learned to distinguish the sound."

He moved his warm hand on the crown of my head, and I watched in bewilderment as his eyes slid closed and his lips began to move, as if in silent prayer. A weighted sense of awe seemed to fill the room as he did so, swallowing up every fear and pouring mercy over me like a sun-drenched sea.

I'd come to murder this man, to steal his life breath. If this formidable High Priest who stood in the gap between the Hebrews and their deity offered such mercy, what did that say of his God?

The gods my father claimed to speak for

offered no pity and no peace. Only suffering and degradation. My father's changeable ideas of justice had been capricious at best, malicious at worst.

But from everything I'd seen of Yahweh's laws over the past months, they were a gift of protection to his people, offered promises of abundant blessings for obedience, and were written in stone. I may not hear the Voice calling my name, but his mercy, and that of the people who represented him, spoke to my heart.

The door to the chamber swung open. One of the Levite guards stepped inside with deferential apologies to the High Priest. "We've captured two men believed to be involved with this plot."

"By all means, bring them inside," said the priest. Then, to my surprise, he assisted me to my feet.

Two large Levite men entered the room, followed by Eitan and Nadir, both with hands bound by ropes. My breath escaped in an astonished rush, and I took one involuntary step forward, but the High Priest snagged my elbow and pulled me backward before putting his arm around my shoulders as if he were *protecting* me.

Eitan's mantle dangled from one shoulder, and his disheveled hair was a wild, one-sided mane. With dirt smudged down one side of his face and a dried trickle of blood tracking down one leg, he looked to have been in some sort of altercation. One look at Nadir made it clear whom he'd been tussling with.

One side of Nadir's forehead was swollen, sporting a painful-looking, purpling lump. A bloody cut on his neck was still oozing, his once-white tunic filthy and ripped at the neckline. As expected, he refused to meet my eye.

Eitan's attention, however, was locked on me from the moment he'd stepped across the threshold. His eyes roved over me again and again, as if making sure that not one hair on my head had been harmed. Slowly, as if tension was unspooling from his center, his shoulders relaxed and his eyelids fluttered shut for two beats of unmistakable relief before his gaze locked on me again with an expression filled with such love that it nearly brought me to my knees again.

"As you can all see," said the High Priest, interrupting my silent reverie with a grand sweep of his free hand from his head to his feet, "I am still very much alive. Perhaps the two of you might explain why that was ever in question."

CHAPTER THIRTY-FOUR

EITAN

The first time I'd seen Sofea, she'd been a tattered little warrior, determined to protect her cousin from whatever savage things she imagined we would do to her. Now she stood in the protective embrace of the High Priest of Israel, all ferocity put aside for wide-eyed concern over me. Her curls were a tangled mess, her face smudged with dirt, and her feet and the hem of her white tunic stained with deep red splotches — and she'd never been more beautiful.

Forcing myself to drag my eyes away from her, I took in the appearance of the man who'd saved my life and given me my mother. The years had leached the remaining color from his long beard, leaving behind only silver, and the maze of wrinkles on his face had deepened, but his back was straight, and the calm authority he exuded had not lessened since the last time I stood before him.

"Eleazar," I said, taking one small step forward that was halted by the sound of six swords erupting from sheaths around me. I lifted my bound hands, spreading my fingers wide in a display of submission before continuing. "Eleven years ago I stood before you as a child when Moriyah bat-Ishai was accused of killing two boys. My name is Eitan. Do you remember me?"

The priest's jaw slackened in surprise, his gaze traveling up and down, as if reconciling the boy I'd been with the man standing before him now. "I do. I remember you well." His brow furrowed. "We sent you to live in Kedesh to protect you, if I remember correctly."

"You did."

"So why are you trying to kill me now?"

"My only concern here is Sofea. I had no involvement in this horrific crime." I gestured to Nadir, whose chin rose in stony defiance. "That man stole her and her cousin Prezi from Kedesh and then coerced her to follow his orders. It seems as though he's been working with Raviv, who is holding Prezi captive in some sort of scheme to exact the vengeance he vowed upon me that day at the trial."

Sofea's knees seemed to go weak at the

reminder of the peril her cousin was in. Eleazar steadied her, whispering a low reassurance as he pulled her closer to his side. A small rush of relief puffed from my lips. Surely if the priest believed her to be guilty he would not comfort her in such a way.

"The man who accused Moriyah of murder is involved in this?" he asked, then looked down at her. "Is this true?"

"Yes," she replied. "Nadir trick us to follow him, and this Raviv, he has Prezi." As she spoke, her voice strengthened and her backbone straightened, her nerve seeming to galvanize more with every word. "Nadir say I must give you the oleander wine or Prezi would die."

"Oleander?" I gaped at Nadir, astonished that even now another of his betrayals could strike a blow. His face was blank, his cold eyes trained on the far wall. Other than Tal and Sofea, I'd never told anyone about the poison I'd inflicted on Zeev and Yared. He'd taken my confidence and wielded it as a weapon, one that would have seen Eleazar suffer a slow, excruciating death at Sofea's hand and caused the woman I loved to be executed.

A bolt of fury flashed through me, breaking my tenuous hold on restraint. I surged toward the traitor, heedless of the fact that my wrists were still bound together. Four guards surrounded me, yanking me to a stop. Nadir had tripped backward at my sudden move and slammed into the wall, his eyes wide and his breath coming fast.

The shock on Sofea's face somewhat assuaged my desire to hear the satisfying crunch of my fist colliding with Nadir's nose. Relaxing my body, I rolled my shoulders back and sucked in slow, measured breaths until assured that my voice would hold steady.

"All over a woman," I said, not taking my eyes off the coward. "He planned to kill you to free himself from imprisonment in Kedesh so he could have his best friend's wife." My lips curved into a parody of a smile. "Except Liora has no desire to marry the man who murdered her husband."

Nadir's chin jerked upward at the accusation, his gaze pinned on me. "You lie," he rasped, and for the first time since I'd met him, Nadir truly looked like the killer I now knew him to be. Every line in his face had gone hard, and hate swirled in the space between us. "It was an accident," he spat.

I shrugged my shoulders. "From her own lips, my *friend*. She claims you drowned her husband in order to have her."

His lips pursed, a flicker of indecision

moving across his brow. "She would never say such a thing."

"Ah, but she did." I arched my brows, baiting him. "She also told me what a relief it was to watch you be marched away to Kedesh in the first place."

Rage burst from his mouth, a string of curses directed toward me that made it clear just what a skillful deceiver he'd been over the past few months. The pretense of a lowly fisherman living in unassuming solitude was camouflage for a soul rotted by lust, jealousy, and bitterness.

Pushing Sofea behind him, Eleazar ordered Nadir to be silent, and to my surprise he complied, midsentence, but any illusion of innocence had already been ripped to pieces.

"If I may speak?" Tal stepped forward, and gratitude swept through me again. His presence here was a reminder that Yahweh had indeed guided my steps over the past few days.

Arms folded across his barrel chest, Eleazar nodded, his silvered brows furrowing in deep contemplation. "Certainly."

"I can attest to the truth of Eitan's testimony. He is the one who warned me that someone meant you harm today. That is why extra guards were placed with you at the feast."

"But we were told to search for a man, not a young woman."

"That is true," I said. "I had no idea Sofea was involved until Nadir revealed it just before we were arrested."

"The guards at the gate saw this man" — Tal pointed at Nadir — "bolting from Shiloh. It was Eitan who stopped his escape."

"I have no wish to harm you, Eleazar," I said. "I owe you my life. I owe you the life of my mother. And Prezi is the only family Sofea has left. She would do anything to protect her."

"Where is Raviv holding the girl?" Eleazar directed the question toward Nadir, who pointedly ignored the exalted High Priest of Israel.

"The accusations against you today are severe, young man," he continued, his powerful voice echoing in the chamber and making Sofea shrink away. "If you are found guilty of this murder back in your village, the difference between a torturous, slow death by stoning or a swift end by the sword very well could be decided by your co-operation now." He stabbed a finger toward him. "If that young woman dies, you will be considered an accomplice in her death as well."

Nadir's bearded jaw twitched as he weighed his response. After a long pause, he relented, but the words came through gritted teeth. "He's holding her near his home at the edge of an apple orchard. He sent a man to Kedesh to spread a rumor that the girls wandered into the valley alone. He's awaiting Eitan's arrival."

Of course. Nadir knew me well enough to guess that I would stop at nothing to find Sofea. Apparently I'd left the city before Raviv's subterfuge reached my ears.

To my surprise, the barest hint of regret flashed in Nadir's dark eyes, making me wonder if not every part of our friendship had been a farce. "I had nothing against you," he said with a slight shrug. "It was always only for her."

Weariness nagged at my bones. The truth gave me no satisfaction. "Then you did it all for nothing. Liora married a man from another tribe the day after I left and moved to his territory so you could never find her."

Nadir's eyes slipped closed as his mouth pressed into a hard, flat line, and his head dropped forward in defeat. A subtle gesture from Eleazar summoned the guards to escort him from the room. Resigned to his destiny and stripped of the last chance to possess a woman who had never wanted him, the man I'd called a friend did not struggle as they led him away to justice.

CHAPTER THIRTY-FIVE

SOFEA

As soon as Nadir was ushered from the room, Eleazar instructed the Levite guards to cut Eitan loose and return to their regular duties at the gate. His casual tone belied the fact that I'd very nearly killed him this night and also made it obvious that he did not hold either of us accountable for what Nadir had done. The rush of relief in my veins was nearly painful.

"I suppose you two plan to head north in the morning," Eleazar said.

"Nadir say if he does not return in eight days, Raviv would harm my cousin." When Eitan had told me the story of the twins' deaths, I'd felt a measure of sympathy for their father, but it seemed the years spent wallowing in bitterness had eroded any mercy in the man. There'd been nothing but cool calculation in the way he'd discussed both Eitan and Eleazar's murders

410

with Nadir. Would my precious cousin even survive the three days it would take for us to return?

Eitan frowned, rubbing at his abraded wrists. "Raviv has proven himself to be ruthless. We must ensure Prezi's safety."

"And you'll solicit help in Kedesh?" Eleazar asked as he sat back down at his table and pulled a fresh scrap of papyrus toward himself. "I'll send a missive to Dov explaining what happened here."

"Thank you. The captain of the guard is a friend. He will undoubtedly lend a few men to help with the rescue." Then, in a practiced move, Eitan unwound the leather cord from his hair and set about taming the mess and retying it neatly at his nape.

With his quill hovering in midair over papyrus, the High Priest tilted his chin, clearly surprised by the length of Eitan's hair. "You are a *nazir*?"

"I am. I took the vow five years ago."

Eleazar continued to appraise Eitan with curiosity. "Five years? Most people choose to adhere to the regulations for only one cycle of the moon. I heard of a Benjamite who determined to consecrate himself for a year but abandoned the notion after a few months. How long do you plan to continue?"

"I have not yet determined the day." Eitan folded his arms, shifting his feet as if he were uncomfortable. And I understood why. *I will not end it until she is free,* he'd told me on the roof of the inn. Not until Eleazar was dead would Eitan shave his head and end his vow.

As if he sensed Eitan's reticence, Eleazar asked Tal to retrieve his wife instead of pressing the issue. "Will you need a place to rest for the night?" he asked. "You both are welcome to stay here with my family."

"No." Eitan smiled, something I'd not seen for nearly a week. I drank in the sight like fresh, cool water. "My grandfather will be glad to have us."

"Ah yes," Eleazar said. "A good man, Ishai. His vineyard has nearly doubled its yield in the past few years. He and Ora will be thrilled to see you, I have no doubt."

Tal reentered the room with an older woman beside him. She was dressed in a finely woven blue tunic and her gray hair intricately braided, and everything about her appearance spoke of elegance. I became conscious of the borrowed white tunic I wore, now stained with poisoned wine and dirt from the alley I'd taken refuge in. I knotted together the filthy, guilty hands that had nearly stolen her husband behind my back.

"Hadassah," Eleazar said with an affectionate smile toward his wife, who seemed to be at least fifteen or twenty years his junior. "I'd like to speak to Eitan alone for a few moments, but Sofea may have need of fresh clothing and nourishment before these two head up the hill to Ishai's vineyard."

"Of course," said Hadassah, concern pinching her wispy brows together and one arm outstretched toward me. "Come, dear, I will fetch you a warm mantle as well. The night is cool."

Although I hesitated to leave the room, desperate as I was to hear more of the plan to retrieve my cousin, Eitan gave me a reassuring smile, so I complied with his silent request for privacy with Eleazar.

The priest's wife fussed over me, clucking like a hen at my disheveled clothing and insisting that I accept one of her own fine tunics to wear. By the time Eitan emerged from the priest's chambers, I was relatively clean and had been forced to eat some bread, cheese, and brined olives by the woman who exuded nearly as much unquestionable authority as her husband.

Eitan's countenance was grim as we left

the home of the priest. I could barely contain my curiosity; only the presence of Tal kept me from demanding that Eitan tell me something — anything — about what he had discussed with Eleazar in his chambers.

From what I gathered from the brief conversation between the two men as we walked through Shiloh, one on either side of me, Tal had received permission to accompany us back to Kedesh in the morning. The easy rhythm between Eitan and the man he'd shared such a long friendship with was fascinating. They were indeed much more like brothers, bantering back and forth as we climbed a narrow road that led up a nearby hill. Tal commented on the beauty of Eitan's long hair, and Eitan returned the tease by ribbing him over the "exhausting" duties of polishing the Menorah and changing out the showbread on the table in the Mishkan.

The good-natured taunting made it plain that their bond went just as deep as blood and that they'd missed each other's company. But even as they traded jests, unease hummed in my bones, and I longed for even a few moments to beg Eitan to reveal his thoughts to me — both about the chances for Prezi's rescue, as well as about what had happened between the two of us.

His palpable relief when he'd seen me with Eleazar had seemed genuine, but had I misinterpreted that relief as love? And did that mean he had changed his mind about marriage? Or had this awful situation only widened the chasm between us? I feared the answer as much as I craved it, his last words to me still hovering in the void like a black-winged specter.

Navigating the night-shrouded path to the vineyard as if by memory alone, Eitan led us to a small one-level home tucked into the embrace of tall poplars that surrounded it on three sides. The dark, rich scent of earth and plant life filled my nostrils as the mellow hoot of an owl welcomed us to Ishai's home.

The tiny sliver of a new moon hovering over us did nothing to light the vineyard that I knew surrounded us here, but still I envisioned Eitan as a child racing up and down rows of grapevines, chasing crows and grackles, his dark hair warm in the sunlight and the fullness of his freckles unhidden by the thick beard he now wore.

At Eitan's third solid knock, the door to the mud-brick home opened wide, a flood of light revealing the anticipation on his face. An older man stood in the doorway, his height filling the space, the silver threads in his black hair highlighted by the oil lamp flickering in his hand. Even knowing who the man was, I was still shocked at the clear resemblance to his daughter. Egypt's blood must run strong in this family.

"What can I do for you?" he said, his tone gruff.

Eitan swallowed hard, and when he spoke the word came out in a low rasp. "Grandfather?"

Ishai stared, openmouthed. "Eitan?"

Eitan nodded, seeming to suppress strong emotion behind the press of his lips. Moriyah's father set the oil lamp on a stool near the threshold and then stepped forward to pull Eitan into a crushing embrace that was returned with equal fervor.

As they parted, Ishai reached up to clasp Eitan's shoulders in a firm grip. "How are you here? And how are you taller than me?"

Eitan laughed, but I caught the distinctive sheen of tears in his eyes. "Ima feeds me fairly well."

Moriyah's father tilted his head back and let out a hearty guffaw. The jovial sound was a surprising balm to my frayed nerves, as was the affection he displayed for the orphaned boy who had been enfolded into his family through tragedy.

"I have little doubt of that!" He craned his neck, looking past Eitan's shoulder out into the black night. "Is she . . . ?" The desperation in his question made it clear that it was his daughter he was searching for.

"No." The humor dissipated from Eitan's expression, and it was clear he regretted squelching his grandfather's hopes of seeing the daughter who had been sent away so long ago. "She is still in Kedesh. I am only here for tonight."

Ishai sighed, then squeezed Eitan's shoulders again, disappointment giving way to curiosity. "It sounds as though you have a story to tell, my boy."

"That we do."

"We?" Ishai glanced around, finally catching sight of Tal and me three paces away. He'd been so focused on his grandson he'd not even noticed us. "Who are your friends?"

Eitan gestured for us to approach. Hesitantly I obeyed, my heart stuttering a wary beat. Who would he say that I was to him? His friend? His love? A stranger? To my surprise, he clasped my hand in his, his fingers weaving into mine as if they'd never left, as if he'd only just dropped the copper ring into my palm and I'd not nearly killed a man tonight.

"This —" he said. "This is my Sofea."

The simple but obvious claim he laid on me curled around my heart in a warm embrace that brought tears to my eyes. His grandfather took notice of the declaration as well, his mouth spreading into an enormous smile. He beamed at me with a sparkle of glee in his dark eyes. "Welcome, Eitan's Sofea."

Eitan's introduction of Tal was interrupted by a female voice behind Ishai. "Who is here, my love?" A beautiful woman with long dark hair braided over her shoulder appeared in the doorway. Although her face was directed toward us, her eyes roved about, as if she could not see us in the dark.

"Ora, it's Eitan! Our boy is here!"

She gasped and pushed past Ishai, her arms reaching for Eitan. Releasing my hand, he stepped forward. Her palms fumbled over his chest and to his shoulders. "These are a man's shoulders," she exclaimed before skimming her hands up his neck and then placing them on his cheeks. "And you have a beard!" Her fingers wandered over his brows, his forehead, his nose, as if memorizing each of his features by touch. Her eyes were open and searching. This lovely woman was blind.

"That I do," Eitan said with a laugh and then bent to kiss Ora's forehead. "You, however, have only become lovelier in the last eleven years."

She patted his cheek again with a saucy grin. "And you, young man, have become a flatterer, just like your grandfather."

"Please," said Ishai, picking up the oil lamp and gesturing for us to follow him inside, "do come in. We must hear how you came to be in Shiloh and all that has happened since we heard from Moriyah and Darek last."

After introducing Tal and explaining that he'd been in Shiloh for over a year training among the *kohanim,* Eitan presented me to Ora, who nearly tripped over herself to embrace me and welcome me to her home. She also whispered an insistence into my ear that we find a few private moments so I could tell her all about myself as soon as possible.

The house was small — the entirety of it would fit within the main chamber of the inn at Kedesh — but hospitality exuded from every corner. A widemouthed clay oven lay at the center of the space, a low fire flickering in its center that fended off the late-harvest chill that threatened to seep in through the cracks. A low table nearby invited guests to seat themselves on the multicolored woven mats and embroidered pillows.

Once we were seated, Ishai produced bowls of stew, with apologies that it had gone cold, and cups of the sweetest, richest wine I'd ever tasted. I'd been fed by Hadassah only a short while ago, but not wanting to thwart their generosity, I nibbled at the stew as Eitan related the details of the last few days to the couple, who listened with rapt attention.

"We must leave as soon as possible tomorrow," said Eitan. "There is no time to waste. We must rescue Sofea's cousin. Although there is one thing I must attend to before we go."

Another cloud of disappointment moved over Ishai's expression, but he nodded in understanding. "As much as I wish you could stay for a few more days, that young woman's life is not to be trifled with."

"You all must be weary to your bones," said Ora. "Sofea will sleep with me tonight, and you three can stretch out in here near the fire."

I stifled a yawn at the thought of a warm bed. Nadir had asked Raviv to provide me a woolen mantle to wrap myself in, but we'd slept on the hard ground for the past three nights on the journey to Shiloh, and my joints ached at the thought of doing so again. But as much as my body screamed for rest, I needed answers about how Eitan planned to save my cousin. Had he sent a message on to Darek? Was the High Priest sending a contingent of men to escort us? Or perhaps he felt as though Prezi's life was already forfeit and did not want to alarm me?

Feeling a rush of urgency, I leaned over to Eitan and nudged him with an elbow. "I speak with you? Alone?"

"We can talk in the morning," he said, his eyes traveling over my face with concern. "You need rest."

I shook my head. "Tonight." My terse whisper made it clear that I would not be denied.

Reaching over to take my hand in his, he appraised me, his thumb absently stroking mine. The slight lift of his cheek told me that the force of my demand amused him. "All right. But then you *will* sleep."

Chapter Thirty-Six

Eitan led me out of the house, then through the small enclosed courtyard, dodging two sleepy goats, and to a stairway around the corner that led to the rooftop. Then he gestured for me to go ahead of him and kept a steadying hand on the small of my back as I climbed the narrow steps.

Ascending into the black night was unnerving, like entering an unexplored cave without a lamp, so near the top of the stairs I paused, turning to ask whether we might instead walk through the vineyard.

Eitan's face was directly in front of me, and even though only dim starlight highlighted the yearning in his expression, whatever question had been on my lips dissolved. His arms went around my waist and he pulled me to him, his desperate mouth on mine telling me in no uncertain terms that he regretted the words we'd parted on and that the days since my disappearance had been as torturous for him as they were for me.

Sliding my arms to his back, I clutched at his tunic, blissfully disoriented as I welcomed the kiss, all thought of sleep seared from my veins. This kind, strong, fiercely loyal man had left his home and his family to travel days to find me. I did not deserve him.

He pulled back, his breathing labored as he leaned his forehead against mine. "Forgive me," he whispered. "What I said at the gate that day was a lie. I want nothing more than for you to be my wife. That is *more* than enough for me."

"I am so glad of it. But, Eitan?" I pushed gently against his hard chest.

"Yes?" he murmured distractedly as he swept my curls behind my shoulder, his fingers warm on my skin as he continued his assault on every one of my senses.

"I do not like to fall." I tilted my head toward the perilous drop only two handspans from my feet.

He chuckled. "Perhaps we *should* continue this conversation in a safer place."

Once clear of the stairs, I peered into the darkness to take in the small flat rooftop, surrounded by a hip-high casement wall. As my eyes adjusted, I spotted a tattered *suk-*

kah leaning precariously nearby, the dried palm boughs drooping nearly to the ground.

Eitan found a wool blanket crumpled beneath the temporary shelter that had been built for the Feast of Tabernacles a couple of weeks ago, and after snapping a few brown leaves out of its folds, he spread it flat on the rooftop. After adding the three pillows he discovered jammed into a basket nearby, he gestured for me to sit.

A chilly breeze rustled through the poplar leaves as I gathered Hadassah's woolen mantle tighter around my shoulders and sank down cross-legged onto the cool fabric.

He sat down in front of me, knees touching mine, and leaned back on his palms. "We will find her," Eitan said, determination in the stony set of his jaw. "I will not give up until she is safe. Do not worry. I have a plan."

Obviously, he had no intention of sharing those plans with me, and I had no choice but to trust him. If nothing else, I had faith in Eitan's fierce need to protect. After all, his desire to fight for his people, even though his life was in jeopardy outside the walls of Kedesh, had been the reason he and Darek had quarreled the day Nadir stole Prezi and me away.

"She had no fear as I leave her," I said,

tilting my chin to take in the stars, which shone all the brighter for lack of moonlight. "She trusts your God to save her." A wry laugh escaped my mouth. "On my island, I was the brave girl. Now Prezi is the fearless one." Not only had living among the Hebrews brought her back to life, it somehow had imbued her with courage like I had never seen.

"Something my mother seems to inspire in those within her circle of influence."

I agreed. The more time Prezi spent with Moriyah, the brighter she seemed to shine.

"Is your mother angry that you go?" I asked.

His brow furrowed. "Of course not. I was forced to sneak out of Kedesh, but she knows that I would do anything to protect you. She will forgive my impulsive decision."

"And Darek?"

"It was Darek's edict to Chaim that prevented me from getting to you earlier." He frowned, his jaw twitching. Whatever had happened between the two was eating away at their already strained ties.

I leaned forward, placing my hand on his knee, wishing I could more easily express myself in his language. "He loves you."

Eitan flinched at my assertion. "He loves

my mother. I was simply bundled into the package."

"No. He is proud. He looks at you like a son." He glanced away, unbelief painted across his starlit features, but I continued. "I know this. My father did *not* have love."

Determined to make him understand, even with my halting Hebrew words, I told him of all I had endured under the tyranny of my father, including his murderous ways and how I'd spent my childhood escaping into the sea to avoid his abuse and to wash away the pain.

Eitan moved closer as I spoke, his hands gripping mine and fury lining his dark expression. "It is fortunate the man is dead or I'd cross the sea to make it so."

"But do you not see? I watch Darek when you do not know. If my father look at me with only a piece of this pride or a small bit of such love . . ." Choking on sorrow, I let the thought trail away.

With a sigh, Eitan released my hands and then lay back on the blanket, hands beneath his head on a pillow. After a few quiet moments, I lay down next to him, our shoulders touching.

The shushing wind in the leaves entwined with the chirrup of a night bird and filled the empty spaces around us, wrapping us in dark beauty as we looked up at the heavens. Months ago, Prezi had told me that Moriyah said the gods did not reside in the sky as we'd been told, but that Yahweh the Creator had spoken each white jewel into existence. Sudden wonderment began to spread through every part of my body as the sheer magnitude of their numbers tangled with the words Eleazar had spoken: *"The Almighty Creator spoke your being into existence. How could you be anything less than precious?"* Did the God who breathed those stars into the sky actually know me by name?

Cutting through the haze of my curiosity, Eitan laced his long fingers into mine but continued looking skyward, his thumb tracing the curves of my copper ring. "Regardless of what I said that day, my decision to ask for your hand was not in any way impulsive. In fact —" he huffed a small laugh — "waiting for you to learn my language so I could beg you to marry me did more for my training in patience than anything Baz ever put me through." He glanced over with a grin. "But don't tell him that."

Guilt crept in, overshadowing the contentment I'd felt since he'd kissed me. "I almost did this thing," I whispered, my eyes latch-ing onto a particularly bright star. "I almost killed Eleazar."

He propped himself on his side and lifted his other hand to my face, skimming his warm palm down my cheekbone. "You *saved* Eleazar, Sofea. You spoke the truth even thinking that Prezi might not survive."

"Will Nadir die?"

His fingers traced light circles on my forearm, which caused my skin to prickle with awareness. "If he is found guilty of the murder of his friend, he would be executed. I do not know whether it can be proven, since there seem to have been no witnesses to the truth that day, but I must trust Eleazar and the council of elders to do as they see fit with him. And ultimately the laws of Yahweh are righteous and perfect, even when men are not."

The stars blurred above me. "If Prezi does not live —"

He cut me off with a stone-etched promise. "I *will* find her. I understand how much she means to you, and I will do everything in my power to return her to you." My view of the stars was suddenly blocked as he leaned over me. His hair had come free of its tie, becoming a curtain of sweet darkness around my face, enveloping me in his familiar cedar-hyssop scent. "From the mo-

ment you appeared in my home, all wild-
ness and blue-eyed fire, I have thought of
little more than making you my wife, and I
will not let you down again."

I breathed deeply of his nearness, my eyes
dropping closed as I lifted my hand to
caress the soft line of his bearded jaw. "I do
not deserve —"

He cut me off with a soft touch of his lips
to mine, his hand wending its way into my
curls as he drew me closer. "You are precious, Sofea. And if Yahweh wills it, I will
spend my lifetime showing you just how
much you are worth to me."

After another tender kiss that ended too
soon, Eitan gathered me close by his side
and we lay on our backs, watching the slow
parade of twinkling lights until I faded away.
I woke early the next morning in a strange
bed with Ora sleeping beside me and the
faintest memory of being tucked in Eitan's
arms as he carried me down the stairs, along
with the sound of his steady heartbeat
against my cheek.

As I watched the sun rise through the
open window, shedding golden light on
every corner of the tidy little room, two
things took root deep in the center of my
soul: not only did Eitan love me in spite of
everything, but the journey to understand-

ing that I was inexplicably valued by the One Who Made the Stars had been worth every painful step.

CHAPTER THIRTY-SEVEN

EITAN

2 Cheshvan

A shiver rippled across my shoulders as the gray dawn breathed across my skin and ruffled my damp, unbound hair. Dressed only in the plain white tunic I'd donned after my cleansing *mikveh,* I knelt on a linen sheet at the entrance of the Mishkan.

The marrow of my bones seemed to resonate with reverent fear as I considered the privilege of being allowed this close to the consecrated sanctuary of the Holy One of Israel.

The smoky-rich smell of my sacrifices roasting on the bronze altar filled the courtyard of the Mishkan — a lamb, an ewe, and a ram purchased by Ishai before the sun had even considered rising. When I'd told him of my plans last night, he'd insisted on providing the necessary animal,

431

grain, and wine offerings and waved off my insistence on reimbursing him for such generosity.

He'd taken me by the shoulders, those dark Egyptian-bred eyes boring into me. "Eitan, you are my grandson. Nothing honors me more than standing by you in this. I will hear no more arguments." He stood ten paces away now, also dressed in white after his own ritual cleansing, and somehow his presence made me feel as though my mother was near as well.

To my surprise, Eleazar stepped forward. I'd not expected the High Priest to be present today, let alone be the one to administer the rite; however, since it was his reproof last night that had brought me to this moment, it seemed only fitting.

"What made you choose to live as a *nazir*?" asked Eleazar after I'd told him all that had transpired over the last few days while his wife tended to Sofea.

Although tempted to skim over my true reasons, I offered him the unvarnished truth, regardless that it was his own death I alluded to. "I have chosen to live this way until my mother goes free from Kedesh."

The priest had lifted his silver brows. "Ah. And what of you?"

"Me?"

"What shackles bind you, young man?"

Taken aback, I had no answer.

"Why do you think I sent you to Kedesh, Eitan?"

"To protect me from Raviv."

"That is true. I saw such consuming bitterness in that man . . . and it seems nothing has changed. And I also sought to remove you from the care of an uncle who neglected you to the point of starvation."

Hot shame sizzled in my veins. I'd not known Eleazar was aware of the extent of my pain in my uncle's home.

"But I also felt it was necessary for you to be away from Shiloh in order to heal," he said. "You were too young to shoulder such guilt for what happened to those boys. Living in Shiloh would only have been a daily reminder of your mistake. I'd hoped that you would long ago have released that burden, but I suspect that you are still punishing yourself."

I began to protest his assumptions but was halted by his large hand on my shoulder.

"Do you think that by beating your body into submission you can erase the memory of that night? That it could absolve you of your part in their agonizing deaths?"

I flinched at the harsh assessment but could not refute it.

"Consecrating yourself to Yahweh is a worthy endeavor, Eitan, one that I would guess you have not taken lightly in any way, but I hope that it was begun with correct motives and not with some misplaced notion of making atonement for what happened to those boys."

I searched back to the moment I'd spoken the words of consecration aloud when I was fifteen. I'd been captured by the idea of setting myself aside, much like a priest, holding myself to a higher standard; but perhaps, if I was honest, my motives had become less worship of Yahweh and more bargaining for my mother's freedom. Ashamed, I dropped my gaze to my feet.

"It was a tragic mistake, Eitan, but one for which both you and Moriyah were offered grace eleven years ago. Why are you trampling all over the gift you were given?"

I jerked my chin upward, meeting his gaze again. "But I do not deserve —"

"Deserve?" His voice rose, echoing in the empty chamber. "Did we Hebrews deserve to be rescued from Egypt when most of us had turned to Egypt's gods there? Did Cain deserve to be pardoned from death and preserved by the mark of Yahweh after he killed his brother? Did Mosheh deserve to become the leader of our nation after he buried that murdered overseer in the sand? No, none of us deserve such kindnesses, especially from the Holy One whose justice and righteousness are beyond all comprehension. If you have freely been given mercy, who are you to question it?"

I lifted my eyes to the High Priest, hoping my expression conveyed my gratitude for his wise council. As I had washed in the frigid creek before dawn, I had allowed those words to take root inside my soul, and now, for the first time since I'd watched Zeev and Yared's lives slip away, I finally took firm hold of the freedom I'd been given.

A faint smile curved his lips as his strong voice rang out. "Is it your desire today, Eitan ben-Nachman, to end your vow to live as a *nazir*?"

I started a bit at the name of the father I barely remembered, my childhood memories of him long having been reduced to vague threads that eluded my grasp more often than not. "It is."

Eleazar moved to stand before me, placed his palms on my head, and began to recite the priestly blessing over me. The familiar words of protection, of grace, and of peace poured over me like the flood that once flowed from a rock in the wilderness.

With the rising sun peering over his shoulder, Tal stepped forward to take Eleazar's place, a razor-edged knife in hand and his expression sober. It seemed that my oldest friend had been selected to perform my unbinding ritual. Although tempted to teasingly admonish him not to let the knife slip, I held still as he began slicing away the hair I had not cut for over five years.

The long strands floated down to the sheet, collecting around my knees, my head already feeling lighter and the cool air raising gooseflesh on the back of my neck. Once Tal had finished cutting most of the length, a razor blade was wielded against my scalp and around the distorted ear that I'd always kept covered. Although momentary regret buzzed in my head, I took courage from my mother's refusal to wear a veil over the Canaanite brand on her face.

As the last of the stubble was pared from my head, Tal and two other *kohanim* training for priesthood brushed the remnants from my garments, then asked me to stand aside as they gathered every last strand of hair from the sheet and placed it in a copper bowl, which was then handed to Eleazar.

As my hair was scattered over the remains of the animal sacrifices, the bread and grain offerings added, and the wine poured over it all, I lay prostrate before the sanctuary of the Almighty, arms outstretched. The smoke rose from the bronze altar in curls, dissipating into the sky and, with it, the shackles I'd clung to for so long.

Sofea took in the sight of me without my hair, her lips parting in surprise as Ishai and I approached the house. It looked as though she had been walking with Ora among the autumn-painted vines this morning, just as my mother had done nearly every day when she lived in Shiloh.

Then, as if Sofea fully understood why I'd shed my vow, resolution arose in her blue eyes. She dropped Ora's arm and walked up to me. Without a word, she reached for my right shoulder and pulled me down toward her. I felt her warm breath against my deaf ear, but her whisper was lost to me. Then her sweet mouth pressed against my deformity, and I realized words were unnecessary. Just like when I called her my own in front of Ishai, her kiss declared that no matter what had happened between us in Kedesh, she was mine, for life.

Our parting from Ishai and Ora was swift and bittersweet. Regardless of the circumstances, I'd been grateful to see them again, but knowing it may well be the last time caused a much deeper wound than it had when I was a child with little understanding of such things. However, anxious to reach Prezi before any word from Shiloh about Nadir's thwarted plans reached Raviv's ears, Tal, Sofea, and I were forced to leave without delay. My grandfather sent us on our way with multiple blessings and Ora with as much food as we could carry in our packs.

Their beloved faces lingered in my mind as we retraced my steps, making our way down into the Jordan River Valley, crossing over south of Beit She'an and following the trade road back to the Sea of Kinneret. Along the way, Tal did his best to distract Sofea from thoughts of Prezi's fate by regaling her with memories of our boyhood mischief.

Whether it was slinging rotten apples off the roof of the inn at an unfortunate herd of goats, stripping off our tunics to run naked through a rainstorm, or setting loose a gaggle of caged geese in the middle of the market, the two of us had found no lack of entertainment in Kedesh. For years we'd barely even noticed that we lived in a prison.

Sofea seemed amused by Tal's stories but had grown quieter and quieter the farther north we walked. It was evident that she grieved every moment that passed without confirmation of her cousin's safety and was losing more hope with every step.

On the third evening of our journey, we took shelter beneath a wide willow tree near the remains of the once-mighty Canaanite city of Hazor. After we'd eaten the last of the bread and cheese Ora had given us, Tal made the excuse of needing to wash in the narrow river nearby, giving me a few moments alone to comfort Sofea.

We sat side by side in the shade of the willow as the sun dipped low in the west over the ruins of the wicked kingdom that was long touted as unconquerable.

"What can I do without her, Eitan?" Sofea's voice barely broke a whisper.

Stricken by the despair in her question, I tucked her into my side and pressed a kiss to her temple. "We will find her, Sofea. Raviv has no cause to harm her. It is me he wants."

She leaned her head against my shoulder, and I savored the feeling of her body pressed against me. "I made her go explore with me," she said. "She like more to help her mother with the brothers and sisters than dive into sea caves or climb rocks. But I was selfish. I want her with me."

Her body trembled as she continued.

"The day the men came, she want to stay behind. Help with the tuna catch. But I make her go with me. I fuss until I get my way. And while we swim like dolphins, our families die. . . ." Her voice drifted, as if she were seeing the horror again in her mind. "But I do not regret this. If I not be selfish that morning, she would be gone. And I cannot think of my life with no Prezi." She drew a shuddering breath.

Slipping my fingers beneath her chin, I lifted her face, needing her to see the determination on my own. "She will come back to you, Sofea." I kissed her tear-stained cheeks. "I promise."

To my surprise, she slid her arms around my neck and kissed me with abandon. Her lips tasted of salt and desire, and her fierce embrace was tinder to my blood. Tangling my fingers in her curls, I slowed the kiss, needing to measure my response but also wanting to memorize the feel of her in my arms.

Knowing Tal would return any moment, I forced myself to release her, grinning at the flush on her cheeks. Then I gathered enough fallen willow boughs to fashion a soft bed on the ground and insisted that she lie down and get some rest for the final leg of the journey home.

I sat beside her, running my fingers through her long silky curls until she fell asleep, and I determined to do whatever it took to fulfill my promise to her.

After a long battle with sleep, I awoke before dawn, firm in my resolve. Quietly untangling myself from my woolen mantle, I stepped over Tal's sleeping body and slipped out from beneath the willow.

Standing on the muddy river bank, I scraped my fingernails across my scalp for the hundredth time, still unused to the sensation of air moving over my bare head. Tal had inflicted a few nicks during my shearing, for which I'd repeatedly vowed retribution during our journey.

My palm went to my ear, curving around the mangled lobe, as I remembered how Sofea had looked at me after I'd returned from the Temple. As I stepped forward into this battle today, it was not the fiery kiss from last night that I would cling to, but that one perfect, silent moment when Sofea had kissed my deformed ear in front of my family with all the solemnity of a lifelong vow.

"You are leaving, aren't you?" Tal edged into my daydream by appearing at my side, his eyes trained on the swirls of water curling and uncurling in their eastward rush to merge with the Jordan.

"I have no choice. Nadir said after today Raviv would make sure Prezi disappeared, whatever that may mean." I did not even want to consider whether he'd determined that I was not coming after all and had already moved her — or worse.

"There is still time to get help from Kedesh. It's only a few hours' walk."

I shook my head. "You don't understand Darek's determination to keep me within those walls. And I have to do this for Sofea. It would destroy her if Prezi died, especially after all she endured to save her."

Glancing back to the willow, I watched her for a few moments, hands tucked beneath her cheek and her wild curls tangled around her face, sleeping soundly on the nest of soft boughs I'd created for her. Lying beside her last night had been equal parts torture and bliss. I'd lain awake for hours listening to her breathe, inhaling her sweet fragrance, and hoping that she would understand that what I did today was only for her.

"I need you to take her to the city," I told him. "You can send reinforcements when you arrive like we planned, but I want her far away from Raviv."

"I won't let you go alone, Eitan —"

I raised a silencing palm. "I am asking you, as my oldest friend, to ensure that the woman I love is escorted safely home."

His jawed ticked as he stared at me. "So, what? You will simply walk into his home and demand he release the girl?"

"Yahweh will be with me." I finally understood what my mother meant when she insisted that sometimes the Holy One spoke truth directly to her soul. The vivid dream that had come to me on the tail end of my fitful sleep had solidified my decision. I'd seen a canopy of blue-white light hovering over me, undulating in the starry sky toward the northeast, and accepted it for what it was — a promise of guidance and protection.

Turning toward Tal, I clasped both his forearms in my hands. He mirrored the gesture, a mutual signal of eternal brotherhood. "I am trusting you with her."

Frowning, he sighed in resignation. "I assured Eleazar I'd see you returned to Kedesh in one piece. Don't make a liar of me."

I shoved his shoulder with a grin. "You still owe me a debt for butchering my scalp. Don't think I won't come back to collect."

He tilted his head toward Sofea under the

willow. "And what do I tell her when she wakes and you have gone?"

"Tell her . . ." With a tight knot in my throat, I absorbed one last glimpse of her through the green curtain of branches that drooped nearly to the ground. "Tell her she is worth it."

CHAPTER THIRTY-EIGHT

SOFEA

5 Cheshvan

Fury pulsed through me with such force that Tal had to lengthen his stride to keep up with me. *Eitan had promised! Promised to never let me go again!* And yet when I'd woken to willow-dappled sunlight on my face, he'd gone without saying good-bye. Without explaining why he would go to Raviv's valley alone, without waiting for men from Kedesh to accompany him into such peril. My frustration at Eitan had overflowed onto Tal, whose all-too-calm demeanor as he revealed Eitan's disappearance caused me to snap at a man I barely knew.

But instead of losing his own temper when I accused him of being part of the deception by not waking me, the young priest had bowed his head in sympathy. "I have known

Eitan since I was ten years old, and although he is naturally impulsive at times and driven by his emotions, he is not a fool, Sofea. You and I will hurry back to the city and send men to help him. Baz and Darek have trained him well. He'll be fine."

However, for as much as he sought to reassure me along the seemingly eternal walk, the closer we came to Kedesh, the more Tal's pretense of calm wavered. When we were greeted at the gates by four stern-faced guards demanding to know our business in the city, his body seemed to hum with tension as he responded to their abundant questions with growing impatience. He was just as panicked over Eitan as I was.

After insisting that he be allowed to escort me to the inn and being denied entrance, Tal handed over a rolled missive sealed with the clay imprint I recognized as the High Priest's symbol. We were ushered through the outside gates but told to wait. None of the men removed their eyes from us, nor their hands from the hilts of their swords, as the message was delivered to the captain of the guard.

"What is this?" I asked. "I go through these gates many times but never such questions as these."

Tal grimaced. "Eitan mentioned that the

night before he left there was an attack against one of the manslayers. Someone decided to exact their own justice."

I caught my breath. "Did he live?"

"It was a woman."

"Not Moriyah," I gasped. Surely if something had happened to his mother, Eitan would have told me.

"No," he said, placing a calming hand on my shoulder. "Not Moriyah."

Although my breath came easier, I had the unsettling feeling that Tal knew much more than he was saying. However, I was prevented from asking anything else when the captain of the guard emerged from the gatehouse, the missive from Eleazar unfurled in his hand.

"Tal," said the broad-shouldered man I recognized as Chaim, another childhood friend of Eitan's. "Where is he?"

Tal grimaced, as if reluctant to speak in front of me. "He's gone to confront Raviv."

Chaim blew out a huff of disdain mixed with a half-formed curse.

"I know where the house is," Tal said. "Do you have a few men to spare?"

"Sofea?" a voice called out from behind me. I spun, shocked to see Darek striding toward us, his sheathed sword in his hand. He must have seen us approaching the city and headed straight here without taking the time to tie it to his belt. "Where is he?"

Beating me to the answer, Tal gave a quick explanation, during which Darek's expression devolved from alarm into white-faced disbelief, accentuating the dusky shadows beneath his eyes that spoke of sleepless nights over Eitan's disappearance. "He went there *alone*?"

Tal's tone was measured. "I'm sure he only went ahead to scout and determine what challenges we face. He told me to wait just a short while before coming here for help."

I glared at him, wondering how long after Eitan had left Tal had waited to wake me, but as I did, the message he'd delivered from him suddenly clarified in my mind. *Tell her she is worth it.*

Although I had instigated that kiss last night, an outpouring of my gratitude for his promise to ensure Prezi was safe, I realized now that at some point it had shifted into a farewell. Horrified, I clutched Darek's arm, the truth splintering my heart. "No — he will not wait for help. He go to give his life for Prezi's."

Darek shook off my grip and sped through the gates.

■ ■ ■ ■

Hastily, Tal escorted me back to the inn. But before I knocked, he leaned over to kiss the top of my head — as if he were my own brother — and murmured a reassurance that he would return with both Prezi *and* Eitan, and then strode away to return to the gatehouse. His haunted brown eyes called those promises into question.

Chaim was gathering a few men to follow after Darek but had vowed not to leave without Tal, so I was left to deliver the news to Moriyah that her son had knowingly walked into Raviv's trap for my sake.

Attempting a few calming breaths before I lifted my hand to knock, I was startled when the door flew open before my fist met wood. Moriyah stood in the doorway, eyes like silver moons. She flung her arms around me, drawing me close and tucking me beneath her chin like she did with her own children. She breathed my name into my hair and stroked my back.

"You are home," she said. "Safe."

Every emotion boiled over. Shame, fear, pain, guilt, anger, and longing mixed together into tears that stained the front of her blue tunic as I clung to her. Although her body went rigid, she did not push me away. She held me closer, murmuring assurances and endearments.

"He go to rescue Prezi," I sobbed, my disjointed thoughts tumbling out end over end. "My fault. He cannot . . . alone . . ."

She pulled back, her warm hands on either side of my face. "Sofea. Slow down. I cannot understand what you are telling me." I tensed at the sharp censure in her voice. Her concern had pulled it taut as a bowstring — with good reason. I drew in a long shuddering breath and tried again, wishing I had more than bad news and halting Hebrew to offer. I looked into the face of the one woman who loved him even more than I did and told her everything.

Moriyah paled as I spoke. She closed her eyes, still holding my face in her palms, and her lips began to move in silent supplication. After a few moments of watching her lift a desperate plea to Yahweh, begging for the life of the son she adored, I too allowed my eyelids to flutter shut and added my own feeble, stumbling prayers to her own.

I felt her thumbs brush beneath my eyes, wiping away my tears. "We can do nothing now but entrust them to the One Who Sees and wait for them to return." She gave me a wan smile as she tugged my wrist. "Now come inside, daughter, and tell me what all has occurred since you disappeared."

I followed her through the inn and into the courtyard, where a chorus of exclamations greeted me.

"Sofea!"

"You are home!"

"She's back!"

Gidal, Malakhi, Chana, and Abra crowded around me, a tangle of arms, hugs, and kisses. However, their exuberant welcome was soured by the questions that followed.

"Where is Prezi?"

"Is our brother with you?"

"Where did you go?"

"What did you bring us?"

The last one was delivered by little Chana, who must have seen my departure as one similar to that of her father, who was sometimes gone for weeks at a time but who nearly always managed to return with some little trinket he picked up along the way.

Hers was the only question I was prepared to answer in the onslaught. I knelt and cupped my palms on her round little cheeks. She reached out to grasp my shell necklace, running her fingers over the rippled back, as she must have seen me do many times. "I have no gifts, little bird, but tomorrow you and I go explore, yes?"

"Can Prezi come?" she lisped.

I swallowed the searing truth and blinked away my tears as I kissed her forehead. "I hope this, my sweet."

Sarai came forward to embrace me as well, welcoming me home. Her face was strangely drawn, a contrast to her normally effervescent disposition.

"What is wrong?" I whispered into her ear.

"It's Binah. The healers have done as much as they can, but an infection rages in the wound. We are all praying that she lives."

Stricken, I pulled back to look her in the face. "Binah?"

Moriyah slipped an arm around my shoulder, drawing me away from the children. "Come, I am sure you are in need of refreshment. Sit at the table and I'll fetch you some food and tell you what happened while you were gone."

Once I was settled on a large pillow with an overabundance of bread, cheese, dried figs, and yogurt set before me, Moriyah told me how Eitan had saved Binah's life from a vengeful young shepherd the day Nadir tricked us into leaving.

So Binah had been the convicted manslayer Tal had spoken of. I was tempted to ask more about why she'd been sent to

Kedesh but Moriyah's next words startled me.

"Although it was terrible that such a thing happened," she said, "and we are all very concerned about Binah, it was the shepherd who revealed Nadir's treachery. Without such knowledge, Eitan would not have known to go after you."

I set down my cup with a jolt, water sloshing onto the table. "What does this mean? He have no plan to follow?"

Moriyah regarded me with curiosity. "He thought you had chosen to leave, dear. He would never force you to stay with him if that is not what you want."

"He hurt my heart, but I don't choose to leave him. Never." I scanned the familiar scene in the courtyard — the children playing a game of chase, Sarai chastising them for coming too close to her loom — and memories of the last months among this family unfurled like a scroll. "And even if . . ." I choked on the words. "Even if terrible things happen today, I want to stay here."

Moriyah's silver eyes bore into mine. "You are part of this family now, Sofea. This is your home, whether or not you marry my son." Her thumb caressed the copper ring Eitan had crafted for me. "It terrified me when he left, but I understood his desire to protect you. In fact, I watched him leave from Dov and Rachel's rooftop and did nothing to stop him. I trust Yahweh with my son, Sofea. And so should you."

CHAPTER THIRTY-NINE

EITAN

I'd been crouching in the brush for too long. Even knowing what I had to do, my reason fought against it. And yet the longer I waited, the more likely it was that Tal would send men from Kedesh before I had the chance to do what I must.

Prezi meant nothing to Raviv. She was simply an expendable piece in the game he was playing with me. If a contingent of men plowed into the valley, swords waving, she would likely not survive. It was my life for hers.

It had been easy to find Raviv's land. I'd seen the nearby lake often enough from Kedesh, and now I surveyed his territory from my vantage point in an apple orchard that sat upon the western ridge, only one of many fruit orchards and olive groves that rimmed this large, fertile basin. Raviv, being the firstborn son, had inherited two-thirds of the land when his father had passed away a few years ago, but Darek was still entitled to one-third. Looking out over the recently harvested fields, I wondered which area was his portion.

This valley was everything he had described. The soil was a deep, rich red, the small lake at its heart shimmered beneath a brilliant blue sky, and trees of every variety entertained myriad birds in their branches — all beneath the white-headed watch of Har Hermon, the range of mountains that dominated the northern horizon.

An unbidden thought strayed into my mind. If they'd lived, Zeev and Yared would be nearly twenty-five now, perhaps married and living with children of their own in the little grouping of homes here in the valley. Their sons and daughters would be playing in this orchard now, climbing trees, laughing. Instead, their generations had been halted by my impetuous hand.

I swiped a palm over my shaved head, reminding myself again that I had laid my shame down in Shiloh. I'd have to replace the daily habit of flogging myself for the boys' deaths with daily reminders of those sacred moments before the altar as my burden was turned to ash.

Although I'd seen two men tending a herd

of cattle and one woman with an infant strapped to her back stirring a large pot over a fire, I was at a loss for direction. A dozen goat-hide tents formed a half-circle around three halfway-constructed homes and one small villa. In the past eleven years Raviv had planted the roots of a small town here and obviously employed a large group of loyal men to harvest and protect his assets.

"Who are you?" said a small voice behind me.

Whipping my head around, I caught sight of two young girls a few paces away. They looked to be similar in age to Gidal and Malakhi, both dark-haired and brown-eyed and looking so much like Abra and Chana that I found myself staring.

With the corners of their outer garments held in their fists, both of them carried a small load of apples in the fold. Their eyes were wary as they regarded me, no doubt wondering about the strange bald man crouched in the weeds.

I sat back on my heels with a counterfeit smile on my face, hoping to assuage their fears. "Shalom! My name is Eitan. I am searching for a friend of mine."

Startling at my voice, the younger one sidled closer to her sister, letting one corner of her garment drop as she reached for the older girl's hand. Her load of apples tumbled to the ground.

"I promise I mean you no harm. I am only looking for a young woman named Prezi. She is tall for a girl, with long straight brown hair and dark brown eyes. Have you seen her?"

Their own brown eyes widened and they glanced at each other briefly, something passing between them that raised my hopes.

"Please, I need to find her. Our family is worried for her safety. Do you know where she might be?"

The older sister kept her expression impassive, her mouth set in a hard line and an unyielding gaze locked on me, her sober nature reminding me of Gidal. The younger sidled closer to the older one, flicking nervous glances between her sister and me. I had no doubt that these two knew exactly where Prezi was.

Tempering my impulse to interrogate them further and insist they tell me exactly where she was being held, I attempted a different approach.

Noticing a reddening scuff on the older girl's shin, one that looked to be caused by a climb to retrieve apples, I sat back against a tree and placed my hands on my knees so they would see that I held no weapons.

I craned my head up to gaze into the green and gold canopy above my head. "There must have been a plentiful harvest this year. I've never seen so much fruit. I was thinking about picking a few apples but it looks like the birds have beaten me to it." I sighed and let my eyelids drop, enough that it would seem that I was simply resting, not peering at the two of them between my lashes.

Although they stayed where they were, it seemed as though the stiff posture of the older girl softened just a touch.

I did not open my eyes as I said, "You two remind me of my little sisters. Their names are Abra and Chana. They are younger than you, but they love to climb trees like this." I held my body still, waiting, breathing in the sickly-sweet scent of the decaying fruit on the ground. "I'll bet you don't climb trees though. Only your brothers would do such a thing, I suppose."

"We don't have brothers, and I climb trees all the time" came the sharp reply from the older girl.

I let my eyes burst open with feigned surprise. "Truly?"

The girl's jutted chin displayed her offense at my manufactured slight. "I climb better than any boy in this valley."

"Did you collect those apples from the top of a tree?"

She nodded, pride in the set of her narrow shoulders.

"Impressive." Smiling in a show of camaraderie, I folded my arms over my chest. I leaned my head back again, eyes closed, determined to wield my newfound patience to glean what I needed to know. "I'll just rest here a few more moments before moving on to continue my search." I sighed heavily, and spoke as if to myself. "Her cousin is soon to be my wife, and she is so devastated. I can't stand to see the woman I love so heartsick. I promised her that Prezi would return home."

After a few long, silent moments, the girl spoke again, her words barely above a whisper. "I saw her."

I pulled in a slow breath through my nose in a feeble attempt at remaining calm and then lifted my eyes. "Can you show me where she is?"

She flinched slightly and then shook her head. "My abba will be very angry."

My insides twisted violently. "Will he hit you?"

"No, but he will yell. Loud." Wide-eyed, the younger one nodded in agreement with her sister.

Their apprehension gave me pause, but Prezi's life was at stake. "I will never reveal to anyone that I spoke with you. I promise you this, on my life." I leveled a sober gaze at them both. "I only want to take my friend home to her cousin. She is alone and must be very afraid."

The girl's eyes fluttered as she contemplated, but then she pointed to one of the small, half-built homes at the edge of the orchard. "I climbed a big tree because I heard singing in words I did not understand. There is no roof yet, so I could see a lady in there. She smiled at me and waved with her fingers because her hands were tied up, but then I heard Abba and I climbed down and ran away."

A voice rang out in the valley, and peering through the brush I could see that the woman with the baby on her back was the source.

"Our mother is looking for us," said the oldest girl. "We have to go."

"Thank you, girls." I smiled at them, one last reassurance. "Shalom."

The younger one shyly returned my smile, displaying a large gap where her front teeth had been and then whispering a lisped *shalom*. The curve of her mouth was the very image of Darek's. My stomach soured as

my suspicions about their parentage solidified.

Needing confirmation, I called out softly
as the girls veered past me, wisely still keeping their distance. "Is your father's name
Raviv?"

Although she flinched in surprise, the
older girl nodded before she trotted off,
dragging her sister along behind her.

These were Raviv's daughters. Sisters to
the boys I'd killed. Cousins to my own
siblings. *We have no brothers,* the girl had
said. So the woman down by the fire, obviously his new wife, carried another daughter
on her back. After all this time, Raviv still
had no male heirs to continue his family
line. No wonder his bitterness had not
waned since Zeev and Yared's deaths. I
could expect no reprieve from a man who
blamed me for ending his bloodline.

Ready to face his wrath for Prezi's sake, I
rose, but someone fisted the back of my
tunic, jerking me behind the bushy apple
tree I'd been using as a hiding place. Grabbing over my shoulder for the wrist of my
attacker, I spun, yanking his arm into one
of the impossible-to-escape holds Baz had
taught me.

"Good," Darek said with a wry grin.
"Quick as lightning and an armlock few

could break." He lifted his brows, appraising my changed appearance with a swift perusal of my shaved head before pinning me with a critical glare. "But I would already have plunged a dagger into your spine. Awareness is paramount, Eitan. It's fortunate I even recognized you."

I released him with a huff. "Not a good time for a lesson."

"Neither is it a good time for suicide." The words were razor-sharp and fury reigned across his lowered brow. "Chaim is coming with some of his men. We'll wait."

"No. Prezi won't survive a full-out assault."

"You don't know that."

"Yes, I do. She is expendable if Raviv doesn't get what he wants. Besides" — I pointed toward the homes, thinking of his girls — "there are women and children down there. I don't want to put any of them at risk either."

"He'll kill you, Eitan, and then he'll kill Prezi anyway."

"I don't plan to surrender until she is free."

He gripped the hilt of his sword, as if considering whether to pummel me with it. "There will be no surrendering. He's my brother, I'm sure I can reason with him to release her."

"Your brother was involved with Nadir in a plot to kill the High Priest of Israel, using Sofea as their weapon. He is beyond reasoning."

Shock made a quick appearance on his face but just as quickly transformed to fiery determination. "Sacrificing yourself will not bring the boys back."

"That's not what this is about. I am not punishing myself. Not anymore." My hand instinctively skimmed my stubbled scalp, and Darek's gaze followed the motion. "This is about saving Prezi."

I could see the questions about the ending of my vow written on his face, but since Chaim and his men might come over the ridge at any moment, explanations would have to wait. "I have to go. Hold them off until you see Prezi walk out the door."

"Eitan —" He grabbed my shoulder, his fingers digging into my skin with desperation.

"You and Baz trained me well. Please. Trust me."

"I do trust you." His fingers clenched tighter. "But I won't lose you, son. We go in together, or not at all."

CHAPTER FORTY

Once within sight of the half-built home the girl had pointed out, Darek and I crawled on our bellies through the high weeds, taking shelter behind separate trees to avoid the roving eyes of the two heavily armed men who guarded the door.

After indicating my plan to Darek with quick hand motions, I kept low to the ground as I extracted my sling from my belt and loaded it with one of the stones I'd gathered from the riverbank this morning. I kept two more tucked into my palm.

Then, clinging to the vision of protective light I'd been given last night, I stood, circled the sling twice in the air with a practiced snap, and released.

One guard fell backward, smacking his skull against the stone wall as he did. I reloaded and sent another missile flying toward the second man, who'd already begun to charge toward me. My second shot missed, but the third did not; the man toppled to the ground with a cry. Darek barreled toward the second guard, who'd already staggered to his feet, then slammed the butt of his sword against the man's temple.

Jamming my sling back into my belt, I sprinted to the threshold of the house. I used my full body weight against the wooden door, and the feeble latch splintered easily. The door crashed open to reveal Prezi sitting on the ground at the far end of a long open-air chamber, her hands and feet bound together but seemingly unharmed. Behind her stood Raviv, a dagger trained on her neck, triumph glowing in his eyes.

I remembered him well, both from the day of the trial and from when I crouched in the shadows as he clutched one vomiting, convulsing son while the other lay still beside him. For the first time when thinking of that night, I felt only bone-deep pity for the man instead of shame over my mistake. How utterly helpless he must have felt as he watched them die.

"At least my daughters are loyal," he said, making it clear that the girls had alerted him to my presence. "Unlike the man I used to call my brother."

I lifted my hands in surrender. "Let her

go, Raviv. I'm who you want."

"Indeed you are. Well . . . one of them at least." He gestured to someone behind me. Two men appeared at my flanks, as if they'd been hiding on either side of the door I'd burst through. They swiftly divested me of my sword and dagger, each taking an arm and pushing me a few paces closer to Raviv. I did not struggle but kept my gaze intent on him. Prezi looked up at me, concern for her cousin bright in her teary eyes.

"Your plot failed. Sofea saved Eleazar's life," I said, as much to calm her as to distract Raviv. "Nadir has been arrested."

He made a dismissive sound. "I had nothing to do with that. He was a fool. I doubted he would return anyhow." With a sneer he pointed the tip of his knife toward me. "But you . . . I've been waiting eleven years to spill your blood."

"You may have the right to my blood, but not to Prezi's. Let her go."

"I can't get to that whore you pretend is your mother. Perhaps I'll take this one instead." He yanked on Prezi's hair, jerking her head back to expose her throat to his dagger. "Perhaps you should watch her life ebb away, the way I watched my sons suffer in the dirt like animals."

Before I could respond that I too had

witnessed that horror, a small voice cried out, "No, Abba!" All eyes lifted to the open space where the roof should be, taking in the sight of Raviv's daughter perched high in a tree.

"Don't hurt her!" she shouted, and at the same moment, Darek hurtled through the open door, knocking aside the captor on my left. I crashed my fist into the jaw of the one on my right and yanked my arm free as I grabbed for the sling in my belt.

Bellowing a curse, Raviv plowed over Prezi to lunge at me, dagger upraised. We clashed at the center of the room, my shoulder slamming into his chest as he brought his dagger down on my arm. Ignoring the ripping pain, I flipped one end of my sling into the air, where it looped over his forearm. I jabbed my elbow into his gut, grabbed hold of the free end of my sling, and yanked hard, hoping to disarm him.

Instead, one of his men collided with me from behind, bringing me to the ground and pinning me beneath his sweaty bulk. Within moments, Raviv's foot was planted on the side of my neck, smashing my face into the stone floor. The other man had both of my arms locked behind me, his full body weight anchoring me in place.

From the corner she'd skittered into, Prezi

locked gazes with me, trembling violently. Her face was streaked with tears and contorted with pain, her hands curled around her bad foot.

"Raviv!" Darek shouted. "Let him go!" I could not see him, but I heard his struggle against whoever was preventing him from reaching me.

Over my head Raviv seethed, spitting words through gritted teeth toward his brother. "You were there! You saw them vomit their lifeblood on the ground. You heard them plead for mercy. They were all I had left of her. . . ." His voice became a strangled roar. "How dare you choose this murderer over your own flesh and blood!"

"He did not know what he was doing! He was *nine*!" shouted Darek. "And he is my *son*!"

I tried to struggle against the brute who held me captive, sweat stinging my eyes as I made a futile attempt to twist my neck and catch a glimpse of Darek's face. That was twice today he had called me his son.

"No." Raviv breathed the word as a curse, undoubtedly, like me, trying to weigh out what such a statement could mean.

Darek's response was equal parts apology and ironclad declaration. "He is legally my firstborn and will inherit my portion of this land when I die."

Jarred by the revelation, I went still. It had to be a pretense. I had stolen his nephews and ripped his family apart. Surely he would not honor me over Gidal, his rightful first-born.

Raviv's heel dug harder against my throat, squeezing my air supply. His next words came out like shards of ice. "I will kill you, *brother,* before I will ever allow such defilement of our father's legacy."

"Then do it." A sword clattered to the ground. "Kill me. If it's blood redemption you want so badly, then take mine."

Raviv went silent, and I desperately wished I could see what was passing between the two brothers above my head.

"You are my brother, Raviv. The same blood flows in our veins." His voice lowered, tinged by sorrow. "Our mother would be destroyed by the rift between us. My heart broke for the boys that day too, don't you remember? I set off to Shechem with every intention of arresting Moriyah and bringing her to justice. But I quickly discovered how wrong I was. I did not choose her over you or the boys. I chose mercy."

Thinking of how desperately I loved Sofea, I could not imagine the agony of having to choose between her and either one of my brothers. It must have torn Darek to pieces.

"And if you kill Eitan or Prezi," he said, "you will be convicted of murder. Instead of your girls growing up to admire their father, to know you as the brave army commander and hero that you are, they will be forced to grieve you and bear your shame. Do not inflict an unjust verdict upon Eitan the way those men did to our mother, Raviv."

After a few silent moments, the pressure on my throat lessened ever so slightly, and I sucked in a painful breath.

"My boys deserve to be avenged," said Raviv. "Who pays the price for their suffering?"

"Moriyah has been locked in a prison paying that price. She gladly accepted the blame and the punishment that came with it. She mourned your sons as if they were her own and bleeds for the chasm between you and me."

A strangled noise came from Raviv's throat. "I won't allow —"

"I will give you the land," Darek said, cutting him off. "I will sign my third of this land over to you, just as I had planned to do before I decided to marry Moriyah. Your new wife is young, you will have more

471

children. Sons will come. They can inherit it all, in honor of Zeev and Yared. But please, let my son go free."

Chapter Forty-One

Baz propped me against a cedar on the ridge above Raviv's home, but my legs wobbled and I slid to the ground, the bark scratching against my bare arms. My head was strangely light and my mouth seemed to be jammed full of raw wool.

Baz, Chaim, Tal, and six soldiers from Kedesh had surrounded the house during the altercation with Raviv, but on Darek's orders had not interfered. When I'd emerged, one arm bleeding profusely and the other around Prezi, they'd plowed through the door to ensure Darek's safety as well.

"You've lost a fair amount of blood," Baz said gruffly as he used his knife to shear off a length of fabric from his mantle. "But I think you'll survive. It's not all that deep."

Chaim stood nearby, blocking the glare of the sun with his body, frowning as Baz wrapped the makeshift bandage around my arm three times and secured it with his bronze toggle pin. "You are lucky he didn't jam that knife between your ribs."

Baz glared at me. "You deserved to be gutted like a deer for the way you ran in by yourself like that."

"Darek was with me."

His nostrils flared. "That wasn't your plan though, was it?"

"I did what I had to do." I glanced over at Prezi. She was leaning against Tal, who'd carried her all the way from the house to the top of the ridge, her ankle swollen after being reinjured during the violent scuffle. But she was alive. And all I could think about was getting her back to Kedesh, to Sofea.

Baz's reply was closer to a snarl. "I taught you to be still for a reason."

"You were just curious to see how long I'd stand there in that courtyard." I grinned, taunting him. "Admit it."

His lips twitched with a hint of reluctant humor, his eyes narrowing. "You cost me a week's pay that day, boy."

"You bet against me? Who did you lose to?"

"Me." My father's voice came from behind my right shoulder as he crested the ridge. "I knew you could last until sundown." He had stayed behind as a scribe whom Raviv employed prepared a document declaring Darek's intention to gift his portion of his father's land to his brother. The inheritance that I'd never guessed had been destined for me was no more.

Although thinking of Darek as my father was foreign, his impassioned plea for my life had convinced me that he had indeed formally declared me as his child. But when had he done it? And why had he kept me ignorant of such a thing?

"Can you walk?" Darek asked. "Or does Baz need to carry you too?" His brow lifted with a hint of mockery.

"I'd rather sit here and bleed out," I said, and Baz and Chaim chuckled at my dry response.

Darek laughed, sounding more relieved than amused. "Someone get Eitan some water. We'll rest a while longer before we head to the city."

One of the soldiers offered me a skin-bag, and I sucked down half its contents before indicating he should pass it on to Prezi.

Darek took a seat next to me, his own back propped against the cedar, and the rest of our companions moved to seek shade beneath their own trees. A smear of ink lined the edge of his thumb, and the grooves of his copper signet ring were stained as well. I'd made that ring for him five years ago, the first piece of jewelry I'd crafted alone in Yalon's foundry. The fact that he rarely took it off held even more meaning for me now.

I let my head fall back against the tree and scanned the fertile valley below us. "Why did you not tell me?"

He released a slow sigh. "When I married Moriyah, you two had only been living in Kedesh for four months. You were still adjusting to life within the city walls after the trial. I did not want to push you into something you weren't ready to comprehend. And, if you remember" — he tossed me a glance — "you were still fairly hostile to me then."

I did remember. I'd been so thrilled to finally have Moriyah as my mother, reveling in being the subject of her lavish attention during those four months, that when Darek married her I'd felt a sharp sting of jealousy.

With so many empty rooms available in the inn, I'd been allowed my own sleeping chamber after the wedding, a luxury for any child, but all I'd wanted was to sleep on the floor near her. For months I'd regretted giving Darek my blessing to marry her, but as I came to understand that he truly cherished her, my resentment began to fade.

"By the time you and I made peace," he continued, "it seemed that perhaps you were too old to begin calling me *Abba,* so I said nothing. But that did not mean that I ever considered you anything less than my son. The fact that I'd signed a formal declaration naming you as my heir on our wedding day was a mere formality. I'd begun considering you my own the day I returned to Kedesh and you practically refused to let me go up the stairs to propose marriage to Moriyah."

I laughed, then winced at the spike of pain in my arm. "I was not about to let some stranger with no beard past me. No matter how much you said you loved her."

He nudged me with an elbow. "I believe a small bribe was all it took to allay your suspicions."

"Ah yes. That little obsidian knife. I still have it." I'd carried that knife with me until I was sixteen and learned to make my own weapons.

My gaze roved over the landscape again, taking in the far-reaching pastureland, the varicolored fields, the shimmering lake, and the blue hills in the distance. "Thank you. For what you did today." I cleared the swell of heat in my throat. "For sacrificing all this."

"You mean *your* inheritance?"

I huffed a low laugh. "But it was yours first. And it was your father's legacy and should have been passed down to your generations, through the boys."

"You are my legacy, *along* with Gidal and Malakhi and the girls. And I will consider your children part of that legacy as well. With or without that land, you have every right as my firstborn son, and those rights can never be taken from you."

"Will the rift between you and Raviv ever be healed?"

"I held to that hope for many years. And I suppose it's possible that his heart will soften one day. He may have relinquished his lust for vengeance today, but bitterness still holds his soul captive." He studied his palms, one finger tracing that smudge of black ink. "After I signed the document, he told me that he will honor the agreement by leaving you and Moriyah alone, but that he never wants to see me again."

A boulder of guilt crashed into my chest. "Forgive me —"

"No." He cut me off, his brown eyes blazing with sincerity. "I meant what I said. I chose mercy eleven years ago. I have never blamed Moriyah and I don't blame you — for the boys, or for Raviv. There is no debt between you and me."

A sensation of liberation, similar to the one I'd experienced in front of the Mishkan, sluiced over me, washing away the final remnants of shame that had been the wall between Darek and me. In its place was the freedom to accept the totality of the mercy I'd been given by both my father and my God.

Swallowing the knot in my throat, I reached out to grasp his forearm, and he returned the gesture with a firm grip, emotion shimmering in his eyes. Remembering what he'd said about my own children, children that my blue-eyed wife would bear someday, I was infused with a rush of energy. I needed to see her, hold her. Now.

I struggled to my feet, clutching my wounded arm close to my body. "Actually, *Abba,* you owe *me* a bride."

Chapter Forty-Two

SOFEA

The jug I'd been holding shattered on the ground, sending up a spray of juice and pottery that I completely ignored as I ran across the courtyard to my cousin. She tottered off balance as I threw my arms around her, crying out her name with a sob of relief.

I pulled her tight, salty gratitude spilling down my face. "I'm so sorry for putting you in danger again. Please, please forgive me for being so easily fooled."

She ran her hand down my hair. "He deceived us both, Sofi. Do not punish yourself over such things." She kissed my cheek. "All is well."

"Your cousin has reinjured her foot," said Tal, making me realize that not only was he standing next to us, he also had an arm around Prezi's waist. "Why don't I help her find a place to sit before she tells you all that happened today?"

"Oh! Yes!" I released her. She took two steps but wobbled, so without a word, Tal whisked her into his arms and carried her to the table, where he lowered her onto a large cushion and then propped another beneath her outstretched ankle.

Astonished by his tender ministrations to my cousin, I let my gaze flit between the two of them. Prezi glanced away, a slight tinge of pink on her cheeks as she accepted a cup of water and a kiss from a visibly relieved Moriyah, and a four-armed, giggling hug from Chana and Abra. It seemed my cousin and I had all manner of interesting things to discuss. . . .

But first —

"Where is he?" I demanded of Tal, stomach churning and fists clenched tightly. He and Prezi had entered the courtyard alone, but surely he would not look nearly so collected if his best friend were not close behind.

"He is wounded," he said, his brows gathering.

The blood seemed to drain from my head into my feet. "Wounded?"

Tal cleared his throat, his eyes darting to Moriyah, whose body had gone very still. "Raviv stabbed him in the arm. He lost some blood, so he was a little unsteady, but

Baz seemed to think it was not nearly as dire as it looked and would heal quickly."

I sagged down onto a three-legged stool nearby, my knees liquid with relief.

"He'll be along shortly. Darek forced him to stop twice along the way to rest." He smirked, a wicked gleam in his eye. "He grumbled, of course, but it was either that or be carried through the gates on Baz's back."

Moriyah came up behind me and grasped both of my shoulders lightly. "And my husband?"

"Darek is unharmed as far as I could tell," Tal replied.

I reached up to cover her hands with my own, an acknowledgment of mutual relief over the men we loved.

"Tell us," she said, looking between Tal and Prezi. "What happened?"

Tal began with his conversation this morning at the river, making it clear that although he had disagreed with Eitan's decision, he understood why he'd made it. It was no wonder that our walk to the gates had been such a silent one. He'd known the whole time what Eitan had planned to do.

Prezi took up where Tal left off, explaining how Eitan had burst into the room like a thunderstorm to demand her release, how cold Raviv was as he threatened to kill him, and how the little girl appeared in the tree overhead, throwing the room into chaos that ended with Eitan pinned beneath Raviv's foot.

Moriyah's hands had become twin vises on my shoulders, her body pressing against my back as if she was suddenly in need of something, or someone, to lean on. Her words came out in a choked whisper. "How did he get free?"

Prezi looked over my head at the woman she'd come to admire so much, a brilliant smile spreading across her face. "Your husband won his freedom by offering his inheritance to Raviv."

Moriyah huffed loudly, as if someone had wrenched the breath from her lungs. "Of course he did." She released a low laugh that vibrated against my back. "There's nothing he would not give up for that boy."

As she spoke, the door from the inn opened, Eitan stepped into the courtyard, and the entire world went hazy.

His mother bent down and wrapped her arms around my shoulders, breathing a prayer of thanks to Yahweh as she squeezed me tightly for a moment. Then she spoke into my ear, her words both a release and a blessing. "Go to him, daughter."

I obeyed, crossing the distance between us so quickly it seemed as though I'd flown. Slinging my arms around his waist, I plastered my cheek to his chest, desperate to feel the heartbeat that echoed my only thought. *Alive. Alive. Alive.*

Eitan brought one arm to hold me closer, his chin resting atop my head. Catching sight of the bloody bandage on his other arm, I startled, concerned that I'd hurt him in my desperation to be near him. But his fingers spread wider on my back, pressing me even tighter against himself. I closed my eyes and relaxed into his strength, heedless of everyone in the courtyard witnessing my shameless display of affection for him.

Behind me, Darek cleared his throat. "Six months, you two." There was a note of amused censure in his tone.

"Two," returned Eitan.

"Four and no less."

A rumble of laughter vibrated against my cheek. "All right. That is only fair, since you had to wait that long for Ima."

When Eitan finally released me, I saw that everyone had moved away to give us a few moments of privacy. Tal was seated across the table from Prezi, enjoying some of the meal Moriyah and I had distracted ourselves by preparing as we waited for the men to return. The children were pestering Baz for details about how Prezi had been rescued, and Moriyah and Darek had drifted across the courtyard, hand in hand.

My mother had been far from perfect, her actions dictated mostly by my father's mercurial moods, yet she'd done her best to protect me the only way she knew how. But Eitan's mother shone like a lone flame cutting the darkness. I could see now why Prezi had been so content to simply be near her, to reflect that light.

"I miss my mother," I said as I watched Darek lead his wife up the stairs to the rooftop for their own private conversation. "But I am glad to call Moriyah my *ima* as well."

With a heated expression that made a four-month betrothal seem very long, and a brief glance around to see if anyone was watching, Eitan pulled me behind the closest column and bent his head to kiss me. I halted him with three fingers against his lips.

"You leave me today," I whispered. "I thought to never see you again."

"I know. I hope you will forgive me."

"But you bring Prezi back to me, just like you promised."

"I said that I would spend the rest of my life showing you how much you mean to me. And even if that life had ended today, it would have been worth it. I will never stop fighting for you, never stop protecting my family — our family. If that costs me my life, then so be it."

Frowning, I weighed the implications of such a declaration. "What of Raviv?"

"He vowed he would not pursue me again, even if I leave the boundaries of Kedesh."

"So you go with Darek? To fight with the army?"

"I must, Sofea. Yahweh blessed us with this land, so we must defend it from the enemies that surround us and from enemies among us who offer false covenants and false gods. Darek and his men are the eyes and ears of Yehoshua, and I am eager to do my part in guarding not only this city, but all of Israel."

Visions of him sneaking into enemy territory and wielding a sword in battle caused my heart to stutter, but Moriyah's encouragement to entrust Eitan to Yahweh rose in my mind, covering over the fear with a strong sense of peace. A deep peace I'd never experienced even when I'd sought solace in the arms of the sea.

I reached up to caress the curl of his deaf ear, idly wondering how long it would be until I could twirl my finger into a lock of his hair again. "Will you always fight back to me?"

"Always." He brushed a slow kiss across my lips, then pulled back as mischief crept into those hazel eyes. "Perhaps we'll finish our sling lessons and then you can go into battle beside me. Baz says you fight like a little wildcat."

Before I could return his teasing comment with one of my own, Malakhi peeked around the pillar, his black hair falling into his big gray eyes. "What are you doing back there?"

"None of your concern, rascal," said Eitan.

Malakhi giggled, one dirt-smudged hand over his lips. "Why did you kiss Sofea like that?"

"We are betrothed," said Eitan. "She is going to be my wife."

Malakhi wrinkled his nose. "But she is a girl!"

"Someday you'll understand, little brother." With a roguish smirk, Eitan slipped his arm around my waist and dropped another swift kiss on my lips.

Malakhi screwed his face into a scowl and made a sound of profound disgust. But then a sly glint came into his eyes. "I'm going to tell Ima," he blurted out before speeding off to make good on his threat.

Eitan released me with a loud laugh and chased his little brother through the courtyard, catching him about the waist and slinging him onto his good shoulder. The other children crowded around them, urging on the older brother they adored with shouts of delight. Leaning over the parapet, Darek and Moriyah looked down on the melee from atop the roof, grinning in obvious affection for all of their children.

Bittersweet gratitude filled my heart. I may have lost my home to Seno and his men and had my mother and siblings stripped away, but Yahweh had provided me with a new home and a new family, one whose generosity and kindness did much to prove what sort of a God he truly was.

Epilogue

Moriyah

12 Adar (Four Months Later)

Across the courtyard, my son pulled his new wife close to his side, dipping low to whisper into her ear. Sofea flushed, her blue eyes flaring wide, and then surreptitiously jammed an elbow into his belly. With a hearty laugh, Eitan looped his long arm about her waist and pulled her curls aside to press a kiss onto her neck. Although she squirmed and playfully chided him for his public liberties, the joy on her lovely face and the sweet camaraderie between them caused a knot of emotion to well in my throat.

It was still difficult to reconcile the long-limbed, muscular man with the gaunt, hollow-eyed boy who had wandered into our vineyard all those years ago. Even as I'd stood by while Eitan pledged his life in

489

sacred covenant with Sofea, I glimpsed leftover shadows of my little warrior in the proud line of his shoulders, the fading freckles over his cheeks and nose, and the bright hazel eyes that regarded his bride with mischievous delight.

In the past few months, Eitan had truly come into his own. Now that he'd finally been able to lay aside the burden of guilt he'd been carrying, the undercurrent of pent-up anger had dissipated, leaving behind a man whose purpose was clear and spirit light. And the woman he'd chosen to walk at his side had all the strength and courage necessary to weather marriage to a warrior of Israel, while still retaining a bright enthusiasm and near childlike inquisitiveness that endeared her to everyone.

May they grow together in knowledge of you, Yahweh.

Darek came up behind me, sliding his arms about my waist and settling his chin on my shoulder. "We could not have selected a more fitting bride for our son. They are a good match."

"Indeed they are." I braided my fingers into his as I watched the small army of women I'd gathered to prepare food and drink this evening. Overseen by both Sarai and Binah, who'd finally regained her strength, they buzzed about filling cups and passing baskets of bread, ensuring that everyone would go home with a full belly.

The laughter and chatter among the wedding guests was *my* food and drink, and I'd never been so replete with gratefulness for this inn. When Dov had offered me a vacant building inhabited only by cobwebs and dust soon after our arrival in Kedesh, I'd envisioned just such a gathering — small groups of people circled together on the ground; children darting between clusters of conversations, playing chase; fresh bread, sweet wine, and every sort of delicacy tantalizing the senses of my guests; and talented musicians weaving their magic into the mix. The satisfaction of a vision fulfilled settled deep into my bones.

And yet I could not ignore the sense that below the surface something was creeping toward us, an ancient something that had taken root in this land long ago and had not been uprooted as it should have been. My dreams of late had wordlessly voiced the notion — at times with vivid images that left me sweating and gripping at my bed linens, and other times with vague murmurings that I could not decipher but weighed on me throughout the day with burdensome tenacity.

These rumblings of unease within my soul were at their strongest when Darek and his men, which now included Eitan, ventured into enemy territory, and it was then that my prayers to the Most High neared the fervency of a battleground. These men I loved were fighting not only against flesh and blood, but also against the influence of the Adversary who sought to destroy this nation at its very core.

Here, within the sheltering walls of Kedesh, that malevolence seemed far away and the residents oblivious to the hovering menace, but I did not believe we could remain blind to it much longer. The generation that would rise in coming years must stand firm on the Torah, must cling to the truth and the Covenant, or suffer consequences similar to the faithless generation that balked at the borders of Canaan nearly sixty years ago.

I surveyed my younger children — Gidal, a sober and contemplative child; Malakhi, strong-willed and full of mischief; Abra, curious and vibrant; Chana, shy and sweet-natured; and Tirzah, just beginning to find her balance on tiny feet — and wondered what place each of them would find in the turbulent times to come. Would they remain faithful to the covenant and the Mighty One who rescued us from Egypt? Or would they relax into the comfortable complacency so many Hebrews had already begun to embrace?

My knees were already callused from many mornings and evenings of battle over such things, and I suspected those moments of supplication would only increase in frequency in years to come.

"You are brooding, my love" came Darek's voice in my ear, breaking into my fretful pondering.

"Not brooding . . . simply contemplating the future."

He turned me around gently, concern pulling his dark brows together. "Are you worried that Raviv will renege on his vow?"

"Are you?"

He shook his head, but his gaze flitted away too quickly, landing on something behind me.

"Darek." I placed a finger beneath his bearded chin and drew his attention back to my face. "Do you suspect him of insincerity in this?"

"No." He offered a reassuring smile. "I do not believe he will pursue Eitan, and he knows he has no legal right to harm you here. I only wish . . ." He paused and sighed. "After seeing Raviv's daughters in the valley, looking so much like our girls . . . I wish that days like today could be shared with my brother's family as well."

A pang of latent guilt struck my heart. "As do I. Perhaps someday what was broken will be mended."

"Perhaps." He sighed as he took in the sight of our son and his new wife speaking with Tal and Prezi nearby, who I suspected were not long from their own betrothal announcement.

"Look around you, husband," I said, my gaze touching on the faces of our children, our friends, our neighbors. "Look at all the beauty that has arisen from the brokenness of our beginning. There is always hope that Raviv's heart will soften. And if Yahweh wills it, it will be so."

Darek looked down at me, his brown eyes traveling over my face with appreciation and his mouth beginning to curve into the smile he reserved for me alone. "Thank you, my beautiful bride." He brushed his lips over the brand on my face. "I will cling to that hope and pray that someday he will embrace mercy as well."

A growl of displeasure lifted over the happy melody the musicians were playing, interrupting the kiss Darek had been about to press to my mouth. Rivkah, Tal's youngest sister, was chasing Malakhi up the stairs toward the roof, demanding that he return her flower garland. Entertained by her overly dramatic response to his teasing, Malakhi tossed the ring of flowers over the parapet, where it broke apart and rained purple and white petals over the crowd below.

"That boy." With a shake of his head, Darek let out a frustrated laugh. "Reining him in will be nothing less than a full-scale battle."

"Shall I retrieve your armor, my love?"

He grinned, yanked me in for a quick kiss, and nudged me toward the group of women who had begun forming a circle at the center of the courtyard. "I'll deal with our wayward son. You go dance."

A NOTE FROM THE AUTHOR

When reading a novel set among the events of the Bible, the last thing one expects would be a pirate attack, so when I stumbled across historical research about the fearsome sea marauders who plagued vessels and villages on the Mediterranean during the Bronze Age, I knew I had to place our heroine right in the middle of that sea.

Little is known about Sofea's people, the Sicani. They were likely the first inhabitants of the island of Sicily, but their origins are contested by historians. However, the few artifacts that remain make it clear that they were influenced by the Minoans and Mycenaeans, so much of Sofea's life on her island is based loosely on what we know of those cultures and their religious beliefs. Therefore, readers may notice that Sofea's main gods, Posedao and Atemito, are similar in name and character to Poseidon (the god of the sea) and Artemis (one of the fertility goddesses) and were the earlier iterations of the same gods. I borrowed these monikers from translations of Linear B, which is the earliest form of Mycenaean Greek, since I found no written documentation of the Sicani language.

There is some evidence of human sacrifice in later ruins on Sicily, and the Bible, as well as many other historical documents, speaks of such horrors in the ancient world. It's not too great a stretch to imagine that instead of bulls being thrown into the sea to appease the god of the sea, as in latter forms of worship practices, a young maiden or two may have been tossed into the waves during times of famine or desperation, especially by a particularly depraved local chieftain like Sofea's father. The mattanza, the annual bluefin tuna hunt where hundreds of the large and valuable fish are herded into nets during migrations off the northern Sicilian coast, is an actual tradition that dates back to the Bronze Age and was continued until recently.

Since the CITIES OF REFUGE series takes place during an interim period between the Conquest and the Judges, there is very little known about this time when the Israelites were settling into the Land, developing farms, building homes and villages, and learning how to apply and incorporate the Torah into their daily lives. But one thing is for sure: It did not take long before things went off the rails. As discussed in *A Light on the Hill,* the tribes of Israel struggled with the command they were given to drive the Canaanites completely from the Land of Promise. Each tribe was responsible to form their own army and rid their new territories of the Canaanites, Amorites, Perizzites, Hittites, and Jebusites.

Instead, we see that the warnings of Moses and Joshua were not heeded. The compromises made with these enemies so undermined the foundations of Israel that within only thirty years of Jericho, they were in severe danger of losing the Lord's protective covering that had brought them such victory under Moses and Joshua. It is within this context that Eitan is eager to fight alongside his Naftali brethren to protect the cities allotted to his tribe against the very real threat of resident and displaced Canaanites and the powerful kingdoms that lay to the north and east.

Was there a band of highly trained spies like Darek and Baz whose job it was to secretly monitor these enemies and feed information to Joshua and the tribes? Perhaps not, although the precedent for such a group has its basis in the twelve spies in Numbers 13, the spies sent into Jericho (Joshua 1), the team sent out to survey the Land (Joshua 18), and even the men sent by the tribe of Dan to Laish (Judges 18), so it's certainly possible — and all sorts of fun to imagine.

As for a plot to assassinate the High Priest, there is no actual evidence of such a thing happening, although I did come across a rabbinic source that said the mothers of the High Priests regularly traveled to the refuge cities with gifts of food and clothing to ensure that manslayers would not pray for the untimely death of their sons. And since justice adjudicated by humans is never perfect, it is conceivable that a few of those convicted of manslaughter actually did get away with murder. The germ of this story idea actually came from an offhanded quip my husband's friend Josh Elsom made about just such a scenario, and once I finished laughing, I thought, "Hey, wait a minute. . . . What if . . ." So, thanks, Josh!

Many thanks to my writing partners, Tammy L. Gray and Nicole Deese. Your commitment to making my stories shine and faithfulness to me personally are an ever-unfolding gift from the Lord. And thanks as well to Amy Matayo and Christy

Barritt, who along with Nicole and Tammy helped me plot the majority of this book in a session during our annual retreat, the recording of which is full of nearly as much giggling as it is brilliance.

My move away from Texas has sadly separated me from my Monday night ladies — Lori Bates Wright, Dana Red, Tammy Gray, and Laurie Westlake — but I am so grateful for all your support, encouragement, and excellent input into Sofea's and Eitan's story. I miss you all so much and look forward to seeing where God is leading your writing careers. Thanks as well to beta readers Elisabeth Espinoza, Joannie Shultz, Jodi Lagrou, and Ashley Espinoza. This story is all the better for your willingness to read unedited drafts and offer your insights.

I can never thank my editors, Raela Schoenherr and Jen Veilleux, enough. They, along with the rest of the Bethany House team, put so much time and effort into editing, designing, and delivering my novels into the hands of readers all over the world. Jennifer Parker and the design team brought Sofea to life on the cover of the original publisher's edition with extraordinary perception and talent. And thanks to my sweet and supportive agent, Tamela Hancock Murray, I can rest assured that my writing career is in wise and capable hands.

And finally, thank you, my dear readers, for spending your precious time between the pages of this novel. I hope you have enjoyed this second book in the CITIES OF REFUGE series and the chance to discover how Moriyah's family has fared over the years. Their story isn't finished yet, I assure you!

QUESTIONS FOR CONVERSATION

1. After enduring horrific loss, Sofea and her cousin are brought from a foreign land to Israel and the city of refuge, which turns out to be a place of unexpected comfort and blessing. When have you experienced a "blessing in disguise" or a situation that may have initially seemed hopeless but yielded significant spiritual growth or encouragement instead?

2. Sofea and Prezi do not know the language of the Hebrews and therefore are terrified of the very people who saved them. When have you been in a situation where you were culturally, linguistically, or otherwise completely out of your element? What things did you learn about yourself and others through this experience?

3. Eitan has been told to keep his past a secret by his parents for his own protec-

tion. Do you agree with their decision? Why or why not? How might Eitan's life have been different if his past was public knowledge? Have you ever been asked to guard a potentially destructive secret? What was the outcome?

4. Eitan consecrated himself to Yahweh by taking the Nazirite vow, but as the story progresses, he comes to see that he may have had the wrong motives. Have you ever made a commitment and then later discovered that your reasons for doing so were not as pure as you thought? Do you think God honors those efforts, even when our hearts are not in line with his will?

5. Sofea does not fully comprehend Yahweh but is drawn to the people of Kedesh, who offer love and protection to her and her cousin. As she grows in understanding, she begins to see that their actions are representative of the God they serve. How have the people of the Church represented God's unconditional love to you? How can the Church do a better job of this?

6. Sofea's culture is drastically different from the one she witnesses in Kedesh, a distinction that opens her eyes to the

righteousness of Yahweh and his Word. Our natural instinct is to try to blend in with others around us, but Christ-followers are called to be "in the world but not of it" (cf. John 17:15–17). In what ways are you living up to this challenge? How do your daily actions and interactions draw others to Christ? In what ways are you struggling to be faithful in this area?

7. As a convicted manslayer, Moriyah is imprisoned in Kedesh but instead of wallowing in self-pity uses her tragic circumstances to glorify God and help Prezi and Sofea begin to heal. What circumstances in your own past can you use to encourage and empathize with others? How has someone else reached out to you in this way?

8. What do you think the scene in which Eitan sets aside his Nazirite vow is meant to symbolize? In what ways are you like Eitan? What struggles do you have with leftover guilt, even if you are already in covenant with Christ through the free gift of grace?

9. Which character in *Shelter of the Most*

High do you most identify with? Why? Which character's motives are the most difficult to relate to? Why? Which events surprised you the most?

10. *Until the Mountains Fall,* the next book in the CITIES OF REFUGE series, will continue with the story of Malakhi, Darek and Moriyah's youngest son, and Rivkah, the girl he loves to tease. What challenges do you foresee for him and Moriyah's other children as the people of Israel become less faithful to Yahweh and wander back into idolatry?

ABOUT THE AUTHOR

Connilyn Cossette is the CBA bestselling author of the OUT FROM EGYPT series from Bethany House Publishers. Her debut novel, *Counted With the Stars,* was a finalist for the Christy Award, the INSPY Award, and the Christian Retailing's Best Award. There is not much she enjoys more than digging into the rich, ancient world of the Bible, discovering new gems of grace that point to Jesus, and weaving them into an immersive fiction experience. She lives in North Carolina with her husband of over twenty years and a son and a daughter who fill her days with joy, inspiration, and laughter. Connect with her at www.Conni lynCossette.com.

The employees of Thorndike Press hope you have enjoyed this Large Print book. All our Thorndike, Wheeler, and Kennebec Large Print titles are designed for easy reading, and all our books are made to last. Other Thorndike Press Large Print books are available at your library, through selected bookstores, or directly from us.

For information about titles, please call:
  (800) 223-1244

or visit our website at:
  gale.com/thorndike

To share your comments, please write:
  Publisher
  Thorndike Press
  10 Water St., Suite 310
  Waterville, ME 04901